CW00687789

FALLING

NORTH UNIVERSITY SERIES
BOOK ONE

JANISHA BOSWELL

Proofreading by Louise Murphy (Kat's Literary Services)

Cover by Layla Brown and Marta Garcia Navarro.

Chapter images from Maurice DT and Pavel Danilyuk.

Discreet cover by Emily Wittig.

BOOKS BY JANISHA BOSWELL

<u>The Drayton Hills Series</u>
Our Secret Moments
Our Secret Game

<u>The North University Series</u>
Falling

More coming soon...

DEDICATION

To those with fragile hearts who still
dream of romance.
Don't stop looking for love in
everything that you do.

"When you are missing someone, time seems to move slower, and when I'm falling in love with someone, time seems to be moving faster."

-Taylor Swift

CONTENT WARNINGS

As sweet and fun as this book is, it also deals with a lot of difficult topics that might be sensitive to some readers. Please read with caution. If you, or anyone you know are struggling with any of the topics below, don't hesitate to reach out for help.

- Explicit sexual content and language
- Mild alcoholism (mentioned mostly in the past)
- Adultery (not between the main characters)
- Emotionally abusive relationship between parent and child
- Grief and death of close friend
- Anxiety, depression, and medication discussed in topics about mental health

PLAYLIST

Feelslikeimfallinginlove — Coldplay
Labyrinth — Taylor Swift
Uptown Girl — Billy Joel
Fuchsia Sea — ZAYN
Sad Girl — Lana Del Rey
Gilded Lily — Cults
Close To You — Gracie Abrams
Jump Then Fall — Taylor Swift
Slow It Down — Benson Boone
Everywhere, Everything — Noah Kahan
Look At That Woman — Role Model
Cheer Up Baby — Inhaler
Sparks — Coldplay
The Greatest — Billie Eilish
The Alchemy — Taylor Swift
Falling — Florence + The Machine

1
WREN

To skate, or not to skate?

"SORRY, COULD YOU REPEAT THAT?" I ask in a small voice, hoping that pretending I can't hear them means that this isn't happening. But the more I talk, and the more I think about the situation I'm in, the more my life starts to feel like a bad sitcom that I like to hate-watch with my friends.

When I was told to come in for a meeting with the head of the sports department and my figure skating coach, I thought I was getting an award. A *well done for not losing your shit at your ex-boyfriend for fucking up your routine, and in turn, your entire life.* In my mind, it was handed to me with an oversized trophy and a bouquet of flowers. Maybe even a certificate with my name scrawled across it to hang in my room.

But that's just as far as my imagination can get me. Instead, I'm getting some really sucky news that I should have seen coming.

"That is the third time you've asked that today. Are you okay, Wren?" Coach Darcy asks in her thick French accent. I can see the sympathy etched into her features, her brown eyes flickering with worry. It's the same look she's given me all year.

I push my shoulders back, hoping that will give me some of

the confidence I desperately need right now. "I'm okay. I'm just… adjusting." I press my lips together at my poor choice of words. I mean, how else am I supposed to respond?

I look around the office, trying to find something to focus on so I don't pathetically burst into tears. I've felt lost as it is for months after a public breakup, losing my regional title, and falling behind on college work. My first year at North University was terrible, and I'm not going to let my second year be as bad.

"You won't need to adjust to anything if you work with us in finding a way around this. It's just a misstep, that's all," Coach explains with a warm smile. It's usually the kind of smile that would calm me down before stepping onto the ice, but now, it's lost it's usual sparkle.

I almost let out an incredulous laugh at the way she's referring to the worst year of my life and the possible downfall of my career as a "misstep." After our winter showcase in December, I might have to kiss figure skating here goodbye and find another way to finish college.

North University is known for its hockey team and figure skaters. We're based in Salt Lake, but we're well loved across the whole of North America. We enter the championships every year, but we also host seasonal events for the students and the wider community. It's a good way to recruit high school students and get people excited for competition season. Over the last few years, figure skating has become less popular, and the hockey team has taken the spotlight.

Surprise, surprise.

After the catastrophe that was the regional championships, the same day that Augustus dropped me and broke up with me in the same breath, no one has batted an eye at us. Neither of them will say it, but I know they blame me. I know they think I should have carried on with my performance like nothing happened, but it didn't go that way, and the decisions that were made that day are coming right back to bite me in the ass.

As much as my creative writing course fills the hole in my heart, I'm not strong enough to stop skating here completely and dive right into that. Dropping skating would mean admitting defeat to my mom, NU alum and previous figure skater, which is the very last thing I want to do.

"How exactly am I supposed to work around this misstep?" I ask, smoothing my sweaty palms on my leggings. They both flinch when they realize I've caught them right out. They could at least pretend to not blame me and have the whole team here to make it seem like we could all fix this together, but no. It's just me, staring at my coach and the athletic director, who has had it out for me all year. If this was some sort of team-building, we're-all-in-this-together bullshit, they've gone about it the wrong way.

Coach Darcy flicks her gaze to Miss Hackerly before sighing, her eyes landing back on mine. "We're still trying to figure that out. We just wanted to make sure everyone knew what the consequences would be before anything else happens."

I sit up straighter in my seat. "Before what happens?"

Darcy sighs again, tilting her head to the ceiling before facing me head-on. "Wren, do you know how many people applied to be a part of the program for next fall?"

I smile brightly. "A lot?"

Darcy groans, and I sense I must have given her the wrong answer, but it's Miss Hackerly's gaze that pierces through me, her steely-blue eyes boring into my own. "Less than a hundred people in the whole fifty states of America." I let out a low whistle. I knew we were gradually losing support, but I didn't realize it was *that* bad. She adjusts in her seat again, her tone strengthening. "Enrollment is low, and we're at risk of getting budget cuts. We're doing everything we can on our end, but you need to do the same. You'll need to create a kind of buzz around the training we offer so people will start turning up to the performances again. Our flyers might do the trick to encourage people to enroll, but we actually need people *there* to encourage them. It should be easy if you really care about skating."

Her words land like a punch to the stomach. Over the last few months, that desire and drive to do my absolute best for this team has slipped. Their faith in me disappeared after regionals, and maybe this was the wake-up call I needed to go back to how it used to be. It's the kind of thought that I've banished into a box in my brain labeled DO NOT TOUCH. Thinking anything negative about skating makes me feel dirty, like I've done something wrong, even when I know deep down that I haven't.

It's been infused into my blood since my mom started skating way before I was born. My sister, Austin, didn't get the same push toward skating that I did, and I'll never know why. Ballet is her thing, and skating is mine.

My entire life has revolved around it, and I don't know what it means to go without it. It's been so ingrained in my brain, in my blood. Sometimes I think it's the only thing that I'm actually good at. It's been proven that I'm statistically one of the best college figure skaters in our country, and if I tried hard enough, worked myself even harder, I could probably make it to the Olympics.

Well, not probably.

I *will* make it to the Olympics.

My mom and coach both count on me. There might not be a lot of us on the skating team, but there's enough to worry about other than me. I don't like being in their spotlight, especially when there are a lot more talented skaters on our team that they can fuss over.

I put on my brightest smile and say, "I'm sure I'll figure out some magical way to make everyone turn up to our performances."

Coach knows I'm joking, but she claps her hands, a large grin on her face, and she beams at me. "I knew you'd figure it out," she says, winking at me and matching my sarcasm.

MY TWO BEST friends envelop me in their embrace the second I'm out the office door. You'd think I just got sentenced to ten years in prison with the way they're hugging me. After explaining the situation to them, we walk back to our apartment off campus.

"They can't do that, can they? Just cut the whole program?" Kennedy asks, her arms still tight around my shoulders, clinging to me as if she's my emotional support animal. Scarlett hasn't said much since I relayed what happened, but she doesn't have to. I know how her business student brain works. She's probably working over plans in her head.

"Well, apparently, they can," I mumble, kicking the crunchy leaves beneath me. I was training this morning and went to the gym right after.

"So, what are you going to do? There must be some loophole," Scarlett says. Her voice is a lot calmer and rational than Kennedy's frantic one.

"I have no fucking clue," I say, rubbing at my temples.

Our walk slows as we get closer to home, the chilly air urging us forward. I must have defeated them with this conversation alone because we all silently agreed to take the stairs to our apartment instead of waiting on the elevator.

"I might have to start a petition or something," I suggest, waving my hand vaguely in the air when we reach our door. Ken hums in agreement, unlocking the door, and we slip into the warmth.

I turn back, and Scarlett is still in the doorway, arms planted by her side, her neat hair a mess from the September breeze. With her eyebrows furrowed and her jaw set, she pins me with a strange look.

"Scar," I coax slowly, gesturing to the apartment.

"You *cannot* petition. I'm not letting you do that," she says sternly, finally starting to walk inside. Ken and I exchange a worried glance before turning back to her as she toes off her shoes at the door. "Take it from the girl who wasted her whole final project last year on a petition that landed her a B. A fucking *B* for collecting over twenty thousand signatures."

"A B isn't bad, Scar," Kennedy says, shrugging. I close my eyes. Trying to argue with Scarlett about grades is like trying to argue with a cat about the benefits of a bath—completely futile and likely to end in scratches.

Scarlett is a lot like a cat in many ways, always with her claws out. Unlike Kennedy and I, who each have only one sister, Scarlett is the youngest and the only daughter of four sons, so she's constantly trying to prove that she is as good as them. You wouldn't need to look at her twice to realize she's smarter than all of them combined. I just wish she could get that in her head. And I wish Kennedy would stop prodding her with these questions.

"It's bad for *me,*" she argues, shuddering as she walks into the open living room and kitchen. "A *B* is like asking for a grande latte and getting a tall black coffee—close, but not quite what you were hoping for."

I just huff at her response, and Kennedy giggles after getting a rise out of her. I throw myself onto the couch, ready to make this my bed for the next few days. The girls walk around me, probably looking for food. "I need to think of something, like, yesterday. If I can't skate, I have no options."

"Why don't you just stick with creative writing and get more benefits that the degree offers? You could get some real feedback instead of getting totally biased opinions from us fools," Kennedy suggests, flopping on her beanbag across from me. She tucks her legs beneath her, a box of Cheerios in her hand.

The suggestion churns in my stomach. It always does whenever anyone brings up the idea of giving up skating to commit to a *real* degree. The prospect of throwing myself into that just feels like I'm setting myself up for failure. That's the annoying thing about me—if I know I'm not perfect at it, I'm not going to try. I've never seen any point in it, and there's no use starting now.

"I'd need to be a good writer to do that, *and* I'd have to admit defeat to my mother of all people," I say with a shiver. The looks she gave me in the office were enough. I've dedicated my whole life to fulfilling the legacy she never got to start. I want to be a living, breathing reminder that her dreams didn't die the day of the accident. I've committed too much time to it, too much effort, too many tears to give up now. And I truly don't think she would look at me the same if I did.

I throw my head back onto the headrest, trying to organize all the thoughts whirling around my brain and tugging on my lungs. I'm going to need to find a way around this. They might be too afraid to say it, but I know this is my fault. I made my bed, so now I have to lie in it.

I don't know how long I stay there, trying to breathe and think at the same time like it's a sport, but when I open my eyes, Kennedy is wheeling in The Whiteboard, a staple in our household. After Scarlett was gifted two large whiteboards for Christmas, she dedicated one to her studies and the other to the number of crises we have per week. It's come in handy for our pros and cons lists for dates, breakups, changing shampoos, or trying to find a place to eat that isn't Nero's Pizzeria. If we didn't have The Whiteboard, our lives would have completely gone to shit by now.

"Scarlett, would you like the honor of being our scribe?" Kennedy announces, holding out the oversized whiteboard pen to her as if it's the holy grail. Scarlett's face lights up as she flashes me a toothy smile.

"I would love nothing more," she replies, jumping up and retrieving the pen. She starts to scrawl words across the board, dictating them as she does. "Operation 'save Wren from dropping out of skating even though she secretly hates it' is underway."

I throw her a sarcastic smile, lobbing a cushion at her.

"Maybe we should just paraphrase?" Kennedy suggests, unimpressed as she returns to her seat in the beanbag.

"That *was* me paraphrasing." Scarlett continues writing out the name on the whiteboard regardless.

"Or, *maybe,* we could stop assuming how much I love skating altogether," I counter. As if they planned it, they both turn around, frowning at me like bratty children.

I can tell this is going to be a long night, and it's only four in the afternoon.

2
MILES

Shots?

"SORRY. COULD YOU SAY THAT AGAIN?"

I shake my head to get my eyes to refocus from the brown walls in the office to her disappointed face. It's not much of an improvement, but maybe moving my eyes will fight off the headache that is threatening to ruin my day. That is, if this doesn't do it for me.

Maybe taking shots before I came wasn't the best idea, but I was convinced I was going to get kicked out anyway. Some liquid courage never hurt anyone. Well, that's what I've been telling myself for the last three months, and nothing bad has happened yet.

"What is wrong with the students today? You're the fourth person to ask me to repeat myself," Miss Hackerly snaps at me, and I slouch a little lower in my seat. This is the very last place I wanted to be today, yet here I am, being scolded about something I have no control over.

All I can do is stare at the photos dotted around the office. The muddy-brown color is off-putting, and not the kind of color scheme that matches the rest of this building. The family pictures she has in her frames are doing weird things to my chest, though, in some pathetic Mommy issues kind of way.

There's a girl in nearly all the photos, around my age, blonde, flushed cheeks, and she's breathtaking. Everywhere I look, her green eyes follow me around the room, and it's fucking distracting. Honestly, I'd much rather get stared at by this stranger than listen to whatever my hockey coach and the athletic director have to say to me.

"Mr. Tucker and I were saying that we think it's best for you to stay off the ice for a while and hand over your captaincy to another player." Hackerly's voice brings me back to reality, and I instantly wish it hadn't. This is probably the third time she's said this to me, but it still doesn't feel real. She takes my silence as an invitation to continue talking, which is probably a good thing. I don't trust myself or what might come out of my mouth. "We've noticed a slip in your grades and in your performance since…" She hesitates, but the three people in this room know what she was about to say, so she doesn't.

I don't know what I would do if I heard someone else say his name again, soaked with remorse. I can't tell which is worse—actually saying it or being too afraid to. I shift in my seat uncomfortably, my jersey suddenly feeling like it's suffocating me. I force myself to breathe, but it only makes the gnawing feeling worse. I've done everything in my power to avoid these feelings, but when I least expect them to, they always creep right back up.

I clear my throat. "I said I would get back into playing when we last spoke, and I meant it. I really am trying."

The words feel bitter coming off my tongue because I know I'm not being one hundred percent honest with them. Saying I'll do something and actually having the balls to do it are two different things. And for a person like me, they're usually not that hard. I've always been a hard worker and prided myself on being North University's hockey golden boy. Now I'm the furthest thing from that, and I doubt anyone even knows that I'm alive.

I thought quitting my job at Nero's Pizzeria would be the first step, the step in the right direction to give myself time to grieve and to focus on school and hockey. It became so easy to say that I'd stop drinking after having one more. *Just one* quickly turns into ten, and I'm passed out drunk before my housemates come back from school at three in the afternoon. It's a pathetic way to live, but it isn't like how it is in movies. I can't just wake up one day and forget him and move on like nothing happened.

"Listen, Miles, we know that you miss him. We *all* do, but you had a few weeks off the ice and class after it happened and the whole summer away from hockey. We hoped that you'd get back into playing, but we're already three weeks into the semester and I've not seen you at the rink once," Coach says.

The last time I was on the rink, I had just finished playing one of the best games with all my favorite people. I've not been fully *there* on the ice, mentally, and I've spaced out enough times to land me on the bench without finishing a shift.

The thought of going out there again, without him, feels like going to sleep *knowing* I would have a nightmare. It's like purposefully bringing a knife to a gunfight. I'd much rather avoid that until my head is in a better place, but it's been five months, and I'm still not there.

I swallow the emotion lodged in my throat. "It's just hard, Coach," I admit, a lot less quiet and ballsy than when I started out. "I swear, I'm trying."

"I know you are, Davis, but I need committed and healthy players on my team. We just want what's best for you. When you're in the position to come back, there'll be a spot waiting for you." His blue eyes meet mine, and he offers me a sad smile. "I'm sure you don't mind Xavier taking over your captaincy in the meantime."

I sigh at the mention of my friend. "Of course not. No one deserves that role more than him."

"I'm glad you agree," Tucker says. "We'll be in touch soon. Just focus on yourself for the time being. We just want you to be healthy."

"I understand." I nod, trying to keep my head held high.

I was in need of a reality check. As soon as I can get him out of my head, finally carve away the infection that has been festering in my heart, I might be able to get over it. People do this all the time. They lose someone, grieve, and they get over it. I don't know how they do it, but I'm going to have to find out, and soon. Hockey is the only thing keeping me at North University, and I've worked way too fucking hard for it to go down the drain now.

THE SECOND I walk through the doors to my house, I question every good reason I had for moving in with Xavier Dawson and Evan Branson last year. It was fine at the beginning with me, Xavier, and Carter. The three of us were all on the same team, and hockey ruled our lives and cemented our friendship. Xavier and I were lucky enough to get in on a scholarship to play hockey, but unlike Xavier, if I fail my classes and my scholarship is removed, I can't pay my way into staying on. It's hockey and a few classes a week or nothing.

When we heard someone was looking for a place to stay a few months into the first semester, we decided to lend a helping hand. We didn't know that millionaire Evan Branson would be the guy moving into our spare room after transferring from Drayton Hills in Colorado. Apparently, some big scandal blew up his reputation there and his dad shipped him off here for a taste of responsibility. He majors in fashion and business, probably so he can take over his daddy's company when he's old enough.

Their obnoxiously loud voices filter in when I get closer to the kitchen.

"You can't put this disgusting cheese next to my shakes," Xavier yells, "It's vile."

"Where else am I supposed to put them when your boiled eggs take up every square inch of the fridge?" Evan shouts back.

As expected, Xavier is standing in nothing but his sweatpants, and Evan is casually wearing a suit and tie on a Friday night. I'm convinced he either has nothing better to do or he's on his way to one of his family's galas.

"Honey, I'm home!" When Xavier's eyes meet mine, his shoulders relax, and he no longer looks like he was about to murder our very good friend.

"Thank fuck. I was about to strangle him," he grits out, making his way over to dap me up.

"Don't let me stop you," I tease, crossing my arms against my chest. I bow down to Evan, knowing it'll get a rise out of him. "What's the problem in the palace today, Your Royal Highness?"

He flips me off before brushing an agitated hand through his blond hair. If he thought the royalty jokes were over by now, he has another thing coming. He's never really fit in with this house at all. While we're chaotic, loud, and messy and always have our friends over to play video games, Evan is quieter and more reserved, often sneaking out to do whatever weird shit his family does. I have to give it to him though. He's probably the only reason why this house is still on all its legs.

"I'd be fine if you could tell your friend to stop putting his eggs in the fridge," Evan says with a groan.

"This might not be my house anymore, so I shouldn't be barking out orders," I reply, trying to make light of my situation and the worst-case scenario as I pluck a beer from behind him. I slide off the cap and take a swig, letting the cooling sensation run down my throat, leaning against the counter.

Xavier's eyebrows furrow. "What do you mean? Is that why you were with Hacks? Are they kicking you out?"

"Almost," I say, winking. He doesn't buy my bullshit and stares me down, waiting for a real answer. "She and coach decided that I can't play until I'm doing better in my classes and when I've got a better head on my shoulders."

"Shit. That sucks," Evan says, dipping a cracker into his weird cheese. Xavier and I look at it, and our eyes connect. I bite on my bottom lip to keep from laughing.

"The good news is you're taking over my captaincy," I say to Xavier, and his eyes go comically wide. He's been my co-captain since last year, and he's one of the best players that this team has. If I'm going to be out this season, I trust him to carry us to victory.

"Still sucks that you're being benched," Xavier says, shaking his head.

I just shrug. "I've been slacking for a while now; it's about time they noticed."

He hums in response, folding his arms against his chest. "I was going to ask if you wanted to go to Ben's party tonight, but if you're bummed out, we can just chill here." He lowers his voice as he mumbles, "Which is kinda what we've been doing all summer."

I think about it for a minute.

I could go and enjoy myself and stop overthinking or sit at home and wallow in my own pity and think about *him*.

I know which one will be more fun.

3
MILES

Pretty girl, dumb boy

I SCAN the house Xavier and I just walked into, and I'm bored and satisfied all at the same time.

I've been wasting away my nights, drinking cheap beer at parties like these until I can't see straight. There's something strangely comforting about intoxicated and happy strangers. I'll get caught up in conversations I don't want to have, and it always settles me a little. It's like a touch of reality in the empty nothingness that has taken over my brain. It makes this whole "moving on" thing feel a little less daunting.

Xavier peels to meet one of his friends, and I take the beers I brought into the kitchen, grabbing myself a cold one out of the fridge. We've not even been here for ten minutes, and the music is already getting to me, thrashing hard against my skull as I take a gulp of my beer.

The liquid goes down the wrong pipe, and I cough over the skin. I gasp and sputter, trying to breathe normally. Maybe this is some sign from the gods that I should stop this pity party I've been throwing myself and get my act together.

A soft hand reaches my back, moving in a slow, awkward circle. My entire body tenses at the contact, and I try to pull away, still trying to catch my breath. Only I would be able to embarrass myself like this today.

"Take it easy, big guy," someone says from behind me, and whoever it is is trying really hard not to laugh just from the sound of their voice.

I turn around, almost stumbling when I see the girl in front of me.

She's got deep-green eyes, the kind that lure you in,, and thick lashes that are blinking up at me, and a gleam in her eyes that shows the humor I thought was there just from the sound of her voice. Her hair isn't just blonde, it looks golden, despite the shitty lighting of this house.

I've been floating outside my own body, watching myself from afar for so long that I can't even pinpoint where I know her from. When I look back down to her, her eyes latching onto mine, I realize it.

I take my time to put the pieces together, shaking my head a little to clear my thoughts. She's Hackerly's daughter. She must be. The resemblance between her and the girl I saw in the photos is uncanny. The same eyes that followed me around that room are staring up at me now, and I should probably say something.

I blink myself back to reality, and when I do, she's closer, her arm by my shoulder.

Wait.

What?

"Sorry. I'm just looking for some water." She lets out a nervous chuckle, snapping me out of my trance, and I move out of the way, clearing her access to the fridge. Jesus Christ. I haven't been that caught up in just *looking* at someone in months. She reaches for a bottle, and I finally think of something to say.

"You're the AD's daughter, right?" I ask, closing my eyes before opening them again.

As the athletic director at NU, no one has really known what to call Miss Hackerly, and if we're not calling her AD, she's usually referred to as "Hacks." She's a stick-in-the-mud, but she's kept the sports department afloat for years.

The girl freezes at my question before pushing a strand of hair out of her face, a tight smile on her lips. "Yeah, I am," she says. I know I'm the last person she wants to speak to given her expression, but that only makes me want to talk to her more. I'm holding out my hand before I can even think about it. She glances at my outstretched hand, narrowing her eyes. "I'm sorry. Who are you?"

"Miles Davis," I say. She hesitates before slipping her hand into mine. It's small in comparison, but I ignore the electric shocks that travel through my brain from where our hands meet. Getting *electric shocks* over a girl is new to me.

"Wren," she replies, pulling back her hand to grip onto her bottle.

Some weird alarm bell is blaring in my brain, saying, STAY, TALK, SPEAK, DO SOMETHING TO MAKE HER STAY. Maybe it's the thing people say when firefighters get attached to people that they save or the other way around. Maybe her saving me from choking just then has forged some invisible string between us. I've never wanted to talk to someone as much as I do her, so, naturally, I don't say anything. I just stare like a weirdo because nothing comes to my brain to start a conversation with a pretty girl.

"Hackerly," she blurts out, her face scrunching up before it relaxes. I blink at her, watching all the muscles in her face smooth out, and a splash of color washes against her cheeks.

"What?"

"My last name. It's Hackerly," she confirms. I already got that, but for some reason, I'm making this way more awkward than it needs to be. She must be thinking it too because she goes on. "I felt like I should have said it since you told me your last name, but given you know my mom, I guess you already knew."

I blink at her again because that's what I'm reduced to as I try to decipher her word vomit. I've only known her a few minutes, but she seems like the put-together, has an itinerary for when she goes to the bathroom type. The kind that schedules every second of her life to perfection, leaving things like parties and random get-togethers in a frat basement at the bottom of her well-crafted list. Having Miss Hackerly as a mom, I wouldn't be surprised.

I clear my throat, forcing words to come out so I don't completely embarrass myself. "Thanks for confirming that. I don't know how I would have coped without that information."

Her eyes narrow. "Well, you were just staring at me and not saying anything."

"I didn't mean to stare, it just started... happening," I say, squeezing my eyes shut to find a better response. Of course, nothing happens.

She laughs, and the sound is unnerving. It's carefree, stupid, and beautiful all at the same time. "No, you just caught me off guard, that's all. I wasn't really expecting to interact with anyone today. Let alone save you from choking on a beer."

"Well, thank you for saving my life," I say, my mouth twitching up into a smile. She just shrugs like it's no big deal, and I can tell she's debating cutting this conversation and making a run for it. I want her to stay. Her company is the most I've had outside my team since we lost Carter, and wallowing in a corner is starting to get old.

"Why would you come to a party if you don't want to socialize with anyone?" I ask.

"My friends can be very persuasive." She shrugs again, locking her hands behind her back, the bottle crinkling beneath the pressure. Her eyes meet mine, and she sighs. "I got some pretty bad news earlier, so they thought this would cheer me up."

"Is it working?"

"I haven't decided yet. I'm—" A loud screech pierces

through the music, and our attention is drawn to the living room, where I didn't notice a very heated game of Just Dance is being played by a group of girls, some of my teammates mingling around trying not to be obvious as they stare. I turn back to Wren as she buries her face in her hands. "Oh my god."

"Are those your friends?" I gesture to the two brunettes dancing with their hands in the air, not at all following the instructions on the screen. The girl with curly hair is doing some weird body roll thing while the other one films her, both of their faces red with heat. Wren peeks through her fingers, shaking her head at them.

"Unfortunately," she replies, grumbling. "They really shouldn't be allowed outside of the house, let alone anywhere near alcohol."

The girls look like they're having a good time, but Wren looks mortified. I can't help the grin that pulls at my lips at her secondhand embarrassment. I bump my shoulder into hers. "Hey, don't beat yourself up about it. Those idiots that are checking them out are *my* friends, Harry and Grayson. I'd much rather have them dance like your friends than be the weirdos in the corner daring each other to do stupid shit."

She snorts, covering her mouth when the sound leaves her. "Right. So, what's your excuse for not hanging out with them? You seem like the type to... What the fuck are they doing? Are they trying to drink beer through spaghetti?"

"Not *trying,* Wren. They are mastering the art of Spaghetti Straw," I say. She shakes her head, watching them with a curious expression. That's just the kind of people Grayson and Harry are. Harry's the youngest on our team, and I'm sure Grayson bribed him in one way or another to do his bidding. "It's the same reason as yours actually. I got some bad news from my coach, and I've been benched, so my friends thought this would cheer me up too."

Turning to me to echo the same question I asked her, she asks, "Is it working?"

I shrug. "Now that I've got someone to talk to, yeah."

She lets out a snobby little "hm" sound, probably assuming I'm doing some dumbass play to hook up with her. If I had the energy, I probably would. She's easy to talk to and fucking beautiful, but I'm not interested in doing anything more than having a good time.

I break the silence between us by saying, "Do you ever just wish you could drink all day, say fuck it to the consequences, and spend all the time you want in your room?"

"You can. It's called alcoholism."

I don't even respond to that because I know how stupid I must sound. I can't remember the last time I had an actual conversation with someone, and it shows.

We watch our respective friend groups from this side of the kitchen, both of them so different yet so similar at the same time. Neither of us have said anything, and I've forgotten how to make friends. How to talk to people without being awkward. It's never been hard for me, but Wren doesn't seem like the kind of person who would want to be friends with someone like me anyway.

When her friends—Kennedy and Scarlett, I figured out when she yelled at them to calm down and neither one of them listened —have moved on to a different dance, roping in some other girls, I turn to Wren.

"Do you wanna dance?"

She looks taken aback at my question, and her eyebrows shoot to her forehead. "What?"

"You got taken out to have a good night. If us silently standing here while we watch our friends have a good time is what you call fun, then excuse me, but I think we should give tonight a shot," I explain. She surveys my features, probably to see if I'm being serious. I sigh, reiterating my point. "You got taken out to have a good night, so you're going to have a good night, Wren. I promise you."

She scoffs. "Is this your thing? You just go around finding girls who are in need of a good time?" I tilt my head to the side playfully, and her eyes widen. "Wait. No. That didn't come out the way it was supposed to."

"Sure it didn't," I say, slinging one arm over her shoulder and pulling her to my side. My arm sizzles with the warmth of her skin, the proximity doing weird things to my insides. She smells good too—like fall and summer rolled into one. I point at our friends, who are now arguing over who should play in the game. "Let's play against them and see who wins. Me and my friends against you and yours."

"What's the point? I'm going to win," she says. So fucking bold and confident. If that isn't a turn-on, I don't know what is.

"You are, huh?"

"Yeah. I've been taking dance classes since I was four, and I'm a figure skater. It's basically in my blood," she explains. I look down at her, and she tilts her head up to mine.

"You skate?"

"Yeah, I'm on Darcy's squad at NU."

That catches my attention. "What do you study?"

"Literature and creative writing," she says.

"Huh," I murmur. I try to place a face on the girl I've seen skating around at the rink when I'm on my way to practice, but I can't tell if it's her or not. It makes sense. She's built like a figure skater, snarky and confident in all the ways that I find stupidly attractive. "Well, I'm captain of the hockey team, so I'm a pretty good dancer."

She laughs again, and I want to keep making her do that. "Those two things don't relate to each other, like, at all."

Her eyes sparkle, and I find myself saying, "Wanna make a bet?"

"That depends."

"If you win, I'll go to a dance class of your choosing. I'll do pole dancing if you want, ballet, hip-hop. I don't care. Anything you want and I'll do it." Her eyes widen with mischief at the mention of pole dancing. I can tell she's imagining what that would look like, and her lips curve into a smile.

"And if you win?" she asks.

"I get to take you out on a date."

She snorts again, and this time, making her laugh hurts a little. I know what everyone thinks the second I tell them I'm a hockey player. They think I walk around campus with a crown on my head, beckoning girls toward me like I have no soul. I usually let people think that. I let them make up their own judgments of me and don't do anything to make them think otherwise. It's better that way. But I don't want Wren to think of me like that. For whatever reason, I want to impress her, and she doesn't seem like the kind of girl that is impressed easily. I want her to see me for who I truly am, even when I'm losing sight of who that is.

"Why would I agree to that?" she asks breathlessly.

"Because you're going to win, remember?" I wink at her, and she mumbles something before walking off to her friends.

I watch as she explains what's going on, and I do the same to my friends. Grayson and Harry are already talking about strategies, and I cast a glance over at Wren. She looks serious, like she really doesn't want to lose. Like she *really* doesn't want to go on this date with me. Her poker face is admirable, really. And downright adorable.

The space in the living room clears out, and Grayson, Harry, and I are up first. The three girls watch us like the Chippettes from the *Alvin and the Chipmunks* movies, arms crossed against their chests as the music starts.

The game loads, and it's all flashing lights and wild avatars dancing across the screen. We line up, our shadows flickering in the colorful glow from the TV. The room around us cheers, a few phones already out, capturing the moment.

As the song starts, we jump into action. I try to mirror the frenzied movements of the dancers on the screen, swinging my arms and sliding my feet, slightly off-beat, but I'm too far in now to care. Harry is surprisingly good, nailing almost every move, and Grayson is all over the place, his long limbs a hilarious hazard as he spins and jumps.

When the song ends, we're breathless, our scores pop up on the screen. Harry throws his hands up in victory, a wild cheer escaping him as he beats us by a narrow margin. Whoever wins out of the girls will have to go up against Harry, and he needs to take this victory home so I can take Wren out.

We step back, and the girls come onto the makeshift dance floor, fiddling with the screen. I'm catching my breath, folded over the couch, and Wren steps between my legs, looking down at me. "I thought this was your thing, Miles. Or are you really all talk and no play?"

I look up to see Wren with a playful smirk on her lips, her arms crossed as she watches me struggle for air. I can't help but smile, the rush of the game still tingling in my veins. "Oh, it's definitely my thing," I reply, trying to muster some of my earlier confidence. "Just warming up, you know? We might have to do a few more rounds to reach peak performance."

Wren laughs, her eyes twinkling with amusement. "Peak performance, huh? So, should I stick around for the grand finale or save myself the disappointment?"

I sit up straighter, waving to her to sit beside me. "Stick around. I promise you won't be disappointed. I might even let you win a round to make it interesting."

She raises an eyebrow, accepting the challenge as she settles down next to me. "Let me?" she echoes, her voice full of shock. "Miles, you're out in the first round. You didn't even come second place." I roll my eyes, and she pats my chest before standing back up. "I'll show you how it's done, don't worry."

And she fucking does.

The dance is ridiculous and over-the-top, but she looks good doing it. Scarlett and Kennedy aren't that bad either, but it's Wren who steals the show and has the whole crowd cheering along with her. When she's up against Harry, I almost forget which team I'm on. I find myself stealing glances at Wren when she's not looking, marveling at the way her eyes light up with each dance move and the way her laughter fills the room.

She catches me staring; something switches in her expression, and she stumbles a little. Her gaze snags on mine, and I tilt my head to the side, but she recovers quickly, shaking her head to try to get back in the game. Harry uses the opportunity to dance his little heart out, doing the best he can to catch up with her. After her misstep, she falls behind, and Harry takes the lead.

Grayson and I jump up in unison, cheering on our friend while Wren and the girls sulk at the side of us. Wren walks toward me, cheeks flushed a rosy pink, and her blonde hair that was slicked into a tight ponytail now flows loose on her shoulders. Kennedy points at Harry and starts accusing him of cheating even though we all watched the game and he won fair and square. Scarlett tries to back her up, and Wren just studies me.

"Now what?" She bites out the words like they've personally offended her.

"Now, you give me your number and I'll pick you up on Friday at 5."

Her eyes widen for what must be the tenth time tonight. "Are you being serious?"

"As the plague." I hold up my fingers in the Scout's Honor, my other hand on my chest. I pull out my phone, handing it to her, and she blinks at it before taking it up.

"I can't believe I'm doing this," she mutters, typing her digits in.

"You better believe it, Wrenny. I'm going to rock your world," I say, the nickname fitting her perfectly. She looks like sunshine, all cute and pretty, but her attitude is more like a storm.

She swats me on the arm. "Please don't call me that."

I nod at Gray and Harry to come with me so we can get going. "Friday at five, princess."

"Did you just call me princess?" She runs a frustrated hand through the ends of her hair, shaking her head like she can't believe this is happening. "You don't even know where I live."

I turn on my heels, and she lets out a frustrated breath-growl thing that has me laughing to myself as I walk toward the door. She shouts after me, and all I call back is, "Friday at five, Wrenny girl. I'll see you."

I walk out of the house, feeling a lot better than I did when I walked in here. For one of the first times in months, I know I'm going to be able to sleep without a drink in my hand and the memories of March might start to float away.

4
WREN

Pole legend in training

THE WEEK FLIES by in a blur of early mornings and late nights, the usual chatter with the girls reduced to nothing more than half-asleep grumbles. So tonight, reuniting on the couch feels like a celebration. I've just tucked my phone away after ordering our favorite greasy indulgence from Nero's when *Matilda* begins to light up the flatscreen.

"Wait!" Kennedy's voice cuts through the opening credits, pausing the movie. She swivels from her spot on the floor, directly below where Scarlett and I lounge on the couch. In a swift motion, she gathers her curls into a makeshift bun, then pins us both with a look that manages to be both stern and teasing. "Before we start," she begins, pointing dramatically at each of us, "we need to set some ground rules for movie night. No phones, no distractions, just us and Matilda. Agreed?"

Her playful seriousness draws a laugh from both Scarlett and me, but we agree. I reach for the remote, but she stops me. "Okay, first, we need to give our two updates."

Our first semester at NU was sheer perfection. Our schedules synced up so well that we could hang out regularly, not just during early breakfasts or late-night cram sessions. A scheduling snafu with Kennedy's classes and mine threw us off our game in the second semester.

We scrambled to find a new rhythm, and once we did, Kennedy came up with a plan for the rare times the three of us could meet up. She suggested we each share three highlights from our separate college experiences to keep everyone looped in. But as assignments piled on and time became a luxury, we streamlined our updates to just two each, cutting out any repetition and keeping our meet-ups fresh and engaging. It's a highlight of my week whenever we can all manage to hang out, and it brings me a kind of joy nothing else can. After spending the past few days trying to make different posters for the winter showcase and giving up, I've spent most of my time either at the library, the rink, or at the gym, hoping that maybe the team will pull through and fix itself.

"Okay, I'll go first," Scarlett says. "I no longer have that *horrible* UTI, and I finally beat Evan in the class Kahoot on Monday, so a win is a win."

We all burst out laughing at the absurdity of her updates. "Two very disconnected but clap-worthy updates, I have to say, Miss Voss," Kennedy says, and I agree, clapping too.

"I try." Scarlett sighs, her body melting into the cushions. "What about you, Ken doll?"

"Can you stop trying to make that nickname happen? It's not going to happen," Kennedy retorts, rolling her eyes. Scarlett just shrugs, reaching forward to pick out all the purple candies from the jar on the coffee table. "Well, I finished our portraits, but before you ask, no. You can't see them until they're ready."

She's been working on and off our group portraits, but she's constantly saying she's getting close to finishing them and then completely scraps the painting. I think I've posed for more photos for Kennedy than I have for myself. She's the most creative out of the three of us and everything she makes is beautiful. She's designed all of her own tattoos and Scarlett's too.

"Which isn't going to be for another year," I mutter under my breath. Scarlett hears me and snickers before thinking.

"I heard that, you impatient bitch. True art takes time," Kennedy states proudly. "And my second update is I finished the new season of The Crown."

"What? Without me?" Scarlett exclaims, throwing a pillow in her direction.

"I had to! You take, like, a gazillion bathroom breaks whenever we watch anything. You're the worst person to watch a movie with."

"You're the one that stopped Matilda. You can't spoil it for me now," Scarlett says.

"I can't spoil it. It's literally history. Just pick up a book, you nerd," Kennedy argues, rolling her eyes. She turns to me, her expression calming down from their short-lived argument. "What about you, Wren? You've been awfully quiet."

"I'm just thinking about my updates. Nothing exciting has happened," I say with a sigh.

The second the words leave my mouth, I feel like I'm lying. Truth is, I haven't done anything exciting. All I've done is go to my classes and train my ass off until I feel like putty. The only thing that comes to mind is Miles and his stupid fucking face and his stupid fucking voice and his stupid fucking teasing. And the stupid fucking date he has been hounding me about since last weekend.

The party was the most fun I've had in a long time. After being stuck in a metaphorical jail with Augustus Holden for four years, going out of the house has been a chore. I never went out much when we were together, so after we broke up, I never had a reason to. We weren't the outdoorsy type of couple, and we were way too busy with our skating schedules to entertain that idea. I liked that about us for the most part. We always put our work first.

Scar and Kennedy will find any excuse to go to a party, and

I'll find any excuse to stay inside and read. We've always worked like that, and I've come to terms with it. I didn't expect that having a dance battle with three random boys and my friends would turn into one of the most exhilarating nights of my otherwise boring life.

I've always felt like my life is constantly going on a loop, doing the same three things every day for the last ten years. It's like I've been stuck in a mundane rhythm, each day blurring into the next with no sign of change. But recently, something shifted. It's as if someone pressed pause on the monotony and flipped the script, breathing color into my once predictable existence. I've always felt like the boring one of my friends. The mild one. The tame one. I don't know if I want to be that anymore just because I've got so comfortable with it.

Kennedy leans in, her eyes drilling into mine like she's about to unlock my deepest secrets with a stare. "Oh my god, spill it. Right now," she demands.

"Spill what?" I deflect, stretching my arm behind her to snag whatever snack I can find. I shove a handful of chips into my mouth, hoping to stop any actual words from escaping.

"It's definitely about a guy. I can tell," Kennedy says, jabbing a finger at me for dramatic effect.

Chewing loudly, I ask, "How can you possibly know that?"

"Because you're blushing like you've just run a marathon in the Sahara," Scarlett chimes in, grinning. "Come on, this is a safe space. You can tell us anything."

I roll my eyes, dodging their questions as I say, "My first update is that I finished another chapter of Stolen Kingdom last night."

Kennedy gasps, and Scarlett's eyes widen with excitement. "Oh my god," they both scream at the same time.

"See, I knew it wasn't about a guy!" Kennedy says, completely contradicting her last comment. Scarlett shakes her head.

"No, you didn't. And you didn't let her finish," Scarlett explains. "But we need to return to that. I have been dying to know what happens next."

I started writing Stolen Kingdom, a fantasy series, when I was sixteen.

It follows a young princess, Carmen, who finds out her whole life is a lie and she is not actually the real heir to the throne. She is sent anonymous messages and is stalked around her small kingdom in Estonia, and she is on a quest to find out who knows her real identity and what they're going to do about it.

It falls into many different categories, and the plot takes ridiculous turns, but Scarlett, Kennedy, and our friend Gigi have managed to keep up thus far. It's stupid and ridiculous in all the best ways and it's the passion project I throw myself into when life gets too much.

"And my second update..." I hedge, not sure how to say this. I get it out in one go, hoping that the word vomit will do the trick. "So, that dance-off at the party last weekend wasn't just a coincidence with the timing. I met Miles, like, ten minutes before that, and we accidentally made a bet that if his team won, he could take me on a date, and if I won, he would go to a dance class. Somehow, Harry won, and now I have to go on a date with Miles."

They both blink at me for a second, neither one of them saying anything.

Scarlett narrows her eyes. "How do you accidentally make a bet with someone?"

I shrug. "I don't know. It just... happened. If anything, it's your guys' fault for leaving me unattended at a party I didn't want to go to."

"You're a big girl, Wren. You were fine." Kennedy laughs. I frown at her.

"Besides, Miles is a hot commodity. You should be lucky he

even graced you with his presence," Scarlett says, rolling her eyes. I had assumed he was popular since he's a hockey player, but the fact that Kennedy and Scarlett are both nodding like this is common knowledge makes me feel stupid. Scarlett registers the confusion on my face and says, "Do you guys remember Jake? That dickwad I dated a while back?" We both nod. "Well, he's on the hockey team too. He and Miles are friends. And he's Evan's housemate."

"It's interesting how you hate Evan so much, yet this is the second time he's made an appearance in today's conversation," Kennedy teases innocently.

Evan is two things: filthy rich and blond. He's a gorgeous man, and no one could deny that, but his personality is where the faults lie. He's managed to get a rise out of Scarlett every day for as long as I can remember. They're in most of the same classes, and he has been trying to upstage Scarlett since we started college. There's been constant competition between them since day one, battling for the best grades and the best answers. Scarlett is not afraid of any competition, but there is something about Evan that makes her skin crawl.

I look over to a red-faced Scarlett, her expression lying somewhere between a blush and pure anger. "You're getting us off topic," Scarlett hisses at Ken. She turns back to me, smiling. "Anyway, he's a hockey player, so I'm sure he's just doing his playboy ritual."

"Really?" I ask, the surprise coming off way too strong. "That's hard to believe."

"What are you talking about?" Scarlett asks.

"I dunno," I mumble, "He didn't give off dickish energy. Just sad, brooding, miserable energy when he wasn't trying to flirt with me."

"Oh, that's hot," Kennedy says, nodding.

"Not really." Scarlett grimaces. "He was the nicest of Jake's friends, I'll give him that. Since Carter passed away, I think the whole team has been on edge, so that checks out."

Kennedy nods again, and I feel totally out of the loop. Have I really had my head so far up Darcy's and Augustus's asses that I don't know the basic social standings of people in my school?

"How do you know about these things, and I don't?" I ask them.

Scarlett rolls her eyes. "Because you refuse to gossip about people who don't concern you."

"Right, and that's a bad thing, how?"

"Because now you don't know about one of the most important things that happened last semester," Kennedy adds in, stuffing her face with Cheerios that somehow materialized in her lap.

"I know about Carter," I argue, my throat burning at the thought. I didn't know him, or anyone on the hockey team for that matter, but what happened was terrible. I didn't have to know him for it to hurt when we were told what happened. He sounded like a nice guy and was way too young to die. "I just didn't know he was friends with Miles."

"Best friends," Kennedy says through a mouthful, nodding at me.

"Right. Well, I didn't know they were *best friends*. It's not like he was going to bring that up to me at the party. All we talked about was how he got benched and how I had some bad news from my mom," I say. They both hum in agreement. "I feel shitty for not knowing, but it wasn't my utmost concern last semester."

"I guess you were too busy with Gus-related things," Scarlett says.

I groan. "Can we not? Just thinking about him gives me the creeps. I can't believe I stayed with him for that long."

"I can't believe you stayed with him, period. He was a

walking red flag when he tried convincing you to cut us off so he could have you all to himself," she adds.

I sigh, feeling the regret rot in my stomach. "Well, sixteen-year-old me didn't know that."

"Neither did eighteen-year-old you," Kennedy mutters. I throw a cushion at her, and as she throws it back to me, my phone pings from beside me.

Miles and I have texted a few times since the party. It was fine at first when we were trying to get to know each other, but now, I never know what to say. He just sends me random memes and songs he's listening to. It's usually something stupid and related to whatever TV show he's watching. The other morning, he sent me a link to "The Only Exception" by Paramore and captioned it, *I feel like an indie pop princess in a coming-of-age movie for teenagers on Netflix. Send help.* I asked why I needed to know that, and he just said that I did. There was no argument, and we fell into some weird rhythm of sending each other songs and how they make us feel.

There's a weird comfort in the randomness of our chats. It's like we're both tossing bits of our day at each other, seeing what sticks. It doesn't feel like much, but there's something about these snippets that makes me look forward to a text from him. I only ever text Scarlett, Kennedy, or Gigi, so having a new contact in my phone feels like a win.

This time, there's no text, and it's just a video. I shake my head before it even starts playing. Miles backs away from the camera, and I notice the room that he's in looks like a dance studio with three poles in the middle. A few older women are in the background, cheering him on before *Needed Me* by Rihanna starts playing in the speakers.

No.

No.

I watch Miles back up to the center pole, a determined look crossing his face. He's wearing the most ridiculous neon-pink gym shorts and a tank top that says "Pole Legend in Training." The bass drops, and he starts his routine, a series of awkward shimmies and hesitant spins that have me desperately gasping for air. His hands clutch at the pole, his feet trying to find rhythm where there's none.

The older ladies in the background are clapping and hooting —clearly the cheer squad he never knew he needed. As the song hits the chorus, Miles attempts to hoist himself up the pole. His efforts are more comical than sexy, his face scrunching up as he focuses. Then, with a grunt, he manages to lift himself off the ground for a brief, glorious second before sliding down with a thump that probably didn't feel as funny as it looked.

The camera shakes a bit—probably because the person filming is laughing too. Miles looks directly at it, blows a kiss with a huge grin, and says, "For you, Wrenny girl. Bet I've got your attention now."

I'm laughing so hard that tears are streaming down my face. This video, this ridiculous, endearing effort just to make me laugh—it's the stupidest thing I've seen all day. It's not just funny, it's weirdly endearing. And as I wipe the tears from my eyes, I ignore the looks Scarlett and Kennedy are giving me and type out a message to him.

> What the fuck is this?????
>
> I'm CRYING.

MILES
In a good way, right?

> In a ridiculous way, yes.

MILES

Luckily for you, my friend's mom owns a dance studio. She let me go in for a taster session. We could pick any style of dance we wanted.

And you landed on POLE DANCING?

MILES

Yeah, it suits me. Don't you think?

It's... something!

MILES

If this is getting you hot under the collar, Wren, you could just say that.

It's doing the exact opposite, actually.

MILES

Sure it is.

Are you going to send me your address or what? I'm trying to play the patient nice guy, but it's really fucking difficult.

Why?

I DON'T KNOW what I'm asking. If I'm wondering why he wants my address or why he's done playing the nice patient guy. Either way, he responds with:

Because I haven't been able to stop thinking about you since that night.

It was less than a week ago.

MILES

Exactly. Five days of pure torture.

You're so dramatic.

MILES

I'm past dramatic, Wrenny. I'm desperate.

I can tell.

MILES

...

I DON'T HAVE any excuse for why I sent him my address, but I did. He responds with a random TV character pumping their fist into their side and a bunch of book emojis. We've talked a few times about my minor obsession with romance books and my literature degree, so now he thinks that it's all I do. I don't stop the snort that leaves my lips, and when I look up, Kennedy and Scarlett are both looking at me with a puzzled expression.

"Who was that?" Scarlett asks, leaning over to peek at my phone.

I push it to my chest. "Just Miles being an idiot."

"Is he your new best friend? Are you going to make matching friendship bracelets and replace us?" Kennedy asks, sulking.

"What?"

"I haven't seen you smile that hard in *months*, Wrenny baby. Honestly, it was kinda terrifying," she mumbles.

"That's not true," I say, knowing it is.

After the breakup, things got hard. It was difficult to do all the things I used to love, and Scar and Ken were constantly watching over me like helicopter parents. If your ex-boyfriend and skating partner dropped you on the ice and ruined your reputation, you would swear off men too. I just didn't expect to fall into one of the worst depressions of my life. Doing mundane tasks became hard, and shutting myself off from the world to keep my heart safe felt like the best option.

It wasn't my finest moment, and I've slowly been making my way out of the fog. *Very* slowly. Focusing solely on my performance and my classes has given me an excuse to ignore my non-existent sex life, but with the added stress of trying to work a way around the new bump in the road on the team, I know I'm going to need some sort of fun in my life.

"Whatever," Scarlett says, waving her hand at us. "Can we circle back to Stolen Kingdom? I need my Carmen and Marcus fix immediately."

Since I started writing this series, we've established a ritual: Every new chapter I finish, I perform a live reading for Kennedy and Scarlett. It's like our own exclusive book club, keeping me motivated to write and leaving them on edge for what's next. Initially, reading aloud felt a little awkward, but they love how I bring the characters to life, and it helps me spot any gaps in the narrative.

Tonight, we sprawl on the living room floor, blankets beneath us, forming our cozy little circle, movie forgotten. Kennedy flops her head onto my lap, her curly hair a ticklish contrast against my skin. Scarlett faces us, chin cradled in her hands, eyes eager for the story to continue. I open my laptop and dive into the world we're all hooked on.

When I get another text from Miles reminding me to be ready on time, I swipe it away from the screen. Not before Kennedy looks up at me with a knowing grin. I don't know how I'm going to convince them that he's not been all I've thought about since the party. I also don't know how I'm going to manage to sit through an entire date when I have no idea how to act on a first date. The old Wren would have run off and said "fuck no" to this idea, but the new Wren is moving closer and closer to saying yes to everything. Even the things that scare me the most.

5
MILES

First date jitters

I RUN my sweaty palms down the front of my jeans for what must be the tenth time as I stand awkwardly outside the door of her apartment.

I thought taking the stairs would help me work off the nervous energy that is working its way through my veins, but it didn't. If anything, it just intensified the fact that I have no clue what I'm doing. The liquid courage at the party no longer exists, and now I have to somehow charm her with my dazzling personality. "Dazzling" is not how anyone would describe it, but it's something.

I doubt Wren even wants to spend any extra time with me after the countless times I've texted her, but she gives me something else to focus on. If I'm not staring into the abyss and wondering how I'm going to get back on the team, I'm texting her. It's been months since I've had to try to convince a girl to give me the time of day, and I'm a competitive motherfucker. She might not realize it now, but I can tell she'll warm up to me at some point.

I knock twice before the door swings open. I barely get to look at Wren's face before she ushers me in and rushes around her huge apartment. "Sorry. I just got back from the gym, and I'm still getting my life together. I'll be two minutes," she shouts, walking down a corridor.

"Okay," I say even though I don't feel it. I step into her kitchen. "I'll just stand awkwardly in your kitchen and pretend this isn't the first time I've been here."

"So, you're not just a pretty face? I knew you'd get the hang of it," she shouts back.

"All I heard was that you think I'm pretty," I say, and I hear her snort.

I do exactly that and stand awkwardly in her kitchen. She's mentioned that she lives with her two best friends, but I don't see or hear them anywhere. The kitchen is as clean as I would expect. The granite countertops are glistening like they've never been used before. Some of the cupboards are made with glass doors, and funky-looking body-part-shaped glasses stand on the shelves.

The fridge is full of pictures of Wren and her friends, most of them in different countries. I trace my finger over one of them that catches my attention. Wren's face is red as she hangs over the toilet seat, her curly-haired friend Kennedy sitting next to her with her hand on her back and Scarlett holding the camera up to take the photo with the three of them in it.

"That was in Barcelona," Wren says, standing on the opposite side of the island. My breath catches in my throat when I take her in. She's wearing a thin cami top, a cardigan, and low-rise jeans. Her blonde hair is tied back into a loose ponytail, and her bangs curl in front of her face. "It was last summer. I think that was the last time I drank alcohol."

"You were drinking water at the party," I point out. She nods. "Is there a story behind this that has led to your sobriety?"

"Is there a story behind your mild alcoholism?" she challenges, crossing her arms against her chest.

"Touché," I say, holding a hand to my heart as if her words

hurt. She rolls her eyes, trying to avoid my gaze as we both just look at each other. I haven't seen her in person since the party, and though texting has been fun, I've been dying to see her again. "You look good."

Her smile widens. "Thanks. So do you." I'm wearing baggy jeans and a shirt. It's really nothing special. But with the way she's clearly eye fucking me, I feel like a million bucks. "Now, can we get on with this date and never see each other again?"

I tut as she walks around to meet me by the door. "I really don't think that's going to happen, princess. You'll be dying to see me again."

"If you keep calling me that, I don't think we'll make it out this door," she mumbles, but she's taking smaller and smaller steps toward me and the door.

"I'm taking you on your dream date and giving you free food. You can at least *pretend* to be happy about it," I argue, opening her door. She looks around her apartment for the last time, double-checking her bag before she gives me a cheesy grin. More like she's baring all of her teeth to me like I'm her dentist and I'm deciding which ones I should pull out.

"You see this?" She points at her face. "This is me pretending to be happy about it."

"Jesus. What are you doing with your face?"

She frowns. "Smiling."

"Maybe try it with less teeth. That was terrifying. You look like a Cheshire cat."

"You sure know how to compliment a girl, don't you, Miles?"

"If you wanted me to compliment you, I would have told you how fucking hot you look, but that didn't seem appropriate. So you know what I said instead?"

She rolls her eyes as I stare at her, waiting for her to play my little game. "You said I looked good."

"Exactly, because that's the *polite* thing to say. Now, come here," I say, tugging on her bag that's slung over her shoulder to pull her into me. I press two fingers on each side of her mouth, trying to pretend the skin-to-skin contact isn't driving me insane. She looks up at me a little wide-eyed, but I fix the frown on her face into something less terrifying. "There you go! That's a real smile."

She keeps her lips pressed in the weird shape I put them in as she mumbles, "This is really uncomfortable."

"You're right. Go back to scowling at me. I like that better," I say, nodding. She laughs, pushing me in the shoulder. And then she does it. She really smiles at me. And a fucking dimple pops out. A *dimple*. Kill me now.

She shakes her head. "You're ridiculous."

"You're gorgeous." I don't even have time to register the surprise on her face, and I usher us out of her apartment before she can say anything. "The library awaits, princess. Let's get going."

FROM THE WAY Wren gawked at me when I said we were going to the library, I thought she was going to scratch my eyes out. I don't know if this is the best place to take a girl for a date, but considering what she studies in college and the complete lack of bookstores in our town, I thought this would be a good idea. Drake's Library is the biggest one we have, and I'm sure it's every bookworm's dream.

I don't think I've seen Wren look happier. Or I *think* she's happy. Every time she passes a book she's read, she makes a weird angry grumbling sound like she hates it before she picks it up, shows it to me, and then tells me the entire plot from start to finish. She doesn't leave a single detail out, and I couldn't find anything more attractive.

"Sorry, I feel like I'm being really annoying, and this isn't exactly what a date is supposed to be like," she sighs, walking beside me after placing another book down. We've been in the romance section since we got here, and I doubt anywhere else in this place would interest her.

"Don't worry about it. I like hearing you talk," I say, bumping my shoulder into hers. She just scoffs. "So, do you come here often?"

She laughs quietly, her whole body shaking with laughter. "To the library?"

I give her a sidelong glance. "Yeah. Why is that funny?"

"I'm an English and Creative Writing major, that's all. I thought you knew that," she explains. I swear my brain stopped working the second I met her.

"Right. Yeah. Sorry. I did know that. I'm just—"

"Nervous?" she finishes, raising her eyebrows at me. I swallow, nodding. "You don't have to be. I don't bite." I'm so fucking captivated by her that I don't even make a joke. She continues talking, and her voice is like literal music to my ears. "But yeah, I do come here quite often. My dad used to take my sister and me here every weekend after our parents got divorced. I think my dad was just unsure what to do with us, so we spent most of our days together just walking around here, and we'd take out books that we liked. We'd come straight after school sometimes just for story time. We would have just preferred hanging out with him, but it was more fun than going to dance classes or going to the rink with our mom."

"Are you guys close?" I ask.

I watch the way her whole face lights up when she says, "I'd say so. He's a real goof sometimes, but it's a nice balance with how strict my mom can be." I hum in response. "What about you? Are you close with your parents?"

I try my best not to seem uncomfortable with her question. My shirt suddenly feels like it's suffocating me, but I just shrug it off. "Not as much as we used to be, but it's cool."

Recently finding out that my mom has been cheating on my dad for years is anything *but* cool. The fact that they're still together, pretending to be in love with each other, is even less cool. They've even convinced my sister and me that it's totally okay and that we don't have to worry about them getting a divorce anytime soon, but I'd honestly rather them just get it over with. It's hard to watch. I've been avoiding them for months and I really don't know when I'll be able to face them again. Not only did I lose my best friend in March, but I lost my parents too.

"I'm sorry," Wren says. "That must suck."

I sniffle. "It's fine, honestly. We've never really been some big, let's all talk about our feelings, kind of family anyway. It's cool this way."

"I get that," she says. It's like refreshing. She doesn't immediately go into fixing mode and try to figure out what's wrong with me. She just lets it go because I said I didn't want to talk about it. "How about this? I pick you a book, and you can pick me one. Whoever finishes it first gets a prize."

"I never knew you could win prizes for finishing first," I tease.

"Are you projecting because your last girlfriend didn't give you a medal and congratulate you for jizzing in your pants while she was still dry?"

"I—" I stop myself because I was not expecting her to catch up with my humor so quickly. I just smile. "I accept your challenge. But I'm not getting you a romance novel. You can read a *good* book."

"You mean a hockey player's autobiography?" she asks.

"Yes, Wren, a hockey player's autobiography is what I consider to be a good book."

Her head quirks. "See, it sounds sarcastic, but I really don't think you're joking."

I frown. "I-I'm not joking. The McDavid Effect changed my life."

"Of course it did."

"Just let me buy you your books, princess, and stop arguing with me."

I hook my arm around her shoulder, leading us out of the romance section, but she's still got a ton of books in her basket, which she's probably going to force me to read. "Miles?" she asks, turning to look up at me.

"Mm-hmm?"

"You do know that all books at libraries are free, right?"

My eyes widen. "Are you kidding me? I was going to brag to all my friends about how I treated you to books and food."

She snorts, the most unladylike sound I've ever heard. God, I could get drunk on it. "Next time, you can take me to an actual bookstore. Then I can spend all of your money."

I smirk. "Sounds like a date if I've ever heard one, Wrenny."

6
WREN

Hot commodity

AFTER MILES GETS me an autobiography of some hockey player I've never heard of, and I give him one of my favorite romance book recommendations, our deal has commenced. I never expected to agree to talking to him or *seeing* him more after today, but he's not bad company.

I've found it exceptionally hard to make friends at college. I've always been so busy with my classes and practice that I've never really ventured out of my circle with Kennedy and Scarlett. I'm too exhausted to go out and make friends, and the fear of rejection has made me want to hide myself from everyone forever. Sometimes, being friends with Scarlett and Kennedy makes me wonder why I'd bother trying to make other friends in the first place.

Miles and I end up in an old 50s-style diner not too far from my apartment and the library. Weirdly, I've had a really good time today. Talking to him feels easy. There's no pressure attached to it. There's no weight on my shoulders that I have to mold myself into fitting into the perception of myself that he's probably conjured up in his head. I can be myself around him and talk his ear off about books he's never going to read. It's weird how easily he's inserted himself into my life and how natural it all feels. I can't remember the last time I made a friend, and whatever we have going on is nice. Comforting.

I take another bite of the burger my mom would murder me for eating as Miles asks, "So, tell me, Wren, did I absolutely rock your world today, or what?"

I study him as I chew, watching the way he covers the entirety of his fries in ketchup before shoving them in his mouth. "I've had worse dates," I say.

"If this is the best date you've ever been on, you can easily just say that."

"I *could*," I say, lifting one shoulder, "but I'm not going to." He groans dramatically, pushing his brown hair out of his face. He mutters something to himself before stuffing his face with more food. "Can I ask you something?"

"Of course."

"Why did you go to the pole dancing class when it wasn't part of your terms for winning the bet? You only would have had to go if *I* won, and we wouldn't be sitting here if that was the case," I explain. It's been bugging me for the last few days. I don't know any other person who would willingly put himself through that humiliation unless he had a good reason.

His mouth tugs into a grin. "Did you smile?"

"What?"

"When I sent you the video," he explains, "did you smile when you saw it? Or, dare I say, laugh?"

I snort. "Yeah, I laughed. It was the stupidest thing I've ever seen."

He leans back, crossing his arms against his chest. "Well, there you go."

"There I go, what?"

"My reason."

"You did it so you could make me laugh?" I ask slowly, really trying to get the hang of this game he's playing. Is it a game? Or have I just convinced myself that any guy that wants to get close to me is only doing it to fuck with my head?

"Sometimes, people don't need any other reason," he says.

Just those words alone make my heart do a weird stutter thing. A thing it hasn't done in a *long* time. He says these things so easily, so naturally, as if it's just supposed to make sense. Everything about our dynamic is still foreign to me. It's fun, but it's still strange.

I shake my head at him, fighting off a smile. "You're ri—"

"Ridiculous, I know. Can we just get to the part where you say that you're cold, I give you my jacket, I walk you home, you pretend to forget something in my car and I run back up the stairs, and then we make out?"

I almost spray my mouthful of soda over my food but I stop myself. "What kind of rom-coms have *you* been watching?"

"Only the good ones," he says. "When I was a kid, my sister would literally strap me to a chair and force me to watch rom-coms with her. She'd point at the screen and make it very clear who I should follow in the footsteps of. I think this was right after One Direction broke up, so she thought Zayn had broken up with *her*."

I can't help but laugh. "Is that why you're so charming and respectful?"

His entire face glows with pride. "That's one of the reasons."

"Yeah? Why else?"

"Because I want to impress you, and I'm trying my hardest not to fuck this up," he says, the words coming out with such sincerity it hits me right in the gut. I don't have the mental capacity to deal with a relationship, let alone a crush right now. Those things consume me. They turn me into a pathetic, horny monster, and I have too much riding on this year at NU to compromise it.

As I go to eat another fry, a few guys hover beside our table. This must be the third time this has happened in this diner alone.

I've passed by here a few times with the girls, but we usually just grab a takeout. Maybe if we ate in, we would realize how much of NU's population likes to hang out here. And we would have realized how much they *love* Miles Davis.

You'd think he's walking around with a fucking crown on his head and has twenty-four-hour security surrounding him. I just see him as a conventionally attractive hockey player who seems to have more to him than this playboy personality I've been told about. To everyone else, he's a god.

"Hey," a ginger guy calls, his group following him over. They seem too young to be in college, and way too nervous to be talking to a normal guy.

"Hey, man. What's up?" Miles says—the same thing he said to the other two people who interrupted our meal earlier.

The ginger guy stutters for a second before his buddy elbows him. "Hey, sorry to bother you. I just wanted to say how much our team appreciates you. We were watching your game at practice last night and the highlights from the Frozen Four last year."

"Thanks, I appreciate it," Miles answers, nodding at the guys who might piss themselves with excitement. "You guys planning to go to NU?"

"Yeah, if we get in," one of the guys says, and the rest of them hum in agreement.

"You guys go to Hollis, right?" Miles asks, nodding at their letterman jackets. They let out a chorus of "yeahs." "Your coach is one of the best in the division. You'll be fine. Just listen to what he says, and you'll be good."

They all let out a breath of relief as if Miles just admitted them onto North's hockey team just like that. They make basic hockey small talk as I continue to eat my fries. Miles tried to involve me in the conversation, but I'm as clueless as they come when it comes to hockey. I'm more than happy to listen to him talk about it though. It's the least I can do after I've spent the entire date talking about books.

A brief pause wedges in the conversation, and one of the Hollis kids says, "We're really sorry about Carter too. He was such a talented player. He would have made it to the pros if he…"

Miles stiffens, and I have the urge to hold his hand. I know the mention of his best friend makes him visibly uncomfortable, but he tries to keep his cool. He clears his throat and says, "Yeah, he would have."

They easily change topics again, and after a few more minutes, they say bye and leave the diner. Miles and I finish our food in silence until he sighs, saying, "It's so weird talking about him and he's not here. I keep thinking in the back of my head that he's going to be there when I get home."

A wedge forms in my heart, and I wish I could do something about it. I've not experienced many losses in my family, not with any close relatives, anyway. I can't even imagine what it must have been like to lose his best friend.

I swallow, meeting his gaze. "I'm so sorry that happened to you, Miles."

He shakes his head. "I'm sorry for dumping that on you."

"It's okay. We don't have to talk about him if you don't want to."

"Yeah. It's— Yeah, let's not."

So we don't. We spend the rest of the night talking about everything and nothing until the owner tells us it's ten minutes until closing time. We're talking so much I'm afraid that my throat will get dry before we run out of things to discuss. We talk about classes and hockey and his idol, Josh Raymond, and I pretend I know what he's talking about while he does the same to me as I tell him about my favorite figure skating stars.

As we walk on the sidewalk toward my apartment, I bump my shoulder into his. "Looks like everyone knows you, huh?" I've never seen people treat anyone like a celebrity like they do with Miles. Honestly, it was fascinating to watch.

He shrugs shyly, scratching the back of his head. "I guess so. I think it just comes with being the captain and all."

I turn to him slowly, watching the blush spread across his cheeks. "Oh my god. You love it, don't you?"

"I don't hate it."

His admission only fuels my glee more. "I can just imagine it," I say, turning my fingers to make a square in front of me like I'm a director bringing a scene to life. "I bet you dream about all these women feeding you grapes while you take turns deciding which one you want to eye fuck."

He tilts his head down to me, grinning. "That sounds more like your dream than mine."

"Yeah, whatever," I mock, shaking my head. I spot my apartment toward the end of the block and I stop, pointing to it. I hook my thumbs into the front pocket of my jeans, rocking back on my heels. "This is me."

Miles's eyebrows furrow, pointing at the townhouse behind us. "You live right here? I know it was only a few hours ago, and I've got such a teeny tiny brain being a hockey player and all, but I could have *sworn* you lived in a fifteen-story apartment, Wren."

I roll my eyes at his sarcasm. "No, you're right. It's the apartments right there, remember?" I tap his forehead before pointing down at the end of the block. I start walking, and he follows me. I turn back to him. I thought that signaled the end of our date, but apparently not. "Where are you going?"

"Walking you home, what does it look like? I'm not letting you walk back in the dark. I'm more gentlemanly than that, princess," he argues.

"It's literally a five-minute walk. I can practically see it from here."

He shrugs. "Well, I can't. I think it's best I just walk you there." He continues walking, and this time *I* have to follow *him.*

"So, you really *are* more than just a pretty face then, huh?" I say when I catch up to him. He slings his arm over my shoulder again, a casual move he's been doing all day that stupidly makes me swoon.

He sighs, shrugging like he's just way too fucking cool for this. "Something like that."

When we reach my apartment, he insists on walking me inside and up to my floor. I don't bother arguing with him. It's like having an overprotective golden retriever follow me around, and I don't hate it.

I lean against my door and say, "For losing a bet, I had a really good time today."

He grins. "Yeah, me too." I turn to unlock my door, but before I can slip inside and hide myself away for the rest of the night, Miles grabs my wrist and tugs me back into him. The contact of his fingers wrapped around my wrist sends a hum of pleasure through my entire body. It feels a lot like butterflies. Something I haven't felt in a long time. "Good night, Wren."

My eyes flicker up to his, and I have to hide the smile that is twitching on my cheek. "Good night, Miles."

7
MILES

"It's a slow burn, Miles."

> Morning, Wrenny! How are you?
>
> I think I'm just going to chill today.
>
> Wanna hang out?
>
> Being benched really sucks. I knew it would, but it's really starting to get to me.

WRENNY

> I'm omw to practice. Bye!

I GET to the rink just in time.

I know I shouldn't be here. I can think of a million other things my coach would rather I was doing. Like, I don't know, going to practice and doing things that could possibly get me back on the ice. I'm sure he'd prefer me to be on *our* rink instead of watching Wren skate.

I've not been able to get her out of my head, and watching her skate in circles is exactly like how she's been running through my mind since that date. It almost feels unreal the way she managed to grab my attention so quickly. I feel greedy when it comes to her already, and I've never felt like that about anyone before. She feels like this special secret that has been hiding in plain sight this whole time.

Before I met her, hockey was my only focus. It was the thing that got me up in the morning and occupied my thoughts when I was in class. I've been dreaming about making the pro team since I was a kid, and nothing has ever gotten in my way before. Especially now, in my second year at NU, I'm already falling behind by being too caught up in my head and too fucking anxious to make it onto the ice without suffocating. I promised myself, Carter, and Coach Tucker that I'd get my head in the game, but I think that flew out of the window the second I met Wren Hackerly. She's like a magnet, and she doesn't even know it.

I stand at the edge of the rink, completely and utterly captivated, watching her glide and turn. She speeds up her pace, doing some complicated as fuck spin before she lands hard on the ice, curling her small hands into fists. Everything she's doing looks perfect to me, each movement sharp and charged with an intensity that I can't take my eyes away from.

She's wearing black leggings and a gray NU sweatshirt with "North Sports Department" written on the back that is a few sizes too big for her. A weird pang of jealousy curses through me, and I wonder if her ex gave it to her.

I might have reduced myself to a bit of internet stalking after our date. She's not really mentioned her ex-boyfriend, Augustus, who was also her skating partner. Especially after what he did to her, I wouldn't be surprised.

She must know I'm here because it's empty and I know her

practice doesn't start for another ten minutes. She's like me in that way. I always used to drag Xavier and Carter to the rink an hour and a half early to get some drills in before our morning skate. It always paid off in the end, and that kind of mindset is so fucking attractive on a girl.

Wren comes to a stop, her chest heaving as her eyes connect with mine across the rink. She's still standing in the middle of the ice when I call out, "Why have you been avoiding me?"

"Avoiding you?" she echoes, her voice strong like she hasn't been skating around for God knows how long. She glides toward where I stand on the outside of the rink, leaning on the barriers. "I have classes to go to, Miles, and practice four times a week. Just because you're benched, doesn't mean everyone else's lives are on hold too."

Harsh but true. "Are you sure? I was pretty sure that's how it worked." It's clearly too early for my bullshit because she just rolls her eyes at me, crossing her arms against her chest. "How's skating going? Your mom still on your ass about the team?"

Her eyes flash with surprise. "You remembered I told you that."

I shrug. "Let's not make it into a big thing. You're the one that remembered I was benched."

"It's quite literally the first thing you text me when you wake up," she argues, deepening her voice to sound like more as she adds, "Morning, Wrenny, how's your day going? Oh, mine's great, thanks for asking. I'm still benched, and it sucks, but it's all good! Double thumbs up."

"I do not do a double thumbs up, and that is not how our conversations go," I say, trying not to laugh at her very off depiction of my voice. She gives me a bored look. "We have some very productive chats."

She sighs. "Miles, I don't even respond most of the time. It's like you're talking to yourself."

"You're making me sound like I'm crazy."

"You *are* crazy," she says, failing to contain her laughter. "And no, I'm still workshopping ideas with Kennedy and Scarlett."

"Any ideas taking the lead?"

Wren sighs, pushing her braid over her shoulder. "Kennedy thinks I should start an OnlyFans and see if that draws some attention to me. Scarlett thinks I should lead a peaceful protest even though I'm not too sure what we're protesting for."

"I like Kennedy's plan better," I answer immediately. Her eyes widen in shock because she definitely did not ask for my opinion. "I will literally get on my knees and beg you to do it."

She grins. "I'm more than happy to see you begging on your knees, but I'm not doing shit."

"Fine, I can settle for a private lap dance. It stays between us two, and no one has to know," I suggest.

She opens her mouth, ready to say something, but something stops her, and she pauses, looking me up and down. I'm wearing a similar hoodie to hers but mine is dark blue—the school colors —and says "North Sports Department" on the back.

Wren sighs, shaking her head. "Tell you what I've just realized?"

"What?"

"You're the stupidest person I've ever met in my life." I groan. All that lead-up for nothing. I'm pretty confident bullying is her love language, and I'm sure I can get behind it. "How about you? How's your problem going?"

"It's… going," I say, "Coach isn't letting me back on the ice until I've cleaned up my act enough, and I have to go to these fucking meetings where we have to talk about our feelings."

I shudder, and her eyebrows crease. "You mean… class?"

"Worse."

"Oh, gee, what could possibly be worse than going to class to get a degree?"

"Group therapy," I say bluntly.

Her lips press into a thin line. "Oh."

I scratch the back of my neck. I have no problem talking about it. Honestly, I'm surprised it didn't come up when we talked about Carter on our date. I just hate the way other people get weird about talking about therapy. It's a normal and natural thing, especially when you're going through a hard time. It's felt like some big, bad secret that the whole team has been keeping since it started. There's nothing wrong with getting help, and if it's accessible to us, we should use it.

"We have to go once a week," I explain. "The school organized it. They started doing them after we lost Carter, but most guys dropped out after a few weeks."

"Then why are you still going?" she asks quietly.

"I feel like I owe it to him, you know?" I say, and it's not the only thing; I owe him so much more than that. "When people drop out, it just shows who actually cared about him. Yeah, it might suck having us all break down while a stranger tells us how valid our feelings are, but those guys are my family. I'd rather cry in front of them than do it alone." Wren smiles softly, and I can tell she doesn't know what to say. I shake my head, wanting to change the subject. "Anyway, I came here because I wanted to update you on how the book is going."

Her face lights up, and that dimple I've missed pops right back out. "How is it? Are you *loving* it? It's my favorite enemies-to-lovers book to recommend."

"Oh, for sure. It might be the best book I've ever read. Truly life-changing," I say with as much conviction as I can muster, but it's fucking difficult.

The excitement dies on her face, and she frowns. "You hate it."

"Wrenny, baby, I'm *trying*. I'm two hundred pages in, and they haven't even kissed yet. Or even held hands. You said it was a romance. That was false advertising," I argue.

I don't know what's more surprising—the fact that I'm two

hundred pages into a romance novel or the fact that they haven't even kissed.

Wren sighs. "It's a *slow* burn, Miles. They're building up the tension, and when they eventually fuck each other's brains out, the wait is worth it."

"They *fuck?* I thought they were otherworldly beings from the fifth dimension. Do they even have the necessary body parts to fuck?"

She holds a hand up to me. "Okay, I'm going to pretend that you didn't just butcher the language used to describe the book and you're going to stop pretending that you didn't know the book had sex in it."

"I *didn't* know that!" I whisper-shout as people slowly start to filter into the huge space. Her eyes flash with worry, but I continue talking, leaning in closer to her. "I read books about sports, Wren. And let me tell you, there is no kissing and fucking involved."

She leans in and whispers, "And that's why they're so boring."

She smiles smugly, and I can't help myself. I grip both sides of her face, shaking her head slightly, and she giggles. The sound is enough to kill me.

When I stop shaking her and we're just smiling at each other, I say, "You're so wrong I want to kiss you." The words are already out of my mouth, and I'm staring at her like I might do exactly what I said. She stares back at me, and for a second, I think she might want me to. I clear my throat, dropping my hands from her face. "In a very platonic and friendly way, of course."

"Of course," she whispers, nodding. More voices fill the room, and she steps back. "You should probably get going. Darcy *hates* hockey players, and I don't know if you know this, but you're kind of a big deal around here."

"You're right. I didn't notice. Thanks for the ego boost." I chuckle, drumming the barrier before walking away. "I'll see you around, Wren."

"I hope not," she calls, but I can tell she's smiling.

8
WREN

"I want to see his lady parts."

EVA

We're so fucked.

MARY

Tell me about it.

AUGUSTUS

I think the bake sale idea isn't too bad.

That's a terrible idea.

EVA

I agree.

INDIA

Darcy is going to kill us. We've not thought of anything.

MADELYN

I'm dropping out. I can't deal with this stress.

EVA

Can't you ask your mom to do something about this, Wren?

I'll try, but it seems like it's up to us to drum up some support for the team. I'm not quitting.

AUGUSTUS

You might as well.

See you at practice.

SOMETIMES, I wish me and my friends could enjoy a casual lunch together without someone or something ruining it.

We're sitting in Florentino's, Kennedy's workplace, and the on-campus café that sells the best food and drinks that anyone student could want. I'm pretty sure Ken is two more shifts away from getting fired because even though we're in the middle of the lunch rush, she's taking her break now, chatting away like she doesn't have a job to do.

"I think you should just fuck him," Kennedy says, shrugging.

"We're barely even friends, Ken, no."

"Friends can fuck," she argues, shrugging again. Scarlett and I exchange a glance and then look at her. "Come on, don't try to act like you haven't thought about it. Friends with benefits situations totally all work out."

"And you're basing that analysis off experience, right?" Scarlett asks, smiling smugly. We both know that Ken isn't as sexually active as she wishes she was. She loves to give us sex advice but will never take it for herself. Which is a shame because she's one of the most stunning people I have ever met, and if she gave any guy the time of day, they'd be falling at her feet.

"I'm basing it off *vibes,*" is Kennedy's response, looking at me. "He asked you out on a date. He's clearly so into you."

The *he* she's talking about, of course, is Miles.

I think they're more interested in whatever it is that's going on than I am. I think he's a good guy, and the date was really sweet, but I don't have the mental stability for a crush or a relationship. Liking people from afar has been my go-to response to anyone of the opposite sex since Augustus, and I really don't want to think about that right now.

"And you're into him," Scarlett adds.

"I'm..." I fight for the words because I can't lie to them and say I don't find him attractive. That would be a crime against humanity. "I'm indifferent."

"Indifferent means you want him to see your lady parts and you want to see his," Kennedy says, bouncing in her seat.

I give her a pointed look. "I want to see his lady parts?"

She scoffs. "You know what I mean."

"No, Ken, I don't know what you mean. Please enlighten me."

She huffs, folding her arms against her chest. "Scarlett, can you take over? She's being difficult, and I'm clearly the only one doing all the heavy lifting."

"She's also right here," I say.

"She's also talking about herself in third person," Scarlett says before she turns to me. Her eyes sparkle as she reaches out and grabs my hand. "Okay, Wrenny baby, what's the issue?"

"There is no issue. You just think any guy who pays attention to me wants to get into my pants," I say, trying not to laugh. The faith these girls have in me and my ability to casually hook up with someone is admirable.

"That's because it's true. Have you looked in the mirror?" Scarlett says, shaking her head. "Look, you think he's a cutie, he thinks *you're* a cutie. Ken and I both vouch that you get some sort of dick that *isn't* a dildo so you can stop being such a grump."

I gasp. "I am *not* a grump. I'm a delight."

"A delight?" Kennedy snickers. I narrow my eyes at her and then to Scarlett, who is nodding in agreement.

"Yes, I am an absolute joy to be around," I say. No one has ever outwardly said I'm a delight, but I can feel it radiating off the energy I put into the universe. Most of the time...

"Yeah, when you've had some chance to work off your energy. When you're a bundle of nerves and anxiousness, you're snappy. Like you have been all day," Scarlett says. I groan. "Give me some reasons why sleeping with him is a bad idea."

"Because he's *him*. He's a popular hockey player. Everybody wants him, and if people see me sneaking around with him, it's just going to draw attention to me, and that's the last thing I want."

"Wren, you *love* attention. You forced us all to enter every high school talent show just so they could call our names out and we'd walk out to the intro to 'Crazy in Love.'"

"Because we're amazing performers if we put our minds to it," I argue. High school Wren was convinced we could be pop stars, and I saw nothing in the way to stop us.

"We were *horrible* dancers," Scar says, shuddering.

"Well, I'm sorry I believed in our collective talent," I grumble. They both laugh, shaking their heads. "Look, I just don't see how getting involved with him physically is going to do anything good for me."

"Getting your brains fucked out of you by Miles Davis isn't something *good*? People would pay to kiss his feet, Wren. You do know just how big of a deal he is, right?" Scarlett explains.

"That brings me back to my first point. It's just going to draw unnecessary attention to me and give me more stress than I need."

"You're no fun," Kennedy mumbles. She sulks, and I don't have the energy to tell her that she can stop trying to live vicariously through me.

I've not been with anyone since Augustus, and the prospect

of hooking up with anyone casually is terrifying. Even when we broke up, it had already been a few weeks since we had sex. He refused to sleep with me during competition season because of some stupid superstition he has and that only led to more friction in our relationship until it blew up.

Scarlett's eyes slowly lift to mine, and a fire lights within them. "This is perfect."

"What is?"

"You can use him."

"I'm not you, Scar, I don't use boys for the shits and gigs."

"Well, you should. It's really fun," she mumbles. Scarlett laughs like an evil genius whose favorite pastime is torturing boys for fun. "Anyway, what I'm saying is you could date him, and maybe that way, people will be focusing on the skating team again. Just use him for a bit of fame and drop him when the showcase is done."

I stumble over my words at her suggestion. "I'm not going to lie to him."

"Fine. Tell him or don't tell him you're going to use him," she concedes. "Honestly, I'm sure he'll take it as a compliment."

Kennedy's eyes widen as she leans forward on our tiny table. "That plan is genius. Why didn't I think of that?"

"Maybe because you should be thinking about things like, I don't know… your job!" I cry, keeping my voice as quiet as possible. It seems like I'm the only person who cares if Kennedy gets fired or not.

She waves me off. "It's fine. Grace can survive on her own for five minutes."

"You've been sitting here for nearly an hour, Ken," I mumble.

"Whatever." I narrow my eyes at her, and she sticks her tongue out. It's like being best friends with a child. "So, are you going to do it?"

"I don't know. I'll have to think about it."

The idea doesn't sound bad at all. I'm already having a fun time hanging out with him, so it wouldn't be hard to pretend to like him. I'm not an actress by any means, but getting the attention out of it would be good. My mom has been calling me nonstop over the past week, and I've been avoiding her like the plague. Not like I have much choice now though. I'm supposed to be going to see her for a "check-in" when I leave the girls.

I've spent the rest of my time in the gym, at the rink, or in the library. They're the only three places I go to nowadays. I can't even remember the last time I had a good night's sleep without having to tire myself out by working too hard.

Trying to think of a plan to get people interested in me and the team has not been working out very well. We had a team meeting last night at Madelyn Briar's house. She called it and said that we all had to do something to raise more awareness for the team and get people interested. I was there for three hours, and the best we came up with was a bake sale. I wasted three hours of precious reading time for a *bake sale*.

We've not been able to come up with any solutions, and trying to focus on classes as well as all of this isn't helping. I need to do something about it, and quick.

"Well, as long as you don't go all Millie Trainor on him, you should be fine," Kennedy says.

"You always blurt out names like I'm *supposed* to know who these people are." I groan, pushing my head into my hands.

"Wren, we've been going to this school for a year, and you don't know who some of the most talked about students are, and it shows," she argues.

"Why would I spend my time gossiping about people I don't know?"

"Because it's fun?" Kennedy stares at me, and I stare back. She rolls her eyes. "Millie catfished her boyfriend for three years in high school, and he only just found out now thanks to Mason

Greer." I give her another blank look, and she sighs. "He's the creator of that gossip page on Instagram. They have a bunch of accounts for different cities to expose couples and just post about drama that doesn't involve them. It's like TMZ. And, no, I'm not explaining who TMZ is."

"That much I can understand, thank you," I say dryly.

"Anyway, as long as you're upfront with him about the terms and conditions, you should be fine. If anyone gets a whiff of this beyond the three of us and Miles, even if you're just *thinking* about it, it'll be used as an excuse to expose you," Kennedy explains. My eyes widen. I don't like the sound of that. "Again."

"I wasn't 'exposed' with regionals," I say, knowing exactly what they're referring to. My fall on the ice was filmed like the competitions usually are, and someone posted a clip of it online. I've been more careful about what I post and who I share my account with since it happened, but the only thing it did was make me a laughingstock for a few weeks and push people even further away from the skating team. "Well, thank you for that insight, Kenny girl. I'll think about it."

"Well, you should probably think quickly because he's right here," she says. The words fly out of her mouth, and before I can even register them, she's beaming up at Miles as he stands by our table. Of course, he's here right now. Kennedy's smile doubles in size. They haven't seen each other since the party, and I planned to keep it that way. I don't want him to get the wrong idea and think we're the kind of friends who have friendship groups merging together. "Hi!"

Miles's smile is all confidence and ease as he says, "Hi. It's Kennedy, right?"

She beams, holding out her hand for him to shake it. "Wynter, like the season but with a 'Y.'"

Miles nods, turning to Scarlett. She sits up straighter, if that's even possible—she has the posture of a ballerina—holding out her hand to him. "Scarlett V—"

"Voss," he finishes, shaking her hand. "Trust me, you don't need an introduction. You and your entire family are millionaires. And I'm sure you remember me from when you were fooling around with Jake."

She beams with pride at the "millionaire" part before scowling at the mention of Jake. "Yeah, I do. I don't remember you being this polite."

"Well, turning over a new leaf and all. Really trying to impress this girl," he says, turning to me. His entire face lights up, and I resist the urge to roll my eyes. "Oh. I didn't see you there."

"Bet you didn't."

He grins. "How are you?"

"I was good until you showed up," I lie.

He frowns, taking the spare seat on the table next to me and Kennedy. "Let's not do the whole song and dance."

"What song and dance?" I ask, pretending to be more interested in the tea in front of me.

"You pretend to hate me; I pretend to not be turned on. It's our thing, Wren."

"Right."

"We were just talking about you, actually," Kennedy says.

Miles gasps, looking around at the three of us. "You were? How sweet of you to talk about me to your friends. I haven't got a text back from you all day."

I roll my eyes. "I spoke to you last night."

"And I texted you again this morning," he argues. I stare at him. He stares back at me. "I'm clingy, okay?"

"I can tell."

We stare at each other, talking with our eyes. His face is puzzled but amused, searching my face for something as the crease between his eyebrows deepens. He's frustrating me just from the fact that I can't get inside his head.

What are you doing? I'm trying to say.

I don't know, he would say, *but you're staring at me.*

You looked at me first, I'd retort until we're in an intense staring contest.

He opens his mouth to speak, but nothing comes out and he clamps it shut.

Kennedy whistles, pushing out her chair from the table. "Well, I better get going, you know, to my job."

"Oh, so now you want to go," I mumble as she scrambles to her feet, rushing behind the counter. I look at Scarlett, and the traitor is packing her notebook back into her bag. "Scar, seriously?"

"Yeah, I've got, uh, business millionaire duty to attend to," she says. She's the worst liar I've ever met in my life. She slings her bag over her shoulder, pressing a kiss to my forehead. "I'll see you tonight. Love you."

I flash her a look, whispering, "Don't leave me," to which she responds, "Play nice."

Miles hooks his foot around the leg of my chair, pulling me impossibly closer to him, and it takes all that I am to pretend not to be affected by his proximity. Not only is he easy on the eyes, but he also *smells* good. He's got that signature man scent, all woody and earthy like he bathes in it.

I hate it.

He drops his face into his hands. "And then there were two."

"Do you get some weird pleasure out of ambushing me?"

"Do *you* get some weird pleasure out of me ambushing you?"

"No." I narrow my eyes at him, trying to figure him out but I get nothing. "Why do you always do this? You're making me jittery."

"How? I'm not even doing anything."

"You're *here,* in my safe space. That is you actively doing something."

He holds his hands up in defeat, the goofiest grin on his face.

"I'm sorry. I didn't know you claimed the campus café as your safe space. Should we rename it Wren's Café so no one else walks in?"

"If it keeps you out, why not?" He smiles, and I smile too, and it's like all the ice around my heart is slowly being thawed. Just like that, we're back in this weird friendly flirty thing I have no clue what to do with. "So… any solutions to your problem, or are you still warming up the bench?"

"For your information…" He trails off, drumming his fingers on the table. I can't help but notice how good they look too. They're not chubby and dirty like a lot of men's fingers are. They look strong and long. His knuckles are a little red, and I can imagine that his fingertips are calloused. "Yes, I am still warming up the bench. You?"

"We tried to have a meeting with the team, but they're all useless. I thought the hockey players were the ones with talent and no brains, but it turns out it might be us."

Miles crosses his arms against his chest, shaking his head. "This clearly isn't our year, Wrenny. We should just make out and forget about it."

"Why is making out always your first option?"

"Why isn't it *your* first option?"

"You have a habit of doing that, you know?"

"Doing what?"

"Flipping every question I ask you back onto me," I explain, trying to stare him down, but it doesn't work. "It's annoying."

"You're annoying," he retorts. I blink at him, and he sighs, shaking his head. "You're not annoying. I don't know why I said that. You're gorgeous."

I scoff, rolling my eyes. "You know, Scar and Kennedy actually suggested something earlier…." I trail off, waiting for him to lose interest or tell me to continue. He does neither. He just continues looking at me, so I say, "They think it will help me out if we pretend to date each other. I know how weirdly obsessed people are with you. I mean, I've gotten at least half a dozen side-eyes since you sat down with me, so everyone clearly thinks you're a big deal. I know it's stupid, and you don't have to agree to it but—"

"I'll do it."

I frown. "You didn't even let me finish."

"That was rude of me, but it doesn't matter. If it'll get you to stop ignoring my texts and we can hang out more, I'll do it."

"I've been busy," I say.

I don't know why I'm being defensive about it, but I don't like the thought of him thinking I'm *actively* ignoring him. I get swamped easily with homework, and my schedule is tight with classes and practice. I don't even get to see my best friends as often as I'd like, and I live with them. I've always felt like I owe people explanations as to why I always have to cancel plans with them at the last minute. Most of the time, they just disappear from my life completely and I never get a second chance. Not with Miles. He's fucking determined. It's refreshing, actually.

"Look, we'd only have to do it for a few weeks until the showcase at the end of December. I know you might not be getting much out of this, so I can help you train more and help with your classes if you want," I explain.

He leans back in his chair, crossing his arms against his chest. "No offense, but how are you going to train me? You're barely five-five."

"For your information, I'm five-seven, and height has nothing to do with physical strength, genius," I mutter. "You saw me on the rink the other day. I get access to the rink early because of my mom, which means an extra three hours of practice before Darcy even steps foot into the building. I take that shit seriously. I don't mess around with my diet or my training. I'm committed to my sport, Miles."

He studies me for a moment, probably to see if I'm joking,

and he knows I'm not. I've always taken skating seriously, even when I feel like I'm slowly falling out of love with it. With my mom's expectations to always be great, I'm determined to prove her right.

"Huh." Miles lifts his chin up, grinning. "I think your friends might be onto something."

9
MILES

"I'm fucking obsessed with you."

"SO, you'll be my personal trainer *and* I get to be your boyfriend?"

"Finally. Now you're getting it." I smile, my cheeks starting to hurt with the number of times I've smiled since I've asked her to repeat herself to me. She points a finger at me, reiterating, "*Fake* boyfriend."

I almost scoff at that. Some girls would die to have the chance to be my *real* girlfriend. Not like that's anything I'm interested in. I don't do relationships, and I don't sleep around as much as everyone thinks I do. Just because I wear a jersey and a lot of my teammates decide to be assholes, doesn't mean I'm one. I've always kept a clean record, and I don't let any girl drag me into shit that I don't need to be involved in. It's one of the reasons I was made team captain. That, and my stats are some of the best this school has seen in years.

From what I've gathered, Wren wants to make everyone believe that we're dating so they will give her and the skating team the attention they need to get more funding and attend the winter showcase. In return, she's going to help train more, reshape my diet plan, and basically become my personal trainer.

This could help her a lot with this ice queen facade she's trying to pull off. She acts like she can't stand me, huffing and rolling her eyes whenever I'm near, but I know that deep down, there's a part of her that enjoys my company.

I don't blame her.

I'm irresistible. And the second people find out I'm taken, her popularity across North is going to skyrocket. I'd be doing her a huge favor, but I think I might be getting the better half of it than she is.

Since I met her at the party, no one has made me want to get to know her more than she does. The fact that she makes me work for all these little pieces of information about her only drives me closer to her. It makes me want to spend all my time around her, getting to know her, and figuring out why she is the way she is.

As if she can tell I'm thinking about her, she slaps me on my arm. "Hey, loverboy. Don't start dreaming up some magical fantasy where we start dating for real. That's not going to happen. Neither of us is in the position to even *think* about that, alright? You're just hyper-fixating on me to avoid fixing your problems."

I narrow my eyes. "Hyper-fixation is an insult to how I feel about you."

"Really? Can you please provide me with a more accurate assessment?"

"I'm fucking obsessed with you, Wren," I say. There's no other way to describe it. Not having hockey to focus on has severely messed me up mentally. It's not given me something to work for or work toward. Trying to get motivation is like trying to find water in a drought. The only thing that feels worth thinking about that isn't my inability to play or my grief is *her.* Sometimes, it feels like she's the only thing I can think about that makes me breathe.

"See, hyper-fixation," she says, gesturing to me.

"Obsession," I correct. I pull out my signature grin, thinking she'd smile too, but she doesn't. She slips her bag over her shoulder and stands. "Hey, where are you going?"

"This clearly isn't going to work. It was a stupid idea," she huffs. She tries to walk past me, but I circle my fingers around her wrist, pulling her back to me. She gasps at the contact, her eyes flickering to mine.

"Says who?"

"Says me."

"Don't I get a say in this?" I ask. Her teeth sink into her bottom lip as she clearly tries to mentally argue with herself about doing this. I swipe my thumb against her skin, and she sighs. "I want to help you, Wren. I swear."

"You've got to take this seriously," she whispers.

"I am," I say, "I will. Let's just talk about it."

"We need to make some ground rules."

I nod. "Okay. What else?"

"You can't tell anybody we talked about this and what we're *considering* doing," she says, her tone sharp and authoritative.

"Okay. Are you going to sit down so we can talk some more, or are you just going to stand?"

She rolls her eyes. "I've got to go and—" Her phone vibrates in her bag, and she fishes it out, groaning when she sees the caller ID.

"Is it your nightmare ex-boyfriend?"

I don't know why I ask. For all she knows, I don't know anything about Augustus, but after all the boyfriend talk, I'm curious. I don't know why they broke up, but from what I found out, they were dating for *years*. He's a fucking fool for letting her go. If I had Wren Hackerly for real, she wouldn't spend a second doubting if I really cared about her. I'd worship the ground she walks on. I already do.

Her body stills at my question. "What do you know about Augustus?"

"Nothing. I just know you two broke up."

Her shoulders drop. "Right."

"What? What was that? Why'd you say his name like we're talking about Voldemort?" I quiz, searching her features. Her walls are back up again, her green eyes growing darker. Anger unfurls in my stomach, and my fists grip on to the arm of the chair. "What the fuck did he do to you?"

"Nothing, Jesus. There's no need for you to go all caveman on him," she says, patting my shoulder, but it doesn't help me relax. She could just be making excuses for him. "Kennedy's got in my head about the whole social media thing. Pages like NoCrumbs spread some shit about me and Augustus. Just..." She takes a deep breath. "Just don't believe everything you read, okay?"

"You're not secretly a murderer, are you?"

"If I were secretly a murderer, you would have been dead already." I hold my hands up in surrender, and she laughs. "It's just my mom. I'm going to meet her and get some older and wiser advice about life. You know, the usual."

"I bet Hacks gives the best advice," I say.

She flashes me a sarcastic smile. "The best."

"We'll talk later, yeah?" I don't know why the question makes me feel anxious. It really shouldn't. I know I've been clingy, almost desperate to get her to talk to me, but it finally feels like we're stepping in the right direction, and I don't want her to pull away from me. I want to see where this goes.

"Yeah. We'll talk soon. Bye."

When she leaves, a rush of air leaves my lungs before they fill back up again.

This might finally be the thing to pull me back to the surface after months of feeling like I'm drowning. I've tried everything to get rid of the aching in my chest, and nothing has worked. I've played mind games with myself so I could get back onto the ice without having a panic attack. I thought I'd be better by now, but apparently it doesn't work like that. I can't just snap my fingers and hope that everything will be fine just because I'm telling myself it is.

As I'm about to clean up the mess the girls made, my phone rings in my back pocket. I take in a deep breath when I see Clara's contact name fill the screen. I don't remember the last time I spoke to her. The few days after I found out about my mom cheating were a blur of heated conversations and memories I've tried my hardest to block out. Honestly, not talking to my sister every day has been hard.

We grew up almost like twins in the weirdest way. There's a seven-year age gap between us, but we did everything together. I think my parents were worried that we'd make the gap too large, so they pushed us into doing everything together the second I could walk. It felt like a treat to hang out with my cool older sister who showed me how to skate and would take me to the Ski Village that she worked at.

My parents worked a lot, and it gave us more time to hang out with each other. My mom teaches at a middle school, and my dad is a radio host for one of the local channels. I always thought it was a weird combination, but they made it work.

Until they didn't.

Apparently, my mom had been cheating on my dad since I was in middle school. She managed to convince him that she was just working it out of her system as if she hadn't been married to my dad for almost thirty years. Clara knew, and she didn't tell me until after Carter's funeral. I spent a whole seven years of my life without the knowledge that the person who has always preached about loving their family and being loyal has been fucking my dad over for years. And he still stayed.

I pushed myself further and further away from the three of them while I tried to wrap my head around it, and I've still not come to terms with it.

"Miles, what the hell are you doing?" is the first thing my

sister asks when I answer the phone. I have to close my eyes and feel my chest rise and fall, allowing it to calm me down before speaking.

"Hello to you too, sister," I deadpan, knowing that if I sass her in some way, she might save us both the torture of pretending that everything is fine. "I'm just having coffee in a cute café on campus."

"Don't be smart with me, Miles," she spits out. "No one has heard from you in months, and in case you forgot, I'm still your emergency contact. Miss Hackerly called me. Why aren't you going to your classes? And how the hell did you get benched? Hockey is the only thing keeping you there."

I feel the bile rise in my throat, but I swallow it, rubbing my temple. "Since when do you care? It was easy for you to lie to me for years. Excuse me if I want some mystery in my life to remain." I know it's a low blow, but it's too late, and the words are already out. I hear her huff over the phone, growing more agitated.

"Get your shit together or you'll lose your scholarship. Just go to your classes, and don't fuck this up," she warns.

I don't know how many more people are going to say this to me before it fully sinks in. It's so easy for me to say, "Yes, fine," but it's the *doing* that I can't do. I can't even pick up a hockey stick for God's sake.

"I'm going to figure it out," I say after a while. "Bye, Clara."

"I hope you do. And Miles…" She pauses, taking in a breath. "I love you. Always."

My chest suddenly feels tight. Suffocating. This feeling has been happening a lot since Carter died, and I can't get rid of it. It makes my breathing quicken, and it feels like something heavy is weighing on my chest, like I won't be able to get up.

Since we were kids, Clara and I would end every "I love you" with "always." It became a thing within our family, and even when times were hard, *especially* when times are hard, we are supposed to say it.

But right now, the words dissolve on my tongue before I can get them out.

I can't bring myself to say anything other than "Always," as I end the call.

I take in a deep breath, dropping my head to the back of the chair, and vow to do something about this. If Wren is willing to help me get back on my feet, I'm not going to take this for granted. I need to get back on the ice this season. I need to do it for myself and for Carter.

10
WREN

Mother dearest

SINCE MY PARENTS' divorce six years ago, Melanie Hackerly has been on the quest to establish herself as a woman who can conquer all. She wanted to be the type of person people write articles about—the type of woman who could have hundreds of girls lining up to play her in a biopic. That was her plan for so long that when she was injured and went into coaching and teaching, she still found some loophole to get her to whatever stage she needs to be at in the future.

My mom has always treated me like I'm her student first and her daughter second. Sometimes, I wish she actually continued being a coach instead of becoming the head of the sports department at North.

There's always been this immense pressure on my shoulders to perform for her. To fulfill this legacy that she never got to. My friends think that she pushes me too hard, but Mom thinks Darcy is too easy on me. I need the structure. I need the routines and someone telling me how to improve or I'm never going to get any better and the only talent I have will all be for nothing. I don't just want to be good, competing in championships and competitions. I want to be *great*. I want to be someone great and important instead of this stupid wallflower that I've reduced myself to become. Being so immersed in my skating, I've never had time for anything else. The little time I do get away from it, I try to spend with my friends, reading or writing.

My mom's words might be biting and harsh, but I need to hear them. If anyone is going to be brutally honest with me, it's going to be her. I used to think she ruined skating for me, that she took the fun out of it, but these last few years, I've started to breathe my own life into it. I've set high standards for myself and for what people expect of me, and the fear of letting them down is nowhere near as bad as the fear of letting myself down.

As kids, Austin and I never really saw anything wrong with my parents' relationship. They seemed happy. Whole. They had the kind of love you thought would last forever. We had weekly family outings, birthdays were always a blast, and we had regular vacations. There was nothing that we could see to tell us they weren't in love.

When you're told your whole life that your parents love each other, it's hard to tell that the kind of marriage they really had was lacking it. You don't know that until you realize what real love is. Their love was nothing to idolize or aspire to. It just *was*.

They kissed and said goodbye on their way to work; they always tucked us in until we reached our teens. Until one day, they just fell out of love. It was quick and simple. There were no arguments or name-calling, they just stopped. My dad told me it wasn't our fault—because it never is—and they went their separate ways.

My mom's current hyper-fixation is another recent divorcee, Mike, who has two kids from his last marriage. She moved out of our family home into a Spanish-style house in Centreville. My dad still lives in our family home, our childhood bedrooms still covered with the same One Direction posters I've had for as long as I can remember.

With Austin away, dancing for a prestigious ballet school in

Russia, I'm my mom's sole focus. Which is probably why she's being so hard on me to help the team pick themselves back up. I'm not completely confident in Miles's boyfriend abilities, but I'm going to have to trust him. I sent him a quick message to meet up on Friday, so I have to give us a chance.

"Any updates on the progress with the team? Darcy told me you all had a meeting last night," my mom says, pouring me another glass of orange juice while she tops up her wine. It's not that warm out, but we're pretending it is, sitting by the pool in her backyard. Her house is huge for only two people, but it makes it a good spot to pretend to be vacationing every day.

"That meeting was a shit show," I say, shaking my head. I know she doesn't like it when I curse, but I can't help it sometimes. I've never felt more useless than I did last night. "I can't believe how terrible we are at coming up with ideas."

My mom laughs. "Darcy wasn't very happy that she didn't hear back from any of you."

I shrug. "There'd be nothing to say."

We're both silent for a few beats. The silence between us always feels deafening, even when we're not talking about anything bad. There's just never been that comfortable silence that I get when I'm with Dad.

"You are taking this seriously, right, Amelia?" my mom asks, using my first name to get under my skin. Amelia has never really fit me. I don't know what it is about that name that I didn't like, but the second I figured out my middle name was Wren, I made sure that's what everyone would call me. There's only a handful of people who actually call me Amelia, and I hate it.

"Of course I'm taking it seriously, Mom." She holds her hands up in defense. I wasn't trying to attack her; I'm just sick of feeling like I have to do everything all the time and I can never get a minute to do something I actually want to. "I think I might have something working out."

"You think so?"

I nod, meeting her gaze. "I don't want to get your hopes up, so nothing is set in stone, but it could work."

Just thinking about spending more time with Miles sends a rush of excitement through me. I never know what I'm going to get with him. It feels like there's always some element of surprise when we hang out, and I'm guessing that pretending to date is going to make that become more regular.

"Are you seeing someone?"

My mom's question makes me jolt. "Where did you get that from?"

She grins, her lined dimples popping out. "Your cheeks are pink."

I stumble over my words, gesturing to the pool and the gray sky. "It's hot."

"Not that hot."

Telling her directly that I'm dating someone is like begging to get shot in the foot.

She's always been protective over me, but when I started dating Augustus, those chains slightly loosened. She adored him. He was charming and funny, he always made jokes at the right time, and he was what my mom thought to be the perfect boyfriend for me. He was a pretentious ass, but I think that's what my mom loved about him.

He pushed me too. Sometimes, it was a little too far, but I learned to brush off the sly comments he'd make about weighing too much to lift or when he would tell me all my favorite colors to wear weren't flattering on me. I ignored them because I had to do what it took to win, and having him as my partner was my best shot at that.

He was the best male skater in our team for duos, and I have been skating with him since I was fifteen. Our on-ice chemistry was palpable and everyone knew it. When our relationship turned into something more, I liked the idea of having a boyfriend. I liked the affection and the attention, but deep down, he wasn't anything special. He never *did* anything special, and I was stupid and broken enough to settle for that. My mom doesn't know how he treated me in private and she probably never will. I'm happy with her thinking that he was the love of my life and that losing him was the most devastating part of the breakup and *not* losing the championship. I'd much rather have a shiny medal to add to my shelf than a boyfriend.

"It's nothing serious," I tell her, and she hums. "If it gets serious, you'll know."

She hums again, tilting her nose up, and she changes the subject. "Have you spoken to Gianna recently?"

"Why don't you just call her Gigi, mom? Gianna sounds so formal," I say, laughing. It's become a running joke between us. My mom calls her Gianna, and Gigi still calls me Amelia. It's silly and stupid, but most things are with us.

"Fine. Have you spoken to Gigi recently?" she amends, and I smile. "She and Diana came over for dinner the other night, and they were wondering if I'd heard from you."

"You do know they both have my number, right?"

She shrugs, taking another sip of her wine. "Well, it wouldn't hurt if you called them sometimes. They think you've forgotten about them."

The guilt festers in my stomach. I know how busy I've been since starting college, but since Gigi doesn't go to public school anymore, it's been harder to hang out with her in person. We try to call a few times a month, but we're both so busy. Coming to visit my mom just reminds me of how we used to hang out as kids and how having dinner with the Kowlaskis wasn't as irregular as it is now.

"I haven't forgotten about them. I've just been busy," I say, pushing my hair out of my face. I tug on the ends of it, a nervous tick I haven't been able to get rid of. "I'll call Gigi on my way home."

"You should. She misses you," my mom says softly. That just

hurts my heart even more. She turns to me, her blue eyes boring into mine. "I've missed you, too. I feel like we don't see each other that much."

And she's gone straight for the kill.

"I know," I whisper, dropping my gaze from hers. "When I've got this skating thing under control, I'm going to try harder, I promise."

"Good because not having your sister here has been hard for me. I miss my little girls."

My throat pinches, and I don't know what to say.

Our views on my childhood are very different.

When I think about how it was when I was a kid, I think about competing in skating competitions when I was four years old. I think about missing out on schoolwork and seeing my friends because I was always training. I think about being swamped with homework because I couldn't catch a break even when I wanted it. I think about having to wake up at three in the morning to drive out of state to a competition. I think about burying my head inside a paperback and wishing I could live inside a fantasy world instead. I think about having to worry about my diet at six years old. I think about not having anything in common with my friends until halfway through high school and forever feeling like I dedicated my whole life to something that could disappear the second I get into an accident like my mom. It's like I've been skating on a fault line for years and at any second, I could fall through the cracks.

And I instantly feel guilty because all those memories gave me what I have today. It built the strength that I have and the talent that is going to get me to where I want to be. I refuse to let myself believe that this was all for nothing.

We change the topic, and my mom goes on a rant about Mike and the vacations they have coming up. She talks about her job like it's the best thing in the world, and I wonder if I'll ever get to a point in my career where, despite all the bad things that have happened, I can still see the good in the everyday.

Still, her comment pricks at me, and the guilt makes a home in my chest.

When I'm safely strapped into my car, I try my hardest not to cry. I'm not a big crier. I've always thought it was weak. It just reminds me of the times I would fall on the ice and my old coach, Donaldson, and my mom would shout at me to get back up. I'd brush myself off and carry on skating with tears in my eyes.

I shake my head, fiddling with the screen in my car to press Gigi's contact. The second the call connects, I feel like I'm transported right back into the comfort of her house: the millions of certificates that line the walls of her writing achievements, the photos of us as kids, and the smell of pierogies. God, I miss it. I miss *her*.

"Hey, G. How are you?" I ask, a smile finally forming on my lips when she answers.

"I'm good. Just in bed, staring at the ceiling and contemplating life, you know?"

"So, the usual?"

"Pretty much." She sighs, and I can already picture her bedroom lit up by her lava lamps that illuminate the Marvel posters on the wall. "I've been writing all day, and my agent thinks I'm burning myself out."

I get a stupid jolt in my chest at her words. I wish I had the courage that she does. I wish I had the balls to self-publish my novel like she did a year ago. Her fantasy series, The Last Tear, went viral last winter, and she got over ten thousand sales within the first month. She was quickly signed to an agency and has been working toward getting a traditional pub deal for months.

I know how hard it is for her to make friends and socialize, but writing has been that escape for her like it is for me. With her learning difficulties, she and her mom made the decision to keep her out of school. Her books were making enough money to live off, and she's more than happy to commit to being a full-time author while her agent works on getting her a deal.

"You should probably take a break," I suggest, my shoulders relaxing as I stop at a red light. "Maybe you should come hang out with me, Scar, and Ken. We haven't had brunch in a while. It could be fun."

"It could also be hell," she mutters. I know she's not being harsh. It's just how she is, so I just laugh. "Thanks for the offer though. How are you? Are you one step closer to becoming the next biggest figure skating star?"

"I'm... getting there," I say. I launch into a five-minute rant about the team and the funding and the lack of support, and she listens to everything, offering her own solutions. A bake sale, again. "I think I've got something figured out though," I say.

"Yeah?"

"There's this guy—"

"There's always a guy."

"He's, like, the most popular guy at college. North's golden boy. High school kids treat him like a hockey legend," I explain, and she just laughs. "I was thinking that we pretend to date, get some buzz around our relationship, and see if that helps with drawing more attention back to the skating team. Do you think that's a good idea?"

She's quiet for a minute, no doubt mulling over the idea in her head. "That's the best idea I've ever heard come out of your mouth, Amelia."

I snort. "It was Scar's idea."

"That makes more sense," Gigi says, and I laugh. "It sounds like a good plan. Why are you worried about it?"

"I-I'm not worried about it."

"You wouldn't be calling me to tell me that if you weren't worried about it."

I forgot just how well she knows me. "I think it's going to

work out, seriously. It's just going to be a little weird adjusting to pretending to date someone when I haven't dated anyone seriously other than Augustus."

"What's this guy's name? Can I internet stalk him?"

I snort. "Miles Davis. Do your worst. He's got an annoyingly clean record."

I hear some shuffling on Gigi's side, and I turn another corner. I was going to go straight home, but I need to work off this energy. Yes, it might be nervous energy but I'm not admitting that to her. If I can't get the support the team needs, I can at least be a good asset to the team for as long as it lasts.

"You're right. He seems like a boring, conventionally attractive guy who plays hockey," Gigi says with a sigh.

"I know. It's a real shame our society has come to this."

"What's worse is that *this* is your upgrade from Augustus. I mean, how do you go from him to this *god?* You're hot as shit, and you settled for Mr. Porcelain Doll." I laugh, pulling into a parking space outside the rink on campus. "I love you, Amelia, but I seriously don't get how you put up with him for so long. I've dated more men and women in the time you've dated this mediocre douchebag."

Laughter racks my entire body, tears springing to my eyes. Nobody makes me laugh as much as this girl does. She has absolutely no filter, and I love that about her. I love that she doesn't feel like she needs to switch off parts of herself for me like she does with other people.

"I love you too, Gianna, which is why I'm not going to say anything to that," I say, shaking my head as I pull my gym bag from the backseat of my car. "Look, I'm at the rink now. It was great catching up. I'll see you soon."

"Not if I see you first," she says hauntingly.

"What does that even—"

The call ends, and I don't know why I expected anything less from her. I slide out of my seat, pushing my headphones over my ears, and I know I'm going to be here for most of the night. I don't mind it one bit. I need to tire myself out. I need to clear my thoughts and get them to stop running away like they do every time I see my mom.

I skate until my head starts to hurt.

I skate until my palms ache from where my nails have dug into my skin.

I skate until my legs wobble from the number of times I've tried to land my triple Lutz.

I skate until it feels like it's all I'll become.

11
MILES

Rule Number 3

"CAN everyone get out so I can sterilize the environment before she comes over?"

I've lost count of the number of times I've tried to get my friends and their BO out of the house before Wren turns up.

I knew it would be a bad idea letting my teammates come over tonight. Usually, Friday nights are pretty laid back with me, Xavier, and Evan, but I was persuaded into letting Harry and Grayson come over too. I haven't seen them much since I've been avoiding the rink, and they put up a good fight about how much they've missed me. They've been playing on the PlayStation for the last three hours, and I don't think they've looked away from the screen once.

"So, are you going to tell us who this mystery girl is?" Grayson asks through a mouthful of mini pretzels as I pick up an empty chip packet from next to him.

"Not really," I say, moving into the kitchen.

"It's Wren Hackerly," Xavier says. I shoot him a look through the open kitchen, and he shrugs. There goes my plans to keep it a secret until we announce our relationship. I haven't told Xavier about our plan yet, but he knows I'm hanging out with her tonight. If Wren tells me I can let him in on it, I'll consider it, but right now, it feels like something that should stay between the two of us.

"Wait. Is that Miss Hackerly's daughter?" Harry asks in his thick Australian accent, which I still haven't gotten used to. He's a freshman, and he's ridiculously good in goal. He's probably been the best addition to our team this year. We met a few times during hockey camp over the last two summers, and he quickly became one of my closest friends.

"Yeah. We played Just Dance with Wren and her friends at that party, remember?"

His eyes widen as he turns to me. "That was *the* Wren Hackerly?" I nod and he shakes his head as if he can't believe what he's hearing. "I saw what happened at that competition last semester where that idiot dropped her. It was all online the second I turned up here."

I hum in response.

Her words have been ringing in my head since I bumped into her at Florentino's. I know what happened circled around social media, but she always seems so unaffected that I didn't even question how badly she must have taken the hit. I can only imagine how it would feel to have everyone talking about you and your relationship.

"Yeah, that looked like it sucked," Grayson adds. "She's hot, but she acts like she's got a cork stuck up her ass." Grayson laughs, and my chest tightens.

I flick him on the back of his head. "Shut your mouth, Gray."

"I'm just saying, if you're finding someone to sleep with, you're better off looking somewhere else," he says.

"Well, it's a good job I'm not trying to sleep with her, isn't it?" The room erupts into laughter like they think I'm joking. I don't think Wren even tolerates me just as a human. I'm sure sleeping together is the last thing on her mind. I sit across from them and pull out my phone.

. . .

ME

Hey, are you on your way yet?

I WAIT A WHILE FOR A RESPONSE, but ten minutes go by without anything. Panic slowly starts to build in me as I pace around the house, making sure everything looks presentable. She's either bailing on me or something has happened. I consider reaching out to one of her friends, but I don't want to seem desperate, so I sit and wait for something to happen.

An hour goes by, and the house is empty when she finally responds.

WRENNY

Fuck. I'm SO sorry. I'm on my way now.

TEN MINUTES of more completely chilled and not dramatic panicking later, I'm opening the door to a sweaty and puffy-faced Wren. She's wearing cycling shorts and a sports bra, a duffel bag in her hand. Her blonde hair is tied back into a messy ponytail, flyaways sticking to her forehead. With the way her chest is heaving, I can see the faint outlines of her abs, and I've never seen anything more attractive.

My smile widens as I open the door, letting her walk in. She waves her hands around frantically, shooting out apologies. I stop in front of her, resting my hands on her shoulders to force her to take a deep breath. She's still panting, and it takes her a while to focus on my eyes.

"I'm so sorry I'm late. I was at practice, and I went to the gym after and lost track of time. And God, I smell like ass." She rambles, all of her words merging into one. She scrunches her nose, shaking her head, and I can't help but laugh.

"Hey, just take a deep breath," I whisper. I rub my thumb against her collarbone, and she relaxes slightly, taking in a deep breath. "Are you okay? You seem a little..." I give her another once over.

"Tense? On edge?" I nod. She rolls her eyes. "My mom's just getting in my head this week. It's nothing. I was planning on working off my energy on the ice, and it just got too much. I'm sorry, again."

"You don't have to apologize; it's okay," I say. I drop my hands from her shoulders, leading her into the kitchen. I try not to focus on the fact that this is the first time that she's been in my house. I've got nothing to worry about now that I've spent the last two hours stress-cleaning. "We can do this at another time if you want."

"No! It was my fault I was late." I turn, raising my eyebrows at her outburst. She closes her eyes and shakes her head. I pull out a glass and pour her some water, handing it to her. She downs it in three gulps and places it back on the countertop. She wipes the back of her hand across her mouth and sighs deeply.

God. It's like she's *begging* me to fall for her.

"Sorry, that was gross."

"It was hot."

She scoffs, rolling her eyes. "Can I use your shower? I came straight here, and I really don't feel comfortable talking about our plan as I'm drenched in sweat."

"Of course," I say. I nod at her to follow me up the stairs. It's weird with the house being so quiet and even weirder having Wren actually in my space. I've always thought my house was some sacred cave that I could escape to, and now she's here, and nothing has ever felt more natural.

She gasps when she enters my room.

The walls are painted a dark gray, filled with movie and hockey posters. My dresser is stacked with textbooks and sports magazines, and the romance book that Wren got me is on the side of them. I highlighted a few of the scenes I actually enjoyed, and I plan on giving it back to her for her to see when I'm done. I got rid of the alcohol in my mini fridge, and it sits in a corner, stocked with soda and water.

"Did you clean this just for me?" Wren asks as she walks over to my pile of books. She snorts when she sees The McDavid Effect sitting proudly on the top. She turns around, leaning against the desk as she crosses her arms against her chest.

"This is actually the only room I *didn't* clean," I admit, stepping toward her. "Clean room equals clear mind."

"Is that right?"

"Yup," I say. She nods, tilting her head up to me, and her green eyes lock with mine. My hands itch to do something. To touch her. To help erase whatever stress she feels in this moment. "Are you surprised?"

"Actually, yes," she says, "You're making it very hard not to like you, Miles."

I tuck the few strands of hair that have fallen out of her ponytail behind her ear, and her breath hitches. "As a friend?"

"Yes, as a friend," she says, flashing me a sarcastic grin as she slides away from me. I turn to find her ruffling through her duffel bag, her ass molded in those tight fucking shorts. She groans, dropping her head between her shoulders. "Fuck me."

Believe me, I want to.

I clear my throat. "Is everything okay?"

She turns. "I left my clean clothes in my locker. You're going to have to put up with me smelling like shit."

"You don't smell like shit, and you can just wear something of mine."

"Are you sure? I don't want to, like, invade your personal space," she mutters, looking through her bag again before giving up. I'm already looking through my drawers before I reply.

"Yeah, it's not a big deal. You can invade my personal space whenever you want as long as you let me invade yours," I say, turning to her with a towel, faded white NU Bears tee, and some shorts. I hand them to her and nod to the door in the corner of my room. "The bathroom is just through there."

She walks over, and I drop back on the bed, dragging my hands down my face. I'm going to need to learn how to focus when she's around. If I want this to work, I can't get caught up thinking about her ass or the millions of places I want to touch her.

"I don't usually do this," she says softly.

I sit up. "Do what? Shower at your fake boyfriend's house?"

"I mean, I'm usually more put together than this," she explains, grimacing at herself. I nod in understanding, not sure what else to say. I don't care if she's messy or not put together. I think it's one of the most admirable things about her.

MAYBE LETTING Wren shower here wasn't the best idea.

It was an even worse idea letting her borrow my clothes because she looks too good in them, and she smells like me. My shirt clings to her body in places that haven't dried properly, and I can see through it.

Right through it.

She walked out, crossed her arms against her chest, and told me not to laugh. I don't think I could even get any words out with how hard I am. This celibacy is not doing me any favors the more that I think about it.

Now, she's sitting beside me on the bed, and I was smart enough to put a pillow in my lap.

"No one can know that this is fake apart from our closest friends," Wren says, writing down another rule in her notebook. We could have just typed them up, but she says this will help her remember better. "Scarlett and Kennedy only know because they suggested it."

"Fair enough," I say. "Xavier will probably figure it out eventually, and I trust him to keep quiet about it."

She hums, writing that down too.

We've agreed to do this whole fake dating thing until her showcase at the end of December, which gives us around two months. If it doesn't work, we'll reevaluate to prepare to get me into some of the winter games so I can help get us into the regional semis and the finals. The hockey season is just beginning, and the quicker I can get myself back into training, the faster I can get back on the ice. I've got more than enough time to convince Coach Tucker to let me back onto the team.

"Okay, so what about our families? Are we fooling them, too, or should we rule that out?" she asks.

My body stiffens, and I shrug. "We can come to it when the time comes."

Her eyes soften, and she nods. "My mom kind of already knows. I didn't even tell her anything; she just knows these things. My dad is probably going to be interested, too, and I haven't caught up with him in a while. Are you okay with that?"

I nod. "The last time I spoke to your mom, she was close to kicking me out, so I'm sure she'll be thrilled that I'm dating her daughter."

"Trust me, no one is going to live up to her precious Augustus," she mumbles, and I pretend that the comment doesn't get to me. From what I've gathered, the guy is a dick. He was stupid enough to let go of the best thing that probably ever happened to him. "We should make a big deal of us hanging out a few times a week and staying over at each other's houses. It just shows it's more serious than casual sex. If we go to parties, we need to attend *and* leave together to give no one a reason to suspect anything is wrong."

"That's good," I say.

This whole thing is making me feel stupid. I have no clue what's on-and-off limits, but Wren has been taking the lead on it. I've just been agreeing to everything and trying not to look at the outline of her tits under her shirt.

"What about PDA?" I ask, clearly thinking with my dick.

"What about it?"

"Is it going to be a problem?" I ask. She continues writing whatever it is in her journal. "I'm an affectionate person, princess." Again, she doesn't say anything. "Okay, so I'm just going to assume that making out, hand-holding, ass-grabbing, and anything up to second base is on the table."

That grabs her attention. Her head shoots up, her cheeks flushed, and I can't help but smirk to myself.

"Only if absolutely necessary," she says, pulling down the shirt to cover more of her thighs. "And we don't need to be affectionate with each other if we're alone unless we're taking photos. Got it?"

I ignore her last addition as she writes it down. "Shouldn't we at least kiss once so we know what we're doing?"

I press my hand to her knee, and she tenses beneath my touch. Her skin is warm and smooth and so fucking tempting. She closes her eyes, taking in a deep breath before placing her hand over mine. She lets out a noise between a groan and a laugh as she takes my hand off her.

"Have you ever kissed a girl before?"

"Plenty."

"Then we should be fine." I roll my eyes, pushing myself up against the wall beside my bed. "Okay, my last and most important rule." I dip my head to her to continue. "Rule number five. If things get too real for either of us, we have to tell each other. I mean *real* feelings beyond attraction. It could mess things up, and that's the last thing either of us need."

A wicked grin spreads across my face as her cheeks heat up again. "Worried you'll fall in love with me, Wrenny girl?"

"No, Miles. It's you that I'm worried about," she replies.

I hate how right she is. All she has to do is look at me and I'm a goner. One look and I'd devour her. If she wasn't so committed to keeping our friendship purely platonic, we wouldn't be sitting on my bed *talking* right now.

"What about my side of the deal?" I ask.

"You'll come to the gym with me, and we'll figure out a good food plan for you to follow. I'll do my own research on hockey training in the meantime and see if we can get you back on the ice," she says, grinning. She's clearly very enthusiastic about working out, and I couldn't think of anything worse right now.

"Sounds good to me," I say. "It's Sophia Aoki's birthday party this weekend, so we could go to that as our first public outing." The second I say the word "party," she groans. "What? Don't tell me you're against parties."

"I'm not *against* them, I just don't like them. I hate the feeling of being drunk, and I hate being around strangers who are," she admits, shuddering. She leans into me and whispers, "Barcelona."

"What the fuck happened in Barcelona?" I ask. She shrugs. "You keep giving me these tidbits of information, Wren, and it's not that useful when I'm trying to get to know you. Please tell me what happened in Barcelona."

She laughs. "It was the last time I got drunk, and I haven't been to a party since."

"You were at one the day I met you."

"That's because my friends forced me to go and it's their idea of a good time," she argues, and I don't push her on it. "I'm fine with going along, but just don't expect me to drink and have a blast of a time."

"A blast of a time?" I echo. She nods. "Is that what you think I'm having when I go to a party?"

"I mean, yeah, don't you? You go, have a few beers, take off your shirt, and run around with your friends. Some girl will find that pathetically attractive, you'll sleep with her, go home, and then do the same thing every weekend."

A laugh rumbles out of me. "Wow, you've really got me all figured out, huh?" She shrugs again, but I can tell that the idea of going to a party is worrying her. She must think she's got this whole I-don't-give-a-fuck attitude down pat, but I can see right through her. She's been on edge since she got here, and I'd do just about anything to help her feel less alone. To help ease any worries she has. "If I ask you something, will you promise to answer me?"

Her eyebrows crease as she traces a pattern on her knee. "It depends what it is."

"Is everything okay?" I ask gently, not trying to pry but to get her attention.

Her eyes lift to mine, and I catch the hurt in them. It's only now, with how close we're sitting, that I notice that one of her eyes is more blue than green. Is she just going to get more beautiful every time I see her?

"What?"

"You said you're going through something with your mom, and today is the first time I've seen you out of control," I explain. "You're always in control. You're always organized and put together. Even on the ice, your movements are sharp and perfect. I want to know that you're okay. If I can help you in any way beyond this, I just want you to know that you can ask me."

I watch her features transform and her lip quiver. "Fuck, Miles," she says, tilting her head back. My heart races, and I reach out to comfort her because she's clearly about to cry. I squeeze her knee reassuringly, but she crosses her legs, pulling her knees to her chest and hugging them. "No. Don't. I just— If you touch me, I'm going to start crying, and I hate crying."

I nod in understanding. "Will you talk to me at least?"

I hate the idea of her thinking that she's alone or that she can't talk to me. We can joke around, and she can make fun of me all she wants, but she's got to know that I actually care about her. I value her. I care about her opinion and what she wants.

"You've met my mom. You know how she is," she starts, resting her chin on her knees. "She's basically been my coach since I was four. She's always had my back when my other coaches would push me too far, but I think it just gave her an excuse to handle the situation. She had a bad accident when she was in her early twenties and there's no way she could dance or skate again. So when my sister and I came along, we wanted to follow in her footsteps. Austin does ballet, and she's one of the best in the world. Figure skating always stuck with me. It always just felt like *my* thing, even if my mom tries to overpower it. There's just this constant struggle between who is in control of *my* life, and sometimes, it doesn't feel like it's going to be me."

My heart breaks for her, and she continues talking, the words rushing out of her. "I don't think I'm being used by my mom because she loves me, and she cares about me enough to know what my limits are, and she wouldn't do that to me. But sometimes, instead of her holding my hand, it feels like she's got her hand on my neck. She'll say things, leave little comments about how she wishes I was still her little girl where I'd spin for *her,* dance for *her,* and do everything for *her.* But my perceptions of my childhood and the ones she's tried to paint for me are two very different things."

My hands itch to hold her. "Jesus Christ, Wren. I'm sorry."

She shrugs, a smile twitching on her lips as she meets my

gaze. "I don't know why I've let her get under my skin this week. I think it just makes me do better. It pushes me to keep going, you know?" She sighs, shaking her head with a wry laugh. "Maybe I should unpack in therapy."

I swallow. "You should."

"Are you telling me to go to therapy, Davis?"

"I go to therapy. It's not that big of a deal, and it could help," I suggest.

"But that's different," she says. "You lost your best friend, Miles. I just have stupid mommy issues, and I often think of emancipation."

"And you don't think that deserves a therapist's attention?"

She shakes her head firmly. "Not if it takes away spaces from other people who really need it. I'd hate to be the reason someone else doesn't get the help they need because of the problems I've pretty much brought on myself."

"What about you?"

"What about me?"

"Who takes care of you?"

She shrugs. "I do."

I stare at her, and she looks at me like she really means it.

I want to change that. In whatever way I can, I want to be the reason why she doesn't have to be alone anymore. I can't even fathom the idea of this girl believing that she always has to be responsible for taking care of herself instead of sharing that burden with someone else.

She drops her knees from her chest and slides off the bed, picking up her duffel bag. "I think I should go. This therapy session has been great and all, but I've got to get up early tomorrow."

"And we're on for the party next week?"

"Of course."

"And you'll tell me if you change your mind?"

"I'll tell you if I change my mind." She smiles. "Thanks for the shirt. I'll give it back next week."

"Don't bother. It looks better on you anyway," I say. She rolls her eyes, smiling before turning to leave. I jump to my feet, gripping onto her forearm, pulling her toward me. "Wait." Her eyes flicker to mine, searching my face for an answer. "Can I give you a hug? You look like you need a hug."

She nods, and I think she doesn't speak to stop herself from crying. I hold my arms out, letting her make the decision, and she steps into me. It might be the best feeling I've had in my entire life.

Her body melts into mine, and her head rests against my chest, where my heart is beating fast. She inhales, and when she sighs, it's like I can feel the weight slowly being lifted off her shoulders. I wonder how many times she's been hugged in her life. How many times has someone seen the sadness in her eyes and taken the initiative to give her a hug?

I don't ease up on her, and I let her take control. I hold her tight and let her decide how long she wants to hug me for, and I don't care if we stand here all night. She clings to me like she's never been held before, and just that thought is enough to break me. Her arms tighten around my back, her nails digging into my shirt like she's afraid I'll let go.

She sniffles, and I cup the back of her head, smoothing my hand down her hair, and her shoulders shake. "I've got you, princess," I murmur, holding her as close as possible. The sound of a sharp sob rips through my heart. I keep her pressed to me, whispering, "I've got you."

We stay like that for a while until she's stopped crying, but her face is still pressed into my shirt. I thread my fingers through her hair, and she doesn't tell me to stop. Her hair is soft and silky, and I can tell doing this relaxes her. She lets me do it for a few more seconds before she pulls apart from me, swiping at her eyes, and she gives me a weak smile.

"If you tell anyone about that, I'll murder you," she croaks out, her voice heavy with emotion.

I hold my hands up in defense. "I wouldn't dream of it."

When I walk her downstairs and to her car, I make it a personal mission of mine to be the support she's never had.

12
WREN

"You're, like, the size of a child."

I WOULD PAY VERY good money to be able to get last week's events erased from my memory.

I used to think that I could keep pushing forward, that I could ignore every weird feeling that passes through me, but after allowing myself to break down in Miles's arms, something shifted. I didn't feel the need to run to the gym or find some way to get rid of my thoughts without actually dealing with them. I just *felt* them, and that's been the most emotionally exhausting thing I've ever done.

Well, that and trying to run around my apartment now to find a decent sports bra to wear to the gym with Miles.

Turns out that going to the gym twice a day for an entire week means you run out of clothes to wear. I didn't realize how badly I needed to work off my problems until I found myself trying to run away from them on a treadmill. I've burned through more workout clothes this week than usual, courtesy of my mom's constant check-ins, and I haven't been on top of the laundry.

Working out has always been therapeutic to me. I've been dancing and skating since I was a kid, and staying in shape has always been important and has improved my mental health without even realizing it. Time passes by in a haze when I'm in the gym, and the relief I feel afterward is so rewarding. I'm hoping to encourage him to see the benefits that I do, but he was reluctant when I texted him last night to make sure he was ready for it.

I finally find a black Nike sports bra that I haven't worn since high school. And not to my benefit now, my boobs have grown a ton since then.

"Did you shave?" Scarlett asks through a mouthful of toast when I make my way into the kitchen. She's sitting at the island, eating her breakfast while balancing her phone on the back of her water bottle as a very intense study video plays.

"No, Scar, I didn't. We're going to the gym. I'm not trying to sleep with him," I argue. She just shrugs and goes back to watching her video. Since I came back from Miles's house and the rules were set, Scar and Kennedy have been pushing me to break them already. I have no interest in sleeping with him any time soon, and these rules were made for a reason.

"Can't you do both?" Kennedy asks, walking into the kitchen as she rubs sleep out of her eyes. If she didn't have classes to go to, I'm convinced she would spend all of her time in bed. She sits beside Scarlett, stealing a piece of her toast. "He might just trip and fall right between your legs."

"Do you both have to be on my case right now?" I groan.

"It's pretty much our job," Kennedy says.

"Yeah, who else would encourage you to make good decisions?" Scarlett adds, grinning.

"*Bad* decisions," I correct, "You encourage me to make very *bad* decisions." I point at the picture on the fridge, and they both shake their heads. "Barcelona."

"Yes, yes, we know. But that wasn't our fault. That guy we followed into the bar sounded very legit and *we*"—Kennedy gestures toward Scarlett—"didn't get any sick, so maybe you just got a bad egg."

I rub at my temples. "Can you hear yourself right now?"

They both laugh, and the rapid knock on the door cuts it short. "Is that your loverboy?"

"Yes, so be nice," I say, turning away from them to walk toward the door. They blow raspberries at me, and I shake my head at their immaturity.

Scarlett snickers. "It's you that needs to be nice to him. I've never seen a guy more smitten, and you've never looked more… annoyed? Turned on? It's hard to tell."

"Annoyed," I say to her before I open the door.

Miles is sporting gray shorts and a worn white tee, his NU duffel bag slung across his shoulder. He looks good. Annoyingly so. It makes sense why girls are doing everything they can to get him to notice them and why he's such a hot commodity. It's frustrating that he's just *that* good at being the charming funny guy without even trying. He steps into the apartment and raises a hand in greeting to the girls, who are trying to stifle their laughs.

"Hey, princess," he says, his voice extra sweet and silky. He dips his head to my tiny sports bra and shorts. "You look hot."

"You don't have to pretend to like me. They already know we're pretending," I say, walking away from him to grab my bag from the couch.

"I know." I turn to find him smirking, and it takes everything that I am not to roll my eyes. The girls flash me a glance, but I ignore it, grabbing water from the fridge and stuffing it into my bag.

I look up at Miles, and he's already got his eyes on me. "You ready to go?"

He nods, and we exchange goodbyes with my friends and head out the door. When we get to the parking lot, he walks straight past my car and continues walking down toward the main road. I call after him, "Where are you going?"

He turns, looking around him before taking the steps to close the distance he put between us. "To the gym. Where are *you* going? It's, like, a five-minute walk."

I tut, shaking my head. "Oh, you sweet, innocent child. Get in." I open my car door, and he goes to the other side, sliding into the passenger seat. He looks so out of place in my car. His larger-than-life shoulders barely fit in the seat, and he has to adjust his chair multiple times to give his legs more room.

We barely make it out of the drive before he starts quizzing me.

"Where are we going? There's not another gym for at *least* a few miles. Are you going to murder me? I know you said you would've done it already, but maybe you're just in it for the long haul." I glance over at him, and his eyes are wide and panicked. "Is this a kidnapping? Are you going to kidnap me?"

I laugh. "If I wanted to kidnap you, why would I ask you to come to *my* apartment?"

"I don't know! It's still a possibility," he argues. "If you are going to kill me, can we make out at least once before I die? I want to die a happy man, Wren."

"Can you chill the fuck out? I said we're going to do *real* training," I say, focusing back on the road. His face is getting more and more comical to look at the wider his eyes get. "If there's one perk to my dad owning hotels, it's that I get access to all the private, quiet gyms."

"That's insane," he mutters.

I shrug. "I'm just being practical. Why would we waste our time in a gym where the equipment is mediocre at best when we could go to a luxury one that has just been built?"

He doesn't ask me any more questions while we drive, and thank fuck for that. It's like I've got to convince our college that I'm dating a real adult and not a toddler. I don't know what demon possessed me to let Miles have the AUX because he plays the most obnoxious music I've heard in my life. I almost crashed multiple times while he screeched every lyric to the *Hamilton* song *Non-Stop*.

His singing and talking is nonstop, that's for sure.

"Remind me never to carpool with you again," I say when we walk into the hotel.

"I've got the voice of an angel, Wren," he whispers when we stand at the reception desk. His breath tickles my neck, but I ignore it, pushing away from him.

"Whoever told you that is a liar."

"No one had to tell me that for it to be a fact," he argues.

"The more you talk, the stupider you sound," I mutter, rolling my eyes. "You could do yourself a favor and shut up."

"You could do me a favor and make me." His voice rumbles low in my belly, and I push off the desk when the receptionist finally hands over our day passes, not before flashing me a sympathetic look. I'm going to need all the help I can get to help this fool with his training.

Secluded gyms like these, that nobody knows about, are my favorite. It's one of those weird things that make my heart insanely happy. They always smell fresh, and I'm usually one of the first people to use the equipment. It's like opening the cap of a fresh orange juice carton.

Miles and I drop our bags in the corner of the room and start with a light warm-up.

I usually stretch at home, but I don't know what kind of level he's at with his training if he hasn't been playing regularly. He might not be regularly working out, but he's still built like a hockey player. He's tall and broad, his thighs and calves are almost god-like, and he's got the personality to match. I did some of my own research into what constitutes a good workout for someone of his age and build, so I'm hoping today can ease him into it.

We settle into a smooth rhythm of doing a couple miles on the treadmill and on the Step Master. We move over to the weights, and start with our legs, pulling back the weights with our feet on the machine. My thighs burn, but it feels fucking fantastic.

I usually work out with my headphones in and keep social interactions to a minimum, but it's Miles. And he'd rather talk my ear off than listen to his outrageous music alone.

"How much can you bench?" I ask when we take a small break. I pull out my water from my bag, gulping it while he catches his breath.

"Isn't that the same as asking a girl what their bra size is?"

"That's not the same thing," I say, "and you don't have to tell me if you don't want to. I was just wondering so I knew what you could handle, that's all."

I position myself on the bench press, and he stands behind me, ready to spot me.

"I don't know. Maybe one-seventy," he answers, looking slightly embarrassed. I let out a "huh" in recognition, and he raises his eyebrow. "What about you?"

"Around the same. I do up to one-ninety on a good day." My cheeks turn red, and I don't know why I even have the feeling of being embarrassed. I'm proud of that. I've worked like a maniac to build up my strength, and being able to press that much has been a personal goal of mine over the years.

"How the fuck can you do that? You're, like, the size of a child," he says, shaking his head at me. I just shrug. "Don't get embarrassed, Wren. That's a good thing." He leans over and pokes me in the stomach, and I squirm.

"Hey, what was that for?"

"Just checking if those abs are real."

"And?"

He smirks. "They are. Hot as fuck too."

My cheeks heat, and I don't think I can blame it on the work-out. There's something about the way Miles compliments me and my body. He never sounds sleazy or gross. He sounds like he *admires* me. Like he cares about me.

Augustus thought everything was a competition between us, which is why we never worked out together. He'd complain that I was trying to show off, or that I should go to a women's-only gym so he could hog the spotlight. He made me believe that was the way things were supposed to go. And now I realize how wrong he was.

After alternating on the bench press, we move back into the floor space, changing between weighted squats and sit-ups. I'm trying to give him a feel of everything and what I typically do, and he meets every challenge with ease. I'm so used to working on my own, but the more time we spend together here, the more I realize it's a lot nicer than I thought it would be.

I watch him through the mirror where he's squatting, and I finally mutter, "You're doing it wrong."

I've been trying to let him do it on his own, not wanting to be annoying or controlling, but it's starting to piss me off.

"I think I know how to do a squat, Wren."

"Do you? Because you've been doing it wrong for the last ten minutes," I say, making my way toward him. I stand in front of him. "Watch what I'm doing."

He blinks at me, and I spread my legs into a decent position, making sure my back is set and I squat down low. I didn't think about the proximity until I felt my ass brush against his shorts, and he sucked in a sharp breath. I grab his hands from behind me.

"What are you doing?"

"You clearly aren't a visual learner," I mutter. I place one of his hands onto my lower back and the other on my stomach. My senses tingle at the feeling, but I ignore it and push it down. It's been way too long since a man's hands have touched me, and my body does not need to be getting confused right now. I clear my throat. "Can you feel how my back isn't leaning completely forward?"

He makes a noise in the back of his throat, nodding at me in the mirror. "You do see how this is a problem, right?"

"Why? Because you're incapable of keeping your dick in your pants?" I can feel it pressing into me, but I'm smart enough to ignore it. He just rolls his eyes. "Just feel what my body is doing when I go down. You're leaning too far forward, and your back isn't set in the right position."

I lower myself down, holding position for a few seconds before coming back up. I watch him watch me as I repeat the motion again before moving away. I watch him do it himself until he's got the hang of it.

"Wasn't so hard, was it, big guy?" I tease, dropping back onto the floor.

"It wasn't the squat that was hard, Wren."

I just shake my head and continue doing my sit-ups until he eventually joins me. We work out in silence, and I've never found anything more peaceful.

That is until he slides his phone over to me and I stare at it. "I found some questions on BuzzFeed," he explains, "I think we should know the answers to these if we're going to pretend to be a couple."

I click his phone, and it opens immediately. "You should put a password on here, you know?"

He shrugs. "I've got nothing to hide. The questions are in my Notes app."

I scroll and open the app. I skim through the first one that pops up. They're all relationship-based or weird icebreakers to get to know another person.

"Did you spend the entire night typing up these questions? It says you made this at three in the morning," I say, laughing.

"I couldn't sleep, and I copied and pasted them."

"You're full of surprises, aren't you?" I murmur, shaking my head until I land on a question. I smile, looking back at him. "What was the first thing you thought about me when we met?"

Miles runs a hand through his hair. "All I could think about was how hot you were."

"You've got to take this seriously or you wasted your night doing this for no reason," I argue, poking him with my foot.

"I *am* taking this seriously." I poke him again. "Fine. I just wanted to keep you talking to me. Keep you interested. I could tell you didn't really want to be there, so I had to think of things to say to keep you talking to me. I just wanted you to like me, and I knew it wasn't going to be easy."

His honesty catches me off guard.

I know I'm not the most fun to hang out with at parties, but there's something about the fact that Miles went out of his way to make sure I had a good time and to talk to me that makes me feel... better.

I smile. "Well, thanks for being honest."

He nudges his foot into mine. "What about you?"

"My first thought was: God, I really hope he doesn't die right now because that would suck. And then I thought you were pretty annoying, and then you *begged* me to go on that date, but you're more tolerable now."

"Just tolerable, huh?" My lips roll between my teeth, and I try not to smile. He doesn't need to know how much having him in my life has actually made me happy. I don't give him an answer, and he pulls his phone out of my hand. "Did you have any phases growing up?"

I shove my face into my hands. "Way too many to count."

"Tell me. I want to know what my little Wrenny girl was like." He pulls at my hands, and I close my eyes, shaking my head with embarrassment.

"Well, my first phase was making everyone call me Wren instead of my first name," I admit. A crease forms between his eyebrows.

"See, I knew something was off about you."

"My first name is Amelia, and my middle name is Wren. Amelia Wren Hackerly. I hated the way Amelia sounded too formal, and it's what my mom shouts at me when I'm on the ice. My mom didn't take my dad's last name when they got married, so Wren Hackerly always sounded better to me. When I started school, I just told everyone that my name was Wren, and it stuck."

He blinks at me. "*Okay,* that's a shocker."

"It's really not that big of a deal," I say, flicking my hair out of my face. "I went through my One Direction phase, a lot later than I'd like to admit. I once went through a British phase, where I forced everyone in my house to speak with a British accent for a week. I forced my family to eat my terrible creations that I thought were gourmet meals after watching MasterChef, but they were really just random condiments that I found in the refrigerator. I was just a general nightmare. I thought that I didn't have friends in middle school other than Scarlett, Kennedy, and Gigi because I was skating all the time, but it's because I was a little weirdo."

"I think I might be falling for you," he blurts out.

"What?"

"How are you going to say all that and not expect me to fall for you, Wrenny? You're perfect and I think it's ruining my life," he says. I laugh because that is the weirdest reaction I have ever gotten to someone hearing about my childhood stories. "Well, I was definitely a lot tamer than you. I don't think I went through any real phases. The only thing I can really remember loving as a kid was hockey. Carter and I lived and breathed it. It was all we talked about. We could go weeks at a time talking about the same game over and over. I guess I'm still in that phase though."

I see the way his eyes dim when he talks about Carter, and if I could do anything to help, I would. He might make me see red and annoy me on a day-to-day basis, but he's *hurting.*

I don't think about it, and I reach over and put my hand over his. It's the least I can do after I sobbed in his arms the other day.

He flips over his hand, his palm facing upward. We both stare at our hands as if daring each other to make the first move. I slip mine into his and instantly regret not doing this before. It feels strange and unknown, but so welcoming at the same time.

"Sorry. That didn't really answer the question," he murmurs, still staring at our hands.

"That's okay," I whisper, stroking my thumb against his hand. "I can tell you miss him. We don't have to talk about anything you're not comfortable with. I'm not going to push you on that just for the sake of this fake relationship."

"Thank you." He swallows, nodding. His hand is warm, his touch gentle, and it sends a strange, comforting warmth through me. I've always hated feeling emotions so intensely, but right now, feeling connected to him, I don't mind it as much. "Hey, Wren?"

"Yeah?"

"Am I dreaming right now or are you willingly holding my hand?"

I chuckle. "Just shut up and let me be nice to you."

"Thank you."

"You said that already."

His gaze meets mine, and I swear I could get lost in those eyes. "I know."

THE REST of the workout goes smoothly, and I think I might have finally found a workout buddy. The journey home ends up being more chaotic than the one there. Miles sings horribly the entire time, and I'm too tired to even fight him on it. When we pull into the driveway of his house, he stops the music and looks at me.

I look back at the house.

Then back to him.

Back to the house.

And then back to him.

He's still staring.

I narrow my eyes. "What?"

"How many guys have you slept with?"

His question startles me, but I don't show it. "Is that one of the questions?"

"No."

"Then why do you need to know that?"

He lifts one shoulder and then drops it. "I'm your boyfriend. I think I'm meant to know."

"*Fake* boyfriend," I correct, "And I'm not answering that."

"Why?"

"Because it's none of your business." I laugh when he pouts.

"*You're* my business, Wren." I stare at him, and he doesn't miss a beat, grabbing my hand out of my lap and pressing the stupidest, sloppiest, most ticklish kiss to my wrist. He blows a raspberry, and I laugh, the sound so ridiculous in the confines of my car that he just keeps on doing it until I'm writhing against my will. "Please, princess."

I can't help the giggles escaping me. "Stop doing that. It tickles."

I try to pull away from him, but he's even stronger than he looks, and he grips onto both of my wrists this time, torturing me even more. "I'm not stopping until you tell me," he whispers around the kisses on my wrist. "Are you going to tell me, sweet girl?"

Sweet girl.

My stomach bottoms out at the nickname, and I stop fighting him. The kisses on my wrist stop being playful and become more deliberate. Slow. Sensual. And I've never found anything more attractive. He keeps his eyes locked with mine as he does it, and my lips part. He kisses one wrist until it's covered in him, and it might be my new favorite perfume.

"Come on, Wren," he taunts, "Just tell me." If I could form coherent words, I would have said something by now, but I physically can't. "You want me to stop, don't you?"

Do I?

My mind is saying yes, but my body is saying no.

"Yes. I want you to stop," I say, breathing out.

His voice lowers. "Then tell me."

He blows a raspberry, and another laugh tumbles out of me, erasing the tension. "Two and a half," I reply.

He pauses, dropping my hands from his mouth but still running his fingers against my wrists where he kissed me. "A half?"

I pull my bottom lip between my teeth and nod. "He couldn't make me come."

Miles's throat works, and I lean over him. I inhale the annoyingly attractive smell of him until I bury my face in his neck. He groans, but I don't give in. I open the passenger side door, and he almost falls right out of the car.

I lean back in my seat. "I'll see you tomorrow, bright and early."

He scrambles to his feet, pulling his bag out from the backseat. "You're seriously leaving me like that?"

I glance down to see the very obvious erection in his shorts. "Seems like you've got business to take care of. I don't want to intrude." Before he can say anything else, I lean over the console and shut his door, backing out of the driveway.

13
MILES

House of Horrors

WHEN WE PULL up outside of Sophia's miniature mansion a few days later, the music surrounds us on all sides. The lawn is littered with people talking loudly over clouds of smoke. Cars line up the driveway and down the block.

It's been a while since I've been to a party. Before I met Wren, I was living a hell at frat houses, doing anything I could to distract myself from my thoughts and my pain. It was comforting to be around people who weren't there to ask me if I was okay and when I was going to start to get my act together. It was somewhere I could just go to forget, but now I've got a real reason to go.

I turn to face Wren, and she's been quiet since I picked her up. She's wearing a cute as fuck blue dress, and I've been trying not to eye fuck her, but her legs are long and toned and they look like they go on for miles.

She scans the surroundings, one hand on the door handle as she hesitates.

I place my hand on her knee, pulling her back to the moment, and she turns to me, her teeth sinking into her bottom lip. "If you want to leave at any time, just say the word, and we'll go," I whisper, and she waits a beat before nodding. The last thing I want is for her to feel uncomfortable. "I'm going to keep you safe tonight, okay?"

She nods.

"Okay?"

"Yeah, okay, let's go," she says, rolling her eyes playfully but smiling.

We walk up to the house hand in hand, and I try not to let my nerves show. It's been forever since I've brought a date to a party. I've been single for years, and my ex-girlfriend Emily used to drag me to every party at the school I went to when I'd visit. We were on and off during freshman year of college, and I wasn't willing to drive nine hours every few weeks just to go see her. She liked that I wore a jersey and that was about it.

But with Wren, people need to know this is serious. I need to do right by her, and if my stupid popularity can also help her out, I'd gladly hold her hand all night and spin her around until she's sick of it.

Music blasts from speakers in all directions, and people are standing aimlessly with SOLO cups in their hands. Fruity smoke from bongs and vapes infuse my senses, and it takes me a second to adjust to the sudden change in scenery.

I take my hand out of hers and slip it around her waist, pulling her into me as we go into the kitchen. "Are you okay?" I whisper-shout in her ear.

"I've been better," she mutters, smiling tight. "Is it always this loud and obnoxious?"

I raise an eyebrow. "What do you think?"

"It's like I'm inside of a really bad Netflix show about high school and someone is going to spill beer on me." She shivers at the thought, and I laugh.

"Just relax. I've got you, okay?"

"Just relax," she says, scoffing and shaking her head.

I pull her further into me, kissing her on the forehead as if it's the most natural thing in the world. She blinks up at me. Shit. Should I not have done that? Is it too soon? We're supposed to look affectionate, but was anyone even watching for me to have done that?

Someone taps me on my shoulder, and I turn around to a cherry-faced Harry. He's soaked head to toe, most likely just coming out of the pool. Knowing him, it was either a dare or someone pushed him in. Harry's not the type of person to willingly get into a pool that hundreds of people have already been in. He's pretty quiet and reserved, which is why I like him and think he's a good addition to the team.

"Hey, Miles," he says before registering Wren next to me. "Wren, right?"

"Yep," she says, popping the "p." She's either nervous or she just doesn't like me very much because that's the sweetest I've ever heard her sound in my presence.

"This is Harry. You remember him from the party, right? He's the one who kicked your ass at Just Dance," I say, gesturing toward him and Wren. They exchange a playful look and I continue my introduction. "He's the goalie and arguably one of the best players on our team. He talks a lot of shit, so don't believe everything he says."

"I don't talk shit," he mumbles, sounding as adorable as ever in his Australian accent. Wren marvels at him like he's the most charming guy in the room. He leans forward, hikes a thumb in my direction, and whispers to Wren, "If you ever want to know any stories about him, just let me know."

"I will take you up on that," she whispers.

"I'm right here, you know," I interject, but they continue talking like they're old friends and I don't exist.

"I've learned a few things about him myself," Wren says, a smug smirk on her lips as she lifts her head higher.

"Oh, yeah? Like what?" Harry asks, throwing me a look. I don't stop her. I'm glad she's trying to talk to my friends after putting up such a fight about wanting to come here.

"He's got an awful singing voice," she says, her gaze drifting from Harry to me and then back to him. I can't hide the grin that's spreading across my face. If taking jabs at me is what makes her comfortable, I'll let her call me every name under the sun.

"Does he? I didn't know that," Harry replies, clearly amused. "You've got to sing the national anthem at the next game, Davis."

"That's not going to happen." I laugh.

"Oh, but it should." Wren beams. "Have you heard how terrible his music taste is? It's like dating a—"

"Okay, that's enough," I say, cutting her off with a laugh. Harry's eyes are wide with curiosity, dying to hear what she has to say. "We're going to go see what's over there."

"I didn't even get to the best part. The other day—"

I put my hand over her mouth on instinct, and it almost covers her entire face as I slowly walk her backward out of the kitchen. I turn back to Harry, and he shrugs happily before walking off. Her eyes widen with alarm before softening and staring into mine as we continue sidestepping through the hallway.

I can feel her breathing quicken beneath my hand as her green-blue eyes pinch together as she looks down at my hand on her mouth. I drop my hand and shove it into my pocket. Her mouth opens and closes as she searches my face, her eyebrows still scrunched together in the cutest way.

I know she's wondering whatever that just was, but I don't know either. Being affectionate with her—whatever that means —is a lot easier than I thought it would be. Everything feels instinctual and natural, and I don't have to second guess myself when I'm with her.

She opens her mouth again, but before she can speak, Grayson wanders into the hallway, swaying slightly.

"Miles. Is this your girlfriend? The one you tried hiding from us."

He gestures his cup toward us, his beer almost sloshing over the edge. The change from being around Harry to Gray is so obvious on her face. I remember what she said about being around drunk people, so I pull her into me, nodding at him.

"The one and only," I say, and he chuckles with a hiccup.

"I'm Grayson, but you can call me Gray."

Wren's smile is tight and clearly forced. "Hi, I'm Wren."

"Let me get you some water, dude. You're already wasted," I say, trying to find Gray's eyes, but he's too busy looking around. I grip his shoulder to steady him as he continues swaying, but it doesn't do much to help.

He snorts. "Since when were you such a prude?"

"I'm not drinking tonight, and if you don't want to be benched at the next game, I suggest you drink some water."

"Fine, Dad," Gray mumbles.

Wren laughs.

Finally.

It's like a breath of fresh air. I can only imagine how irritating it must be for her to be here with me, but she's trying her best. I look down at her, watching her face transform into sunlight as she laughs at my expense.

Gray mumbles something that neither one of us can understand, and the conversation dies down.

Wren brings her hand across my stomach, nestling into my chest as if we aren't close enough already. The gesture makes my heart constrict when it shouldn't. I know it's been a while, but my body is acting like it's never had the attention of another woman before.

"Well, it was nice to properly meet you, Wren," Gray

mumbles when he remembers how to speak. He gives me a messy wink before disappearing back into the crowd. She bursts out laughing, pulling away.

She stands across from me, leaning against the wall. "Now what? Are we going to just stand around here all night until another one of your friends comes up to us?"

"This is all on your terms, Wren," I say. "If you want to stand around here all night, we can."

She hums. "Where's the birthday girl? Don't you want to wish her a happy birthday?"

"Sophia's probably got her tongue down her girlfriend's throat, and she wouldn't even notice if I'm here or not," I explain. She nods, looking around the small hallway where more people are starting to filter in. "Let's go to the pool."

She laughs. "You can go in and I'll watch. Then, I'll drive you to the hospital when you get a disease from whatever is in there."

I smile. "Deal."

I grab her hand and lead her out to the back of the house, where the pool is just as disappointing as Wren made it out to be.

Each inch of the rectangular pool is filled with semi-naked bodies, beer cans floating, and beach balls making their way across the water. The water has turned a strange brown color, and I don't want to find out why. We stand next to a wall close to the glass door, our arms touching.

It's a strange kind of intimacy that I didn't realize I enjoyed so much before tonight. It's like every touch from her is like the first time I'm experiencing it.

She erases every woman in my life before her, and I'm only left with her. Her touch. Her smell. Her laugh. Her smile.

And a part of me is starting to think that I won't need anything else in my life.

She bumps her arm against mine.

"And you wonder why I don't like parties," she says, looking up at me. She's so unimpressed it's almost funny. I lean my head against the door, laughing. I really am starting to get it. I can't remember what I found so comforting about being at a place like this.

"Yeah, it's not as fun as I remember. But I guess I found them more fun when I couldn't remember them," I say.

She frowns, her mouth twitching. "How's that going? The sobriety."

"I'm not actually an alcoholic, you know?"

"No, but you were getting there," she says, "I don't want to pretend to be dating an *almost* alcoholic."

"You're not."

"Are you sure?"

"Yes, Wren, I'm sure," I say, pinning her with a look. "It was just hard. I didn't know how else to cope with it, and drinking was the easiest option. I've cut back now, and I haven't had a drink in weeks."

Her eyes are hopeful. "Really?"

"Yeah, really."

We settle into a rhythm of comfortable silence as pop music blasts out of the speakers, reminding me of a scene from a movie. Except, we're not screaming and shouting and running around. Instead, we're lingering around like high schoolers who are too afraid to dance.

The silence between us isn't uncomfortable like it is with most people. It might be the most peaceful thing I've ever encountered.

"Do you want to go find some of your friends?" she asks after a while.

"Do you?"

She sighs. "Not really. I'm bored. I know I didn't want to be here, but I thought we'd at least witness a fight or something. I could have stayed home and done something fun."

"Yeah? And what do you do for fun, Wren?"

"Read."

"And that's... fun?"

Her entire face lights up, and I swear I've only ever seen her get this excited over ink on paper. "The most fun," she says, "and I can assure you if you threw out all those trashy hockey books and picked up some of my recommendations, you'll be staying up until three a.m. just to read."

"Has anyone ever told you how insane you are?"

She frowns. "You have. Twice, actually."

"And I mean it, princess," I say, bumping my arm into hers. "You're insane, but you're my kind of insane, so it's okay."

"Say that word one more time and I'm going to gouge your eyes out."

I lean down, tucking a strand of hair behind her ear. I hover over her, and she shivers. "Insane," I whisper, extra smooth and extra slow to see what she does. She tilts her face toward mine, and her lips are a breath away. I could kiss her. I *should* kiss her. I can just imagine how good it would be. How good it would feel for the both of us.

Her lips curve up into a grin, and she laughs.

She bursts out laughing in my face, and I can't even take the blow to my ego because it's the hottest sound I've ever heard. "You really are stupid," she wheezes. I just shrug, letting her laugh it out. I can practically see the tension leaving her body, and I'll happily be the butt of the joke if it gets her to laugh like that.

Her head shoots up from her feet, and something across the pool catches her eye, and she stops laughing.

"What's wrong?" She looks up at me as if she's seen a ghost. My heart starts beating rapidly against my chest, the sound roaring in my ears.

"Augustus is here," she says, turning to me so she's out of his view. I search over her head, and I spot him. He's slender and blond, wearing a button-down shirt to a house party. I almost laugh at the sight of him. Wren stands in between my open legs.

"Put your hands on me."

"What?" I , basically gasping for air as I blink at her.

She sighs and grabs my hands to rest on her hips as she snakes hers around my neck. She turns us around so her back is against the wall instead of mine. Her back arches slightly, her front flush against me.

Fuck me.

"Can you see him?" I ask, swallowing. Her face is a few inches below mine now. She looks behind me and nods before looking up at me. My breathing turns shallow when her green eyes drift aimlessly around my face, and I'm trying to compose myself enough to not just go out and kiss her.

"Just pretend you're whispering in my ear," she suggests, pulling at the hair on the nape of my neck, playing the doting girlfriend as she looks at me with fucking stars in her eyes. She guides my head until I'm breathing hard on her neck. I use one arm to brace myself on the wall so I don't crush her with my weight, and she shifts beneath me to get more comfortable.

"What do you want me to say?"

"I don't know. I don't care. Just do some—" she pleads, but her words turn into a sigh when I kiss her neck.

It's barely even a kiss. Barely even a touch. My mouth merely skims the soft skin on her neck, but when the goose-bumps arise across her, I can't help myself.

I kiss her jaw tenderly, once, careful not to contact her mouth. The feeling instantly makes me feel light and airy as I breathe her in. She smells like Gucci perfume mixed with sweet lavender soap. She's all fresh and summery, and I just want to drink her in. Her hands move from my neck to my chest, her small hands fisting my shirt, drawing me in closer so I can taste her.

"Is this okay?" I ask, biting softly against the space just

beneath her ear. She doesn't respond. Only a soft gasp leaves her mouth. So, I press again, "Wren. Is this okay?"

"Mm-hmm. Just keep..." she says, her chest rising and falling. "Just keep doing that."

While my mouth explores the side of her neck, Wren guides my hand that has gone limp at my side to her sweater. She slowly lets me slip it under the material, my hand spreading across her stomach.

She lets out a low noise of approval when the heat of my hand hits her cold stomach. Her abs tense beneath my hand, and I can't help but run one of my fingers over them. I kiss and bite gently on her neck, and she moans quietly.

She fucking *moans*.

Her breathing quickens when I accidentally rock against her, and she gasps.

She's going to be the death of me. But at least I'd die a happy man.

"Is he gone?" I ask into her skin. If she doesn't put a stop to this, I might spend the rest of the night just like this.

Her voice is hoarse when she asks, "What?"

"Augustus. Is he still there?" I ask again, taking my hand out of her shirt. I suck in a breath at the sight of her. Her eyes are closed, and her cheeks are red. I turn back, and I can't see him anywhere. "Wren. He's gone."

When her eyes open, her pupils are dilated. She searches my face, her chest rising and falling as she looks over me. Her eyes explore mine before she drops them to my lips. Her gaze hovers before she drops it, turns around, and runs away.

It takes my brain a while to register that she's just disappeared from in front of me. I run after her, but she's a lot quicker than I thought. I push through the crowds of people, trying to keep my eyes on the gold claw clip in her hair, but it's fucking difficult. I shoot out quick apologies as I almost knock people over as I run past.

I catch her sprinting toward the bathroom, but there's a small queue. She skips it, earning her a few grunts, and runs into the room before the next person can even open the door.

"Hey, what are you doing?" the guy at the front of the queue garbles. He's clearly drunk, but I apologize anyway.

"Sorry. My girlfriend's in there, and I need to check on her. Can you wait a few minutes?" I say, trying to open the door handle. He groans and walks away. The rest of the queue slowly follows after they realize that this might take a while.

"Wren, can you please open the door? I need to know you're okay."

I lean my head closer to the door, trying to hear better, but all I can hear is my heart hammering against my chest.

"It's nothing," she responds, but her voice doesn't sound the same. "It's fine. Everything's fine. I'm just— I'm fine, I swear."

"You don't sound fine, princess," I say through the door. "Can you open the door, please?"

I hear her sniffle, and it tears me in two. She's clearly not a big crier, and if she's crying right now and it's because of him, I'm going give Wren the fight she clearly wanted to see here.

After what feels like forever, I hear a click, and I push the door open, slowly.

The bathroom is all marble, and the bright lighting is startling compared to the dark neon lights on the other side of the door. The music is almost completely muted this far into the house, so I can hear the trickle of the tap and the sharp breaths Wren takes in. She's standing with her back to me, her arms tight around her middle, looking out the window as if she's completely immobile.

I walk toward her cautiously.

"Wren. Are you okay?" I ask quietly. I put my hand on her shoulders, and they drop with a shaky breath. "What happened?"

She turns around, her eyes filled with tears that haven't fallen yet. She blinks up at me, tears slowly falling down her face.

Instinctively, I swipe my thumb across her cheeks, futile attempts to help ease her pain, resting my hand on her face for a second before dropping it. Maybe I'm the problem. Every time I'm alone with this girl, I keep making her cry.

"I think… I think I'm having a panic attack," she says. Her eyes drop to her shoes as I place both my hands on her shoulders, steadying her. "This is, like, my third or fourth one this week. My second one today."

Her hands shake when she brings them to her face, rubbing at her cheeks.

How can she still look so beautiful even when she's crying?

I try to bring my hands to her face, but she backs away again, moving her hands frantically.

"It's already enough that I'm crying in front of you again," she says, "I really don't need you trying to comfort me too." She steps away from me until she's sitting on the toilet seat, shoving her face into her hands. I sit down on the edge of the bathtub, looking up at her.

"Can you smell that?" I ask, scrunching my nose up.

She sniffles. "What?"

"It smells bad in here, don't you think?"

"Miles, what are you—"

I cut her off, pretending to sniff in the air around us. "Just really try to smell it. It's awful."

Her teary eyes flicker between mine until she sniffs, taking in a huge breath. It doesn't smell bad here. It's honestly weird that it smells *good* for a bathroom at a house party. But it got her to take a deep breath, and that's all I need from her.

"I can't smell anything," she whispers.

"That's the whole point. You needed to take a deep breath," I say, running my hand across her knee reassuringly. She covers her face again, shaking her head like she wants to make me disappear. "Wren. Talk to me." I try to peel her hands away from her face, but she doesn't budge. "I've got you, alright? I know you don't want me to, but I'm here for you." She takes in a deep breath, the exhale shaky. "What do you need from me? Tell me how I can help you."

"It's just in my head. I'm getting anxious over things I don't need to get anxious about, and then it crushes me like a weight on my chest when things get too much, and I freak out." She blurts out the words, still not looking at me, and she takes another deep breath. "I think something's wrong with me. This… weight, this pressure, it doesn't feel normal."

This girl is breaking my heart. If I didn't think she'd push me away if I went to hold her, I would have her in my arms right now. I'd be smoothing my hand down her back, holding her as close to me as possible until she manages to pass all the pressure she feels onto me. I'd take it on and more if it meant she could be okay.

"There is nothing wrong with you, Wren. It happens to the best of us. A lot of people panic and have anxiety, but everyone just deals with it in different ways," I say. She looks up at me now, and a part of me wishes she didn't. I've never seen her like this before, and it breaks my heart. "I used to drink until the tightness in my chest went away, but a good friend of mine told me that I'd become an alcoholic if I didn't stop."

She sniffles. "They sound very smart."

"Smartest person I know," I confirm. She gives me a weak smile. "I know you've got a lot going on with your skating team and your mom, and clearly, there are some unresolved issues with Augustus, so we can leave. We can get out of here and get some food and pretend tonight didn't happen."

"But what about our plan? The pictures. This was supposed to be our big debut as a couple," she says, rolling her eyes.

"You," I say before I tap her skull, "and this brilliant brain of yours are far more important than any party, any photo, or any opportunity to show people that we're dating. What you want matters, Wren, and I'm sorry if it's never been proven to you that it does."

"Please stop talking or I'm going to cry again," she mutters, laughing.

I stand to my feet, holding out my hand to her, and she slips her hand in mine. "Let's get something to eat."

14
WREN

Fries with a side of trauma

I'VE ALWAYS HATED CRYING.

I've always hated the feeling of being weak and vulnerable, and I've put those walls up for a reason. But since I've met Miles, it's like he's been slowly hammering away at my walls and trying to get me to open up to him.

I don't think he's doing it intentionally, but he's got this annoyingly calm presence about him that makes me want to spill secrets to him and have him give me another hug. It's stupid and the most pathetic thing I've indulged in, but it feels good, and I haven't felt that in a while.

We end up in a secluded diner not far from the one we went to for our date. According to the very short menu, they only sell fries or fries (exploded). We sat across from each other in a back booth after ordering our fries and drinks.

I take a long sip of my Coke, drawing out the inevitable. "Hey, I'm sorry about what happened earlier. I know it's not a big deal or whatever, but it kind of is to me. I hate freaking out like that on other people, and I should have warned you or something. I don't know. I'm just embarrassed that you had to see me like that."

He stares at me for a minute, and I wonder why I didn't just keep my mouth shut. "You've got nothing to apologize for. Things happen. I'm just glad you didn't leave me shouting outside the bathroom door the whole night." I snort. "I meant what I said the other night, Wren. I want you to know that you can be real with me, and I like knowing that you're okay."

"Why?" I find myself asking.

"Why *wouldn't* I want to know that you're okay? When you're with me, and even when you're not, I just like knowing that you're okay. *Especially* when I'm not there. So, you running off from me earlier? Yeah, that doesn't really work for me."

The seriousness in his tone catches me off guard. No one has ever seemed so like they care much about what I feel or what I have to say. No one checks in on me as much as Miles does and I haven't known him for that long. It's all so weird to get used to.

"Okay," I whisper. He raises his eyebrow and I smile and say, "Okay."

"Do you find it hard to talk about?" Miles asks. His words are soft, but he has this intense way of looking at me. It isn't like he's judging me or thinking of ways to make fun of me. It's like he's trying to understand me, and it baffles me why he would want to do that.

I shrug. "Not really. I think I've always been anxious since I started skating at a competitive level. When I was a kid, I didn't really know what it was. I'd just start to feel really sick before competitions, and no matter how many times I'd tell my coach or my mom that I felt like that, they just said it was normal. It stopped feeling 'normal' when I was around eight and every time I felt like that, I couldn't breathe. It just felt like I was constantly drowning, and the more I thought about it, the more I'd panic and the worse I'd feel. When it's really bad, I throw up, which is what I thought was going to happen back there. Usually, the nausea is a tell-tale sign that I'm going to have a panic attack, but sometimes it just happens, and I can't control it."

Miles nods. "Do you ever talk to anyone about it?"

I shake my head. "The girls know, and I've mentioned it to my doctor. She diagnosed me with anxiety and depression a few months ago, so I've been taking medication to deal with it, but it doesn't mean it just stopped existing. It's hard to adjust to, but I always knew there was something wrong and I just needed to draw some real attention to it."

"Was it because of the fall? With Augustus?" he asks, his voice low and quiet like he's too afraid to ask me.

I nod, biting my lip. "I didn't think it was going to effect me as bad as it did, but it really took a toll on my mental health. I thought I could move past it since it was coming to the end of the semester and summer was around the corner, but it all just crushed me. I couldn't eat. I didn't leave my room, and the girls had to do all the basic things for me because I couldn't do anything on my own even though I desperately wanted to be left alone." I take in a deep breath. "There are still days when I think about it or I get overwhelmed with everything, but it's definitely not as bad as it was before. I think I'm getting better, but it's not something that just goes away, and I just have to be okay with it."

"You know you're not alone, right?" Miles says, and it feels like a punch to the gut.

I nod, swallowing. "I know. I've got my girls."

"And you've got me," he says.

I smile, wishing it could just erase the last few hours from our memories. "Yeah, I do."

There's a comfortability about Miles that puts me on edge. He lets me talk about things without an ounce of judgment, even the hard stuff. I always found that the second I tell people how it feels to be inside my head, they freak out or act differently toward me. My mom pretends that it doesn't exist even though she was with me when I first started taking anxiety medication when I was sixteen. It's become such a regular part of my routine that I don't think about it anymore. That's until I have moments like today or even when I look in my mom's face and she can tell that I'm not her perfect little girl anymore. She tries to ignore it because it's easier for her to conjure up a version of me she prefers in her head. I've never felt so much shame for just existing when she looks at me like that. But when I look up to find Miles's eyes on me, I have a weird feeling like he actually cares. Like he values me more than just my talent.

Our fries arrive, and sure enough, his exploded ones look disgusting. It's even worse that he has the biggest grin on his face while I grimace at them. They're covered in melted cheese, bacon bits, mustard, and hash brown bites. If I wasn't so hungry to eat my own food, I would have thrown up by now.

I cover my fries in ketchup, and when some drips down my finger, I lick it off, making the stupid mistake of looking up at Miles while I do so. He smirks, and I grab a napkin, cleaning up the mess in a more appropriate way.

"I take it you don't get to do this much," Miles says, nodding at our meal.

"My mom would have a heart attack if she found out I was eating food this greasy."

"Does she monitor what you eat or something?" he asks.

I shake my head. "Not really. We both know how important it is for me to stay healthy, so I've kinda adapted what I eat around that. It was worse when I was younger, but since I got so used to it, I don't really think about it that much," I say, shrugging and poking around at my fries.

He nods in understanding, not pushing it any further. He eats more of his fries before pulling out his phone from his back pocket. "Question time," he announces.

"My absolute favorite time of the day."

Honestly, it's not the worst idea he's come up with. They've helped ease a lot of the tension between us and are fun to talk about when we take breaks at the gym.

He breaks out into a smile. "Do you have a flaw that you think I might not be okay with? Any kinks I should know or weird fetishes would also be appreciated."

I narrow my eyes. "Does it actually say that?"

"Just the first part," he mumbles. "Wait. It'd be harder to point out your own flaws. How about you tell me what *my* flaws are?"

I nod. "It's just something I've noticed," I start, waiting for a reaction before I continue. He just blinks at me, still eating his fries. "You get very attached to things." He doesn't move, and I'm guessing this isn't the first time he's heard this. "I mean, you had a meltdown when we changed gyms."

"It was a very nice gym."

"My point still stands."

He throws his head back and groans. I get a good look at his throat, and it makes mine go dry. What is so hot about a man's throat? I would love to know why it drives me fucking crazy.

"What was it that you said? That I was hyper-fixating on you to avoid fixing my problems?" I nod. He shrugs, leaning his forearms on the table. "I guess you were right. It's just something I do. But if it wasn't for that, we wouldn't be here right now. So it's really a win."

"It's definitely something," I mumble. "Okay, my turn. Tell me something horrible about me."

"Whoa, it's nothing *horrible*. The only horrible thing about you is that I can't spend every minute by your side." I don't think I'm ever going to get used to how smooth he is. How easy it is for him to say these things and expect me to act normal about it. He leans forward and I do, too, and he finally whispers, "You're a very stubborn person, Wren Hackerly."

I roll my eyes, but I still stay close to him. "Tell me something I don't know, genius."

"See, you refuse to be nice to me. You were putting up a

fight about doing this until you realized how irresistible I am, and now look at us."

"And how well is this working out for us so far?"

He frowns, clearly not finding my joke funny. "Wrenny baby, we had *one* setback and—"

"Stop calling me that."

"*And* we've been out *one* time. It's going to take a while for us to get used to being around each other like that. Especially if you're so committed to not liking me."

"I know," I say with a sigh, "I just really want this to work."

"And it will," he says, and he has the audacity to wink at me before leaning back in his seat, crossing his arms against his chest. "Just trust me."

WE CONTINUE ASKING each other more questions on the drive home, and I find out that his favorite quality about me is that I'm not easy to win over like the girls he's been with in the past. I thought that was stupid because I'm actively trying not to let myself get caught up in him. It's like he's put some pathetic spell on me that makes me itch to be with him. I tell him about the upcoming showcase and how I can't wait to get my leotard back from my designer that Scarlett hooked me up with.

As he drives me back, he points out where his house is, and I'm only just realizing how close it is to my apartment. It's almost like he's been hiding in plain sight this whole time.

When we park, he insists on walking me to my door, and he talks the entire time.

"Should I buy you a muzzle for Christmas? You really need to learn how to shut up," I mutter when we step out of the elevator.

"I'm sure we could have a lot more fun with that than you think," he murmurs, bumping his arm into mine.

"Okay, I have a question for you, loverboy." We get to my apartment door, and I lean against it. Miles raises his eyebrows for me to continue. "What's your love language?"

"Isn't it obvious?"

"Okay," I whistle, "So, physical touch. Got it."

He smiles. "What about you?"

"Physical touch and words of affirmation," I say, and my body tingles for no other reason than I haven't had sex in eight months. Or maybe it was the feel of Miles's hand on my stomach at the party. He studies me for a second, and my cheeks flush. "What? Do you think I'm lying?"

He steps closer to me, dipping his head toward the side of my face, his mouth close to my ear. His hot breath tickles my throat. His thumb traces small ovals from the sensitive part of my collarbone to the side of my neck, where I'm sure he can hear my pulse hammering. I take in a shaky breath, my legs suddenly ready to give out beneath me.

"No, I'm not surprised. I heard the noise you made when I touched you earlier," he murmurs, each syllable reverberating through my body.

"And what noise was that?" I ask.

"You moaned like you haven't been fucked in years, baby," he whispers, and I hate how right he is. I hate how sensitive my skin is and how in tune it was with his body. I close my eyes before placing my hands on his chest, gently pushing some space between us.

"You just called me 'baby.' Non-ironically, might I add?"

Miles grins. "Sure did, baby."

I shudder and pretend to gag. "I think I just threw up in my mouth a little." He laughs, shaking his head. "If you call me baby, I'm going to call you Milesy."

"Call me whatever you want, baby. 'Daddy' is also acceptable," he replies, smirking. I laugh at him and shove him in the arm, and he laughs too. There's something so carefree about laughing with him, and a huge part of me wishes I had this earlier when I really needed it.

When we calm down, I say, "I had a good time today. Shitty food and all."

"Me too, but I don't think the food was that bad."

"This is why we changed your diet," I say, patting him on the chest. I push the door from behind me, keeping it open with my foot. "Good night, Milesy."

"Good night, baby," he whispers before turning on his heels.

When I slip into bed later that night, I feel lighter.

I'm trying to convince myself that these sorts of panicking feelings just happen. They aren't going to determine my life and this fake relationship. I tried to get rid of all those feelings in the shower, but my hands still shake a little when I reach for my phone.

When I unlock it, it's flooded with followers and tags. I knew Miles was popular, but I didn't know the extent of it until now.

Fucking hell.

Is he secretly a prince or something?

I've got follows on Instagram from people who I've never spoken to before and likes from the people who shunned me after regionals. A strange sensation runs through my body when I click on Miles's profile, and there it is.

The most recent post in his grid is a picture of me in the diner we went to: a candid of me nudging around my fries as I look down at them, my hair almost covering my face, but you can tell it's me. I don't know how I missed him taking the photo. I look over it again, taking note of what I can see before my eyes wander down to the caption.

Eating bad fries in the middle of nowhere with my girl 🖤.

. . .

MY HEART BOTTOMS OUT.

Jesus Christ.

My girl?

Why do those two words make my heart stop? They shouldn't. He doesn't mean it, obviously, but I don't hate the feeling of pretending he did. I wander down to the comments, which are a mixture of *You guys are so cute, When did this happen?* and *Who is she?* From this picture alone, I've gained a shit ton of followers.

Despite the setback today, things might be finally looking up for me.

When sleep pulls me under, I have the biggest and most ridiculous smile on my face.

15
MILES

Fake boyfriend perks

I DIDN'T KNOW how lonely I was until I felt what it's like to be around Wren. Even with all her walls, being with her feels less empty than being alone.

I used to have Carter for that. We were inseparable, always together, whether it was on the ice or just hanging out. He was more than a best friend—he was like a brother. We had this tradition of getting burgers at Joe's Diner after every game, win or lose. We'd sit there for hours, analyzing every play, arguing over missed shots, and laughing about the stupid stuff that happened during practice.

I've spent so much time alone since then, sinking into this dark hole. But Wren—she's like this unexpected light. She makes me feel less alone. Even though she's guarded, her presence is comforting.

Now, I feel like smashing my head against the wall out of boredom.

Every day after classes, I've gone home and done nothing. Going to the rink feels like the stupidest thing I could do because whenever I see my teammates I can just see the empty space where Carter used to be. The rink feels so empty without him, like a part of me is missing. Every time I laced up my skates, I'd see him there, grinning like an idiot, ready to take on the world. There's this deep, unsettling feeling that I get whenever I consider going to skate, knowing he's not here anymore.

I see him in everything, and when I don't have anything to distract myself from, I start to feel myself slipping back into old habits. I can't go back there. I've been working hard with Wren in the gym, and I don't think I've been in better shape. I can't fuck that up now because I've had a couple of bad days.

It isn't helping that I've not gotten a call from either of my parents or my sister. I can't blame them. I shut them out completely after what happened, and I can't stomach the thought of talking to them again like everything is fine when it's so far from it.

I put myself out of my misery and throw on jeans and a hoodie and jump into my car. I connect my phone to the Bluetooth and put on the playlist that I've started to put together for Wren.

Okay, it's not for her, but it's also… for her.

It's just songs that not only remind me of her, but songs that I know she likes from going to the gym and hearing them on repeat. I know she hates my usual music taste, but I've altered it so it fits more of the music she likes, but it's still got me written all over it.

When I'm not on the ice, I love discovering new music. Carter and I would have a pre-game pump-up playlist, and it was our own superstition that we were sure would guarantee the win. Now, just hovering over that playlist makes my stomach flip.

I put on *Jump Then Fall*, by Taylor Swift, and it immediately puts me in a good mood as I drive around my side of town, desperately trying not to go straight to Wren's apartment.

I mean, technically, I should be able to go and see her when I want since she's my girlfriend, but I have more self-control than that. I'm delusional enough to think she must be thinking of me too because the second the song finishes, my phone lights up with a text from her.

> **WREN**
>
> Campus library. Study sesh. Now.

> Not even a 'please???'

> **WREN**
>
> I'm asking you to come study, not to go to prom with me.

> I don't think I want to study with you and that attitude.

THE BUBBLES APPEAR, but they disappear again, and I laugh to myself for getting under her skin. I can't help it sometimes. She's just too easy to wind up, and lucky for her, I like it when she gets mad at me.

> **WREN**
>
> Miles, would you please come study with me so I don't fail my exam? Not to be dramatic, but you're my last hope.

> That's my girl.

> Wait. What is that supposed to mean? I'm supposed to be your first choice.

> **WREN**
>
> Just get to the library.

. . .

I CAN COUNT on one hand how many times I've been to the campus library, which says a lot about how much I care about my studies. Choosing sports sciences was the easy way out, but actually having to study sucks. Kinesiology sounded fun when I was applying for colleges, but I'm already a lost cause. I've been attending classes per Miss Hackerly's request, but Wren hasn't been keeping up with her side of the deal to tutor me. She just sends me links and hopes that it helps. Besides, she's way too busy to try to get my pea brain to focus.

I walk through the large doors, scanning my NU card onto the machine to go through the security gates, and I'm in the middle of unknown territory. There are floor-to-ceiling bookshelves, filled with deep-brown paperbacks and textbooks. I know it's a library, but it's too quiet here. So quiet that the second I accidentally step on the wrong piece of wood, the few people that are in here snap out of their study focus and give me a death glare. But it also draws my attention to the one person I wanted to see.

Wren is sitting at a table tucked in the back of the study zones, the only person in her section. She has a pile of books on the right side of her, and her laptop is on the table.

She looks different in this setting. She's not sweaty and panting from skating or working out. Instead, she's wearing the cutest owl frame glasses, her hair is tied into a high ponytail, and she's wearing a white tank top and shorts, her knee pulled up to her chin.

I walk over to her with the biggest grin on my face, and I step on another wrong plank of wood. You'd think that they'd try to make the floors as soundless as possible, but no. Wren shakes her head at me, pulling up her glasses to rest on the top of her head.

"Could you be any louder?"

"Hello to you too, girlfriend." I reach over to tap her glasses and pull them over her eyes. "These are cute."

Her nose crinkles as she rolls her eyes. "Thanks," she mutters, looking down to her laptop and then back to me. "I need you to test me with these questions." I raise my eyebrows at her lack of manners, and she whispers, "Please."

She turns the laptop toward me, and I see the list of questions she has in her Word doc about a book called "Atonement." I have no idea what that is, but the questions seem interesting. Well, interesting if you're into literature.

"Is this all you need me for?" I ask, scrolling through the endless list. She nods, scribbling something down into a notebook. "Couldn't Kennedy and Scarlett do this? As much as I know I'm going to enjoy asking these questions, I know I wasn't your first choice."

"Do you have any volume control?" she whispers, pinning me with a look. "Scarlett has an exam today, and Ken's working."

"And you don't have any friends from your class?"

She shakes her head. "Just ask me the questions, Milesy."

And I do.

I learn all about the cultural and social setting of the novel and a bunch of other random shit that I don't need to know. I don't know how she's worried about passing this exam when she answers every question immediately and exactly with the answers that she's written down.

When I finally get to the last question, I turn the laptop back around to her. "What's next?"

She scrolls through it, picking up her very annotated copy of the novel before typing something down. "I need to write down some last-minute notes and then I'm going to do a timed essay."

"And you need me here for that, why?"

"So you can confiscate my devices. I'll get too distracted if I have them in front of me. It's what me and the girls usually do," she explains.

"Do you really have that little self-control?"

"I have a lot more self-control than you do," she argues. "I'm just gonna make these notes and then do the essay. You should go and explore while I write."

"And risk getting death-stared by every person in here? No thanks," I say, leaning back in my chair, crossing my arms. "I can just watch you study."

Watching her study is slightly motivating me. I know I should have brought some of my own stuff with me to study for exams that aren't for months, but I would have just got distracted anyway.

Have I mentioned how beautiful this woman is? How is she managing to read, write, and listen to a podcast all at once? I can't figure it out for the life of me, but her dedication to studying as well as skating is one of the most attractive things I've ever seen.

I've been making paper boats with her spare paper for almost an hour. She's written her essay and has moved on to making more notes, and I'm *this* close to dying of boredom. I tap her pen with the fluffy end next to the laptop as she types away.

"Wren. Wren. Wren. Wren," I press, and I know it's about to irritate the fuck out of her. "Wrenny, Wren, Wren."

She stops typing, slamming the laptop shut. "What!?"

I smile wide, popping my dimple out and everything. "Hi."

Her face almost breaks for a second, but she sticks her tongue in her cheek before opening her laptop again. She starts typing as she says, "Don't do that."

I bash my eyelashes at her innocently. "Do what?"

"Annoy me like a puppy."

"Isn't that what boyfriends are for?"

"Real boyfriends," she clarifies. "Real boyfriends can annoy me. Real boyfriends carry my books for me. Real boyfriends take me shopping and buy me anything that I want. Real boyfriends fuck me in bathrooms just because they can. But you, Miles Davis, are my fake boyfriend."

"We can change that."

"No, we can't."

"We can. Just say the word and I'll carry your books, spoil you with whatever money I have left, and fuck you into oblivion in every bathroom in the city," I whisper. Her cheeks turn the slightest shade of pink, and I smile to myself. "Does that sound like something you're interested in, Wren?"

She swallows, dropping her gaze back to her work. "Not at all."

WHEN WREN finally finishes her intense study session, she picks up all of her shit and we walk across to Florentino's. It's busy here, as always. If there is one good thing about NU besides hockey, it's this café. We walk up to the counter, my arm around her shoulder, Wren's books clutched to her chest, and I'm sure we look like every clichéd couple in a teen drama.

"What's your usual order?" I ask when we join the line.

"It depends what the special is. Ken is always making something crazy back there," she says, nodding to her best friend who is working frantically behind the counter. "Her mango smoothies are fantastic."

"It's freezing outside and you want a mango smoothie?"

"What would you suggest?"

"Deluxe hot chocolate, obviously," I say. "It's expensive, but it's so fucking good."

"That's not the most expensive thing on the menu," she whispers, shifting from one foot to the other as we move further down the line.

"Really? What is?"

"The caramel crunch cappuccino," she concedes, avoiding eye contact with me.

"Let me guess. That's your usual order," I say, laughing. She nods.

"Even with Kennedy's discount, it's still ridiculous," Wren replies. "It is the best drink though."

"I'm a nineteen-year-old student. What makes you think I can afford a seven-dollar coffee?" I spit out, and she laughs, shrugging.

"You said you'd spend the money you have left on me. This is a clear opening," she argues.

"If we're playing that game, does the rest of what I said stand?"

She shrugs, avoiding my gaze as she faces forward. "We'll see."

"You're lucky, princess. You are the only exception."

She shakes her head and snorts, a combination of mannerisms I'm sure she reserves just for me. I nudge her in the shoulder to move forward since we're next in the line. When Kennedy sees us, she smiles wide, clearly our biggest fan.

"There is my favorite couple," she cries, leaning on the countertop. "What can I get for you?"

"The most expensive drink you have," Wren chimes in, smiling at me. I'm going to be fourteen dollars more broke than I was this morning, but if it makes her smile like that, I'd do it again in a heartbeat.

Kennedy beams, winking at me. "Coming right up."

We walk out of Florentino's sipping our drinks and head toward Radnor Hall, where Wren's classes take place. I'm holding both of our drinks in my hand while Wren hooks one arm into mine, holding her books with the other. It's probably the most PDA I've ever engaged in as I give Wren regular sips of her drink. I swear every time we walk past someone, they do a double take. I don't think I'm ever going to get used to this. The stares. The whispers. The looks.

"Hey, I forgot to ask you something," Wren says after a long stretch of comfortable silence. I hum, and she continues, "My dad's hosting a charity event at one of his hotels, and he wants us to come. We were talking the other day and I slipped, saying I was seeing someone. He's excited to meet you."

I swallow the lump in my throat. "He is?"

"Yeah, he likes hockey, and you like hockey. You've already got so much in common," she says, laughing. "It's a laid-back event, but people get really into it, so you'll have to wear something nice."

"Something nice?" I bite out the words like they've personally offended me.

"Yeah, a nice suit or something," she says. She grabs a hold of both our empty cups, throwing them away. "You don't have to go if you don't want to. I just thought it'd be fun and probably the only time you'd get to meet my dad. He's pretty busy."

"You really think he'll like me?"

I shouldn't care so much, but I do. Whether it's fake or not for us, this feels like a big deal, and I can't mess it up. Wren shrugs. "Yeah, he likes everybody. The only thing is we'll have to stay the night. It's a couple hours' drive, and he doesn't like the idea of me driving back so far at night. Is that okay?"

"If this hotel is anything like the gym we go to, then hell yeah, I'm in."

She looks up at me. "Really? You seriously don't have to go if you don't want to. It's just a stupid event and everyone's going to be—"

"Hey, I want to go, okay? If you're just saying that because you don't want me to go, you can just say that."

She bites her bottom lip. "I do want you to come."

"Then it's settled. I'm going with you."

She smiles at me, and I don't know why I'm already feeling nervous. Her dad seems nice from what I've heard, but meeting someone's parents is a big thing. The kind of milestone I never reached with my ex.

"Wren! Oh my god. I was just looking for you." A girl with dark-brown hair rushes toward us as we walk back past the library. The girl I've never seen before in my life hooks Wren's arm into hers, taking her away from me.

"You were?" Wren asks, looking back at me as her friend walks in front of me with Wren in tow.

"Yes! I was trying to find you to talk about the exam we've got coming up," she explains. "Aren't you going to introduce me to your boyfriend?"

Wren turns around, looking at me skeptically, her eyes suddenly wide and unsure. "This is Miles Davis. Miles, this is Katie Buxbaum from my creative writing class."

"So you guys really *are* dating?" Katie asks, looking between the both of us. We nod. Her eyes narrow for a second before she nods again, slowly. "Cool. So will you guys come to my party tonight, then? It's a low-key thing, but most people from class are going."

I'm about to respond, but Wren awkwardly unlinks her arms with Katie's and slips her fingers into mine instead. This is much better.

"Thanks for the offer, but we're busy tonight. We're like newlyweds. Just can't be apart from each other," Wren says, her voice an octave higher than usual as she snuggles into my side. "I'll see you in class."

Wren practically runs down the corridor, pulling me along with her, turning the sharp corner until we're away from her and panting.

"What the hell was all that about?" I ask when Katie is out of sight.

"I don't want to go," Wren replies, her big green eyes boring into me.

"We don't have to, but you didn't have to run away."

She huffs, running her hand across her forehead. "I swear I've never spoken to Katie before today. The thing is, she's really nice, but I don't want to build our friendship around the basis that I'm sort of popular now because of you. I'm sure she's great, but I just—"

I cut her off, placing my arms on her shoulders as she clutches the books to her chest. "Then you don't have to be friends with her, Wrenny. Just relax, okay? You're letting yourself get worked up over nothing."

"I know, I just—"

"Breathe," I say slowly, and she stops. She takes in a deep breath, breathing out of her nose. "Good. Now give me your books."

Her eyebrows crease. "What?"

"Let me hold your books for you, princess," I say, plucking them from her. "Oh, and your bag too." I sling her tote bag over my shoulder, feeling ridiculous and proud all at the same time. She shakes her head at me, laughing.

She hooks her arm through mine again, walking us down the corridor toward her class. "These are the kind of fake boyfriend perks I need."

"I can give you all the perks if you want."

"I'm good," she replies, scrunching her nose. Her phone rings, and she reaches into her back pocket and pulls it out. "I've got to take this. It's my dad. I'll let him know that you're coming with me. My class is just there. I'll see you later."

She collects her books and her bag from my shoulder. She starts to walk, leaving me behind, but I call after her. "I think you're forgetting something."

"What? I have all my books."

"My kiss." I grin.

"Right. How could I possibly forget?" Her shoulders slump, and she walks back up to me and presses the softest kiss to my cheek.

This is going to be perfect.

I get to watch her study. I carry her books. I walk her to class and then I get a kiss on the cheek. Fake dating Wren Hackerly might be the best thing to ever happen to me.

16
WREN

Stormy weather

THE MORE TIME I spend with the skating team, the more I wonder why I'm even at this college at all. After the disaster that was regionals last year, going solo has been the best decision I've ever made. I used to love competing in group skates when I was younger, but there's less control when I'm working with a group. Partnering with Augustus helped that, and I actually enjoyed the routines Darcy would help us choreograph, but after I realized how easily one mistake could set my career back, I decided to put myself back in control.

Today's practice session wasn't too bad. I had a chance to run through my program with Darcy and talk to the other solo skaters on the squad, Eva and Madelyn, about what they're planning to do for the winter showcase. My mom sometimes sits in on the practices, but she wasn't here today, and the energy in the locker room after we all return shows that.

Madelyn flops onto a bench, pulling off her skates with a dramatic sigh. "I swear, if I have to do that double axel one more time, my legs are going to fall off."

Eva laughs, sitting down beside her. "At least you landed it. I'm still tripping over my own feet on the footwork sequence."

I join them, feeling a rare sense of camaraderie. "You both looked great out there. Darcy seemed pleased. Luckily, my mom wasn't here to start barking orders."

India sighs, shaking her head. "No offense, Wren, but she always takes over our practices. I don't know what makes her think she's our coach. Darcy shouldn't let her walk all over her."

I laugh. "I know. She just needs something to do with herself. But don't worry, seriously, you all looked so good today."

Madelyn grins. "Yeah, but now we just need to get the rest of the world to care."

Eva nods, her expression turning serious. "Speaking of which, we need to talk about the showcase. If we don't get more support, our program might get cut. No sponsors, no donations, no team."

The mood shifts as the reality of our situation sinks in. We all know what's at stake. I always wish I had a better relationship with my teammates, but we're all so busy with school and skating that we hardly get to hang out. It's nice though. We all have this one thing in common, and when it's necessary, we can pull things together.

"I know," I say. "We need a plan to drum up support. Maybe we could do some kind of promotional event or a social media campaign?"

Madelyn perks up. "That's a good idea. It's better than a bake sale. Maybe we could do a live Q&A on Instagram or TikTok, show off some of our routines, and get people excited about the showcase."

Eva nods enthusiastically. "And we can invite some local schools to a practice session, get the younger kids involved. Parents love supporting things their kids are interested in."

There's a brief silence as we all mull over the ideas. Then Madelyn smirks at me. "Speaking of support, Wren, how's it going with Miles? You two have been hanging out a lot lately."

I feel a flush creep up my cheeks. "It's great," I say, trying to sound nonchalant. Telling them that I'm faking it could be risky, so I try to give them some details but not enough. "Since we started hanging out, people have been talking about us more, if that helps."

Eva giggles. "Yeah but are you sure it's not just for popularity."

I roll my eyes, but I can't help the smile that tugs at my lips. "It's not like that. We're just helping each other out."

Madelyn raises an eyebrow. "Helping each other out, huh? Sounds like a convenient arrangement given the timing. Are you sure you're not just rebounding from Augustus?"

I can't stop the laugh that escapes me. "No, Jesus. I got over that a long time ago."

They all look at me like they think I'm lying. I *am* over it. Just because I was going through a hard time after we broke up doesn't mean that I'm still thinking about it. He's given me the opportunity to finally work on myself and what I can do to make myself a better skater. Mine and Miles's arrangement is just going to prove that even more.

I shake my head, laughing softly. "It's not like that. Miles and I... we just have an understanding. He needed a distraction, and I guess I did too."

Eva's eyes twinkle mischievously. "A distraction, huh? You know, sometimes, distractions turn into something more."

I shrug, trying to play it cool. "Maybe. But for now, it's just nice to have someone around who gets it, you know?"

Madelyn gives me a knowing look. "Rebounds can get messy."

"Thanks for the advice, Dr. Phil," I say, rolling my eyes.

Eva claps her hands together. "Alright, back to business. Let's make a list of everything we need to do for this social media campaign. We'll need videos, photos, and maybe even some behind-the-scenes content. It shouldn't be that hard."

We spend the next half hour brainstorming ideas, and by the

time we're done, the mood in the locker room has lifted. There's a sense of purpose, a feeling that we're all in this together. And as I look around at my teammates, I realize that maybe, just maybe, this team is exactly where I'm supposed to be.

After we all go our separate ways, I find myself itching to speak to Miles. We've got the event at my dad's hotel in a few days, but I haven't heard from him today, which is concerning. He's usually blowing up my phone and demanding to hang out with me. The fact that he hasn't sent me a link to a song he's listening to all day is worrying.

I make my way to the hockey facilities across from the skating rink. If he's not at home, he might be here. I've tried to suggest we go skating together sometime instead of going to the gym, but he brushed me off. I would have been offended that he didn't want to skate with me if I didn't see the hurt in his eyes when I suggested it. There's clearly something holding him back from getting back on the ice that has nothing to do with his physical strength.

When I push open the doors to the arena, the comforting chill of the ice hits me, and the thump of the doors echoes when I step through them and they swing back. It's completely empty here, and I don't know why I'm surprised. There's a timetable between our rinks that shows when the figure skaters and the hockey players have practice, and I know there wasn't one today. What I'm not expecting to find is Miles sitting on a bench outside of the rink with his head in his hands.

"Miles?" I call out, even though I know it's him. I could probably recognize him out of a million clones. There's something about his presence that draws me to him, and I keep on walking until I'm standing in front of him. Then I notice that he's not just got his head in his hands to listen to music before skating, but he's *crying*. Popular Miles Davis with the flirty jokes and the cocky personality is sitting in here, alone, and he's *crying*.

I bend down to crouch between his legs. He's wearing his skates, but they're not laced up, and his gloves and stick are discarded on the floor.

I grip his wrists, rubbing my thumbs against them like he does to me to calm me down. "Hey, are you okay?" I whisper. It's a stupid question. Obviously, he's not okay. He wouldn't be sitting here crying if he was. "Miles, look at me."

His shoulders shake with sobs, and I just want to take away his pain. "I can't."

"You can," I press, swiping my thumb against his wrist again.

"I'm pathetic, Wren."

My heart lurches in my throat at the vulnerability in that one sentence. "You're not pathetic."

"I'm a fucking mess," he mutters, finally looking up at me. His eyes are red and swollen, and I'm struck by the pain that's etched into his features. "I can't even put on my helmet or my jersey without feeling like I'm going to throw up. Everything I do just makes me feel like I can't breathe, and even when I try, it's not enough. I try not to think about him. I try not to think about the last game we had together, but it's the only thing on my mind. Everywhere I go, he's right there, and I'm not doing enough to make him proud. I'm just walking around with a hole in my heart, and I don't know how to get it to go away."

My hands shake as I reach for his face. I hover over his cheek, and he presses himself into me like he needs my warmth. He closes his eyes, tears still spilling down his cheeks and onto my hand as I cradle his face.

"Things like this don't just go away," I whisper, swiping my thumb under his eye. "You're allowed to think about him. You're allowed to be upset, or angry, or *anything,* because everything you feel right now is valid."

He takes in a shuddery breath, and it breaks my heart. "I just want it to stop."

"What do you want to stop?"

"The pain. I keep feeling *everything* all at once, and it's like it just keeps festering in me and getting worse instead of getting better. I have moments where everything feels okay and then it just comes crashing down on me and I just—" His voice cracks. "I don't know if I can handle it anymore. I know I shouldn't think like that, but I can't help but think it would be better if I wasn't here. If it was me that went instead of him. He didn't deserve what happened to him, and it would be so much easier if it was me. Maybe then—"

"What makes you think you deserve that?" I ask, my own voice heavy with emotion. He shrugs, more tears falling. "Miles, what happened to Carter should never have happened. Just because he's gone, doesn't mean that you should have taken his place. You're still here for a reason, and you're going to continue making him proud on and off the ice."

"He deserves a better friend than I am being right now, Wren," he says, throwing his head back and trying to collect himself before facing me head-on. "I should be playing with our team right now, and I can't even do that. Do you know how hard it is for me to even *think* about hockey without thinking about him?"

I shake my head. "I don't think I could ever understand what you're going through, but that doesn't mean you should be alone. You can always talk to me about whatever you're feeling, and I'm never going to judge you. You're an amazing player, Miles, and the team is always going to be there for you when you make your way back."

He lets out a self-deprecating laugh. "You've never seen me play."

I lift one shoulder before dropping it. "I watched a few of your game tapes."

"You watched my games?"

I smile. "Research."

"Research," he echoes, a smile playing on his lips. As if he's just realized I've been stroking his face, his fingers circle around my wrist, his thumb rubbing against my skin. "Thank you for being here."

"Of course," I say, wiping away the last of the tears. "You don't have to do anything until you're ready. If you want to just sit here and stare at the ice until security kicks us out, we can do that."

"Yeah?" he asks, swallowing.

I nod, brushing my thighs before I stand. "Yeah."

I sit on the bench next to him. He rests his hand on the inside of my thigh, his touch one of the most calming and grounding presences of my life. I drop my head to his shoulder, and he sighs like there has been a weight lifted from him. I feel a sense of peace wash over me. It's like the weight of the world feels that much less when he's around, and I know he can feel it, too. All that's left is this moment, and we spend hours just listening to the gentle hum of the empty arena, holding each other until the storm passes.

17

WREN

Stupid, horny, and stupid

MILES

I've got a game coming up in two weeks that I'm thinking about sitting in on. Wanna come?

Will I have to pretend I know how hockey works while I'm there?

MILES

I can teach you, baby.

I won't be going anywhere if you keep calling me that.

MILES

Arguing feels like foreplay to me, so please, keep going.

Shut up.

MILES

I love it when you talk dirty to me.

"I'M NEVER GOING to forgive you for this, Wren. I have so many emotions inside of me I think I might explode. Actually, I'm moving out." Kennedy groans, dropping onto the floor.

"I'll be moving out with her," Scarlett adds, falling to the floor on top of Kennedy. They laugh hysterically as they roll over each other, getting all up in each other's personal space.

I've just read the latest chapter of Stolen Kingdom to them, and I killed off one of the main love interests, Erik. He was a personal favorite of both of them. I kind of liked him too, but I needed to add some oomph to the story. It's been a while since I've sat in my room and wrote for hours, and this is the first thing that came to me.

I poke them with my feet from the couch as they squirm.

"You guys are so dramatic. He's not even real," I say, joining them on the floor.

"He was real to me!" Kennedy sobs, throwing her hand across her face. "I already fan-cast Austin Butler to play him in the movie."

"It's not going to be a movie," I mutter, and Kennedy pretends to sulk. "It won't be anything if I don't have any time to actually finish it."

Trying to finish a novel is a lot harder than I thought it would be. I thought it would get easier after I finished my first one, but it feels like I just learned how to write yesterday. Some days, I just stare at my empty document and hope that daydreaming about writing will finally get me to write something.

I hardly have time to do anything these days between going to practice, the gym, and having my mom hound me with questions. Not only is she stressing me out about my position on the skating team, but she hasn't heard from Austin in a while, and she's started to get worried.

Austin has always been a lone wolf, and I've always admired that about her. She's stronger than I'll ever be, and she's doing insanely well for herself in Russia with her boyfriend Zion. The more my mom stresses out about it, the more I get stressed out. It's how we work.

"Speaking of things that aren't real... How are you and Loverboy?" Scarlett asks with a shimmy.

"Things are good. He's getting better with training, and I got a ton of Instagram followers. Things are looking up already," I say proudly.

"Cool, but how are...you know...things?" Scarlett repeats with more emphasis, gesturing suggestively toward my private areas. Kennedy shoots up now, looking at us with expectant eyes, mischief dancing in them.

"What she's trying to say is, have you fucked him yet?" Ken asks without batting an eye.

"I wasn't going to say 'fucked,'" Scarlett argues, rolling her eyes playfully. I snort. Her face suddenly turns serious. "But yes, have you?"

"No, I haven't. And I'm not going to anytime soon." I sigh. "But the sexual frustration is slowly eating away at me. I've burned through two sets of batteries for my vibrator in the past two weeks."

I hate to admit it, but it's true.

Seeing him nearly every day has not helped the throbbing between my legs. He's an attractive guy, and we have to go to the gym together. Listening to him grunt and groan is not making this any easier. He's hot, and he knows he is. And for a girl who has been involuntarily celibate for almost nine months, it is not going well for me.

"You dirty bitch," Scarlett mocks, her face wide in a smile. I shove my face between my hands. "You need to sleep with someone and quick. It doesn't even have to be with Miles. It isn't in your contract, is it?"

I lift my face up to them. "Technically it's not, but I don't want to do that. It feels too close to cheating, and I feel like I'd have to tell him, and it would be a whole thing."

"So you're going to mount that tragic vibrator every night until you can't afford batteries anymore," Kennedy says, scrunching her face up.

"Pretty much. At least it can make me come," I say, getting up from the floor.

We all burst out laughing until our stomachs hurt. Kennedy is the slapper, hitting us until we're basically bruised while she laughs hard. I'm the one with the wheeze, and Scarlett just sounds like an evil baby genius.

"Poor Augustus," Scarlett says between her hysterical laughter. I remember coming home from staying over at Gus's and telling them how tragic it was that he tried to go down on me and absolutely nothing was happening. I thought I was broken or something, but it just turns out he didn't know what he was doing with his tongue. I can't believe I spent years faking orgasms for that man.

My phone starts to ring beside me, and I see my dad's caller ID, so I wave my hand around to keep them quiet.

"Hi, Dad."

"Wrenny! I thought I wouldn't be able to get hold of you with how busy you were the last time I called," my dad replies, being the drama queen he is.

I laugh. "I had to go to class, Dad. I'm not busy now. What's up?"

"Your Miles is still coming to my event, right?" he asks.

My Miles.

I don't know why my heart stutters at the way he says that. Miles isn't mine in any way, but sometimes it feels like he is. Something shifted the other day at the rink, and knowing that we've got each other's backs in a purely platonic and friendly way is helping me put that barrier up between us. When I get looks around campus or comments on my post, I feel a weird sense of pride that I get to call Miles mine in front of the world.

"Yeah, he's coming," I say.

"Great! I've sorted out the room, so I hope he can make it. If not, it's totally fine. I understand how you kids are these days, but I'd love to meet him," he says. I shake my head, and I wish he could see me rolling my eyes right now. "I've got you a luxury suite, so you don't have to worry about sleeping in different beds. There'll be one big enough for you to share."

"Yeah, Dad. About that. We don't need to share a bed because—"

"Wren," he presses. "I want you to know that I trust you. And I know that you and your mom butt heads, but I don't want that for us. If you and your boyfriend want to cuddle, who am I to stop you? As long as you're being safe, that's all that matters."

"Dad, seriously, you didn't have to go to all that trouble," I say. "Two beds are fine."

"You deserve this freedom, Wrenny."

"But, Dad—" I try again, but he cuts me off.

"Wren. It's settled."

"Mom would never do this," I murmur.

"Good thing I'm not your mom. Isn't it, kiddo?" he adds before cutting the call on me.

"What did Daddy Hacks want?" Scarlett asks, beaming up at me.

"Stop calling him that, it's gross." I shudder, and they both laugh. It's even stupider that they use Hackerly as his last name even though it's my mom's. My dad's surname is tragic, and I like to pretend that it doesn't exist. "He was just double-checking that Miles is coming with me to that event."

Scarlett's eyes go wide. "He is?"

"Yeah." They exchange a look, and I sigh. "Don't be weird about it."

"We're not being weird," Kennedy says, "I mean, the two of you are going to be in a hotel for a night. The possibilities are endless."

"Yeah, I say buy a cute lingerie set and flash him before you go to bed," Scarlett suggests.

I bark out a laugh. "I'm not doing that."

"You should *so* do that," Ken adds. "He'd lose his fucking mind."

"I don't know about you, Ken, but if—and I mean *if*—I were ever to sleep with him, I'd want his mind intact."

She shrugs. "I wouldn't. I like my men a little tortured and miserable."

Scarlett's grin turns evil. "I like mine a little pathetic and a lot rich."

We all burst into a fit of giggles. "What the fuck is wrong with us?" I ask, trying to catch my breath.

"I don't know. You started it," Kennedy says, swiping a tear from her eye.

The next thing I know, we're all involved in a very intense case of whodunnit, shouting "j'accuse!" at any given moment and rolling on the floor in laughter.

I couldn't think of anyone else I'd rather laugh at stupid shit with.

18
MILES

Cream cheese

I HAD no clue what to wear to this thing, and all Wren said was to "wear something nice." If she had given me more instructions, I would have had more to work with. I can't show up to a fancy event with my fake girlfriend's dad looking like an orphan, so I had to go to my last resort.

Evan got me a link to a good tailor who wasn't too expensive, and I dug into my savings to buy myself a suit and bow tie. It's nothing flashy, but it should be enough for the occasion and, considering the price, maybe even my wedding.

"Please tell me you brought your outfit in your bag," Wren pleads the second I slip into her car in my dark jeans and faded tee. I throw my bag into the backseat.

"No, Wren, I'm going to wear this to the event," I reply sarcastically, gesturing toward my outfit.

"Knowing you, you probably would," she mutters.

"What's that supposed to mean?"

She grins, looking at my outfit and then back to my face. "Have you looked in the mirror? You give off rough around the edges,   I-don't-wear-suits-unless-it's-for-a-wedding-or-a-funeral vibes."

"Gee, I didn't know you paid that much attention to me," I say, running my hand through my hair. She gives me a blank look. "Obviously it's in my bag."

"Good. Did you get something nice to wear?" she asks as she checks her mirrors while backing out of my driveway.

"Define what you mean by nice…" I tease, leaning over to play with the radio until something good comes on.

Listening to Wren's Taylor Swift playlist while we work out has had its effects on me. Now, I can't do anything active without some *1989* or *Reputation* action. Her music cures the soul. It has to be magic or some shit.

"I don't know. Something charming, smart, dazzling," she lists, staring out at the traffic we quickly merged into. I watch her dark-blue nails tap onto the steering wheel as she sighs.

"Aren't I all those things anyway?" She gives me an unimpressed look. Maybe it's too early for my bullshit. "Yes, I brought something nice."

"Okay, good," she says softly. She murmurs something under her breath as she taps her fingers impatiently. The car in front of us stays still when the light turns green, and her face heats up as she pounds the steering wheel with her tiny fists, avoiding the horn. "God! Can you drive your fucking car!?"

"You seem tense," I whisper, turning down the music. She turns to me for a split second before focusing on the road.

"I haven't slept properly in almost two weeks," she bites out, her knuckles turning white as she grips the steering wheel.

"Why? What's keeping you up?"

"Oh, nothing," she says cheerfully. I can tell she's about to go on a sarcastic tangent. Luckily for her, it's my favorite thing. "Just having a quarter-life crisis over my career in figure skating. Oh, and my sister has been off the grid for almost two months, and my mom is starting to project all of her frustrations onto me, so I'm just waiting for the other shoe to drop."

I blow out a breath. "Jesus."

"Yeah, it's starting to get to me."

"Makes sense why you made me eat shit at the gym yesterday."

She scoffs. "That was nothing. I could work you harder if I wanted to."

"Please, be my guest," I say, crossing my arms against my chest. "Are you and your sister close?"

"We are. Sort of. She was like my mom's test run before I was born, so if I thought I had mommy issues, Austin has it worse. She's been in Russia for the last four years at a ballet program. We haven't heard from her in a while, and everyone's a bit worried."

"Are you worried about her? Is that why you're stressed?"

She groans, shrugging. "I am, but I'm not. Austin is tough. A lot tougher than me. She's always been independent, and she takes care of herself first, so I'm sure that whatever she's going through, she'll get through it. It only stresses me out because when my mom doesn't have two kids to fuss over, all the weight lands on me. That's why she's been so hard on me about getting the skating stuff sorted as soon as possible. I just wish she would at least communicate with us more so we don't have to worry."

My mind instantly drifts to Clara. How I've been pushing her away over something she was trying to protect me from. How she might be feeling like Wren in her situation. Maybe I should reach out to her. As much as these last few months have sucked, she's been the best big sister

"She'll come around. Family is hard. Believe me, I know," I say as reassuringly as I can.

"You never talk about your family, and you talk about everything," she points out, glancing at me. Her green eyes flash with worry before she turns back to the road. "But just so you know, you can talk to me about them. When you want to, that is."

"I know," I reply. "I just don't like talking about them much. We're all in a weird place right now."

"I get that," she says, smiling softly. "Well, that door is always open if you ever do want to talk about it, just so you know."

"I know. Thank you, Wrenny."

She flashes me a smile that's both teasing and sincere. "You're so welcome, Milesy."

On the drive there, I try to remember the countless stories she has told me about her dad. From what I've heard, he's probably the only person that Wren truly loves apart from her friends. When she talks about him, she doesn't hold back anything like she does with her mom. She doesn't talk about him as if he's simply just the person responsible for creating her.

She told me about how much she adores him and how grateful she is to have him as a dad while her mom was hard on her. Over the last three days, she's been quizzing me on the things that her dad likes and what he doesn't.

"Cream cheese," she says, keeping her eyes focused on the road.

"Like or dislike?"

"Loathe," she growls, slowly turning to me, her eyebrows knitted together.

"Okay," I whistle. 'No cream cheese."

"*Never* any cream cheese."

THE HOTEL IS a lot fancier than I imagined.

I have to crane my head back to take in all the stories of sleek black glass from top to bottom. The inside is a mix of gold and black, and it's fucking breathtaking.

Wren navigates us around as if she works here. She seems so natural at this, linking her arm in mine and walking us around. She talks to the staff as if they are old friends that she needs to catch up with. Honestly, I wouldn't be surprised if they are.

We make our way through the glass elevator to our luxury suite. There are three main rooms: the master bedroom with a California king, a huge bathroom, and a living room space with a mini bar. Obviously, we're not legally allowed to drink so everything is empty, but it's still cool.

"So, I guess I'm sleeping on the couch," I say when I return to the bedroom. Wren has started unpacking her things onto the hangers neatly, walking back and forth from her suitcase on the bed to the closet. I don't understand why she insisted on bringing so many clothes for such a short trip.

"Miles, I had to go through the trouble of explaining to my dad that I wanted separate beds. He's doing the whole 'I trust you' thing. Plus, this bed could fit, like, three times the size of us on here and there would still be room. We can share it for one night, right?" Wren turns to me, hands on her hips. "You probably won't even notice I'm there."

"Okay, but no funny business," I say, mainly reminding myself to keep it in my pants. I could never not notice her. She laughs and walks toward me.

"How about you go and repeat that in the mirror?" she whispers.

After we take turns in the bathroom, we're finally getting ready for the event. I'm standing in front of the mirror that takes up most of one wall, watching a YouTube video on how to tie my bow tie.

I don't know how I let Evan talk me out of getting a clip-on one. He said something about making a good first impression even though I doubt Wren's dad would be able to tell the difference between a real bow tie and a clip-on.

I'm grunting with frustration when I catch a glimpse of her in the mirror behind me. Wren's eyes lock with mine, and I forget how to breathe.

She looks devastating.

She's wearing a dark-blue evening gown, her blonde hair is

tied back into a neat bun with a small silver clip. Her silver earrings dangle elegantly, matching with her heels. She walks toward me slowly, and my hands fumble around my tie when I remember that it's there.

"Need help with that?" she asks, gesturing toward my bow tie. I nod, basically foaming at the mouth. When did I forget how to speak? "I asked my dad to teach me how to tie ties once and it just stuck."

Her hands come toward my neck as she unties the knot I made. Very slowly. Too slow. I watch as her hands work at the mess I made, and I try to swallow. She looks up at me, smirking before looking back down to my tie.

A soft smile tugs at her lips. "What?"

"Promise me you'll come back here with me tonight," I get out when I find my voice. Her eyebrows furrow. She looks up at me, but I watch her in the mirror.

"What do you mean?"

"You look fucking stunning, Wren," I whisper, and I make the mistake of looking her in the eye. Her wide eyes stare into mine, her lips slightly parted. "I'm just saying, I won't be surprised if someone tries to take you home with them."

"The only person taking me home tonight is you," she murmurs. My heart skips multiple beats. I know it shouldn't take this long for her to tie my tie, but her hands are still on me, even when I can see it's done. "You clean up nice in a suit. You look good."

I grin. "Say that last sentence again."

"You look good?"

"Just wanted to double-check I'm hearing you correctly," I say. She rolls her eyes and drops her hands after smoothing out my shirt. "Are you sure your dad will like me?"

"Yes, I'm sure." She looks up at me as she takes a little step back. Her heel catches with the carpet, but I wrap my hand around her waist to steady her. Her hands come to the lapels of my blazer, pulling herself up into me. "Now stop worrying."

"What if I bring up cream cheese?"

"Why would you ever need to bring up cream cheese?"

I shrug. "I don't know. I might get nervous and say something about it."

"If you do, I *will* go home with someone else tonight right after I murder you."

19
MILES + WREN

Give a sex-deprived girl a hockey player

MILES

WITH MY SHITTY timing and my even shittier luck, it seems as if I've managed to will my worries into existence. In the short time we've been in here, there has been this one guy with his eyes on Wren the entire time.

He's dressed like all the other men in this place except he's one of the few who look our age. Even when we're sitting, my hands tight around her waist and her head nestled in my shoulder, he still doesn't stop trying to fuck her with his eyes.

Not that she notices.

It turns out these things are pretty boring when you can't drink. All the people around us are drunk, laughing loudly, and finding everything funny after the auction went down. Wren and I are eating pistachios out of a bowl, waiting for something to happen.

"Is this what it's usually like?" I ask.

She sighs, slouching back in her chair. "Pretty much. It was better when the girls would come. It was more of an excuse for us to dress up, and we'd make up stupid games to pass the time."

I tilt my head at her. "Oh yeah? Like what?"

"Just people watching, making up lives for strangers that we see. That sort of stuff. Wanna play?"

I'll do just about anything to pass the time at this point. "Show me how it's done, baby."

"Okay. You see that guy over there?" she asks, her gaze setting on a group of men, but one guy in pants and a button-down stands out as he's the only one without a blazer. I nod. "Middle class. Divorced his wife because she watched a movie he introduced her to without him. He likes it soft and timid in bed, but she was an animal. He couldn't admit it to his buddies so he lied and said she was the one who couldn't take his sword of thunder."

I roar out a laugh at the randomness, and she does too, smiling at me. "Your brain is brilliant."

"Why, thank you," she mimics, flicking her hair over her shoulder. She nudges me in the arm. "Now, your turn."

"Okay… The guy next to your guy. He lives a very happy life. Wife, kids, the whole shebang. But he has a secret. He probably has a porn collection or something from the way he's fidgeting like that."

"Or he's a murderer," Wren whispers.

I turn to her. "I know you revealed your true identity to me, Miss Amelia Wren Hackerly, but if you really are a murderer, please just put me out of my misery."

She sighs. "Do you always assume the worst in people or is it just me?"

"Just you," I say, smiling.

She flips me off before turning back to the crowd. "Okay, that woman over there with the pixie cut definitely has twins. I can just tell from the lines on her face. They give her hell, but she loves them. She has an older son, though, who looks like Schmidt from *New Girl*, and he is for sure robbing her without her knowing. But she'd let him get away with it. Freud and all that."

"How am I supposed to beat that?" I ask, gaping at her. She smiles smugly. I scan the room for somebody, and then my eyes connect with the creep who has been staring at her all night. "That guy, our age, he's obsessed with you."

"What?" Wren chokes out.

"I'm being serious. He's been eye fucking you all night."

"Now you're really not understanding the game," she mutters, shaking her head.

"I'm telling the truth," I argue, turning to her. Her green eyes narrow at me. "He can tell we're together, and he's not stopped looking at you. It's like he's begging me to strangle him."

"Jealousy looks good on you, Davis," she murmurs before she turns away from me, leaving us in another round of silence.

WREN'S DAD arrives a little later, and it's clear that she adores him.

"Dad!" Wren shouts, pulling my attention away from the pile of pistachio dust we've created. She jumps out of her seat, and he pulls her into a hug. He's wearing a dark-blue suit and white shirt, and he's not that much taller than me when I stand too. When she pulls out the hug, she turns to me with the biggest smile I've seen on her face. "This is Miles Davis. My boyfriend."

Boyfriend.

I don't fight the smile that splits across my face, filled with pride. Being called Wren's boyfriend, fake or not, might be the peak of my existence. I stretch out my hand for him to shake it, but he pulls me into a tight hug instead.

"It's a pleasure to meet you, Mr. Berger," I muffle. He presses me into him further, and my face is squished against his chest. I widen my eyes, looking at Wren for help, but she just laughs.

"The pleasure is all mine, son." He pats me on the back hard when we pull apart. "My last name sounds stupid, doesn't it? No wonder her mom didn't want anything to do with it."

"Dad," Wren scolds, and he just laughs, shaking his head. I wonder what is up with everyone in this family changing their names. Wren stands at his side, with a smile, giving me a double thumbs-up and a wink. That went a lot smoother than I thought it would.

He sits down across from us, his deep-brown eyes flickering between the two of us as Wren moves her chair closer to mine, our arms brushing, and our thighs pressed together. There's something so comforting about her contact, about the way she naturally gets closer to me.

"So, what do you do at NU, Miles?" he asks, folding and unfolding his hands at the table. I'm doing the same because I have no idea what to do with them.

"I play hockey. I'm benched for most of the season, but I'm getting back out there soon," I reply with a shrug. Wren's hand covers mine, and the tension slowly eases its way out of my body.

"That's good to hear. I used to play back in my day, but I wasn't any good," he replies with a vague waft of his hand in the air.

"I've seen the videos, Dad. You were insanely good," Wren challenges.

"Ah, I guess so," he replies, shrugging shyly. "How are you finding your second year at NU? The sports department is apparently one of the best in the country, so Wren tells me."

"It's going really well. It's better than the first year, but the classes are getting harder," I admit. If I could play hockey all day, I would. Having to go to classes and pretend like I know what they're talking about sucks.

Wren's dad nods. "This one over here thinks her classes are too easy." He nods over to Wren, and she rolls her eyes. He turns back to me and smiles. He's got one of those genuine smiles. Not ones you give to people when you'd rather not talk to them. It's nice and comforting, and I wish my dad would have smiled at me like that. "Hey, would you fancy having a few rounds on the ice sometime? You can help me get back into shape, I'm sure."

"Yeah, that would be cool," I say, trying to hide both my discomfort and my excitement.

"Just let me know when you're available," he says, and I nod.

When her dad is gone to talk to more people, I start to notice how comfortable she is around him in this environment. She doesn't tense or freeze up when she's talking to him. She talks animatedly with her hands, expressing her excitement in a child-like way. I fucking love this look on her.

She doesn't need to be anyone other than Wren. Not Wren the Future Olympian. Just her. The person I can see myself liking more and more each day. The person whose whole face lights up like sunlight as she talks about the things she loves with her dad.

When she leaves to go to the bathroom while I get us drinks from the bar, her dad stands beside me. He studies me for a minute, and I clear my throat, doing my best to seem okay with his kind of attention.

"Are you making her happy?" he asks, his eyes narrowing.

I nod. "I'm trying to."

"Every day?"

"Every day."

He nods at me and pats me on the shoulder. "Good man," he says, winking at me before disappearing again.

I didn't realize how big the world of hoteliers was until tonight. It looks like people from up and down the country come to these events.

It reminds me a lot of my family and how loud and chaotic

we are. Birthdays in the Davis family are wild. Thoughts and feelings are always at full volume. They look a lot like this but with more drinking, cheesy music, and more burned food.

"So, Mr. Berger, I have a very important question to ask," I begin when her dad returns to the table. We've been engaging in small talk about hockey and classes for a while, and it's about time I make it more interesting. Wren must know exactly what I'm up to because she glares at me.

He finishes his Scotch and looks at me. "Please, call me David. I can't even stand the sound of that name anymore," he pleads, waving his hand around. Wren laughs a little, still glaring at me. Honestly, it's a little creepy.

"What do you think about cheese? Just in general. Like? Dislike?" I ask, feigning curiosity. Wren elbows me in the ribs, and I smirk at her. "Oh, or loathe, as your daughter likes to say."

David laughs. "You know what, Miles? I cannot stand cream cheese. Everyone thinks—"

"Miles hates cream cheese, too," Wren says. She blinks up at me, her eyes silently screaming at me. "Don't you, Milesy?"

"Yep, sure do," I bite out, turning back to Wren's dad, leaning on the table. "Now, tell me, David, what is it exactly that—"

"Dad!" Wren basically shouts. She must really not want her dad to talk about cream cheese. "Why don't you tell Miles about how you almost made it pro?"

"You're too kind, Wrenny. I was nowhere near making it pro," he replies, shaking his head.

I almost choke on air as I spit out, "Kind? I'm sorry to tell you this, sir, but your daughter is everything but kind."

Wren glares at me as her dad laughs. "I am kind. People are always delighted to meet me."

"Delighted? No. Frightened, maybe." I shrug, hiding my smirk. She pokes me in my ribs and returns her attention back to her dad, asking him about his hockey career again.

Of course, Wren gets what she wants, and her dad forgets about the cream cheese debacle and tells me all about his days as a young athlete in nearly every sport.

I laugh at his terrible jokes and ask him follow-up questions, and I play my part as the doting boyfriend. Wren eats up every second of it, smiling at me like she wants to hug me and kill me at the same time.

He disappears again, speaking to some reporters.

"So, what do you think of my dad?" Wren asks, her head resting in her hand on the table. She looks at me with dreamy eyes, and I can tell she's exhausted.

"He's nice. Kind. Very different to your mom," I admit.

"Yeah, she can be pretty intense," she replies. "It's nice to have a balance."

"I can see where you get both sides of your personality from. You're brutal, but you're a little softie on the inside," I coo, scrunching my nose up at her. She rolls her eyes before smothering her smile in her hand, trying to hide it. "See?"

We melt into my favorite kind of conversation: the one where we get to learn more about each other. She talks more about her sister and what a good cook she is. She over-explains her dynamic with Kennedy and Scarlett, telling me what their sun, moon, and risings are. Whatever the fuck that means.

In return, I tell her about me and Carter as kids and how we created our own annual Olympic tournament called the Reyes-Davis Games. I avoid talking about my parents and tell her about how I peed myself at my first hockey game as a kid. She listens intently, slowly leaning into me as I speak.

Until the dark-haired boy comes into my view again.

I give him, what I hope to be, a look to back away, but he stalks closer, his face twisting into an evil grin. He's just seconds away from our table, his eyes completely focused on Wren's exposed back.

I hook my finger into her chair and pull her closer into me, our legs intertwined. She yelps as I interrupt her rant on what my zodiac sign means about me. I place my hand on the exposed skin on her shoulder, and she looks at my hand and then back at me.

"What are you doing?" she asks.

My heart races.

Fuck it.

I grab her face between my hands, and I kiss her.

WREN

I can feel myself melting into him. His large hands slip around my neck, his fingers curling in my hair as he dips my head back, deepening the kiss. Our mouths move against each other in sync. Like we were made to do this for each other.

Miles Davis is kissing me, and I'm kissing him back.

I whimper softly when he slips his tongue into my mouth and his fingers tighten in my hair. My body feels like it's on fire—like there's light bursting out of my chest. I hold onto the lapels of his blazer and pull him into me until he can't move any further.

The only thing I can focus on is how he feels against my mouth for the first time. It feels safe and exhilarating at the same time, and the longer we stay like this, the more real it feels. The more my hands itch to touch his skin. The more my nerves sing with pleasure when he swipes his tongue against mine.

He smiles against my mouth when I sigh, and I pull apart from him.

"What was that for?" I ask when I'm able to catch my breath. I'm panting, chest heaving like I've never been kissed before. He blinks back at me, his mouth parted.

"It was that guy. He was staring at you again, and he was about to come over here. I had to give him a reason not to. And would you look at that? He's gone," he rambles. I stare at him, and he sighs, dragging his hand down his face. "Sorry, I should have asked first."

Heat rushes up my neck when he licks his lips.

"No. It's okay," I say. I push further away from him, clearing my throat. "Are you going to do that every time somebody looks at me?"

"If it takes kissing you to prove to everyone that you're mine, then yes," he mutters before looking away.

WHEN WE GET BACK to our room, we're both defeated from eating terrible food and laughing at my dad's jokes that were so not funny they were funny. Miles carried our conversations with ease, flowing from each group of people to the next. He was a natural. At all of it. Pretending to like me, knowing the right way to make my dad laugh, knowing what kind of jokes to make to the hoteliers.

The second we reach the living room, I slip off my heels, letting the cool marble soothe the throbbing in my feet. I drop onto the couch, lying on my back, my head on the armrest. "Can you just chop off my feet?" I say, sighing.

Miles stands behind me on the other side of the couch, laughing. He's taken off his blazer, and his bow tie is hanging loose around his neck.

"I don't have my amputation equipment with me, but I can give you a massage," he suggests, looking down at me. His brown hair drops a little in his eyes, and I'm fighting the urge to push it away. It should be illegal for anyone to look this good right now after such an exhausting day. Especially him.

"I'd die for a massage right now. I'm sure there's a masseuse around here somewhere. I'll find one in the morning before we leave," I say.

"No, I mean, now. I can do it," he responds, gesturing toward my feet.

Before I can protest, he's sitting next to me, sweeping my feet into his hands on his lap. My feet immediately feel like butter under the touch of his rough and gentle fingers. I lean up on my elbows as I stare at him.

"Miles," I get out, but my breath catches when his fingers run smoothly over the inside of my foot. "My feet are gross. You don't have to do that."

"I don't mind," he says, shrugging. His voice is hoarse when he adds, "And no part of you is gross, so stop saying that. You're perfect, Wren."

I slip in and out of a haze as his fingers work magic around my ankle and my sole, relieving more and more of the pain.

"When did you learn how to do this?"

"I taught myself. My feet would get so sore after practice sometimes, so I just googled stuff. You should learn, then I won't have to do this for you all the time," he says, laughing.

I wiggle out of his grip and nudge him in his stomach, but he grabs my foot again and continues rubbing small circles around the pad of my foot with both hands.

"Hey, I told you that you didn't have to do this," I argue.

"I know."

"Then why are you doing it?" I ask.

He looks up at me, and his smile is deadly. "I don't know if you've noticed, but I like doing things for you. It's like our whole thing."

"But you don't have to."

"That's exactly why I'm doing it, princess."

I try not to let that comment get to me. The more nice things he does for me, the more it confuses me and the firm line I've put between me and anyone I've dated.

Silence washes over us, and I let myself fall into the rhythm of his hands working over me. His fingers are long and clean, and I can't help but think how they'd look on other parts of my body. The way they felt in my hair and how he tugged it roughly when he kissed me has been the most action I've had in months. And the more time I spend with him, the more I want it to happen again even when I know I shouldn't.

I tear my eyes away from his hands, staring up at the ceiling.

"I think I might take the whole beauty is pain thing too seriously," I say after a while. "My mom always said that if it's not hurting then it's not working."

"I don't like the sound of that," Miles whispers. I laugh, but he isn't laughing when I look at him. He stares down at my feet, shaking his head. "Don't you feel like you're too hard on yourself? You work harder than most guys on my team and you don't even play hockey."

"Sometimes, I think I'm not tough enough on myself. I don't know if you've noticed, but skating is like the only thing I'm good at. It's the one thing I can do. So, I might as well be really good while I'm at it," I admit.

My stomach twists when the realization of saying this for the first time washes over me. I've always known that skating is my life, but saying it aloud makes it more final. Indefinite.

"Not that it matters what I think, but I think you're plenty tough, Wren. A lot tougher than me," he says. I look up at him, but he's already looking at me, his brown eyes hooded and relaxed. "For whatever reason you feel like you need to prove yourself, I just want you to know that you don't need to do that with me. I like you enough the way you are for the both of us."

My heart practically doubles in size. "You're not too bad yourself, Davis."

He looks at me. Something dangerous in his eyes as our gazes burn. His eyes dip to my mouth for a second, and I exaggerate a sigh. "I think that's me done for the sappy shit tonight. Come and help me with my dress."

I get up from the couch, carrying my shoes with me to the

bedroom, where I find my sleeping shorts and tank top. I drop my shoes on the floor and walk into the gigantic bathroom, where I'm surrounded by mirrors and bright lights.

I take out my jewelry and place it into the boxes I brought with me and start to wipe off my makeup. I rinse and dry my face before taking my hair out of its clip and brushing it out, leaving it to fall to my shoulders.

Finally, I catch a glimpse of Miles in the doorway in gray sweatpants and a white tee.

Gray sweatpants.

Kill me now.

I clear my throat. "Can you zip this down for me?"

He walks toward me, his eyes locked with mine in the mirror. This isn't the first time I've seen him like this—relaxed, tried, and effortlessly sexy—but something else lingers when he comes up behind me. The proximity of him sends goosebumps up my arms rapidly, and I hate it.

I'm the one that's in control with him.

I always have been.

But since the way he surprised me by kissing me tonight, I've never felt more out of control.

"Did you have a good time tonight?" he asks, his voice rough. He still hasn't touched my zipper, and I'm about to tell him to get on with it. He slowly brings his hands around my hips, his fingers connecting at my stomach and then pulling back to rest on my hips. I close my eyes at the contact, the feeling so foreign and comforting. "Wren?"

My voice sounds hoarse and shaky when I say, "I just want to get out of this dress."

He nods and pushes my hair to one side of my shoulder and starts to zip down my dress, painfully slowly. Like, so slow that I could run down from the thirtieth floor to the bottom at the same time it takes him to move it down a few inches.

He keeps one hand on the top of the zipper, his fingers

grazing my neck, making me shiver. His eyes are focused on zipping me down, but when he realizes there's nothing underneath but bare skin, his breath hitches.

Even when he's finally done, he still keeps his hands on me. I don't tell him not to. There is something wildly comforting about his hands on my body. Something that feels just right, and I'm selfish enough to want to bathe in this feeling for a little longer.

I don't move when he starts to bring one strap over my shoulder, his eyes locked with mine in the mirror. The first one falls, almost exposing my chest. I watch the heat rushing to my cheeks like a tidal wave. He brings his face to my neck, his breath ragged and desperate, his mouth barely touching my skin. My pulse quickens so much that I'm sure he can feel it under his mouth.

He moves his hand to the other strap.

"Miles, you should stop," I whisper, my voice shaking.

"Why?" he murmurs into my skin as he bites onto my shoulder softly. My stomach somersaults. Every single nerve in my body focuses on that small spot on my shoulder, and my brain almost flatlines. "You smell so fucking good."

"I know I do," I get out, smiling at the image we've created in the mirror.

"Such a smart mouth." His voice is all gravel and rough against my skin.

I laugh, but it turns into a sigh when he kisses my shoulder. "Someone has to put you in your place."

"So you're saying I should be lucky that it's you, baby?"

"Something like that." He chuckles, and the sound reverberates through my body, the pressure of his lips on my shoulder driving me wild. His hand trails down my side, brushing against the side of my breast before he grips my waist. "Miles, we can't."

"Just think about how good it would be," he murmurs, still kissing my shoulder, "How good I could make you feel. How good it would be if you just stopped trying to control everything for once. Let me take care of you. *Please.*"

I've banished myself from having Miles-related thoughts, but that doesn't mean they don't creep their way in there sometimes. Like right now as he kisses my shoulder, his hands branding my body in ways it shouldn't and my self-control almost snaps.

I could say yes. I could say fuck it, turn around, and kiss him like he did earlier. Now that I've had that one taste, I want more even when I shouldn't. Give a sex-deprived girl a hockey player to fake date and this is what happens.

I clear my throat, placing my hand over his. "Miles, seriously, we can't." He groans, dropping his head to my shoulder, but he listens despite his dramatics. He tears away from me, leaving me in the bathroom, and I let out a breath of relief.

I don't bother to put my shorts on because it's so hot in the bedroom and I'd end up taking them off anyway. I slip into a pair of panties and put on my tank top, a reckless part of me hoping that he'll still be awake. But when I go into the room, he's deep asleep on one side of the bed.

I sigh and slip into the other end, putting as much space between us as possible.

20
WREN

Wonderland (Wren and Miles Version)

GIGI

I think Miles might be the best thing to happen to you.

What has provoked this conversation, Gianna?

GIGI

Have you seen his post?

The one of us at the charity event? Yeah, G, it's almost like I was there.

GIGI

Still!!!!! He's wearing a tux, and you kept your cool. How are you still alive?

I'm barely holding it together. Trust me.

I WAKE UP IN SWEATS, clutching my chest like I had a nightmare, only it was the exact opposite.

It's been a few days since spending the night with Miles at

my dad's hotel. Which means it's been a few days of intense workouts, desperate studying, and doing everything I can to avoid thinking about Miles Fucking Davis and his stupid fucking mouth.

The more time I spend with him, the more I start feeling things I definitely don't want to feel. Like attraction. Safety. Comfort. He pulls me in like the moon pulls in the tide, and I've tried everything to stop letting myself feel this way. I had to tell Kennedy and Scarlett to sit me down and tell me every good reason why he's not good for me.

They came up with nothing.

So I've spent the last four nights having insanely vivid sex dreams about him. He's invaded my senses and my thoughts. Even my dreams aren't safe from him, and he's not even doing anything. He just exists beside me with his tall frame and deep voice and his dirty jokes, and it makes me want to fall for him. How pathetic is that?

"Rough night?" Scarlett asks, sitting on the edge of my bed while Ken rifles through my wardrobe. I don't know why they love to do this. They treat my room like the designated hang-out spot, like we don't all have our own rooms and a living area.

"You could say that." I rub my temples. "Stupid Miles and stupid dreams." They laugh, and I go to check my phone. I still haven't heard from Austin, and my mom has been asking me for updates all weekend. This is just what Austin does. She disappears for a few weeks, lets everyone worry, and then turns up again like nothing happened.

It's well into the afternoon now, and it's been a while since I've had a lazy day. It also helps that it's been snowing like crazy these last couple of days. Our little town has been covered in thick layers of snow, and we've been bundled up in our apartment watching *Gilmore Girls* and pretending our lives are on hold.

"My point still stands," Kennedy says, turning around to me

with two bikinis I haven't worn yet in her hands. "I say you fuck him and get it over with."

"Yeah, at least then you're not still thinking about what it would be like to sleep with him," Scarlett adds.

"I'm *not* thinking about it." I groan, dropping my head against the headboard.

"Right...." they both say at the same time, looking at each other.

"What are you doing with my clothes, Ken?" I ask as she makes a pile.

"I'm preparing myself for summer. You never let me borrow your clothes unless you don't want them, so I'm starting my collection early," she says, smiling at me.

"Do you ever buy your own clothes?" Scarlett asks.

"Why would I? Wren lends me hers, and you get me clothes from Voss all the time," she argues. Scarlett's family's clothing brand has saved our lives so many times. Kennedy shrugs. "The perks of our friendship are finally paying off."

"Can't argue with that logic," I mumble, slipping out of the bed to finally get dressed. I should probably visit my mom or go to the gym or do something that isn't lying around thinking about Miles. I startle at the knock on the door. "Did you guys order takeout already?"

"Nope, but we are having pizza tonight, right?" Kennedy asks. I snort, walking out of my room toward the door. We've had pizza every night this week. She shouts after me, "Right?!"

I ignore her and open the door.

The wind is almost knocked out of me when I see the one thing I've been trying to avoid. Miles is standing in front of me, grinning like a Cheshire cat, wearing at least three layers of clothing.

"Miles," I greet, nodding curtly.

"Wrenny girl," he says, smiling wide. "I've missed you."

"Wish I could say the same."

"Are you going to let me in?"

"Depends what you're doing here."

"I'm taking you out. Me and you."

I narrow my eyes at him. "We don't have anything planned today."

"I know."

My patience thins. "Then why are we going out?"

He sighs, rolling his head back dramatically before facing me. "Because I want to hang out with you, you idiot."

I gasp, trying not to laugh. "Don't come to my house to insult me, Miles."

"No, I'm coming to your house to take you out because I've missed you, and I want you to put me out of my misery," he says, removing my arm from the door where I've blocked him, and he walks in like he fucking owns the place. "Can you get ready so we can go?"

"Who said I wanted to go out with you?" I argue, crossing my arms.

"Or don't get ready," he drawls, scanning my entire outfit. I'm still wearing the shorts I slept in and a thin tank top. "You look perfect like this."

I huff.

It's either spending an entire day inside daydreaming about Miles, or spending time with him that proves that he's actually annoying and I *shouldn't* need to daydream about him. Really, there isn't much of a choice.

"Fine," I say, holding my hands up in defeat and dropping them. "You better rock my world, Milesy, or I'm not trusting you again."

"You won't regret it," he says, winking at me.

WE GET a good hour into the walk until I'm ready to go home. There's a trail I sometimes take for a run that's not too far from us and has enough hills and turns to get a good workout in. But Miles wanted to take us somewhere else.

"Do you know where we're going?" I ask as he pulls me along, my gloved hand clasped into his. Honestly, the weather is a lot more bearable with his hand in mine. The sun is shining, but it's still cold as fuck, and the snow is taking forever to melt.

"That's the whole point of the adventure, Wrenny girl," he says, flashing me a grin.

"Are you being serious?" I sigh. "You dragged me out of my house to go on an adventure and you have no clue where we're going?"

"You need to be more spontaneous. Live a little."

"I *am* living, and I hate it."

He tugs onto my arm, and I catch up with him. He drapes his arm over my shoulder, pulling me into his side. "Come on, baby. This is a once-in-a-lifetime opportunity."

"It snows all the time, you oaf."

He frowns. "Are you allergic to having fun?"

"What part of this is fun?"

He ignores me and pulls apart from me before swiping up some snow from a tree. He turns to me, and I step back. "No," I whisper, holding my hand up to him to stop.

"Just one."

"No."

His grin turns evil as he squeezes the ball of snow in his hand, making it into the perfect round shape. He lifts his hand slowly. "It's already leaving my hand, Wren, and it's coming straight for you. There's really no stopping it now."

"You've got to catch me first," I shout.

I run in the opposite direction, my boots plowing through the snow as Miles chases after me, throwing snowballs in my direction.

I swipe up some snow from a bush before launching it over my head. I don't know if any of them are actually getting him, but I keep running and making more until he gets closer to me and I'm panting.

"Your aim is terrible, princess," he shouts, and I turn back to see that he's right on my heels.

I throw another snowball in his face. "And you keep hitting me in the ass."

"That's exactly what I'm aiming for." He winks and I shake my head, still trying to run away from him. My foot gets stuck in a patch, and I fall over on my stomach. Miles is right behind me, and he drops onto me before rolling over and tugging me right onto his chest. We're both wheezing with laughter, our faces covered in snow.

I push at his chest, but he keeps me close to him, and my legs wrap around his waist. I sit up, his hands digging into my sides as I straddle him. His face is flushed, and water droplets are dripping down it. God, he looks good.

"Got you," he says, looking at the space between us before his eyes meet mine.

"Looks that way, doesn't it?" He stares at me, and his gaze dips to my lips. I lick them, and his grip on me tightens. I'm too afraid to move but too scared to stay here and do something stupid. I clear my throat. "Should I take a picture?"

He nods, and I pull out my phone.

I take a picture of him from where he's beneath me, getting the way his hands rest on my thighs in the frame. I pass my phone to him, and he takes one of me from his position so we can make a good collage out of it and post it.

"These are good. Do you want me to post them, or should I send them to you?" I ask.

"Send them to me." He rubs his hands against my thighs. "But I'm not going to post it, and I don't want you to either. I want this one to be just for us."

I frown. "But, Miles—"

He shakes his head. "Let's keep those just for us, Wren. Please."

The pleading in his tone catches me off guard, and I nod. Maybe there are some parts of this agreement that we can keep to ourselves. There's no harm in that. Is there? Like how right now we're just staring at each other, covered in snow, and neither one of us has moved.

"We should try to find a way out of here. It's like we're in a maze," I say after a while.

"You're going to have to get off me for that to happen, princess," he mutters before he drops his head back into the snow and crosses his arms behind his head. "Or don't. I like this view."

I groan and stand up. As I do, I collect some snow in my hands and throw it in his face. "Come on, Milesy."

***

I'M REALLY CONTEMPLATING why I let Miles talk me into this because we go another half an hour without getting anywhere. The view is gorgeous, with our entire town covered in white snow and the sun still peeking through the clouds. The snowball fight tired me out, and the sun is still harsh, so the only thing Miles is really good for is keeping my jumper in his bag while I walk around in jeans and a shirt.

"We're lost, Miles," I say for the tenth time. "I'm tired and hungry, and the only end I'm seeing in sight is death."

"You know, you're the most dramatic person I've ever met," he says, shaking his head at me. "Trust me, I've got it all figured out."

He sticks his finger in his mouth and moves it around in the air. This must be the third time he's done that, and he makes us change direction every time. I lean against a thick tree as I watch him do his Boy Scout ritual.

"Do you actually know what you're doing, or do you just like getting your finger wet?" I ask.

He turns to me, hands on his hips. "Why would I like getting my finger wet?"

I shrug. "I dunno. It could be a kink of yours."

"That's not a kink, Wren; that's just weird."

"Whatever you say, pretty boy," I tease. I cross my arms against my chest, tilting my head up to the sky. "You've got to admit that we're lost. Let's just give up. The sun is about to set, and all the freaks come out at night."

He grins. "Oh, so you mean you?"

"Is your love language bullying?"

"You know, over the last few weeks, it's changed. Words of affirmation might be taking the top spot, actually," he says.

"Huh. I wouldn't have guessed. You don't do much of that with the girl you're supposed to be dating," I say, laughing.

"What do you want me to do, Wren?" He groans, dropping his arms from his hips.

"Right now? I'd appreciate it if you could try to get us—"

"No, I mean with the fake dating. What else do you want me to do, to tell you?"

My heart stutters. I thought we were just joking around, but maybe not. "What are you talking about?"

His eyes darken, and he steps closer to me. I'd back up if I wasn't already pressed to the tree. "Do you seriously think I don't compliment you enough?"

"I-It was a joke," I spit out.

"But do you really mean it? If you want me to tell you how stunning you are every day, I'll do it." He steps closer, and his hand grazes my cheek. He's not wearing his gloves, and I feel my entire body melting into him. He tucks a strand of hair behind my ear, and I blink up at him. "If you want me to admit that you're all I fucking think about, this is me admitting that to you. You consume all my thoughts, princess. You consume *me*."

I try to search his face for something. For some sort of sign to tell me that he's joking, but I find nothing. He flirts with me all the time. It's been our go-to banter since we met, but this doesn't feel like it usually does.

"Are you being—"

"Yes," he bites out. His hand curls around my neck, and his other grips my hip. "I mean it, Wren."

I stare up at him, and no words come. I want to tell him he's lying, that he doesn't mean it, that he *can't* mean it, but I'm legitimately speechless.

I let him grip the back of my neck tighter, and he searches my eyes for some sort of answer, but I don't give him one. His breath tickles my neck before he kisses me there. The sensation is so intense and unknown that my head tilts to the side, giving him more access.

"My god, Wren. You're perfect. So fucking perfect, and you don't even know it," he murmurs into my skin, pressing the hottest kisses to my neck like I'm paying him to do it. "Can I keep kissing you here?"

"Yes," I breathe. I clutch his shirt, and I don't have it in me to tell him to stop. He doesn't kiss me; he just keeps worshiping my neck and my chest until I'm writhing beneath him.

He kisses across my jaw, and I laugh when he gets to a sensitive spot. "Keep still, baby," he rasps against my cheek. He drops his knee between my legs, pinning me there, and he pulls my arms up, pinning them together with one of his hands. "Let me do this for you, okay? Let me show you what you do to me. Let me show you how good I could be to you."

I nod, and he continues. He kisses and sucks my skin into his mouth in the most maddening ways, biting and then smoothing it out. I've never had a more sensual feeling in my life, and I don't ever want it to stop.

He nudges his knee between my legs, and I grind into him. The friction between our clothes and his knee pressing into me sends a ripple of pleasure through my entire body. I can feel myself get wet, and the faster his kisses become on my neck and on my chest, the harder I grind into him. My body is spinning out of control, and I don't want to catch it.

"Jesus Christ, Miles," I mutter when his warm hand spreads across my stomach, reaching up to cup one of my tits. His thumb swipes across my nipple, and I arch into him, my hips moving faster. "What are we doing?"

"Do you want this as bad as I do?" he asks into my skin, still not kissing me where I want him to.

"I don't know," I whine. I don't know what I want. Everything about this is screaming yes while also saying no at the same time. It's confusing as fuck. My patience runs out, and I say, "Are you going to kiss me?"

His grip on my wrists tightens. "Do you want me to?"

"I don't know what I want anymore," I pant. This is all too confusing. Too much. He leaves one long kiss on the top of my breast before he drops his hands from mine, smoothing out my shirt and stepping back from me.

"Okay, then we'll stop," he says.

I blink at him. "W-what?"

"You need to be sure, Wrenny girl," he says, tucking my hair behind my ears. "I'm not touching you again until you're sure."

He smiles at me like he didn't just put my entire body through a workout, getting me ready to let him fuck me against a tree. I've never wanted to punch and kiss someone more.

He tilts his head to the side. "Is that okay with you, princess?"

No, Miles, it really isn't fine because I almost let you kiss me just then, and if it happens again, I really don't know if I can convince you to stop.

But I don't say that. Instead, I smile and say, "Fine," before turning in the opposite direction and hoping I can find us a way home. I don't trust myself to be alone with him anymore. When I'm with him, I find myself losing more and more control, and there's nothing more terrifying than that.

21
MILES

"My dick isn't a fucking puppy, Wren."

SLEEPING on the edge of the bed that night in the hotel was fucking torture. So I thought the best way to help with that after she avoided me was to go see her again. The snowstorm was the perfect excuse. Until it turned into something way more than that, and I'm still trying to find excuses for what I did.

I've been replaying that day in the forest nearly every night just to get myself to sleep. The sound of her whimpers haunts my dreams, and I can't get the image of her grinding into me out of my mind. She was a fucking sight, and I have no idea how I'm supposed to act normal around her after that, especially for the game today.

I'm putting on my jacket, ready to leave when my phone lights up with a text.

WRENNY

What do I wear?

I ROLL my eyes with a laugh and shoot back a message.

> Anything. You could wear a garbage bag and you'd still be the most gorgeous person in the room.

WRENNY

> Do you enjoy lying?

> I'm coming to get you in five minutes.

HOCKEY GAMES at NU are the highlight of the week. We always get a full house even when the games are just friendly. Everyone loves the atmosphere, the rush, and the energy that radiates off the players. I can't wait to get myself back out there.

Coach has been checking in to see how I'm doing, and he told me that he'll let me know as soon as he thinks I'm ready to play again. Wren has been easing me into getting back on the ice in my full gear, but it's a lot harder than I thought. Each time I step out there and see the nets, I freeze up. I'm going to have to get there eventually. After we sat by the ice for hours, I started to feel the warmth slowly seeping back into my blood, and imagining myself back out there isn't as scary as it once was.

I drive the distance from my house to Wren's apartment, and when I get to her door, I knock twice before Kennedy opens it. A wide grin splits on her face, and she lets me in.

"She's through there," she says, pointing down the hallway. I look down the hall and then back to her. "When you hear frustrated groans, you'll know which one it is."

As expected, I hear frustrated grunts coming from one of the rooms down the hallway, and I knock on the door.

"Wren?" I ask. "It's me. Miles."

"Yes, I know what your voice sounds like, Miles," she says, sighing. "Open the door."

Entering her room is like looking straight into her brain. A chaotic, beautiful mess.

The walls are covered in music posters, figure skating posters, and pictures of her and her friends. A dressing table in the corner holds a vinyl player and a stack of Taylor Swift records next to it. A shelf is covered from top to bottom in trophies, medals, and certificates. Another shelf is dedicated solely to books, and it looks like it's seconds away from collapsing. I don't know why I'm surprised with all the awards because I knew she was good, but *fuck*. There is almost no room for anything else on the shelves.

And best of all, Wren is sitting in the middle of the floor, surrounded by thousands of clothes in a sports bra and leggings. She looks up at me, and her face drops in exhaustion.

"You're going to have to leave me here. I'm not going," she groans. I crouch down in front of her and tilt my head to the side.

"Yeah, you are. I got you a present," I say, holding out my cap and jersey with my number seven on it. She looks at them and then at me.

"Do you know how tacky it is for me to wear your jersey?"

"If you're gonna wear a jersey, it needs to have my name and number on it. I'm not letting anyone think you're someone else's," I challenge. Okay, maybe I do have a jealous side. Her mouth tilts into a grin. "Plus, it makes you look like you care and that we're in a committed relationship. We are in a very committed relationship, right?"

"Yes," she mumbles.

"Great. Then get dressed, princess."

She groans before grabbing my shirt out of my hand and standing up out of her heap. When she stands, I get a better look at her and the red-and-purple marks on her skin.

She rolls her eyes when she catches me staring. "Yeah, those are your fault," she says, pointing at her neck. "Really appreciate the hickeys, Miles. Are we in fucking high school?"

"How the fuck did you get those?"

"Do you not remember pinning me to a tree and kissing me everywhere *but* my mouth and then telling me you wouldn't touch me again until I'm sure?" I give her a blank look. "Whatever the fuck that means."

I snort. "I mean, I know I kissed you there, but fuck."

I reach out to touch her neck, where she's basically covered in marks from me. She swats my hand away. "My skin's sensitive, Milesy. You would have known that if you didn't go all crazy possessive caveman on me."

"God, I'm sorry, but you've got to admit, it's a little funny," I say, pressing my lips together, but Wren is not the least bit amused. "You don't think it's a little funny that I hardly did anything, and you look like a victim of a vampire attack?"

"No, it's not funny," she huffs, but I can tell she's trying to hold in her laughter. She pulls the shirt over her head and looks in her full-length mirror. The jersey hangs loose on her and falls halfway down her thighs. I stand behind her and put my hands on her shoulders.

I love that she has my name written on her back. I've never given a girl my jersey, and I'm so glad Wren is the first person to wear it. My ex-girlfriend Emily Fraser would love to use the fact that I'm a hockey player to show off, but she'd never wear my jersey. She demanded I get her a fitted one, or else there would be no point in wearing it.

"See, you look fabulous," I say, smiling. She shakes her head and turns to me, my hands still on her shoulders.

"I look like I'm dating a hockey player," she says before a horrified expression takes over her face. "Oh my god. I'm dating a hockey player."

"Should I be concerned that it's taken you that long to notice that?" I laugh while her jaw hangs open. I put my cap on her head and tap it. Her nose scrunches as I put two fingers under her jaw and close her mouth. "Come on. We're going to be late."

"Why are you so worried about being late? You're not even playing."

"I know, but it's not the worst thing to be on time," I retort. "You're the one who likes to take hours to get ready."

She huffs, and we walk out of her room. Kennedy and Scarlett stop us before we can get to the door. They both walk over to us slowly like they can't believe what they're seeing.

"Amelia Wren Hackerly. Respectfully, what the fuck is this?" Scarlett says dramatically, gesturing to Wren's outfit.

"I am speechless. Like, no words," Kennedy exclaims.

"I know. Desperate times call for desperate measures," Wren replies, grabbing my hand, pulling us past them. "We better go before someone gets grumpy."

THE STADIUM IS PACKED when we get there. There's a certain buzz that radiates from each wall as we make our way through the crowds of people. We walk up to our seats, people's heads turning as they see I'm not down on the ice. It's weird having this many people care about what we do.

The season's in full swing, and the pressure is mounting. Our team's financial backing from the parents and investors is always a topic of conversation, and I can feel the weight of their expectations on my shoulders. It's not just about winning games; it's about generating buzz and getting noticed by scouts and sponsors. We're not just a team, we're a business, and everyone's got a stake in our success. Just being in the arena makes me feel like a spectator in my own life, and everything feels off.

I keep my arm around Wren until we're sitting comfortably in our seats with a perfect view. It's still busy in our section, and people are walking up and down on the stands. I pull her into my lap instead, and she flashes me a look.

"This is cozy," she murmurs.

"Well, we've got to look like we're a couple."

"Right, and me sitting on your dick is the most coupley thing you can think of?"

"If you'd rather we remove the layers, that can be arranged," I tease, wrapping my hand around her stomach and pushing her back against my front.

She scoffs. "We could have just made out and made it more obvious."

"You're making some great suggestions here, Wrenny. If I didn't know any better, I'd be starting to think that this is all a big ploy so you can get in my pants."

She laughs. "You don't know any better," she says. She points to the rink where the Zamboni is doing its last round. "Now tell me what is going on here."

I kiss her on the cheek. "Now you're speaking my language."

I've just finished explaining to Wren how the game works for the third time when Sophia Aoki sits down on the seat below us. She does a double take when she sees Wren and me.

"Hi, Miles. Long time no see," she says, pushing her dark hair behind her shoulder, getting a better look at me. "I thought you'd be on the ice today."

"Nah, not yet. I'm still working on my training," I say with a shrug.

"Yeah, I get that," she replies, giving me a sympathetic smile.

Sophia, Carter, and I became close in high school through Grayson, our friend, and her cousin. She's one of those people who is genuinely good, and I need more people like her in my life.

She turns to look at Wren. "You're Wren, right? I don't think we've met."

"Hi," Wren replies, smiling and snuggling further into me, which only rubs her ass against my dick. "It's nice to meet you."

"You too." Sophia grins before turning to me. "I thought you two were coming to my party, but I didn't see you there."

Wren stiffens and looks back at me. I run my hand down her arm quickly before resting it on her thigh. "Yeah, we went for a little while, but we didn't stay for long. Sorry we didn't get to say hi then," I explain.

"No, it's cool. Can I say that you guys are so cute together?!" she exclaims. Wren's face turns red with heat when I slip my hand up to her waist, squeezing gently. "And Wren, you're a figure skater, right?"

"Yeah, I am," Wren replies. Sophia's face lights up, quite literally. Her smile always reaches her eyes as lined dimples form on her cheekbones in a childlike way.

"That's so cool! I always wished I could skate, but I'm so clumsy. So, I like to live vicariously through them by watching the team play." She laughs. Which is very true. She fell into a Koi pond outside the venue of our high school prom, and whenever I see her around, she walks like she has two left feet. "I'd love to see you skate sometime. Do you have any competitions coming up?"

"Yeah, actually. We're doing a winter showcase in December. I'd love to see you there," Wren says.

That's my girl.

As introverted as she seems, seeing her interact with other people makes my heart swell. She gets herself worked up about it, but when she realizes that my friends are not out to get her, she relaxes a little and lets herself enjoy talking to people who aren't Kennedy and Scarlett.

"Great. I'll be there. I'll ask some of my friends to come, and I'll bring Brie." Her smile widens at the mention of her girl-friend. "Are you going to be there too?"

"Of course," I say. "I wouldn't miss it for the world."

Sophia smiles and then pulls her bottom lip between her teeth, a nervous tick I've noticed she's had over the years. "Miles, can I ask you something?"

I sigh, knowing what's coming next. "Soph, we do this every time." Wren looks up at me in confusion. "Sophia's our photographer. You've probably seen her photos all over the school and on the school Instagram account. She takes all of our pictures of the team and tries to get as many candids as she can." She still looks confused, so I add, "She wants to take a photo of us."

Wren smiles shyly, but before she can say anything, Sophia cuts in. "I'm planning on making a mockumentary for this season, and I need some more pictures of NU's star players. I need to schedule an interview with Miles soon, too, but some pictures are a good start."

"That actually sounds really cool," Wren says, "But do I have to be in it? I'm not on the team."

"You're on my team, baby," I murmur, and she rolls her eyes. "Come on. Just one photo."

She groans. "Fine. Just one."

Sophia squeals happily and whips out the camera that she takes with her everywhere and instructs Wren and me to sit closer together than we already are. She leans her head back, dropping it onto my shoulder as I lean into her.

She feels too good like this.

Too much like mine.

"Say, 'Hockey!'" We do as she asks, and the camera clicks. Sophia holds up the back camera to her face and squints at it. "It's perfect."

"Can we see it?" Wren asks.

Sophia laughs. "You'll see it once the video is done."

I wipe the confusion off Wren's face with a kiss to her cheek as Sophia turns back around. The game starts up, and we stay quiet. Well, as quiet as possible because Wren keeps asking me what is happening every two seconds.

She keeps wiggling in my lap with excitement, and all it's doing is pressing her ass into my dick.

I grip her hip with my left hand. "Can you keep still? You're making it worse."

She sighs, turning to me. "Can't you tell it to go down?"

"Tell it to go down? My dick isn't a fucking puppy, Wren."

"I realized that, Miles, thank you."

"If I could, I would have. This isn't very comfortable for me either, princess," I bite out, and her hips roll again. I suppress my groan into her shoulder, shaking my head. "Just keep still and watch the game."

She salutes me, trying to hold in her laugh. "Yes, sir."

I think she's trying to kill me.

WE KEEP quiet most of the game as I watch Xavier and Gray with concentration as they shuffle on the ice. We're in the lead during the first period against Fraser College, one of our more friendly opponents. Most of the guys on my team went to high school with people on their team, so we're all familiar with each other.

During the first intermission, Wren peppers me with more hockey questions before another one of my friends turns up behind me in the queue for the vending machine.

Charlie Jacobs is one of those guys who I don't see often enough to call one of my close friends, but I have seen him at nearly all the parties I've been to over the past few months. He's a cool guy, but he doesn't exactly fit in with my friendship group.

"Davis! I wasn't expecting to see you today," Charlie exclaims, running a hand through his blond hair in disbelief. "It's good to see you in daylight, man."

I laugh nervously as Wren blinks up at me, twisting open the bottle of water. She moves closer to me as I watch her watch him. My friends are not at all like hers, so I wrap my arm around her shoulder, tugging her close to my side.

"Yeah, it's good to see you too," I reply. "This is my girlfriend, Wren. She skates. You should come to one of her performances sometime."

"Jesus, I can talk, you know," Wren murmurs as she looks up at me before turning back to Charlie, a smile playing on her lips. "But, yeah, I do skate. Don't let Miles bully you into coming."

"No, I definitely will go." Charlie laughs with a huge grin. Right answer. "You probably wouldn't believe it, but I used to skate as a kid. I wasn't very good, but I appreciate the sport."

"You're right. I wouldn't have guessed," Wren says.

Charlie smiles at her and turns to me.

"Funny question, actually," Charlie starts, rubbing the back of his neck. "If you're dating Wren, does that mean Em is single?"

"She's been single for almost a year, Charlie," I huff. Wren does flinch at the mention of my ex. There's not much of a story there to be told other than every guy on the team wanted her, even when she was with me. "If you're asking for my permission to date her, then sure. I really couldn't care less."

"Okay, cool. It's just— You looked like you would kill anyone that even looked at her when you were dating, so I wanted to make sure." Wren looks up at me with an evil smile, and I can tell she's going to make fun of me later.

"Yeah, well, I don't care anymore. If you want to date her, go ahead," I say. I know that Emily would eat him alive, but I don't say that. "The game is starting up again. We better get back to our seats."

I don't let him say bye before I turn around with my arm still around Wren. When we sit down, she nuzzles herself right back in my lap, and my breathing stops. For someone who loves physical touch so much, whenever she touches me, it feels different. It's uniquely hers, and it's slightly terrifying.

It feels like a slow, torturous, perfect way to die.

"Jealous *and* protective. Wow, Davis. You really are something," she whispers into my ear. As she draws back, the smell of her clouds my thoughts, and I don't respond.

It would be too risky to tell her that I would protect her with my life. I would never let anything, or anyone, hurt her.

When we score another goal, Wren and I both get out of our seats and cheer, the excitement taking over us completely. Chaos erupts around us as the stadium grows loud with chants and cheers. She jumps into my arms and hugs me tight. I kiss her quickly before pulling away. Her eyes widen in shock for a moment before she returns her celebratory smile to the rest of the team.

This is easy.

We can do this.

THE LOCKER ROOM is loud and chaotic when I walk in. Most of the guys are still in their jerseys, spraying water around as they whoop and yell. There is no better feeling than winning a game alongside your best friends. When they see me, they start cheering even louder.

"Look who decided to show up," Harry announces, gesturing toward me, looking out of place in my jeans and hoodie.

"You guys did good. Could have been better if I was there though." I laugh. Tyler Vaughan stalks toward me, patting me on the back.

"No need to get cocky, dude. You need to get back out there. This season is going to be a nightmare without you," he says, rolling his eyes at the rest of the team before slipping away into the showers.

"It's up to Coach. I'm still training and getting my head back in the game. Coach just needs to give me the all-clear," I reply, shrugging. All of the team nod in agreement.

Then Jake starts laughing hysterically from the corner of the room. Who the fuck does he think he is? Is he a villain in a kid's movie? Everyone's heads turn to him as he makes himself the center of attention. Like always.

Jake and I were good friends in first year. We both got onto the team, and, like all my other teammates, we bonded instantly. Carter was never really a fan of his. He always thought Jake was too much for the team. He has too much chaotic energy and not in a good way. He always took things a step too far, especially during prank week.

Then he started dating anyone he could get his hands on. He dated Scarlett, which didn't last very long when he cheated on her. Considering who her family is, he's lucky he got away without a scratch. He's a machine on the ice, which is the only reason anyone on this team tolerates him.

"Are you, Davis? Because I haven't seen you on the ice in months," he drawls, stepping closer to me. I swallow, feeling the rage and nausea at the same time.

"Dude, calm down. No one has been feeling it since Carter died, especially Miles. They were practically brothers. Just leave it, and fuck off," Xavier cuts in, coming to my rescue.

"Don't give me that dead friend bullshit. If Davis wanted to play, he would have by now. Instead, he's too busy fucking around with his girlfriend," he says, moving closer in my face. I take a breath in, trying to calm myself down. I can't fuck this up for myself now. "What's her name? Wren? Hacks's kid?"

"Keep her name out of your mouth, Callahan," I bite out, my fists clenching and unclenching at my sides. I feel bile rising in my throat, but I swallow it. I've never felt this kind of anger and exhaustion all at the same time. I hate the way it makes my pulse quicken and my jaw clench. I hate the way he thinks he can talk about my girl with no repercussions.

"Or what? You going to go crying to Coach about it? Grow the fuck up, Miles. If you ever want to play in the pros, you're going to have to stop moping over Carter and stop drooling over that whore. If you're not careful, she might follow in her friend's footsteps."

I get closer to him, our faces inches apart.

"Talk about her or her friends again and see what happens," I bite out. An evil smile spreads across his face slowly. "I swear to God, Callahan, if you so much as breathe near her, I'll crack your fucking head open."

"Oh, shit." He laughs. "Does she really fuck that good, Davis?"

I bite my tongue so hard that it almost bleeds. I take a deep breath in before turning around. I can do this. I can take the high road. I can walk out of here and leave him to crawl back into whatever hole he came from. If I mess up now, I could be off the team for good. I walk closer to the door before I hear him again behind me.

"Yeah, go home and cry to your little slut," Jake shouts.

I turn back around.

Fuck this.

22
WREN

Pretty boy, dumb girl

I'M STANDING OUTSIDE in the cold, shivering as I wait for Miles to come back from doing whatever he was doing. I've tried calling him, but he hasn't picked up. I could walk home from here. He drove us here, and if something has happened, I don't want to leave him alone. So the least I can do is be here when he comes out. I sit down on the curb outside the sports center and wait for him.

"Wren." I hear a quiet voice from behind me. I stand up, turn, and I see him. Miles walks toward me slowly, limping like he's been injured. "You waited."

"Of course I did. You're my ride back home." He comes closer to me, and the bright street light shines on his face. That's when I see the bruises. His right eye is shut while marks and bruises cover his face and neck. I reach out to touch his face, but he pulls his head back. "Jesus, Miles. What happened?"

"Can you drive? My eye hurts," he murmurs, holding out his keys to me.

I nod and get into the driver's seat of his truck.

I've never been in this kind of situation before. I've never had to take care of someone like this. Me and the girls take care of ourselves fine, but when we do need each other it's not because we've been punched in the face.

We drive in silence, and it eats away at me.

"Are you going to tell me what happened?" I ask. He shrugs and looks out of his window.

I want to ask him again, to get him to open up to me, but he clearly doesn't want to speak, and I'm not one to push. So I focus on the road and drive back to his house.

It's freakishly quiet as we walk up the stairs to his bedroom, and I wish I could do something to ease the tension.

He sits on his bed, resting his back against the headboard, his legs stretched out straight. He's barely said a word since we left campus. Which is worrying since I can never get him to shut up usually.

I run down into the kitchen, feeling helpless as I put some ice into a ziplock. When I get into his room again, he's still sitting there, his eyes closed, and he's taking in deep breaths.

I put my knees on both sides of his legs, straddling him but still hovering as I press the ice to his face.

He winces. "Sorry," I whisper. I put the ice down, touching and examining his face carefully. "What happened, Milesy?"

"It doesn't hurt that bad. You should see the other guy. I'm fine," he says, trying to be cheerful as his lip twitches. I tut and shake my head.

"Oh, you're fine?" I gently prod my finger on his cheek. He hisses. "This looks really bad. We should get it checked out. I can drive you to the hospital."

"I'm fine, really," he argues, more convincingly this time. The tightness in my chest pinches as I look at him, opening and closing my mouth, trying to make my brain say something. "Can you stay tonight? I need you here."

After what happened in the woods, I told myself to be more cautious around him, but then things like this happen. Where he says that he needs me in that whiny voice of his. Or he says "please" and flutters his eyelashes at me. Or when he convinces me to do things that I said I wouldn't. Like wearing his jersey and straddling him as I tend to his face.

"Okay," I say, and he smiles wide. "I'll stay, but no funny business."

"Funny business? What does that even mean?" He blinks up at me, trying to be as innocent as he can, but I know better.

"You know what I mean."

I inspect his eye, trying to do my best to see what can help. It's gone down since we've been here, but it's still harsh.

I put the packet down again to give his eye a rest from the cold. It's not swollen, just badly bruised underneath. He'll probably have a black eye in the morning though.

I start to climb off him, to put some much-needed space between us when his hands come onto my hips. His touch is electric, and I wish it didn't send sparks flying across my entire body.

"I want you so badly, Wren. Me and you for real," he murmurs, dropping his head to my chest.

I laugh. "This is exactly what I meant by funny business."

He rolls his head against me. "I'm telling the truth."

"You're delirious," I say, trying again to move, but he keeps me there, hovering over him. I lift his head up, brushing his hair out of his face and looking down at him.

"No, I'm not."

"You are."

"Ask me again in the morning," he challenges, "and see what I'll say."

"That's if you can remember any of this in the morning."

He meets my gaze with intensity, and I suck in a breath. "Cut the bullshit, Wren. Stop covering up everything you feel with a joke. You're way too fucking smart to be doing that with me."

"I'm not doing that," I whisper.

"Don't play dumb with me either, princess."

"I'm not playing dumb. I just— We joke around, it's what we do. I just don't believe you're being serious," I argue. "You're not into me, Miles. I *know* that."

His grip on my hips tightens, and he drops me onto his lap. I feel his dick pressing into me from the thin material that separates us, and I gasp.

"Is this believable enough?" he rasps, "Is the way my body has been aching for you since the day I met you believable, Wren? Because I can prove to you in a thousand other ways that this isn't fake."

My heart thunders in my ears, and every reason not to do this is screaming at me. I know him. I know how he operates and the jokes he makes about wanting me or flirting with me. I also know that I haven't had another man touch me in nine months, and every time Miles so much as looks at me, I swear I see fireworks exploding.

"Just kiss me," he repeats, biting on my earlobe, "Just once. If you hate it, we can stop and pretend it didn't happen."

"Miles, if we do this once, we'll just think of another excuse to do it again," I say.

"I can control myself, baby. Can you?"

He looks up at me with passion and intensity, and I shake my head.

"This is a really fucking bad idea," I say, panting.

Every rational thought I had is thrown out the window as I crash my mouth into his.

It's more frantic and exhilarating than the first time we kissed at the gala. Hell, it's a lot more chaotic than the peck he gave me earlier. It's the kind of kiss that'll drive me insane. The kind that I won't be able to stop thinking about days from now.

My hands dive into the curls at the back of his neck, pulling and gripping as his hands explore my ass before venturing up my shirt. His hand is warm and comforting against my skin and so fucking gentle. His touch is a little hesitant like he's trying not to break me.

There is something so addicting about the way his mouth tastes like sweetness and fall. I feel greedy when it comes to him, desperate to taste every part of him.

I press featherlight kisses onto his bruises before sliding down the length of him to get better access to the column of his throat. I kiss and suck frantically like he did to me in the woods, and a low noise comes from the back of his throat when I nip at his collarbone.

He moves his hands out from under my shirt to my ass, grabbing and pulling me back up into a sitting position. I make the mistake of rolling against him, feeling the friction between us, and I whimper.

"Can I take this off?" he asks hoarsely, tugging at his jersey that's clung to me.

"Are you sure? I thought it was boosting your ego."

"Can I take it off, Wren? Yes, or no?"

"Yes," I reply, pushing off him. He pulls his jersey over my head, and when it's free, he dives back into me, kissing my exposed chest. I have no idea what I'm doing, what I'm inviting to happen, but his mouth is too skilled, and it has no business turning me on this much. "God, that's good." He bites me, and I gasp. "Don't give me any more of those stupid hickeys, Miles, I swear to God."

He laughs against my skin. "I can try not to."

"You better."

He replies by slipping his hand up the material of my sports bra, his fingers splaying out across my breasts. My head lolls back when he brings his fingers to my nipples, teasing me in the most maddening way.

"You feel so soft," he whispers, "so fucking good."

I don't know how I'm going to get this to end. I don't know

if I ever *want* it to. The roughness of his hands isn't like Augustus's. They're purposeful and masculine like they know what they want.

I grind into him again, and he groans, squeezing my hips. His nails dig into my exposed skin, and a pathetic part of me hopes he leaves marks there. He moves me over him faster until I'm grinding in his lap, my mind spinning out of control.

"Miles, fuck," I cry. He's masterful with the way he rolls my hips, hitting the pressure points just right until his dick presses into my core. His kisses across my chest get more intense, and his hips buck up, and I need to dull the ache between my legs as soon as possible. "I need more. Please."

He pinches my nipple, and I whimper. "More?" I nod, my lips pressed together. "How much more do you need, baby?"

"I don't know," I reply.

"Wren."

"I don't know," I say again, angrier. I wish he could just take the initiative sometimes instead of pestering me to find out what I actually want when, most of the time, I don't know what that is. I've never felt so powerless while feeling like I could explode at the same time.

"Tell me what you want, sweet girl," he murmurs.

"Just keep touching me. Please," I whisper. He kisses me again, but it isn't enough. My voice shakes as I say again, "Please."

He's clearly reduced me to begging, and I hate myself for it.

He flips us over until he's on top of me, and he slides down the length of me. His fingers hook into my leggings and my underwear, and he looks up at me, "Can I touch you here?" I nod, my chest heaving. "Talk to me, baby. Can I take these off and see that pretty pussy of yours? I want to see how badly you want this."

"Yes. Take them off," I say, watching him slowly take them

off me. His mouth pops open when he sees how wet I am, and I moan just at the sight of him. It's been way too long since I've had someone between my legs, and Miles looks capable enough to do a good job. "Are you going to touch me or just stare?"

"Do you ever shut your mouth?" he groans, kissing my stomach and up my chest.

"Not really," I mutter as his hand presses my legs open, his mouth branding across my chest and my neck. I suck in a breath as one of his hands braces beside my head and the other swipes my clit. I'm soaked. I close my eyes, rocking my head side to side with both pleasure and frustration. "Can you hurry up?"

He laughs against my neck and teases his thumb against my core. My hips buck up, writhing beneath him until he finally pushes two fingers inside me. It's tight, and the sensation is otherworldly. I can't remember the last time I felt this good. With his weight over me, the hypnotizing smell of him, and how full he's making me feel, I might burst into flames.

"So fucking tight, baby," he mumbles into my neck.

I suck in a sharp breath. "I haven't done this in a while.".

"That's okay," he whispers, "I'll take care of you. Will you let me take care of you, Wren?"

"Yes."

He groans when he pushes into me again, and I clench around him. I've never been shy when it comes to sex, but I don't have much experience to compare it to. I didn't think going all the way was such a big thing until Augustus and I first had sex. Before we were official, I had slept with someone that Scarlett had set me up with, and he didn't know it was my first time, and it was nice. It was nice that it just felt like a regular hookup to him and not this huge milestone. But Augustus couldn't let it go. I was eighteen, and he made it into a whole thing, put together a PowerPoint and everything like he was trying to mansplain *my* virginity to me.

But Miles Davis isn't like that at *all*.

He's soft but playfully rough in all the right ways. He nips and sucks at my neck like he's trying to leave *more* marks as I grind into his hand, and I've never been this turned on in my life.

"Were you this wet for me the other day, princess?" he asks, his voice silky smooth as if his words aren't filthy. He pushes into me hard and fast while his lips stake claim to my throat.

"*God*, Miles." I sigh. I can't think of any words right now. All I can think and feel is *him,* and I don't ever want him to stop.

"Don't have such a smart mouth with my fingers in your pussy, huh?" he rasps, nudging his nose against my neck. His thumb brushes against my clit, and I cry out, shamelessly grinding into his hand. "Is this good for you, Wren?"

"Yes."

"Tell me how good," he demands, his voice a rough caress against my skin. "I want to hear you. I want to hear who's making you feel good."

His fingers move faster as if he's trying to make a point, and my heartbeat accelerates. My entire body narrows to a pinpoint of sensation as he continues the merciless thrusts of his fingers and I squeeze around him.

"It's really fucking good, Miles," I say, panting.

"That's it," he murmurs, rewarding me with a drugging kiss to my lips. He pulls apart, pressing a kiss to the corner of my mouth. "Are you going to come for me, my sweet girl?"

I don't know what it is about the nickname that tears me up inside, but I'm struggling to tell if it's turning me on or pissing me off. "I don't know, will I? I don't think I've decided yet," I tease, and my eyes lock with his. His grin turns evil as he thrusts his fingers into me, curling them just right until I cry out. "Are you going to *make* me come, pretty boy?"

"Fuck yes," he replies, his eyes flashing at the nickname.

He picks up his pace, using my wetness to massage my clit,

and I can feel myself getting closer to the edge. I don't want this to end yet. I want to make this last as long as I can, but if he keeps kissing my neck and whispering into my skin, I might combust.

"Miles," I pant, "go slower, baby."

He listens, adjusting his pace. "Like this?" I sigh, melting into his bed as I nod. "You're doing so good. See how good it can be when you lose control for once?"

"You're driving me crazy. Stop. Talking," I bite out, shutting my eyes.

He laughs, but he doesn't speak. We become a mess of desperate moans, and while my hands grip the sheets, his fingers work their magic over the most sensitive part of me. My entire body trembles when I finally shatter, and we stay there for a few seconds as he massages my clit until I stop shivering. He pulls his fingers out of me, sliding down my body and he surprises me by bringing them to his mouth and tasting me.

"So fucking good," he mutters as he kisses the inside of both of my thighs. "You're perfect, Wren."

I'm still catching my breath when he pulls my leggings and panties back on. "You need to stop saying that."

He drops onto his back beside me, pulling me on top of him like it's the most natural thing in the world, and I'm way too tired to fight it.

He presses a kiss to my forehead, and I swear I almost die. "I'm not going to stop saying it until you believe it," he whispers.

I let him hold me for a few minutes. I know it's selfish, and the last thing either of us needs right now is to complicate this, but being with him feels so *good*. Everything about him is comforting and safe, and it's been a while since I've felt like that. I'm desperate enough to want to be held by him that I don't question it and continue snuggling into his embrace.

I clear my throat and push away from him. "Can I borrow something to sleep in?" I ask, and his eyes widen.

"You still want to sleep here?"

"I said I would, didn't I? An orgasm isn't going to change that," I say, shrugging.

He smiles, but it's a sad one. "There's some shorts and shirts in my drawer. Take your pick."

I get out of the bed and pick some clothes out of his drawer, shutting myself in the bathroom until I can regulate my breathing and convince myself that it doesn't need to be awkward.

This is fine.

Everything is totally and completely fine.

I don't have to worry or overcomplicate this any more than it is. It was a meaningless hookup that we don't have to think about again. Sure, the memory will probably be burned behind my eyelids for the foreseeable future, but that's a bridge I'll cross when I get to it.

Neither of us says anything when I slide into the bed next to him, turning my back to him so I don't do anything I regret. I've made too many mistakes recently, and if I look at him, I don't know what I'll do. I can't afford to slip up now.

"I'm not a violent person, Wren," he whispers into the silence.

I don't hesitate. "I know."

"One of the guys was saying some really fucked up stuff about you and Carter, and I just lost it. I should have kept my cool. I shouldn't have freaked out on him, but I did, and I'm sorry," he murmurs.

My heart sinks through my ribs as I turn over to face him. I know better than to ask what they said about me, so I just blink at him, trying to figure him out.

"You don't have to apologize to me. You didn't do anything wrong," I reassure him. He looks so disappointed in himself that it breaks my heart. He's always the confident, funny, charming

Miles Davis when he's around me. And when I get glimpses into this side of him, I just want to hug him like the day he hugged me for the first time. I want him to feel like I did. Like I didn't have to be alone in my feelings anymore.

"If Coach finds out, I won't be able to play. He'll kick me off the team for good, and any chance I had of getting drafted this season will be over. But with what they were saying, I'd do it again in a heartbeat. I'll ruin everything," he explains, his voice cracking. I brush my hand over his cheek before curling it into his hair, and he melts into my touch, closing his eyes.

"That's not going to happen, Miles," I whisper.

"It might."

"It won't," I say. "Tell you why?"

"Why?"

I smile. "We've got this."

"We're a 'we' now? I didn't know we were official."

I roll my eyes. "I think we've always been a 'we,' Miles. We're in this together or whatever."

"Who turned you into an optimist?"

I shrug one shoulder. "I hear orgasms can improve your mood."

He chuckles. "Are we going to talk about what just happened?"

"What's there to say? It's not a big deal. We broke the rule. It was a moment of weakness," I say even though it pains me. It's the easiest option. It's what is best for both of us. My fingers are still in his hair, tugging at his curls, and it's the most relaxed I've felt in a while. He swallows. "We can just forget about it, right?"

He clears his throat. "I can pretend to."

"Miles…"

"I just finger-banged you and you're expecting me to forget about it?"

"Don't *ever* say finger-banged in my presence, and yes, I am expecting you to forget about it," I argue, and he huffs. "We've got a lot coming up in the next few weeks. You've got the play-offs, and I've got the showcase. It would be a bad idea for us to think about whatever this is right now."

"Okay. You're right," he bites out. I roll my eyes again. He shifts in place and shuffles a little closer to me, our noses almost touching. "Hey, if I ask you to do something, will you promise not to be weird or question me about it?"

I nod. I'm starting to think that there's very little I wouldn't do for Miles Davis. "Okay."

He swallows. "Can you keep running your fingers through my hair? Just until I fall asleep." I blink at him, and he sighs before I can say anything. "Never mind. I knew it was stupid. Just—"

I cut him off and pull him into me so his head rests on my chest. I run my hand across his forehead, pushing his hair back before I sink my fingers into the hair at the nape of his neck, and he sighs.

I know how badly he needs this. I know how badly he needs someone to just be there for him, to be in his corner so he doesn't have to be alone. I want to be that person for him. I want to ease his pain in any way I can.

"Is this good?" I whisper.

"It's perfect. Thank you," he murmurs. "Thank you for being here."

"I don't think you're getting rid of me anytime soon, Miles," I admit. He's weaved his way into my life, and I want him to stay no matter what's going on between us. I don't want to push him away like I've done with everyone in my life when things get hard.

"And you'll be here when I wake up?"

"Yeah, I'll be here."

I brush his hair out of his face, running my fingers through the end of his curls until he falls asleep. Even after his breathing has settled and he's deep in sleep, I keep him close to me. Well into the night, I stay there, watching him sleep.

I can't ruin this for him by acting on impulses because that's all they are. They are just parts of this that we have to ignore. He needs to play again more than I need to skate. We're so close to the show that I can almost taste it.

He *needs* this.

23
MILES

It's a long story

A LOUD CRASH startles me out of my sleep, and I'm instantly on high alert. I reach for Wren to find she isn't in my bed. She was basically clinging to me like a koala all night. Or maybe I was clinging to her. It's hard to tell.

When I sit up, my heart roaring in my ears, I find her on the floor next to my bed. She's still wearing the clothes from last night, but her tote bag is around her shoulder, and her hands are flat against the floor as she peers up at me.

"Hi," she whispers.

"What are you doing on my floor, Wren?" I ask, rubbing the sleep out of my eyes.

"I was about to wake you up, and I was rushing and tripped over my own feet, and now I'm seriously contemplating why I took up figure skating if I can't even walk properly," she rambles, slowly standing to her feet. She brushes her hands against the shorts she borrowed, her face pink, and her nose turned up.

God, she's fucking adorable.

"You're still here," is what I end up saying after staring at her for too long.

She shrugs. "I told you I would be." She gestures to the bedside table. "I, uh, made you a sandwich, and there's some aspirin and water too. Sorry. I'm not a nurse, and I really don't know what's going to help. You haven't eaten since before the game, so I knew you'd be hungry, and I wanted to make myself useful."

I clasp her hand in mine. "You didn't have to do any of that. Thank you," I whisper, squeezing her hand, and she shrugs again like it isn't a big deal. "What time is it?"

"It's early afternoon, just after two. I didn't want to wake you. You sleep like the dead." She laughs before pulling her hands away from me, running them down the front of the shorts again. "I have practice, so I've got to go."

I check my phone and then turn back to her. "Didn't you have class this morning?"

She bites her bottom lip. "I skipped to stay with you."

I skipped to stay with you.

"Wren, you animal," I say with a gasp, and she rolls her eyes.

"Well, you needed me, and I didn't want to leave you alone," she explains, her eyes glossing over. I don't think either of us is ready to talk about what happened last night. Part of me still thinks I dreamed it. "Don't die on me, Milesy."

"I'll try my hardest," I say, winking at her before she slips out of my room. I drop my head back onto my pillow, glancing at the sandwich she made me and the three bottles of water she's piled on my nightstand.

She might be one of the most stubborn people I've ever met, but I know she has a soft side. A quiet side. A side to her that I'm desperate to get more of. When she's not busting my balls, she's spending the night running her fingers through my hair just because I asked her to.

I down the water and take a few pills before eating half of the sandwich. I already feel a thousand times better, but the guilt of getting into that fight is gnawing away at me. I've always prided myself on not being a rough or violent player. I can usually hold my own on the ice, and hockey is a violent enough sport without me needing to add any excessive force, especially when it's banned on the ice at college level. Coach Tucker has always taught us to play clean and play fair. But what Jake was saying in the locker room got to me. I was stupid and in a vulnerable enough position to let his comments weave their way into my head.

The rest of the afternoon goes by in a blur, and I'm already feeling restless. There isn't a practice today, so I couldn't go watch even if I had the energy to. Most of the guys are on campus, studying or in classes. I pulled out some work to do and forced myself to get a couple hours in and tried my hardest not to think about Wren.

It doesn't last very long because a couple hours after she leaves, I get a text from her.

WRENNY

Hey, I just got out of practice. I hope you haven't got any internal bleeding.

Not that I know of. Do you think I should get that checked out?

WRENNY

As we established this morning, I am not a doctor.

You'd be a hot one though.

WRENNY

I know I would.

> Anyway, I was texting you because I saw an SUV parked outside your house when I left. Idk. It kinda spooked me, and I don't know if it was the police surveilling your house or a stalker, so I just got in my Uber.

> You thought I was being surveilled or stalked and you're only just telling me this now?

WRENNY

> I was busy. I was already running late for practice.

> Did it have a Bob Marley bobblehead in the front?

WRENNY

> IDK???

I SIGH, ignoring the anxious butterflies that have appeared in my stomach. I grab my phone and make my way down the stairs, peering through the living room blinds and finding exactly what I thought I would.

I drop my head against the front door, groaning when my phone lights up with more texts.

WRENNY

> Is everything okay??? Are you a fugitive???

> Unfortunately not.

WRENNY

> Then who is stalking you??

> My sister.

Your sister is stalking you?

> It's a long story. I'll talk to you later, princess.
> Don't worry about it.

I SHUT my phone off before she can continue harassing me for answers because I don't even know how to explain it. Clara is just like this. My overprotective older sister who apparently has been protecting me too much and had kept the biggest secret from me for years.

This is not the first time Clara has turned up at my house and not come in. She'll park on the street, listen to music in her car for hours, and I'll watch her contemplate knocking on my door or driving away. Most of the time, she drives away. On the few times she does come in, we both pretend that I didn't watch her have to convince herself to leave the car.

I don't know why she does. Why she has to make this so fucking awkward for the both of us. I know our relationship has changed over the last few years, but making a big deal out of it doesn't help matters. This *is* the first time she's done this since she told me about Mom's affair.

I slip on some shoes, make my way over to the car, and knock on the window. My sister has her curly hair loose to her shoulders, her tanned skin glowing as she expertly eats a taco and drinks a Diet Coke while watching a YouTube video on her phone.

"What the fuck are you doing?" I shout, and she yelps, turning to me.

She swallows what's in her mouth, her big brown eyes wide as she rolls down the window. "What the fuck happened to your face?"

"Nothing," I say immediately. She raises an eyebrow. "Just hockey stuff."

"You're not on the team."

"I am on the team, I'm just... taking a break."

"You're benched."

"It's a break."

"They're the same thing," she argues.

"You're trying to distract me, and it's not working," I say, and she shrugs, taking another bite of her food. "What are you doing here?"

"I came here to talk to you," she says.

"Yeah? Well, my girlfriend left *hours* ago, and she saw you, and you're still here," I say, crossing my arms against my chest.

"Girlfriend?" Her jaw drops open, as dramatic as ever, and I sigh. "Okay, we have a lot to catch up on." Then her facial expressions change, a crease forms between her eyebrows, and she points at me. "No, we don't. I'm mad at you. That's why I'm here to talk some sense into to you."

"What have I done now?"

"Miles, you've not spoken to me, or Mom and Dad in *months*. We're worried about you," she whispers, checking the street like she doesn't want anyone to hear.

"Well, stop worrying. I'm fine," I say, my voice rough.

"Yeah, I can see that," she says, gesturing to bruises on my face. She heaves out a sigh, and we just stare at each other for a second. "Get in the car. I'm going to talk and drive. That good?"

She gives me a stern look, and I know better than to say no. She's my sister for God's sake, and I'm still a little terrified of her. I've spent way too long avoiding her and my problems at home. She's done nothing but stick by me, even when she dropped that bombshell.

We barely make it out of my neighborhood before she says, "I didn't tell you about Mom because I was trying to protect you." I guess we're going straight into this. She glances at me, and I nod for her to continue talking. I know she doesn't want to talk about this as much as I do, but the fact that she's here is more than what I would have done if I were in her situation. "I found out in the worst way possible. I was going into the school to surprise her for her birthday, like we had planned the week before. I had just started college, and you were still at school, so we planned that I'd go in with flowers and chocolates, remember?"

I swallow, nodding. To me, that was just a regular tradition that we did every year. "I remember."

"Well, when I got there, she was kissing him. You know, Jean Claude. I guess they forgot I was coming, and I didn't even recognize him at first. I thought maybe Dad had gotten a new haircut or something, and I realized it wasn't him when I got closer."

Her hands tighten on the steering wheel before she lets out a breath.

"What did you do?" I ask, my voice a lot smaller than I thought.

She shrugs. "I did what any eighteen-year-old who had just caught their mom cheating would do. I burst through the door and yelled at her. She told Jean Claude to leave, and she sat me down. I was furious, so it took me a while to process it, but she apologized and told me that it wasn't Dad's fault, and it wasn't any of our faults either."

I nod, but I say, "That doesn't explain why you didn't tell me."

"I didn't want to, Miles," she sighs, dropping her shoulders and resting her head against the headrest. "Mom told me to. She said that I could tell you if I wanted and she wouldn't hold it against me, but I chose not to. I know you, baby bro. I knew it would crush you and set you back. You were only a kid, and I didn't want you to spend the rest of your life hating her. Not like I did."

That last part is the only thing I remember. I remember when they'd argue constantly and they'd go days, and sometimes weeks, without speaking to each other. I was told that it was just because Clara had moved out and it was regular teenage daughter stuff.

I don't have the energy in me to make a snarky comment. To make it out like it's her fault when clearly that isn't the case anymore. If I found out then, I *would* have hated her. I would have held onto it, used it against her in any way I could, and I still wouldn't be over it.

When I know something, it consumes me. It becomes all I think about, and there's no way of telling when I'd get over it.

I clear my throat, and she looks over at me when we get to a stop sign. "So how did you do it? How did you forgive her?"

"It helped that I was at college. If I still lived at home, I don't think I would have done it so easily," she explains. "I just had to let go. I had to move on with my life. I had goals that were bigger than this one setback. At the start, I was angry, and I wasn't sure when I'd stop thinking about it, but I had to. It was the only way I'd be able to move on with everything else in my life."

"I don't know how to do that. I don't know how to let things go," I admit, running my hands through my hair.

She gives me a sad smile. "I know you don't, and that's why I couldn't tell you. Do you remember that one action figure you had? The one with the interchangeable outfits?" I nod, and she continues. "You had it with you *all the time.* At one point, I tried to tell Mom you needed to go see a therapist. You had it in your stroller, you held onto it while you were potty training, and you brought it with you to your first day of kindergarten. It was old and moldy by the time you were nine, and do you remember what happened when Dad tried to throw it away?"

I hold back my laughter. "I screamed at him and said I'd run away if he didn't give it back to me."

"Exactly, because you couldn't let it go, Miles. You convinced yourself that you needed it to survive, that you wouldn't be able to do anything without it, but when you got a new pair of skates, you moved on, and that became your new obsession. Or hyper-fixation." She shrugs, waving her hand about before turning a corner. "That's why I thought if I waited to tell you, you'd be more open to forgiving her. I thought you'd find it easier to move on, but with Carter... I understand that things are hard for you right now, which is why I want to be there for you. I don't want you to push me away because of some stupid decision I made when I was eighteen."

I nod because it seems like the only thing I can do to stop myself from crying. "I want you to be here for me too," I admit, and she smiles. "Do you think that's why I can't get back on the ice without thinking about Carter? It feels like the entire team has moved on and I haven't."

"I think that's a completely different thing, Miles. Losing someone is a very difficult thing to go through, and everybody deals with it in different ways. I don't think you need to worry about how long it takes you because it's not something you just wake up and move on from," she says softly.

"Everyone else has, Clara. I can't even put on my helmet without feeling like I'm suffocating," I whisper. I don't know when the tears started to fall, but any time I even think about him, it all wells up inside me, and I'm one nice comment away from breaking down. I swipe at them furiously, and Clara notices.

"Oh, Miles, fuck. Let me pull over," she says, checking her mirrors before pulling off to the side of the road. She opens her car door, and my eyes widen. Is she crazy? She rounds the car, opens the passenger side, and almost knocks me out when she wraps her arms around me. "You looked like you needed a hug. You told me once that I give the best hugs."

"I was five," I grumble, melting into her embrace.

"It still stands," she whispers. "Please tell me you've been talking to someone about this and you've not been keeping it inside."

"The team has a counselor we speak to once a week, but other than that, it's just Wren," I admit. Even she doesn't know the extent of my pain because I can't even put it into words, and I shut down each time I say his name out loud. I've never felt more helpless than I did when I broke down at the rink, but just being around her makes me feel less alone.

Clara pulls from me, smiling wide. "I'm guessing Wren is the girlfriend."

I nod. "She is, but she's..." I trail off, laughing at myself. How could I even begin to describe her? How could I possibly explain that she's taken over every single thought in my brain since the moment I met her? That she's the only thing I can think about sometimes, her stubbornness and all. "God, Clara. She's everything."

Clara grins. "Wow. We really do have a lot to catch up on."

24
WREN

Crushes are gross

MY MOM once told me that boys are like the wind: some will push you forward, like a strong gust that helps you skate faster and better, but most are just breezes that distract you from your path. After my breakup, she reminded me how my ex helped me focus on my figure skating, and she warned me not to let other boys blow me off course. "Stay true to your goals," she said, "and the right wind will support you when you need it most."

I kind of thought that every boy would be either of those things, but I can't seem to fit Miles into those categories because he does both. He pushes me and encourages me in all the best ways, yet he distracts me. But a huge part of me thinks I need to be distracted sometimes. A little bit of fun wouldn't kill me, and he reminds me of that way more often than I'd like.

After a long day practicing and trying to get Miles out of my head, I'm sitting with the girls in the living room while they ask me more and more ridiculous questions. I've been dodging most of them as I lie down with ice packs on my sore knees.

"*Sooo*, what was it like?" Kennedy asks with a huge smile.

"What was what like?" I sit up further on the couch so I can see them both properly. Kennedy is sitting in the beanbag, and Scarlett is on the floor, lying on her back.

"The kiss. You can't just be like 'yeah me and Miles made out for real' and ignore it," Kennedy explains. I made the stupid mistake of telling them that we made out but left out the fact that he finger fucked me until I forgot my name.

"That's exactly what I'm trying to do. If I think about it too much, I'll do it again, and this whole thing will be over. I can't do that. Not so close to the show and during hockey season," I say, turning over my ice packs before resting my head back on the headrest.

"Fine, don't tell us. But, judging by the look on your face, it was better than the kisses you write about in Stolen Kingdom," Kennedy says, looking at me innocently. I don't have the energy to argue with that. It's true. It was probably the best kiss of my life, hickeys and all.

"It was an above-average kiss," I admit.

"Above average how?" Scarlett asks. "Like a little touchy?"

"Or like close to fucking?" Kennedy suggests.

I sigh, closing my eyes for a second before opening them. "The second one."

They both burst into hysterical screams, clapping their hands as if this is the best news they've heard in their lives.

"You fooled around with him, didn't you?" Scarlett asks, but it doesn't sound much like a question. Sometimes, I think she should be a detective instead of a fashion major.

"Maybe," I murmur, and they both gasp. "But it wasn't like that. He was sweet and kind, and we fell sleep afterward."

They both blink at me, not saying anything. I know how they work. I know they're thinking of every way they can make fun of me until they're satisfied.

"Oh my god," Kennedy mutters.

"What?"

"You like him," Scarlett answers for her.

I scoff, but my heart betrays me by skipping a beat. "No, I don't."

"Yes, you do! You have the hots for him," Ken says, jumping to her feet in excitement. "You *like* like him."

"We're not in middle school, Ken," I murmur.

She shrugs. "We're all in middle school when it comes to things like this. And *you*"—she points at me—"have a crush on a popular hockey player."

My cheeks rush with heat. "I do not."

"You so do."

Do I?

Crushes are gross and nasty and make me feel out of control. I never really had a *crush* on Augustus. He just started getting more flirtatious with me and kissed me, and the next steps to that felt like a relationship. I didn't question it because I was sixteen and stupid, so we had this weird on-and-off thing for years until we started college. But with Miles, liking him doesn't feel weird or out of place. Everything about it feels fresh and nice and more like a hug I can wrap myself in, not something that will choke me.

I'm about to say something to the girls, but my phone chimes and vibrates next to me. I reach into the pocket of my shorts and retrieve it. I smile wide when I see a message from Gigi.

GIGI

Why haven't you posted any pictures with your boyfriend? Did you guys break up?

We didn't break up, G. It's been twenty-four hours since I posted.

Any updates on TLT?

GIGI

If you keep up with my posts, then you would know. But, no, there are no updates yet.

I saw the pictures at the hockey game. How was that?

It was actually fun. I think you would have enjoyed it.

GIGI

I'm sure I would have. There is nothing I love more than crowded spaces.

Ha-ha. So...

That means that you're not coming to my show?

GIGI

I'll try, but I doubt it. If I pull out at the last minute, don't be upset with me.

I would never be upset with you, G. Just let me know. I love you big time.

GIGI

Thanks.

Would it kill you to say that you love me too?

GIGI

It wouldn't kill me; I just don't want to say it.

I LAUGH at Gigi's last message and throw my phone next to me. The second it hits the cushion, it starts to ring again. Just my luck. When I reach for it, I see the unknown caller ID, my pulse instinctively quickening. I swipe the answer button and bring the phone to my ear.

"Hello?"

"Wren? It's Austin. Are you alone?"

My chest tightens at the sound of her voice. It's been so long that I almost forgot what she sounds like. We've had a few calls over the last few years but nothing to remember. She's always busy so it's always a quick "Hi, how are you?" on her way into the studio, and I'm okay with that. I've always wanted a better relationship with my sister like we used to have as kids, but it's changed a crazy amount over the last few years. She does her thing, and I do mine. And I'm fine with that.

"Is it your loverboy calling for phone sex?" Kennedy coos.

"No. It's Austin," I say, the words sounding foreign on my tongue.

They both turn to me in horror as I pick up my ice packs and limp into my bedroom, closing the door. My hands shake as I sit down on the edge of the bed. "No one has heard from you in months. Are you okay?"

"My life is over. My career is over. I won't be able to dance anymore," Austin says, groaning. It sounds like she's crying, but I can't tell. I don't remember the last time my sister cried in front of me.

"Are you hurt? What happened?"

"Worse," she replies.

"Austin, what could be worse than that?" A huge part of me doesn't even want to know the answer. Austin is a lot less dramatic than my mom. She's always been the rational one, but with the complete terror in her voice, I don't think I want to know.

"I'm pregnant."

The line goes silent.

Austin has never wanted kids. It's not that she doesn't like them. But Austin's life plans were very simple. Ballet. Get married. Ballet. Even as kids, when asked what she wanted to do, it was always "ballet" with certainty and "marriage" with a question mark.

She has done everything in her power to make sure that one plan stays consistent and that it actually follows through. In a way, I have a very similar plan to hers. Skating has always been my entire life and will continue to be. I wouldn't be having a meltdown if I got pregnant, but I wouldn't be thrilled either. I have goals and an end in sight, and I'm not willing to let anything come in my way of that.

She's been dating Zion for as long as I can remember, and they've made it work between her schedule and his job as an editor. I knew they were serious when he moved away with her to Russia a few years ago, but *this* was clearly not in their five-year plan.

"How far along are you?" I ask when I get my voice back. As much as I would want to congratulate her, I'm sure that's the last thing she wants to hear from me.

"Maybe four months?" I don't say anything. What am I supposed to say to this? "Emmy, I *can't* do this right now. This was supposed to be my last month here and then I was meant to move to France in the new year with just Zion—not him *and* a baby."

"Wait, you got into the company?"

"Why are you so surprised? I worked hard and I got in," she says bluntly. Right. I forgot how uptight she was. "They won't want me anymore if they find out that I can't dance for at least a year."

"What are you going to do?"

"I'm going to figure that part of it out. I was calling for a favor," Austin says, and my skin prickles.

"We haven't spoken in months and you're calling me for a favor?" I ask.

"Yes."

Well, at least she's honest. I don't bother giving her the whole spiel about how we've not checked in on each other. The truth is, not talking every day is the norm. If something was wrong, we'd know. The fact that we don't talk as much sort of gives each of us peace. I know that she's fine, and she knows that I'm fine too. It's weird and probably fucked up in a lot of ways, but it works for us.

"Can you tell Mom for me? You don't have to make it into a big thing, just bring it up like she already knows. I won't be able to stomach the disappointment if I tell her myself. I've told Dad already, but you know what he's like. He was just happy that there's a possibility he could get a grandson." She laughs quietly.

"Austin, I don't know if I can do that," I stutter. "I don't want all that pressure on me right now. I've got a show coming up and—"

"Great. That's perfect. Just tell her right after the show, when you've done your best performance, and she'll be so proud she probably won't even care."

I wait a minute, not saying anything. My future in figure skating at NU is riding on the back of this showcase. Not only do I need people to turn up, but my mom needs to enjoy it. She needs to see that I've put my blood, sweat, and tears into my training. And now, she needs to be prouder than ever so Austin's pregnancy can fly right over her head.

"Thank you, Wren. I owe you for this one," she says quickly without waiting for my reply before ending the call. I sit on my bed for what feels like hours, dumbfounded, and my body suddenly feels heavy.

This is the last thing I need. The show is only a few weeks away, and I need to stay sane enough so Miles doesn't think I'm going off the rails. I've already changed my routine for him, skipping classes and staying in bed with him when I could have used that time to be more productive. If this stupid, pathetic schoolgirl crush doesn't go away soon, I don't know how long we'll be able to keep up this shtick.

When the anxieties creep up into me, I rush into my bathroom to throw up. When the retching doesn't stop, both of the girls run into my bathroom. Kennedy holds my hair back while Scarlett rubs my back, knowing exactly what to do. I seriously don't know what I've done to deserve them. After I feel like it's all out of me, I go to my sink and brush my teeth, but they both hover around me in the bathroom.

"I'm going to the rink," I say when I turn around to them, clearing my throat.

Scarlett inches toward me.

"Wren, it's past nine o'clock. I don't think the one on campus is open," she says.

I brush past her and go into my bedroom. They follow behind me.

"And not to mention you've been there all day. Take a break," Kennedy suggests as I pack my duffel bag with my leotard and essentials.

"I'll find one that's open, or I'll go to the gym," I bite out before walking out of my room and into the kitchen. They follow behind me again as I grab a couple bottles of water, and I shove them into my bag, avoiding their eyes.

"Wren," Scarlett says, carefully, shifting from one foot to the other. "I don't think this is a good idea. You need to take a breather. You just threw your stomach up. You were like this before regionals."

"Yeah, and look where that fucking got me. I didn't take it seriously enough. I put being with Augustus over skating, and I didn't practice enough. I could have prevented that. If I fuck this one up, it's over. I'm done!"

They both take a step back. Kennedy's eyes soften as she looks at me. Scarlett looks irritated and a little disappointed. She's had to put up with this side of me for the longest, and I'm sure she's sick of it. She's seen me after losing a comp as a kid, she's seen me after winning and still needing to do better. Constantly trying to do my absolute best. To be absolutely flawless.

"Look." I sigh, my voice quieter. "I'm sorry for shouting, but I'm in a really difficult situation right now, and I need to clear my head."

"If this is about Miles—" Scarlett starts.

"It's not."

"Then talk to us. That's what we're here for," Kennedy whispers, her voice weighty with emotion. "You don't run away when things get hard. We don't do that."

I want to grab them both into a hug. I want to tell them everything. I want to tell them how it feels like I'm constantly being held down by a giant, cutting off my blood circulation. How I'm constantly hearing the words, *You're not good enough* over and over. I want to tell them that I hate the person I'm becoming and that I feel like I can't breathe if I think about it too much.

"I can't. I'm sorry. I can't," I stammer as I slip out of the door.

25
MILES

Am I obsessed?

I THINK I've fucked up.

I don't know what I've done, but I have a very strong feeling Wren is ignoring me. I haven't seen her since the day of the game, and even though we've both been busy with classes, I've hardly gotten a text from her. We've worked out together twice since then, but it's mostly in silence since I have a routine I stick to now, and she does her own thing.

Even when I make my hilarious gym jokes, she just ignores them.

"Why did the cheese go to the gym?" I said once while I caught my breath, standing over her while she did sit-ups.

"Why?" she asked with a bored expression, not a single waver in her voice even after doing fifty sit-ups.

"Because he wanted to *cheddar* couple pounds," I replied. She just blinked up at me, not even a crack of a smile on her face. I remember when these kinds of jokes would earn me a toothy grin and a kick in the stomach. Now she doesn't even care. Or even pretend to care. She stood up and looked at me.

"Can you spot me on the bench press?" she asked. She barely looked at me for the rest of the day.

I'm beginning to think that kissing her was a bad idea. In the moment, we both wanted it. She was really fucking enthusiastic about it when she was moaning my name with my fingers inside her, but maybe it was just a moment of weakness. Maybe I'm in way over my head, and what we did really meant nothing to her. She keeps telling me she's busy, but I don't know how much of that I believe anymore.

I just want her to talk to me. To let me in. I feel like I've been floating around her, stuck in this weird cycle of never being fully taken in and it hurts so much more knowing what it *is* like when she lets me in.

Since speaking with Clara, I've felt lighter. I still haven't spoken to my mom yet, but I'm getting there. With having regular classes and attending some practices, I don't feel as alone anymore. When I get home after college, I don't feel this weight on my chest like I used to a few months ago. Everything is starting to feel more manageable, and the thought of getting back on the ice doesn't sound so bad.

I got a phone call yesterday from Coach, asking me to meet him this morning.

He knows about the fight. He has to. Someone must have told him, and this could be the start of the end. I could lose my scholarship, and I'd have to move back home, start community college, and get my old job back.

I walk the distance from my house to the sports center to clear my head. It can't be that bad, right? Fights happen all the time when they're not supposed to. They're taken more seriously when it's on the ice, but since this was out of game time, I don't know what the sanctions are. Coach Tucker is usually more laid back about these things, but I've not exactly been proving to him that I'm still his most valuable player.

I get to Coach Tucker's office, and the door's already open. His office is more like a closet, filled top to bottom with sports equipment. There are tons of equipment for sports that he doesn't even coach and certificates and medals hung on the walls. His desk is piled high with paperwork and folders, but when they're cleared, it's easy to see the pictures that he has on his desk. His most famous photo of him, his husband, and their three corgis, from the day he found out he got the job at North.

When I go in, I'm greeted with a smile, and he gestures toward the seat in front of him. I can't read his face just yet. I can't tell if that's a good thing or not.

"Miles, I'm sure you know why you're here," he begins, strangely cheerfully. He leans his forearms on the table, his dark brows knitted together in a serious expression.

"Uh, I think so," I reply cautiously. He lets his expression drop and sighs deeply.

"I heard about what happened after the game. More like, I *saw* what happened. Butler showed me a video, and I heard about what Jake said to you. I'd like to say that I'm sorry he said that," Coach says, and I shrug, not wanting to relive that moment. I'm going to talk to Harry for narcing on me, the little shit. "I understand *why* you did it, but I'm still disappointed."

"If you're going to kick me off the team for good, can you just say it? The suspense is killing me."

He laughs, shaking his head. "Miles, I'm not kicking you off the team. You think I haven't seen you throw a few punches at other players during the games even when you're not supposed to? These things happen, and neither of you reported it or were badly injured. The fact that Jake's been avoiding me like the plague since it happened, I'm assuming it's not going to happen again. As long as you and Jake can separate what happened from what the team needs, I want you to play during the playoffs. You've proved that you're in a better place. Your grades have improved and it would feel wrong to keep you benched just because of this incident."

"Really?" I exclaim, not able to contain the excitement in my voice. Coach smiles wide, nodding. "You're not going to regret this, Coach. Thank you."

"I still want you to be training over the holidays, and if we make it through the playoffs, you need to bring your all to get back your captaincy. If you need someone to talk to, you know, about Carter... I'm here."

"I know," I say before pulling back my chair and thanking him again.

"And, Miles?"

"Yeah?"

"Whatever you're doing, it's working. I know this has been a hard year for you, but watching you slowly turn it around has been a blessing," he says, nodding at me. "I was going to wait until the new year to let you back on the team, but you've earned this in more ways than one."

I clear my throat, trying to keep in the tears. I can't cry right now. But Coach has always been a second dad to me. He saw me as a wild high schooler who needed real training and took the chance on me. He saw my potential, and he hasn't looked back since.

"Thank you, Coach. I appreciate you saying that," I say.

"Anytime, Davis."

I have the biggest smile on my face when I walk around to the rink Wren is skating on. I know I shouldn't, but I'm too excited to not tell her right now. I know she's been busy, and I have no idea when I'll next get an uninterrupted minute with her.

She's in the middle of spinning, with her foot high above her head in a black leotard. She skates forward before doing a triple turn in the air and landing wobbly.

"Fuck me," she says loudly, and she begins again.

I watch her for a few more minutes, completely in awe. There's something so effortlessly perfect about the way Wren skates. Even if she doesn't think so, I think she's the most talented person I've ever met. When she comes to a slowdown in her routine, I wonder if she's noticed me or if she really is just ignoring me.

"I've got good news," I announce. She stops abruptly and stares at me from across the ice before floating over to me. She stands at the railing, her face red and puffy. "I got back on the team."

Wren's face lights up, and her smile widens. "That's great, Miles. That's really good, honestly. That's great."

"Yeah, you said that twice," I say, laughing and shifting from one foot to the other. "But it's all thanks to you. So, thank you."

"You don't have to thank me. You're the one who put the work in. You just needed someone to push you."

I shrug and we stay silent for a while. She looks at my face in a curious way as if this is the first time and she's trying to figure me out. Her eyes land on my lips, and they hover there for a beat. Her tongue runs against her bottom lip before she shakes.

"How's practice going?" I ask.

"It's good. Could be better," she replies, waving her hands in defeat.

I nod, and we just stare at each other. She's been more on edge recently, and I can't figure out what it is. It might be because we're coming up closer to the showcase, but I don't like that she's been shutting me out too. I know she might not like me very much, but I thought we moved past that. I can't take the silence for much longer, so I say, "Have you been ignoring me?"

"I've been busy."

"Too busy to text your boyfriend back every once in a while?"

"Fake boyfriend, and yes. I don't know if you've noticed, but I suck right now, and the show is in less than two weeks, so I really need to get my shit together," she explains, blowing out a puff of air.

"Are you free tomorrow night?" I ask, awkwardly wringing out my hands.

"I was going to work out tomorrow night. I've got some homework due," she says, but she avoids my gaze.

"I've got that interview with the team for Sophia's documentary. A lot of people are going to be there, and you could invite them to the show," I say. She thinks about it for a minute, twisting her mouth to the side. "Come on, Wren. We haven't hung out in days. You said an orgasm wasn't going to change anything, but it feels like it has."

"I—It hasn't."

"Yeah? Then talk to me. Sit in awkward silence with me, I don't care. Just please stop shutting me out," I say, my tone pleading. "I miss you."

Her eyes finally meet mine, and she whispers, "I miss you too."

I make a show of trying to clean out my ears. "Can you repeat that for me?"

"No." She smiles, and it's the most beautiful sight I've ever seen. A sight I've *missed* and it's only been a couple of days. "I do have to go back to practice though. Congrats on getting back on the team. You deserve it."

"All thanks to you."

I wink at her, and she rolls her eyes, pushing away from the barrier before she continues skating. I walk out of the building with my head high, and a weird feeling settles over me.

Hope, I think.

26
MILES

Sophia's corner

I'VE ALWAYS TRIED NOT to warn other people when they meet my friends. It's usually a surprise when they see how chaotic they are. I've been trying to prepare Wren for when we go to Sophia's house, but she's adamant that we'll be fine.

Becoming the leader of the NU Press has given Sophia the perfect opportunity to make her dreams as a director real. She gets to interview students from different courses, and by the end of our fourth year, she's aiming to create a huge graduation video to show everyone. Since the hockey season is in full swing, she's coming around our team to interview everyone.

The only thing about Sophia and this project is that she's kept it very secret. We've had mini-interviews before that she posts on Instagram and TikTok, but since this is her big project, we don't get to see these ones until the mockumentary has been completed.

She sets up her house into a comfortable interviewing space, and the team and usually their other friends and partners join us so we can hang out afterward. I know Wren's not going to enjoy the whole socializing aspect of today, so I try and get us there early.

As we drive toward Sophia's house, Wren isn't doing that angry humming thing that she does when we drive to the gym together. Instead, she's silent, no doubt in her head about the showcase. Which is even more concerning because Taylor Swift is playing. I turn up *New Romantics,* and her face doesn't even crack.

"Hey, can I ask you a question?" I ask.

"If I say no, are you going to ask me anyway?" I glance at her and catch her playing with one of her French braids.

"Yes," I say. "What would be the first thing you'd do if you won the lottery?"

She laughs a little, the sound rushing through me like a gentle wave. "These questions are getting more and more random," she says. "I'd buy me and the girls a house where we could each have our own wing and then order as much pizza as possible."

I grin. "Not even a salad? Wren, you animal."

She laughs again. "If I win the lottery in the future, then I would probably stop skating professionally. I'd do it just for fun by that point. If I won it today, I'd just put it in savings."

"Do you want to skate professionally? Like, the Olympics and all that?"

She sighs a little. "These last few months have put me through the wringer, but that was the goal when I first started, so I guess so."

We get to Sophia's house, and I park up, not wanting to end this conversation just yet. I turn to her as she stares straight ahead. "You guess so?"

"Okay, I *know* so." She turns to me now, propping her leg up on the seat to get more comfortable. "I want to be the greatest."

"You already are."

She shakes her head, laughing. "No, Miles, I mean I want to be the best in the fucking world. I've dedicated my entire life to this sport. I've spent more hours on the ice than I have in bed since I was four years old. I've done everything in my power to be one of the best in the country. I refuse to drop out or give up when things get hard. I'm not going to stop until I win gold at the Olympics."

I don't think I've found anything more attractive than this. The way she's so passionate about what she loves is so fucking admiring.

I tilt my head to the side. "You're competitive then, huh?"

"I'm not a loser, Miles," she says, and I swear my entire body comes alive. "I'm not a loser, and I'm not a quitter. That's why dropping out of the race for regionals last year threw me off. I'm not letting someone else dictate my future or mess up my routine just because they can. I'm going solo from now on, and it's the best decision I've ever made."

I grin. "You're going to do it, you know. You're going to win Olympic gold."

She shrugs, flashing me the cockiest smile I've ever seen. "I know."

She glances over to the house and then back to me. "I just want to say that I am trying with this. With us. I know I've been distant, but it's family stuff. It's just hard to get out of my head sometimes."

"You can let me into your brain, Wren. I'm never going to judge you."

"I know, but this is something I need to fix on my own."

She's clearly keeping something from me and it's not just stress about the showcase, but I don't want push her on it and scare her away. There are still things about my past that I haven't told her yet, and she's not forced me into confessing my deepest, darkest fears to her.

When we get out of the car, I grab Wren's hand in mine, and she relaxes into me. We step up onto the porch, and I pause for a second, knowing that inside is going to be a hell full of hockey players.

"Why are *you* preparing for this? It's bound to be a lot worse for me than it is for you. This is *your* safe space. The last time I came here, I had a panic attack," Wren mutters, tugging on my hand and looking up at me. Does she have to look so good all the time? Those French braids are making me want to say a huge fuck you the rules we set about PDA. "Come on, Milesy. You're a big boy; you can handle it."

I smile and don't tell her how difficult it's going to be to see the whole team together, knowing that the last interview we all did together was with Carter. I don't tell her that it's going to take everything in me not to rip Jake's head off the second I lay eyes on him. Instead, I squeeze her hand tighter in mine and step up to the door.

The door swings open, and the room erupts into cheers. Music blasts from the speakers, and it's probably Gray's playlist playing. The entire hockey team is here, crammed into the living room and the hallway, along with a bunch of other random people I've never seen before. I know that the interviews take place in the soundproofed basement, so there's no wonder why it's so loud up here. I pull Wren with me through the crowd until we get to the kitchen, standing on opposite sides of the island.

"Is it just me, or are you getting really vivid déjà vu?" I ask, remembering the night of the party. Wren laughs, picking up one of the waters from the island.

"If only you were choking over the sink again," she says, shaking her head at me. I'm about to make a snarky comment but Xavier appears, his arm around Michelle as they sport matching NU Bear's jerseys. Michelle writhes out of his grip and pulls Wren into a tight hug. "Michelle! How are you?"

"I'm fabulous," Michelle replies, pulling out of the hug and holding Wren at arm's length. I'm sure they've only met once in passing, but apparently, girls can become best friends overnight. "I *love* your hair like this, Wren. Isn't it so cute, Miles?"

"The cutest," I say, no word of a lie as I watch her face turn a bright pink. It's becoming so easy to make her blush, and I want to do it all the time.

Xavier stands beside me, smiling, as we watch our girls gush over each other's outfits. Well, my *fake* girl. Because that's all we are. The more I tell myself that, the more I start to believe it and act like it.

Maybe.

Possibly.

Hopefully?

"Those two are going to be best friends. No matter how you guys end things, you can't make my girl upset about losing Wren. She's, like, obsessed with her. She was stalking her Instagram before we got here," he says, low enough for only me to hear. Honestly, I'm not surprised. I've always wondered why Wren doesn't have many friends, but with how guarded she can be, it makes sense. People like Michelle would kill to be friends with this girl if she just let them in.

"Can I be honest with you guys?" Michelle says, turning toward me and Xavier. "Wren is the best person you've dated, Miles."

Wren laughs, throwing her head back. "You can stop with all the compliments, Michelle. You don't have to try to flatter me," she says, twisting the end of her braid between her fingers.

Michelle shakes her head. "No. I'm being serious. You bring out the best in him. I've seen him through many stages in his life, and this is by far the happiest. Losing Carter has been hard for all of us, but you've made make him happier, and I don't think I've seen him more smitten."

Wren stands there, frozen. This is what we want. We need people to be invested in us, but this feels like we're crossing a line somehow. I know she's made me a happier person. Even if this is pretend, the way she makes me feel is so real that it scares me. Not the way that she turns me on or drives me crazy, but the way that she talks to me, listens to me, and even when she's trying to push me away, she still puts in the effort.

Before I can respond and try to save this somehow, Sophia's voice echoes off the walls. Because she's one of the most over-the-top people I've ever met, she's connected a microphone to the speakers around the house.

"Hello, everybody," Sophia's voice booms. "I'm so glad so many of you could make it. If you've just arrived, refreshments are everywhere, and so is the food. We're going to get straight into it, and I'm inviting the first five people into the basement, where the group interview will take place. Afterward, individual interviews will commence. If your name is not called, sit tight and you will be down next. First, can I have Xavier Dawson, Harry Butler, Jake Callahan, Grayson Aoki-Park, and Miles Davis downstairs? Please, and thank you!"

Xavier and I look at each other and then back to the girls. "I guess that's our cue," I say, nodding at Wren to come over to me, and she does. "Do you want to stay up here or come down?"

"If Michelle's going, then I am too," she replies, beaming at her new best friend. We start to make our way through the crowds, and I hold onto Wren's hand as we go down the stairs to the basement. It shouldn't be this nerve-racking. It's just a stupid interview with my stupid teammates. That's it.

"Miles?"

"Mm-hmm."

"You're squeezing my hand," she whispers. "It hurts."

"Shit. I'm sorry, baby," I murmur, releasing her hand and allowing her to curl it over mine. I bring her hand to my mouth and kiss it as she blinks up at me with those killer green eyes. "Better?"

She smiles. "Much better."

When we get down to the basement, it looks a lot more professional than I thought. On one side of the room, there's a white wall with a neon light that reads "Sophia's Corner" behind a couch that's big enough to fit ten of us on there. On the seats of the couch, there is a sheet of paper with our names on, which I'm assuming is the order Sophia wants us to sit in.

I'm on one end next to Harry, Xavier, and Gray, and then Jake is on the other end. I've not even bothered to look in his direction since we got down here, and I don't plan on it anytime soon.

On the other side of the room, there are brown chairs and tables filled with drinks and snacks for the people who have agreed to stand silently and watch the interview up close. Sophia's director's chair also makes this whole thing feel more official. Honestly, it's sweet how much work she puts into these things.

We all take our seats, and Wren and Michelle stand on the other side of the room, lingering around a table near Sophia's chair. I try to get my heartbeat to settle when I notice the team photo that Sophia has hung up on the wall.

She has one of all the sports teams at NU, including the skating team, which she probably took for the yearbook. In our picture, we're celebrating our championship win last year, Carter being held up by all of us with the trophy in his hands. I shake off the uncomfortable feeling and try to settle down. I look over at Wren, and she does the dorkiest, most adorable thing ever, smiling wide as she gives me a double thumbs-up.

If she's there, cheering me on, I can do this.

"Are you guys ready?" Sophia asks, setting up her camera on her tripod and pressing record before mouthing a countdown. "So, we are here with the first interview of the day with some of my favorite players from the North University Bear's ice hockey team. We have Miles Davis on your right, followed by Harry Butler, Xavier Dawson, Grayson Aoki-Park, and Jake Callahan. What a dream team, I must say."

"When you've known each other as long as we have, it's hard not to work together so well," Xavier says, looking up and down the line. Everyone nods in agreement. "Of course, it was different for Haz over here, since he only just joined the team this year."

Harry groans at the nickname we've all got for him, and we laugh. "Just because I didn't play with you guys in middle school or high school, doesn't make me *that* new to the team," he retorts.

"How does it feel being the baby of the team, Harry? It must be a lot different to playing hockey in Australia," Sophia says, crossing her legs and getting into her serious position.

"It feels good. I mean, in my town, ice hockey was pretty uncommon, so when I got offered a place here, it gave me the best opportunity to work harder for a more serious spot," Harry explains.

"And how have you been settling in?" Sophia asks. She gets cut off by a loud groan coming from Gray. "Got something you want to say, Grayson?"

"Yes," he concedes. "You're asking all the boring questions, cuz. No one wants to know about how Harry enjoys the team."

"First names only, Grayson Phillip Aoki-Park," Sophia relays, pinning him with a death stare. "Moving on. How are you, as a team, planning on tackling the opposition in the new year? I hear you've got a very competitive season ahead of you, and if the playoffs go well, you could be up against the best colleges in the country."

"Out hustle, out work, out think, out play, and out last," Xavier says, repeating our mantra that we have been using our whole lives. Coach chants it before every game, and it works like magic. We all have our own superstitions, but that's the one we all indulge in. Obviously, Jake snorts at that.

"Cut out the BS, Dawson," Jake says, laughing. "What we're really going to do is beat the competition with whatever force we have. Hockey isn't just a physical game, it's a mental one, too."

"Great. Thank you for that insight, Callahan," Sophia

mutters, scribbling down notes in her notebook. I look over to Wren, and she is not trying at all to hide the disgust on her face.

"You're welcome," Jake replies proudly.

"Okay, so, you all agreed to talk about this before coming, so here is just a small warning before we get into it," Sophia begins, not breaking eye contact with me, and I know exactly where this is going. "You all lost a vital team member at the beginning of summer, and I know it has not been easy for any of you. Some more than others. I grew up with Carter, and we all knew he was going to do amazing things in the hockey world. He would have easily made it to the pros and became one of the most talked about players in North history. My next question is, how are you planning on honoring him during this season? Xavier, would you like to go first?"

Xavier nods, looking at me before facing the camera. "Unlike some of the tactics Jake likes to use, Carter was the calmest one on the team. I don't know how we managed to win every game with him even though he seemed to be the most chilled out and relaxed on the ice. While the rest of us were pushing into people, knocking them over, Carter kept a leveled head, even when he was pushed to second string. That's how I'm planning on honoring him, by keeping calm and spending as much time out of the penalty box as possible."

We all nod, agreeing with the perfect answer. "It'll be easier for some than others, I assume," Sophia starts. "Ahem. Grayson."

"Yeah, yeah. Whatever. I'm only in the sin bin because I like to play dirty for the win," Grayson says easily.

We seamlessly float into a conversation of Sophia asking rapid-fire questions before going back into the deeper ones. There's a perfect balance between the ones we feel comfortable talking about and the more serious ones. I don't think I could do this if it was anyone else, but because I've known her forever, talking to her feels easy. Fun, even.

Wren's still standing with Michelle, watching me intently. I can tell that she's listening to every word that I'm saying, and I hope that it's taking her mind off skating and whatever is going on with her family, allowing her to be with us in the moment.

Sophia asks us about how we balance hockey and school, where we see ourselves in five years, and more hockey-related questions. I stay quiet for the most part, only answering questions that everyone else gets stuck on. But Sophia's next question catches me a little off guard.

"We all know that hockey is a team sport, but what people *really* want to know is how you stay focused in the game. How do you ensure that you are on the right track and are going to perform your best as well as making sure it's a team effort?" she asks.

I look down the line, hoping that someone is going to pipe up. "I think that this is Davis's question," Harry says, turning to me. Sophia nods, and I feel everyone's eyes on me.

I take a deep breath and start talking.

"As everybody knows, Carter was my best friend. We grew up together, and we were inseparable. I took his death hard, and I didn't let anybody in. I was drinking a lot—sorry Mom," I admit, remembering that if my mom comes to graduation, she's going to know I've been underage drinking. Everyone in the room laughs quietly. "I lost motivation to train, and I hardly ever went to the rink. Everything felt too hard and overwhelming, but then I met Wren." The smile that was on her face drops as I connect my eyes with hers across the room. Her cheek twitches, and a sad smile forms on her face. "She turned my life around, and she really *saw* me. She became the storm to the calm, quiet loneliness that I was in, and in the best way possible. She thought that I was hyper-fixating on her instead of dealing with my problems, but I managed to kill two birds with one stone, and I got through some of my problems while also getting a gorgeous, smart, talented, and just fucking brilliant girlfriend."

"No cursing, Davis," Sophia warns.

"Shit. Sorry," I say, and Sophia gives me an evil glare. "Wait, no. Fuck. Can you take that bit out?" Sophia shakes her head at me. "All I'm trying to say is that having someone who cares about me by my side is what helps me stay focused because I know that I'm doing it so I can be the best version of myself for her."

The room is eerily silent as I look at Wren, watching the way her features soften. Her eyes haven't left mine since I started speaking, and her mouth is pinned into a warm smile, no doubt trying to decipher if what I said was true or not. Hell, I don't even know half of the words that just came out of my mouth and where the truth lies within them.

I break eye contact with her, unable to bear the look on her face, and focus back on the interview. Sophia asks the group a few more questions before letting us branch off before our individual interviews. I go over to Wren, and she's now alone since Xavier has pulled Michelle away.

"You okay?" I ask, standing in front of her. She nods. "Is what I said okay? You know, for the sake of the interview."

"It was perfect. I don't know how you managed to make all that up on the spot," she replies, almost laughing. Her eyes shine.

"It wasn't hard to talk about how much I enjoy spending time with you," I say, stepping in closer to her. I watch her audibly swallow as she blinks up at me. I tug on her braid, forcing her to tilt her head up to me. I lean down to whisper in her ear, "They're watching."

She lets out a shaky exhale. "Of course." She pulls back, trying not to make it obvious that she wants to move out of my grip. "I feel weird."

"Why? Because they're watching?"

She shakes her head. "No. Well, yes. I don't know, Miles. I just— Everything you said out there sounded very real."

I swallow. "Isn't that the whole point?"

She looks at me for a long moment, her eyes tracing every line on my face. I let her take her time and figure out what she wants. She has so many thoughts in her head that I know it overwhelms her, but if she just let me in, let me help her, then maybe we could work through this together.

She blows out a breath. "Yeah, you're right. I'm sorry. I-I think I might go, if that's okay. I really need to get a workout in tonight."

"Seriously, right now? Can't you stay for a little longer?" I ask, shifting my weight from one foot to the other. I don't mean to sound irritated, but fuck, I am a little. I feel like it's been months since we hung out, and I miss her. And she said she misses me, dammit.

"I need to go. I've already missed out on a lot of time just being here," she says, looking up at me. "If you've got to stay to do your individual interview, I can just walk."

"I can do it really quickly and then I can take you. I'll just ask Sophia—"

She cuts me off by rising on her tiptoes and pressing a kiss to my cheek. "It's okay. You stay. I'll see you soon."

She doesn't wait for me to respond before she's already running up the stairs out of the basement.

27
WREN

"I'm not a drink."

I MAKE my way back home after a long day at the rink, ready to avoid the girls' probing questions, and take a long bath before snuggling in my bed with a paperback in my hands. Most nights, Scarlett and Kennedy watch a movie like we used to. But now, I'm so used to walking past them, mumbling a "good night" that I don't even realize that they've spoken to me.

"What?" I say in the near darkness, tugging my duffel bag higher up my shoulder. I step closer into the living room, looking at the makeshift fort they've huddled in. They both pop their heads out of the fort, pulling the blanket around them.

"We're going out tonight, and you're coming with us," Scarlett demands.

"I want to stay home. I'm exhausted," I say.

"You're always exhausted. A night out will wake you up," Kennedy adds with a shimmy.

"The showcase is in less than two weeks," I say, sighing. As much as their friendship means the absolute world to me, sometimes, I just want to be alone. Most of the time, they allow me to do that until it gets to a point like this where it's non-negotiable.

"No, Wren. You're going to speak to us because that's what

friends are for. You're not going to shut us out because you're stressed. Let your stress become *our* stress," Kennedy relays, gesturing between us. "This ignoring shit you've been doing is pathetic."

"Okay, rude," I mumble.

"It's true," Scarlett says, "We know you have things going on, but pretending we don't exist is low, Wren. We need you, too, you know."

I take in a rush of air and blow it out. These girls have always had my back. They've sat through every awkward stage I've had, held my hair back while I threw up, and have been by my side every day since I met them. I've been a grade-A asshole to them over the past week, and we all know they deserve better.

"You guys really don't want to know what's been going on," I whisper, everything that has happened in the last few weeks coming rushing back to me. I've managed to fuck up whatever Miles and I had going on by running away, but these girls won't stand for that to happen, I'm sure of it.

Scarlett rolls her eyes. "Try us."

"WHAT THE FUCK? ARE YOU SERIOUS?" Scarlett exclaims once I've finished explaining everything to them. Everything from fooling around with Miles to finding out about Austin to whatever the hell it was at Sophia's house. It feels good to vent even though most of what I'm saying doesn't make much sense to me anymore.

We're at a secluded bar that Scarlett managed to get us into because of her family's access to getting away with drinking with our fake IDs. This is the first time I've drank something other than a sip of wine since Barcelona. I don't want this to become a habit, and I'll make sure it doesn't. Being around these two, I feel safe enough, and hell, I'm going to need liquid courage.

"Unfortunately, I'm being very serious," I say, sipping more of my cocktail.

"No wonder you've been so distant," Kennedy says quietly, shaking her head. "Does she really just expect you to tell your mom for her?" I nod. "Jesus. If Mia ever asked me to do something like that, I'd tell her to suck it up and do it herself."

"I tried, but she cut me off and isn't answering any of my calls," I admit, feeling helpless.

"So what are you going to do?" Scarlett asks.

"I don't know. I'm going to wait it out and see if she'll tell her herself. I just know that this whole thing is going to come crashing down on me, no matter who tells her."

As if they had planned it, they both trap me in a hug from both sides, and I melt into them. We have always done group hugs like this: the person who needs it the most is almost suffocating in the middle with the others acting as the anchor, keeping us together. When we pull apart, I can still feel them around me, making anywhere become a home with them in my arms. I'm convinced it's their superpower.

"Tell you what you need, Wrenny?" Scarlett asks.

"For you to stop calling me that nickname?"

"Shots!" she shouts.

So we drink.

I don't think I've ever consumed this much alcohol in my life, but it's making me feel alive. As if all my problems can be dealt with tomorrow and all that matters is being in this moment with my friends. My friends who are screaming Taylor Swift lyrics at the top of their lungs. I try to make a mental note to apologize to the bar staff who have had to put up with our atrocious singing for the last two hours.

"I love you guys so fucking much," I scream when *Blank*

Space finishes. They pull me into a tight hug again, their microphones jabbing into my stomach. "Like, so, *so* much."

"Oh no," Kennedy says, frowning as she pulls apart from us.

"What is it? Have I had something in my teeth this whole time?" Scarlett asks, frantically searching for her mirror in her purse.

"No. Your teeth are perfect, babe. I just realized that Wren is an emotional drunk," Kennedy says, pouting at me.

"I'm not emotional, and I'm not a drink," I slur, waving her off.

"*Drunk*, babe. You mean you're not *drunk*," Scarlett says, patting me on the back. Thank God she knows how to speak. "And you are. Watch."

She pulls her phone out of her back pocket and clicks on her home screen, and it's a picture of the two of us at our kindergarten graduation. We look so tiny and small and so cute. We've got the biggest grins on our toothless faces with our graduation caps and gowns on. Then she clicks the screen, and the worst thing happens. It changes to a picture of all of us, Kennedy now included, at our high school graduation, smiling as we hold our diplomas.

"See, that's just cruel," I say, the sob ripping through me unexpectedly. "I miss you guys."

"We're right here, Wrenny. And we always will be if you let us," Kennedy says, looking at me with her gorgeous brown doe eyes. Then the waterworks are really flowing. God, I can't get myself to stop. "More drinks!"

Then we drink more as the last few weeks I've had fade into a blur. I'll have to see my mom at the show next weekend, and I can't even stomach the thought of having to tell her about Austin.

Then my mind goes into a no-go zone. The Miles Zone. Suddenly, all I can think about are his brown eyes, his kind words, and the way his hands felt on my body. I can't stop thinking about the fact that I've been slowly pushing him away and I ran away like a coward at the interview when things started to feel too much.

I do the stupid thing and pull out my phone, which opens up to a picture of the two of us. It's a selfie he took while he was confiscating my phone as I studied. He's got the cheesiest grin on his face and is holding the camera high so you can see me in the background, my head buried deep in books. By the time he gave me my phone back, this was the picture he changed the home screen to, and I haven't had the energy to change it back.

I do an even stupider thing, and I call him.

He picks up on the second ring.

"Milesy," I say cheerfully.

"Wren. You're calling me," he points out.

"I know."

"Are you okay? What's going on, baby?"

"Does something have to be wrong for me to call you?" I argue, playing with the keychain that hangs off my phone case.

"Actually, yes. You've hardly spoken to me since Sophia's," he says.

"I miss you," I blurt out, the words coming out garbled. The girls throw me a skeptical look, and I turn away from them, walking toward the bar to sit down.

"I miss you, too, princess," he sighs. The sound of movements on his end and a few mumbles confuse my senses, and I sit up straighter. "I'd miss you a whole lot less if you stopped avoiding me."

His statement lands the blow he intended, and I sigh but recover quick enough to ask, "What are you doing? Who are you with?"

I hear him laugh low over the phone. "I'm on a late-night grocery run with Evan. What are *you* doing?"

"Drinking at a bar with Kenny and Scarlett," I say through a yawn. I whisper as if it's a secret, "I think I'm drunk."

"Really? I couldn't tell," he replies, also whispering before returning to his normal voice. "Are you okay? I thought you didn't drink. Barcelona and all that."

"I don't drink," I say, hiccuping.

"But you are."

"I am."

He huffs. "What bar are you at? Let me come get you."

"Shhhh. Stop shouting at me, or I'm going to kiss you."

He laughs, but I don't see what's funny. "You're going to kiss me? Do you mean kill, Wren?"

Oh. "Stupid autocorrect."

"You can't autocorrect with your voice, baby."

"Stop calling me baby, or I *will* kiss you," I murmur, but I don't think he hears me. All I hear is a sharp inhale, so I continue. "Can you come and get us, please?"

"Can you turn on your location for me?" he asks gently, and I fumble to change the screen so I can send him my location. "I'm on my way."

Less than twenty minutes later, we're still all very drunk and a little less sad than before, and the boys have arrived. Maybe I should have given Scarlett a trigger warning about Evan because she almost throws up when she sees him. Which I can't tell is because of the alcohol or because of the disgust she has for him. Evan is dressed casually in pants and a crisp white shirt with a black tie hanging loose on his neck, while Miles is wearing gray sweatpants and a white shirt.

Scarlett comes beside me as we stand in a line, staring at the boys as if they've interrupted something. "Why is *he* here? You promised no blonds," she tries to whisper, but she's basically shouting in my ear.

"I promised no such thing. Plus, he was already with Miles in his fancy car," I say back, singing the last few words. I don't think I'm ever going to get used to the fact that I'm friends with people like Scarlett and Evan, who already have more money than I will ever make in my lifetime.

"I can't help it if I'm blond," Evan retorts, running a hand through his hair. "Genes."

"You can dye your hair," Kennedy suggests.

Evan nods. "Done."

"No! Don't do that," Scarlett says, stumbling toward him as if he's about to dye his hair this minute. Evan laughs, holding her as she almost falls into him.

"You *just* said how much you hate my blondness."

"That doesn't mean I want you to dye it, you idiot," she mumbles, trying to get herself out of his grip, but he keeps his hands on her forearms. "Would you really do it if I told you to?"

"If it annoys you that much, of course I would, angel."

What the fuck?

When did this happen? Has he always called her angel? And has she always let him? I'm not going to remember this in the morning, so I will start to erase it from my memory now. They both stare at each other, and it's hard to tell which one of them is drunk at this point.

Until Scarlett finally says, "I'm drunk. I don't know what I'm saying."

"Drunk thoughts are sober words," I say, trying my absolute best to wink at Scarlett.

"That's not how the saying goes. But good job, baby," Miles says, smiling down at me as he wraps his arm around my waist. "Can you walk okay?"

"I think you might need to carry me."

"Really?" He narrows his eyes. I nod, smiling up at him. "Fine."

He picks me up in a fireman's carry, hauling me over his shoulder, and I'm lucky I'm not wearing the skirt that the girls begged me to wear. All Miles can see is my fully clothed ass in my favorite pair of jeans.

He carries me all the way to the car as Evan has Kennedy and Scarlett on each side of him, and they slip into the back with us. We drive home mostly in silence, and Miles insists on walking us up to the door.

After the girls have gone to their rooms, Miles follows me into mine. I'm still a little tipsy, on the verge of falling asleep, but the second that Miles comes into my room, I'm fully awake. It's pitch-black outside, and Miles Davis is in my bedroom, and he's looking at me, waiting for me to do or say something.

A few weeks ago, I would have been close to mauling him. Having him finger fuck me until I almost passed out is more than enough of crossing this boundary we've put up. Everything else that followed has just made it even harder to look him in the eye. My life is a mess right now, and the only thing that might help me get back up is the showcase. My priority. My goal. Not whatever is going on with Miles and what my sister is trying to make me do.

He steps closer toward me, and the back of my knees hit the bed, making me sit down. My heart races as he kneels in front of me and pushes me down.

"What are you doing?" I murmur, his eyes burning into mine.

"I think it's time for bed, Wrenny."

"With my clothes on?"

"You're right. Easy fix," he says, tugging me back up to stand. "Strip."

"I— What?"

"Just get ready for bed," he urges, leaning against my vanity. "Do you want me to step out of the room?"

I shake my head. "You can stay."

"Perfect. Then take your clothes off, Wren."

I blink at him, but I do as he says. It's not like he hasn't seen anything before. There's nothing sexual about this, but it feels even more intense than it would if it was leading to something. His gaze is hungry and filled with desire without being overbearing and uncomfortable. I turn my back to him as I take off my bra and slip on an oversized North T-shirt and shorts.

When I'm dressed, he urges me to get inside my covers and then wraps them around me like I can't do it on my own.

He passes me the glass of water that I hadn't realized was there, and I take a few gulps. He places it back on the nightstand and gets into the bed with me. I'm lying down, tucked neatly under the covers as Miles sits beside me on top of them, looking down at me.

I turn to the ceiling and say, "I'm sorry about that. About calling you and having you pick us up. I shouldn't have had a drink. It was a really stupid thing to do."

"You don't have to apologize to me, Wren," he says. "If you think I'm going to lecture you or tell you what to do, I'm not. I'm glad you're having fun. All I want is for you to be happy. You deserve a break, you know." He slides down onto the bed next to me, our shoulders brushing against each other as we both look up at the ceiling. Honestly, it hurts to look at him. It's like there's a fire in my chest whenever I do.

"I don't deserve anything, sometimes. I don't deserve you, and I especially don't deserve a break."

I know how pathetic I sound, but I can't tell my mouth to stop. He turns to me now, one arm resting beneath his cheek and the other wrapping a finger around my hair, and it distracts me for a second. I like that he does that. That he always needs to touch me or be close to me in some way.

"What makes you think that?"

I shrug. "My brain. My mom."

He closes his eyes for a second before opening them. "When I see you skate, do you know what I see?" I swallow, shaking my head. "I see the most talented, smartest, skilled person I have ever met. I feel like I need to hold my breath when I watch you. I don't even want to close my eyes sometimes in case I miss something, and that's just when you're practicing."

I sigh, trying to let his words register, but my brain is still foggy. "I don't think I try hard enough. If I tried hard enough, my mom would actually like me, and I wouldn't be constantly trying to gain her approval."

"What makes you think she doesn't like you? She's your mom; she adores you," he whispers.

I laugh incredulously. "She can adore me, but she doesn't *love* me or maybe even like me. I think I've known that for a while. She thinks I'm a good skater and I can be what she didn't get the chance to be. But I think deep down, she doesn't see me as her daughter in some fucked up way."

His face is so close to mine now, the light touch of his fingers in my hair grounding me to this moment. "You have no idea, do you?"

"What?"

"You have no idea how special you are, Wren, and it breaks my heart every time I hear you speak like that. I would give up everything I have for you to realize that you're perfect in every way that counts."

I feel like all the alcohol has left my body as the words leave his mouth and puncture me right in the heart. This is exactly what it feels like for my inner child to be healed.

I do what I've been needing to do since I saw him today and wrap my arms around him. It's a little struggle at first since we're both lying down, but once we're comfortable, I nuzzle my face into his neck, breathing in his lavender smell. I think I could stay buried with my head in his neck forever if he let me. His presence is so utterly perfect that I just want it to consume me.

"Can you stay here tonight? Just hold me," I ask into his skin, not wanting him to leave me just yet. Yeah, I really am an emotional drunk.

He lets out a heavy sigh. "Wren, you know—"

I cut him off before he can say no. "Can you, please? I need you. I need you here." I think he's the only thing keeping me calm. The only thing that is keeping my heartbeat at a settled pace. I also think I want him around all the time. I've got so used to having him here that I can't imagine being alone again.

"I was going to say that you should know I'd do anything for you, princess," he whispers. I pull apart from him, leaning on his chest to look at him. He brushes a strand of hair out of my face, smiling, and it might be the prettiest sight I've ever seen. "If you want me to stay, I'll stay."

I bite my lip to stop myself from crying. "You're a really good guy, Miles. Like, almost too good."

"I know." He grins.

"I take it back. You're the worst."

He presses a kiss to my nose, and I think it's the sweetest thing anyone has ever done. "Just shut up and let me hold you."

He gently pushes me to turn around until my back is flush against his front, his arms braced tight around me. I don't tell him about Austin or how stressed I am because it doesn't feel like the right time. All I need is to be held by him, and it seems like he needs it too. So he holds me.

All night.

He's just *there*.

28
WREN

"We're a team now, remember?"

I'VE SPENT the better half of two weeks practicing non-stop. Maybe I've started to go delirious since I've not been eating well, and all my days have become one big cluster. Every time I close my eyes, I see myself falling on the ice again, and I can't get that image out of my head.

I *need* to get it out of my head.

I know I've been distant with Miles since that night at the bar, but I had to. After having a few days off to hang out with my friends, I needed to go back to skating every day. It was fine when they encouraged me to take a break when the showcase was months away instead of tonight.

These showcases are not heavily graded, but they're for fun to lead up to the real competitions and can sometimes reflect my final grade. In a way, it's good practice to be in front of an audience before the holidays. This way, if people turn up here, they're more likely to turn up to the real events. Darcy says it's vital to do things for fun in between comp seasons, and I usually enjoy them.

But nothing is ever fun with my mom. When it comes to skating, the steady relationship we've built over the years turns into something a lot more serious. She gets back into her coaching mode and forgets to be my mom.

"Good luck today." I hear a voice from behind me as I walk toward the locker rooms. All I want to do is get the smell of sweat off me before indulging in my pre-skate ritual before the showcase later. For a second, I think it's Miles, but when I turn around, I see him.

Augustus Holden.

I have not missed his face at all. He's a few inches taller than me, a typically uptight Russian with dark-blond hair and scarily sharp cheekbones. He's attractive in a way he shouldn't be. It's almost unfair. It's just my luck that I see him before my performance.

I've hardly seen him around since the party, and I'm glad. All he does is mess with my head and try to convince me that I'm not as good as I was when we first started skating together. If we're no longer a duet, I don't need to put up with his pesky comments and his blows to my self-esteem. I like to think I'm stronger than that, but here he is, walking right toward me, and I'm momentarily frozen.

"What?" I ask after I compose myself.

"I *said*, good luck. We both know you're going to need it," he says as he towers over me, that smug as fuck smirk on his lips. My back presses against the wall, trying to put some space between us, but he moves in closer.

"Don't give me that bullshit," I retort. I don't know why I'm even entertaining this. We rehashed what happened at regionals for weeks, and he's still refusing to believe that it was *his* fault that I fell. "We both know that you messed up our routine on purpose."

"Amelia, that's not what happened, and you know it. I told you I didn't want you anymore, and you couldn't take it. It's not my problem you let your feelings get in the way of the performance."

"I don't give a fuck that you dumped me. I care about the way that you handled it, you moron," I shout, frustrated. "You could have done it in any way, but you wanted to mess with me for whatever reason, and it just reflects badly on the *both* of us."

He snickers. "Seems to me like you've been better off."

"You know what? I have been."

"You sure? I saw you at practice last week. You could hardly stand straight," he mocks. I had *one* bad morning amongst the chaos Austin has caused. *One.*

I curl my hands into fists and take a deep breath before shoving him in his chest, but he doesn't move much. "Go fuck yourself, Augustus."

"Oh, you'd love that, wouldn't you?" he snarls, leaning further into me as his expensive cologne invades my senses. "I know you like to watch when I get myself off."

I have the urge to tell him that I was only into that because it made him feel better after all the times he went down on me with no result. I take in another deep breath, and I meet his icy-blue eyes and whisper between pushes at his chest, "Fuck. You."

I didn't even realize there was someone else in the hallway until I saw Miles's tall body next to me, towering over Augustus.

"Wanna say that louder, baby? I don't think he heard you," Miles says, turning back to wink at me before blocking Augustus from my view as he pushes him, and he stumbles back.

Is it just me or has the temperature climbed up in this hallway?

Augustus laughs incredulously, looking at me from the side of Miles as he points at him. "*This* is your boyfriend? The hockey player with a god complex?"

I nod.

Augustus gives Miles a once-over, snickering like a child. There must be something that I'm missing because my fake boyfriend is gorgeous in comparison to Augustus. No matter how irritating he can be.

311

"Got a problem with that, *Gus?*" Miles asks, and I can literally see the blood drain from Augustus's face. Calling him "Gus" is like poking a bear, and I've never known why it bothers him so much. If they were to fight right now, my money would be on Miles. Augustus is tall, but he couldn't hold a candle to Miles. He has a different kind of strength. He's impossibly tall, but he's broad too, which Augustus isn't.

"Not at all," he bites out, shaking his head before sauntering off down the corridor. I let out a real breath of relief this time, and Miles turns around to face me.

I immediately burst out laughing. *This* is why Augustus couldn't take him seriously. Hell, even I can't. Even though this guy oozes sex, he also has poor fashion choices. His T-shirt has "I 💜 my girlfriend" written across it in bold letters.

"Come here," he says over my hysterical laughter. I do just that. I walk into his open arms and wrap myself around his middle, falling into his lavender smell. His arms feel like coming home after being away for years. He rubs his hand down my spine reassuringly. "You okay?"

"I'm perfect. Better now," I muffle into his shirt.

"Good."

I give him one last squeeze before pulling apart from him as he catches both of my hands, beaming at me. "I'm sorry you had to see that."

"I'm glad I was here. Someone needed to put him in his place," Miles says.

"I could have dealt with him on my own."

"But you shouldn't have to."

"But I could have."

He grins. "I know." I stare at him because I know it's coming. "But you shouldn't have to."

"Miles."

He laughs. "We're a team now, remember? Me and you?"

I nod solemnly, but I can't hide the smile that's on my face. "Me and you."

He smiles back at me, letting go of my hands. "The show's starting soon, so I'll let you get ready."

I nod. "Thank you, Milesy. I appreciate it." He smiles at me again before nodding to the locker rooms, urging me to go.

I appreciate you, I want to say, but the words get stuck in my throat. In some way, I feel like he already knows that.

I keep my composure when I get out my black-and-emerald outfit in the locker room. I stay calm when I take off my leggings and sweatshirt. I'm fine when I step into the shower, but as soon as the heat hits me, I break down.

I allow myself to cry. I give myself fifteen minutes before I have to suck it up and move on.

I cry out of the pressure, the constant torment of trying to always do my best.

I cry for Austin, knowing that I have to do well in order to tell my mom after the show.

I cry over Augustus's stupid comment and Miles's sweet words. Over his hugs and how I could have had more of them this week.

I get out of the shower and put on my costume. I look into the mirror as I apply subtle makeup to my inflamed face. I braid my hair into a bun and secure it with some bobby pins before I head out of the door.

The only pre-skate ritual or superstition I have is making sure the water is hot enough before I go on the ice. As long as I've showered, almost scalded my skin with the heat, I'm good to go. I accidentally turned up the heat once before a junior competition, and I won by a landslide. It was the best I had ever performed, and I've used a hot shower, some music, and the same hairstyle as good luck ever since.

When I get back into the small arena, people are already

starting to fill the area. A lot more people than I thought would turn up. I search the slowly emerging crowd, but I only spot Sophia with a few other girls sitting around her. I can't see where Miles has gone, and I can't see my girls either. Before I can worry about that, my mom starts strutting toward me in her dark-blue pantsuit: a black handbag in one hand, and her phone in the other.

"Oh, Amelia. I'm glad I could catch you before the show," she says frantically as she places her hands on my face, inspecting it. She tilts my face up to the side as she stares into the space between my eyes and underneath them.

"Hello to you too, Mother," I muffle, as her hands squeeze my cheeks before she drops them. "Coming to wish me luck?"

"Yes, and I need to speak with you afterward." My stomach drops. Maybe she already knows. Maybe Austin sucked it up and told her herself, saving me the torture of doing it.

"I need to talk to you too, actually," I say.

She pulls out her phone and scrolls through it, ignoring me as she mumbles to herself. She always gets like this before performances. More jittery and antsy than I am. I call her name to snap her back into reality, but she's still scrolling.

"Ah, it's better that we talk afterward," she says dismissively when she finally looks up at me, her pupils huge. "Remember to stay focused. Stay sharp."

I nod, and she rushes off to her seat. I look up into the stands, and now, even more people are here. It's still not as full as it would be at the hockey games, but it's something. It's better. I search the crowds and I see them. Miles is standing, no doubt, searching for me too, still wearing that stupid shirt.

When his eyes connect with mine, he smiles wide. I lift up my hand sheepishly and wave. He waves back before tapping on Kennedy and Scarlett's shoulders and pointing to me. They both get up and wave their hands as if they're trying to flag down a taxi. I laugh to myself before the lights start to dim and Eva starts her routine.

She's phenomenal as I watch from the railing, basically drooling. She glides and spins to *I'd Like You for Christmas* by Julie London, not missing a step or a beat. It's hypnotizing watching her gracefully work around the ice, and it just reminds me why I love this sport so much. There's something so addicting about figure skating. Something so incredibly mesmerizing that you don't want to miss out on a second of it. She finishes with a flourish, and the crowd cheers, and I whoop. I move toward the entrance, knowing that I'm next.

This is it.

They announce my name on the intercom as I glide onto the ice, getting ready in my starting position as *Video Games* by Lana Del Rey begins.

29
MILES

That's my girl

I MEANT it when I said that she was mesmerizing.

Watching her in her skating costume, the music blaring from the speakers, and the rink almost full of people just makes that statement even more true. She performs her routine flawlessly, and I swear I'm still holding my breath. Her face is concentrated but effortlessly beautiful. She glides across the ice gracefully, each spin and turn landing smoothly.

I can't tear my eyes away even if I wanted to. There is something so elegant and satisfying about watching her skate. I watch as she gets lost between the lyrics and the movements. I look around to see everyone else with the same expression: pure hypnosis. Even though playing hockey is similar to the adrenaline and the thrill, this feels so different. When we're on the ice, we're fighting, roughing each other up as we try to score a goal.

But this?

This is completely magical. I could watch her like this for hours and I would never get bored. I could spend the rest of my life just sitting in this seat while she moves around the ice.

She looks so peaceful while she skates, her body moving seamlessly with the music. I can tell there are so many intricate patterns and details that she puts into this routine. Like the way she rolls her head back slightly and the way her arms right down to her fingers flow with the music. Even when her eyes close for a few seconds, there are no faults.

She looks up at me for a split second, and I smile at her, but her smile wanders somewhere else in the crowd, and it drops. Her face turns sour as she turns back around, skating in the other direction. My heartbeat quickens, and my stomach twists. I try to find who she is looking at, but I can't see anyone else other than Kennedy and Scarlett, who are watching her beside me with adoration.

Her routine comes to an end, and we stand up to clap and whoop. Wren gives a shy smile in her finishing position before skating off the ice. I walk down to her as she's stepping off the ice, itching to see her. People are still clapping by the time I get there.

"You did amazing. Like, so fucking good, Wren," I say when she steps off. I slip my hand around her waist and kiss her on the cheek. She doesn't throw me a confused look like she usually does; instead, she slips out of my grasp and pushes away from me, which is worse.

"Thank you," she replies bluntly as she catches her breath. "I didn't land my Lutz as well as I did in practice, but it's fine… I think. Did you see my mom up there?"

Her words come out in a weird, breathy clump. "What? Uh, no. I didn't know she was here." I look around the stands as people watch the duet on the ice.

She makes a *humph* sound as she sits down on the bench outside the rink. "Well, she's here, and I know she picked up on my mistake."

"What mistake, Wren? You were perfect."

Her head whips toward me, and she lets out a sad laugh. "I wasn't perfect, Miles. I was far from it. You might not notice that, but my mom definitely will."

"She wouldn't," I say, but I know it's no use.

"I watched the literal second she lost interest. I saw the disappointment on her face, and she didn't watch the second half of my set," she explains.

I rest my hand on the small of her back. "Fuck, I'm sorry."

She shivers and pushes my hand away before straightening. "It's nothing. It's fine."

I know she says it's fine, but I don't believe her. I think that the more she tells herself that, the more likely she is to believe it. I know because I've done it before. She hasn't told me to leave yet, and I don't think I would leave if she told me to. She's just going to have to get used to the fact that some people always want to be with her even when she's going through a hard time. So we sit in silence until all the performances are over and everyone surges out of the stadium.

Even when Kennedy and Scarlett come over to say congratulations, she gives them a smile before dropping it and turning to face the empty rink. They don't make a fuss, and they walk away. They must know if there's something wrong, but I don't want to intrude, and I know she won't open up to me if I bug her.

Heels click behind us, and we both turn around.

"Mom," Wren says curtly as she stands up. She turns and walks toward her mom, who is rather dressed up for the occasion.

I stand up, brushing myself off as I walk toward her, standing next to Wren. I didn't know I would be meeting the AD as the guy who's dating her daughter. If I did, I would have worn something that isn't jeans and a shirt saying how much I love her daughter.

"I had to take a phone call," Miss Hackerly says, holding her chin high.

"In the middle of my performance?" Wren asks, her voice tight. Miss Hackerly nods, and I wince. "You couldn't have waited until after and at least *pretended* you enjoyed it?"

"What good would it do either of us if I pretended to enjoy it?"

Silence falls between us.

I don't know what to say, because all the thoughts I have right now are not very nice. What kind of mother treats their kid like that? Especially one like Wren, who is kind and selfless and talented and smart and way too fucking *good* to be treated like this by her mom.

I remember what she said to me the other night about how she doesn't think her mom loves her or sees her as her daughter. How she's probably the pawn in some game for her to relieve her glory days. It's a fucking shame that someone so kind and loving could have someone so heartless as a mom.

Miss Hackerly directs her attention to me, her gaze not friendly in the slightest. "Is *this* your boyfriend everyone has been telling me about? I thought you would have at least told me in person."

"I've been busy," she mutters.

"It seems like it," she says, "It makes sense now that your performance was off. You've been distracted."

"I haven't been distracted," Wren argues, huffing out a breath. I don't feel like I should be here for this. They're talking about me as the distraction, and I'm standing right in front of them.

"You were never like this with Augustus. He pushed you to be better."

"Yeah, and look where that got me," Wren snaps. She takes in a steadying breath. "Look, Miles is a good person, and he's a really fucking good boyfriend, so I really don't care about what you have to say about that."

That's my girl.

If we weren't in front of her mom, I would have covered her face in kisses by now. She probably would've rolled her eyes and pushed me away from her, but still.

Miss Hackerly doesn't even acknowledge what Wren said, or me, and it pisses me off. "Listen," she says, sighing, "your performance was fine. I know I was distracted, but it doesn't take a genius to point out your Lutz needs more work."

"Of course, you found space in your busy schedule to critique me. You're unbelievable," Wren says, scoffing. She hooks her arm into mine. "We're going."

She tugs at my arm, looking up at me with teary eyes before walking in the other direction. I don't say anything because what am I supposed to say? I knew they had a difficult relationship, but I don't think it's my place to step in. She doesn't need me to save her. All I can do is just follow after her like the lost puppy I am.

"You said you needed to speak to me about something, Amelia," her mom shouts after us. Wren stops walking and turns around, her cheeks red as if she's been caught.

"It's nothing. I'll call you," she murmurs.

"Okay, fine. I was going to go away to Palm Springs after Christmas and into the new year with Mike," her mom begins, but Wren interrupts her.

"Great. Have fun."

"*But* he has an important surgery coming up, and he doesn't want to disrupt his schedule. That's why he called me. We were going to reschedule, but he suggested that we let the two of you go. If you'd like," Miss Hackerly explains, not seeming happy about the idea at all.

"I need to practice as you so clearly pointed out," Wren argues. I look down at her, and her face is hard. I put my hand around her waist and pull her into me.

"You need to take a break," I whisper for only her to hear. She tenses at the way my breath tickles her skin as she inhales a shaky breath. "You deserve it, Wren."

"Did you hear what she just said? Clearly, I don't."

"You do."

"I do—"

I quirk my head to the side. "Do you really want to do this right now?"

She rolls her eyes. "Okay. Okay, fine," she murmurs before turning to her mom, her voice stronger. "Thank you. We'd like that."

THE SECOND we get back to her apartment, we order Thai food. Well, *I* ordered Thai food, and she took a salad out of the fridge. We've been sitting on the floor around the coffee table in silence until she finally speaks.

"You do know she's only doing that so I won't be mad at her, right?"

"What?"

"The vacation. I doubt she and Mike had plans. I bet she booked it right there in the stadium," Wren mutters, laughing at herself.

"Has she done that before?"

"How else do you think we got to Barcelona?" Wren says, shaking her head. "I lost out on a comp because I wasn't eating properly. I passed out on the ice. Before you say anything, it hasn't happened since, and I'm not stupid enough to do that to my body again. One of the more mortifying points in my career, but I turned it around. But right after it happened, my mom could hardly look at me. So she booked me and the girls an all-inclusive vacation to Barcelona. I don't know why she thought that would make everything better, like it was to show she still cared about me, but it never felt like that. I always knew deep down that she was doing it to be like 'Hey, I'm not mad at you. Here, have some freedom as proof.' But when I'd come back, it was back to the same shit, the same routine, and the same fucking comments about every single thing I do wrong."

Her words sound like a sucker punch, and I wish I could do something to make it better for her. I wish I could give her a whole new mom all together. "Have you ever brought this up with her?"

"Once," she says. "She sent me a new pair of skates for some stupid mistake I can't remember. They were the most expensive ones she could find, and when I confronted her about it, she gave me this whole spiel about how ungrateful I am and how she wishes I was still her sweet little Amelia."

"Fucking hell," I mutter. "I'm sorry."

"Yeah." She lets out a short laugh. "It's fine."

"It's not. It's manipulative, Wren."

She shrugs. "You know, saying it out loud to you has been the first time I've actually thought about it like that."

"Jesus," I murmur, shaking my head. I hate how okay she is with all this. How she's so fine with everything being wrong with the relationship with her mom.

She sighs. "It's cool. She's my mom, you know? It's hard to stay mad at her sometimes. It's just… Let's talk about something else so I don't freak out."

"What are your Christmas plans?" I ask instead, changing the subject. I grin, and she tries to hide her own smile.

"Nothing. Our flight to Palm Springs is the day after, so I guess I'll spend Christmas Day here with Kennedy and Scarlett. My family aren't very Christmassy people," she mumbles between chews.

"How come?"

"Since the divorce, it's felt kind of unnecessary to celebrate as a family. Neither one of them remarried, but they're always dating new people, so it's always felt a little awkward."

"Do *you* like Christmas?" I ask, nudging her under the table with my foot. A smile creeps up her face.

"I love it. I like the seeing my friends and family part the most. It's nice when everyone's together."

I hum. "My parents are having Christmas Eve dinner at home this year. They invited us since I skipped Thanksgiving, but I wasn't going to go because my mom and I are in a weird place. But if you want to, we can go," I ramble, unable to stop the shit spewing out of my mouth. "You know, only if you want," I add.

I wasn't going to mention that I was invited because as soon as I got the message from Clara, I was going to decline the invite, but hearing this, I had to ask. Besides, it'll give me an excuse to finally see my mom again and hang out with my sister without her cornering me in her car.

"Of course I'll go. How could I miss the opportunity to see baby pictures of you?"

"Are you sure? My family is a little unhinged."

"They can't be any more unhinged than mine."

"Let's test that theory, shall we?"

Wren gives me a wide smile before shoving more salad into her mouth. She chews thoughtfully, looking down at her food and then at me.

"You never talk about your parents. Is there anything I should know before we go?" she asks cautiously. "Are they axe murderers or have weird taxidermy animals in the living room?"

"My mom had an affair a few years ago, and I only just found out," I spit out. "It's over now, but it's still weird to me."

"Oh." She clears her throat. "I kinda wish she was an axe murderer now."

"Me too." I sigh.

"That sucks. I'm sorry," Wren says, smiling sympathetically. "But your parents are still together, right?"

"Yeah, *that's* the weird part. My dad forgave her almost immediately. When I thought they were going on date nights, it turns out they were going to couples therapy. They've been hiding it from me for years." I laugh but it's forced.

"And you haven't forgiven her?"

"I'm trying to. I'm just scared that if I see her, I won't know how to act," I admit. "We haven't really spoken since I found out, and I don't know what I'm going to say. It's just awkward as fuck."

"I'm going to be there. If you want to leave at any time, I can pretend I have diarrhea or something," she suggests, and it sounds so genuine I laugh, shaking my head.

"Generous offer, but I couldn't let you do that. I don't think Clara would ever let us live it down," I say, and her eyes widen. She scrambles from her side of the table and kneels in front of me, her hands on my shoulders, shaking them slightly.

"Shit, Miles. I forgot you have a sister. She's going to *hate* me," she says frantically. I chuckle and put my arms on her shoulders like she's doing to me.

"She's going to love you, Wren. You've got nothing to worry about."

"Yeah, but she's a *girl*. She'll know. She'll find something she doesn't like. I know she will."

"There is nothing about you that she wouldn't like. You're perfect." She inhales, about to say something, but I stop her. "Don't."

"Don't what?"

"Don't try to tell me that I'm not telling the truth or that you're not perfect because you are, okay?"

She shrugs shyly. "I mean, if you say so," she mocks.

"Yes, I do say so." We stare at each other for a minute until we finish eating our food in comfortable silence. I don't want to overstay my welcome, so once I've thrown out my trash, I get going and hope Wren can be my good luck charm for facing my mom.

30
WREN

Christmas tree farm

I'M ALWAYS surprised by the Christmas decorations in Salt Lake. There's something about the holidays that always makes me happy, and I wish my parents made more of an effort after their divorce. I might have been a teenager, but it would have been nice to have something to celebrate while all my friends did. The upside to getting to celebrate now is that each year the decorations get more and more extravagant.

The girls and I like to keep our decorations simple with a small silver tree and decorations to match. The second we venture out of our part of town, the houses get more glamorous. This year, I've seen one house transformed into a giant present and another with a Christmas tree almost bigger than the one in Rockefeller.

When I walk up to Miles's truck, he's blasting Mariah Carey's Christmas songs, singing along like a maniac. Nothing new coming from him. I laugh as I open the door and slide in, watching him with adoration.

I couldn't bring myself to say it the other night, but I am so grateful for him. He sat with me for what felt like hours after the show when I waited for my mom to turn up. He does things without me having to ask him, and that's more than what Augustus had ever done.

He still brought me home and ate dinner with me after he saw how bratty I was acting with her. I'm not proud of it, but I was pissed about her missing the end of my performance. She's been pulling stunts like that for years, and I find it hard to stay angry at her for long every time. The anger she fuels in me makes me work harder just to spite her and prove her wrong. I hate that it works every time. Austin's problem is going to have to be on hold for a while.

"Merry Christmas, my love," he says as if he has only just noticed I got in the car.

I turn down the music and frown at him. "Hey, what happened to Wrenny or baby? They were starting to grow on me." He laughs as looks at me and then back at the road. Then he gives me another glance.

"You look hot," he says, ignoring my comment.

I grin. "I know." I watch his smile tug up on his lips, and I have the strangest urge to kiss him. I don't know where we stand after we breached the rule about the things we do alone, but that shouldn't be on my mind. I gesture to his jeans and thick jumper and say, "You could have told me to dress down."

I'm wearing a red skater dress and black boots with a long black puffer jacket to keep warm, assuming this would be more of a formal thing. I'm meeting his parents for God's sake. I don't exactly know what the uniform to meet your boyfriend's parents is, but I feel way too dressed up for this.

"What part of 'you look hot' don't you get? If you look better than me, they'll know that you care, and they'll focus on *you* instead of me."

"I don't want them to focus on me," I moan, sulking back in my seat.

"You could be wearing a paper bag over your head with the eyes cut out, and you'd still be the most gorgeous woman in the room, Wren." He looks at me intensely when he says it, his eyes taking another sweep of my outfit. I hold up the bag that I brought in my hand awkwardly.

"I bought your mom a necklace, and I couldn't find anything for Clara or your dad. I didn't know what they'd like, and it was too late to ask you, but I'm sure—"

"It's fine." Miles cuts me off. He glances at me, flashing an annoyingly charming smile in my direction. "Thank you. You really didn't have to do any of that, but my mom will appreciate it."

"Are you sure?" I ask, turning to him while he drives. "I didn't even ask if she prefers gold or silver. What if—"

He stops the car abruptly, and he's lucky we're in the middle of an empty estate. He turns to me, his eyes narrow. "Amelia Wren Hackerly. Stop worrying for five minutes and just live in the moment. Can you do that for me?"

I stick my tongue in my cheek, trying not to laugh at his sudden seriousness. "I can try."

"Good," he replies sternly.

"Fine," I say back.

"Great."

"Perfect."

He holds my stare for a few beats before he smiles, smoothing out the tension, and then he continues driving. I pick up Miles's phone from the holder and look through his playlists, trying to put some decent music on. I find one called "Songs for Wrenny," and I laugh.

"What's this?" I ask, looking through it. There's a lot of Taylor Swift, Paramore, Gracie Abrams, and Florence + The Machine. "If I didn't know any better, I'd say all this terrible music you've been playing is just a front."

"What are you talking about?" he laughs.

"There's a playlist called 'Songs for Wrenny.' The songs on here are actually good. What's all this about?"

He laughs a little, glancing at me and then back to the road. "You weren't supposed to see that yet."

"I mean, it says the songs are *for* me. Why can't I look at it?"

"It's not meant *for* you. More like, songs that you like and songs that remind me *of* you," he says, and I can feel my cheeks getting hotter just at his words. No one has ever made a playlist for me before.

"Can you tell me which one is your favorite that reminds you how amazing I am?"

"*Christmas Tree Farm*," he says.

"That was quick."

He shrugs. "I add to it a lot."

The comment is so simple and matter-of-fact that I try not to overthink it, and I'm left speechless. There's always been this sweet, sensitive side to him, and I wish I got to see this more when we first met, and I wouldn't have been so committed to pushing him away.

We don't say anything else, and I press play while we sing along to the music. Everything about it is so stupid that I'm laughing more than I'm singing. I seriously don't know how many more times I'll have to tell him he's a terrible singer for him to stop.

When we get closer to his house, he stops singing, and I can tell something is wrong. When we're pulled up outside his house, he doesn't get out of the car, and he taps his fingers on the steering wheel.

I place my hand over his, linking our fingers together. "If you don't want to go, we can drive away and never look back." He shakes his head with a weak laugh, and his hand flexes on the wheel. "How about this? If you feel irritated, angry, or upset, just squeeze my hand, and I'll squeeze back. That way, you'll know that I'm here."

He nods and squeezes my hand. I squeeze back.

We keep our hands linked together as we walk up the gravel

path of his childhood home. It's a small bungalow in a quiet suburb an hour away from campus. It's the kind of house you drive by, knowing a happy family lives here. The house is a gorgeous dark brown, and the lawn is covered in freckles of snow. It already feels cozy and safe. It's much nicer than my mom's new house, and I haven't even stepped inside yet.

He knocks on the door twice before it opens. Miles's dad is a tall, light-skinned man with kind and almost boyish features. He's at least five heads taller than Miles's mom, a breath-taking woman with dark-brown locks flowing long past her shoulders.

"Merry Christmas, you two," Miles's dad says as if we met before, with a huge smile on his face. He pats Miles on the shoulder and nods at me with a smile. "I'm Ben."

"Hi, I'm Wren. It's a pleasure to meet you both," I say, looking between the two of them. Considering their past, they don't look like a couple who have been through a hard time and have a rocky relationship. They look exceptionally happy. Which is probably why it unsettles Miles so much.

"It's so nice to meet you, Wren," his mom exclaims, smiling at me. Miles's hand tightens around mine, and I squeeze back.

"Thank you for inviting me, Mr. and Mrs. Davis," I say.

"Oh, just call us Portia and Ben. There's really no need for the formalities." She turns to Miles, who has been avoiding eye contact with her. "Miles, love. It's good to see you."

"You too." His words don't mean to sound harsh, but I can tell he's struggling to keep it together. He smiles down at me, and the line between his eyebrows smooths out. "Wren got you a present."

Of course he's going to try to throw me under the bus to avoiding talking to his mom. I clear my throat as Portia smiles at me. "It's only something small," I say, handing her the gift bag.

She beams at me, her mouth forming the same dimples as Miles. "Oh, that's so thoughtful. Thank you, Wren."

I'm about to respond, but before I do, a tall, curly-haired

woman I recognize as his sister Clara comes around the corner in a pink tracksuit. Maybe I *am* too dressed up. Her face lights up when she sees us. She pushes past her parents and pulls Miles into a hug.

"I didn't think you'd show up," she says through a grin when she pulls apart from him. He shrugs and looks over at me, his eyes wide. He warned me about his sister, but all I can see is someone who is excited to see her little brother. "Wren! I've heard a lot about you. I didn't know you'd be as pretty as he said."

I laugh awkwardly. "Thank you. You're stunning."

Clara's face gets impossibly brighter. "You're flattering me already," she coos, flicking her hair behind her shoulder as she looks at Miles. "She's perfect."

"I've been trying to tell her that, but she's allergic to compliments," Miles says, squeezing my hand again, and I squeeze his harder.

"Why don't you take off your outdoor clothes and come into the kitchen with us girls?" Portia asks, smiling wide.

Everyone else slips away, and I can still hear Clara talking about me and making fun of Miles. I start to unzip my coat, but Miles stops me, pulling it down for me. I watch him work slowly at the zip at my front, his eyes focused on it. He comes behind me and pulls on the sleeves.

"You don't have to do that," I say, almost laughing at this gesture.

"I want to."

I smile. "Are you going to be okay?"

"I will be, Wrenny."

He hangs up my coat with the others, and I get a peek of some of the baby pictures hung on the wall. I start to walk in the direction of Clara and Portia before Miles's hand grabs mine.

He squeezes, and I squeeze back.

This whole time, I've been worrying about what's going to

happen with Miles instead of worrying about what's going to happen if I'm left alone with his family. He gave me a small rundown on the way over, but I don't exactly have much experience with meeting my boyfriend's parents.

Clara sits on the kitchen counter, her legs swinging and her tall stature overcrowding the kitchen, while her mom chops vegetables on the other counter. Her head shoots up when she sees me.

"You and Miles seem very happy together," she says, smiling like a maniac. She's talking to me like we've known each other for years, and the thought of her brother being happy clearly makes her happy. "I can tell by the way he looks at you. I know he's a little unhinged, but I'm glad you're able to handle him."

She slips off the counter, and I laugh awkwardly. "I definitely made him work for it, but he's grown on me," I admit.

"Atta girl. It's all about the chase." Clara laughs. "Sometimes, he needs to be dealt with that way though. He thinks he can get what he wants without working for it. It's a hockey player thing."

"Ay. Miles *is* a hard worker in some respects, but sometimes, his heart is a little misplaced," his mom says, shaking her head lightly.

"What do you mean?" I ask as casually as I can. I've wanted to know more about Miles's family and his childhood, but I haven't wanted to push him.

She sighs, pausing her vegetable cutting, looking off into the distance. "He loves a lot, and he loves *hard*. He always has, and he always will. Sometimes, he can't let go of things and he latches on. It consumes him." She sighs. "I'm sure that is partly my fault."

"Mom," Clara presses, rolling her eyes as if they've had this conversation before. I stay quiet, letting the new information about Miles settle in.

"Enough talk about him," Portia says, wafting her knife

around. "You girls are going to have to help me dish out this food."

EATING CHRISTMAS EVE dinner with Miles's family was a lot less awkward than I thought it would be. Although Miles doesn't talk much to his mom, everyone else is getting along great. Miles's dad is a man of few words, but he drops these sarcastic one-liners that I know Miles and Clara both take after. Clara basically carries the conversations on her back with her work horror stories.

She works on low-budget films with her friends and enters them into festivals. You wouldn't believe how many of her stories end with getting booked for a job, but it turns out to be some weirdos wanting to film a porno. Even with the inappropriate jokes she makes, neither one of her parents seems to bat an eye at the candor. If something like this was said around my mom, she would have had a stroke.

"Oh my god, Miles, have you told Wren about Felicity?" Clara asks when we're eating dessert. Their parents have gone into the kitchen, leaving us to talk in the dining room.

I've never felt fuller of laughter, food, and everything good about this place. Miles might not see it, but this place is clearly filled with so much love. I'd kill to spend time with a family that makes inappropriate jokes and eats too much dessert to then sit by a fire and recall stories from our childhood. If I ever get the opportunity to be a mom one day, this is exactly what I'd want.

My mind instantly drifts to Austin, who is probably going to kill me for not telling my mom about her pregnancy, but this is my life too. I shouldn't have to carry that burden just because she's too chicken-shit to do it herself.

"Clar, don't," Miles replies, shaking his head with a blush.

I've never seen his face go so red before, and it's downright adorable.

"Who is Felicity?" I say, dropping my head into my hands to look at Clara. She takes a long swig of her wine before speaking.

"She was Miles's first crush. He was probably around five or six, and there was this girl in kindergarten who he thought was cute. So he came to me, asking for my help. And as the hopeless romantic tween I was, I suggested that he write a song for her." She gestures to him to continue the story, and he's still shaking his head with laughter.

"Long story short, I sang her the song at recess, and she started crying. *Not* out of happiness," he admits, shoving his face into his hand.

"Oh my god, is this where your love for music came from?" I ask, my eyes wide, and he shakes his head again, chuckling. "I must hear this song immediately."

I look over to Clara, who is smiling wide, but Miles's expression is serious. I nudge him with my knee, and his face cracks like sunlight bursting through the blinds. I don't think I've ever seen a sight more beautiful.

Felicity, will you be with me? Felicity, do you like cream cheese? Felicity, your eyes are so green and so pretty, he sings at the top of his lungs in the most operatic tone possible.

I start hysterically laughing, tears springing to my eyes. I've always known he was a bad singer, but Jesus he's *terrible*. That poor girl who had to hear this at recess probably still has nightmares about it. He takes a deep breath as if he's about to continue.

"No, please stop," I scream, covering his mouth with my hand. An evil smile spreads across his face as he nips my hand with his teeth. I swear it feels like I'm dating an untrained puppy. I pull my hand away, shaking it out as I glare at him.

"I think he's learned a few moves since then if he's managed to get *you* to date him," Clara comments, tipping her glass toward me. I look up at him, and he's already looking at me. I hide the smile on my face by snuggling deeper into his side; the perfect day washes over me like wine. "Do you want to know what he said when he first told me about you?"

"I'm genuinely frightened to find out," I say.

I feel his warm hand slowly move from his thigh to mine, just beneath my dress. He squeezes it gently before leaving his hand there. It's comforting, and I'm *just* tipsy enough to let him do it.

"He mentioned you for the first time, and I had no idea who you were. Then he said that you weren't just his girlfriend, but you were *everything*."

I can feel my heart racing as soon as the words leave her mouth. *Everything.* Why does everything he pretends to say make my heart swell? I can feel the tears prickling at my eyes, but I blink them back and turn to him.

"You said that?" I ask.

"I did," he murmurs. Again, it's so simple and not up for debate that I don't say anything because for the second time tonight, he's practically rendered me speechless.

31
WREN

"A woman's pleasure should not be an embarrassing topic."

DECIDING to host Friendsmas is probably the best decision I've made all year. When we lived with our parents, we always spent Christmas day together. After spending the morning with our family opening presents, we'd all go over to Gigi's house and eat as much shit as we could.

The holidays have been hard for Ken because her mom and sister still live in South Carolina while we're here in Utah. It's too expensive for her to fly out and too far for her to drive, so last Christmas, it was just us three, and it was perfect.

I always call my parents on Christmas Day, but to Mom, it's seen as a day off work more than anything special. I had a long call with my dad, wishing me and my girls a Merry Christmas, as well as sending me a new pair of skates and some money. My mom's "Merry Christmas" came in the form of a three-foot bouquet with an impersonal Christmas card.

We decided to do Secret Santa, which wasn't very secret since there's only three of us. We sit down on the living room floor in our Christmas pajamas, which we intend on wearing all day, each with a present in front of us. It's a stupid tradition, but we're all terrible at giving each other gifts. Scarlett spoils us too much on our birthdays with the casual fact that she's a millionaire, and we didn't think it was fair, so now we give each other one gift each that we know we'll like. I honestly wouldn't need anything from them. Being surrounded by their energy is more than enough for me.

"I wonder who had me," Kennedy mutters with an eye roll, shaking the box in front of her. I look over at Scarlett, who is beaming. She opens the box and pulls out two hardback books. "Oh my god! Shut the fuck up. Who had me?"

"Doesn't that take away the whole purpose of Secret Santa?" I ask.

"Okay, so it wasn't you, you grinch," Kennedy says, giving me an evil side eye before turning to Scarlett. "How did you get these?"

She holds up two special editions, signed copies of her favorite author Jasmine James's new novel, which she has been obsessed with all year. They've been sold out everywhere, but somehow, she managed to snag two.

"I have my sources." Scarlett shrugs as Kennedy drools over them. "Now me."

She picks up her present, which is in a small envelope from me.

I try to hide my smile when she opens it. The anticipation surges through me as she takes out the small, handwritten note.

"To Scarlett," she reads aloud. "'Here's a present that you can use for the next year, and you don't have to lie about sleeping with the hotel owner to get in.' Wren! You sneaky motherfucker. How did you do this?"

"I have *my* sources. Plus, if you keep pretending to get access to the hotel without a real ID, you're going to get thrown in jail, or worse, your family will find out. Now you can stop lying about it. You can use it for a whole year too," I explain. She jumps into my arms, and I almost topple over as she suffocates me, pressing kisses to my cheeks. "Okay, get off me, you animal."

She giggles, and we pull apart. I get back up into a sitting position and pick up the gift bag in front of me. I know it's Kennedy who got me this from the process of elimination and the terrible wrapping. I take out the hundreds of tissue papers before digging my hand into the bag and I pull out...

"Batteries?" I ask Ken. She nods and gestures toward the bag for me to keep looking through it. Then my hand finally hits a big box. I pull it out and start laughing.

"What is it?" Scarlett asks from across me, her knee bouncing like a child. I turn the box around so she can see the front of it. Scarlett also bursts into hysterical laughter. "This is the most Wren thing I've ever seen. Now I wish that Ken had me."

"I had to do a lot of research for this. And the week when the Wi-Fi was down, I had to go to the library to search up where I could get a good one. You wouldn't believe how many times my account got blocked for searching, 'Where can I buy the best vibrator?'" Kennedy explains.

"Thanks, Ken. You always get the best presents," I say when my laughter dies down.

"Well, I thought if you're not going to sleep with Miles, you might as well get some action elsewhere." She shrugs, and I couldn't agree more. Having Miles's fingers inside me was more than enough, and I can't let myself get that out of control again. I'd rather slowly set my body on fire than let him kiss me again for real.

MILES and his friends arrive soon after. Xavier arrives with a bottle of expensive champagne, and Evan, rich boy of the century, arrives in jeans and a button-down.

And Miles looks fucking sexy.

He's wearing a dark blue button-down, his shirt sleeves rolled up, giving me the most delicious view of his arms, and black pants. This is the most I've seen him dressed up since the event, and if I wasn't so committed to keeping things friendly between us, I would have told him that. So instead, I just eye fuck him until he walks toward me.

He immediately snakes his hands around my waist and presses a kiss into my neck even though the only person who doesn't know this is fake is Evan.

"I got something for you," he whispers into my skin as everyone walks into the living room, where Kennedy is setting up board games.

I take a step back. "Why?"

"Because it's Christmas," he says.

"But why?"

"Because it's Christmas *and* you're my girlfriend," he says, but it still doesn't make any sense. We never agreed on getting each other gifts, and I sure as fuck didn't get him anything. "Do you need everything explained to you? You're a lot smarter than that, Wren."

I cross my arms against my chest. "Tell me why you got me something."

"Because I wanted to."

I don't say anything else, and he rolls his eyes. He drags me by the arm into the corridor to my bedroom, and when we get inside, his woody cologne clouds my senses as he towers over me, my back pressed against my closed door.

"What are you doing?" I laugh, looking up at him.

He smirks. "Close your eyes."

I raise one eyebrow slowly. "Why?"

He takes a step back, hiding the small bag that I only just noticed behind him. "Do you trust me, Wren?" I nod because I do. Probably more than I should. And I'm excited to find out what he got me. "Then close your eyes."

I do as he says, all my other senses heightened as I feel him move closer to me. The fresh lavender smell of his soap crowds my mind and my senses as I feel his hand come to the top of my chest where my collar is opened slightly.

My breathing picks up as the tips of his fingers skim the exposed skin on my chest. His touch is so soft and light that it drives me crazy, but I keep my eyes closed as he starts to button down my shirt.

When I feel the cold air of my room hit my stomach, I know the shirt is unbuttoned. This whole ordeal feels insanely intimate, like he's undressing me to lead to something more when I know he isn't.

He catches my wrist in his hands and pulls at the sleeves of my shirt, dropping it to the floor. I hear the rustling of tissue paper and then I feel a soft fabric stretch around my head and he pulls my arms through it gently, tugging it down on my stomach. "Can I open my eyes now?"

"Yeah."

He's grinning at me with that smug face of his when I open my eyes. I look down at the shirt he pulled over my head. It's a white shirt, the same one that Miles wore at my showcase with a bright-red heart. Instead, it says, "I 🖤 my boyfriend." He dusts off my shoulders, holding onto them as he looks down at me.

"Now we can match," he says.

"This is ridiculous."

"*You're* ridiculous."

I can't control the laugh that escapes me as I look up at him. "It's perfect. Thank you," I say, and I can tell how hard I'm blushing. I shift from one foot to the other, feeling irritatingly uneasy under his gaze. "I didn't get you anything."

He tucks a strand of hair behind my ear, smiling so hard that lines form on his cheeks. "You didn't need to. I'm spending the next week alone with you. I think I'll survive."

AFTER WE FINISH COOKING DINNER, we set up a mini buffet on the kitchen island. Everybody lines up, taking a paper plate to save washing dishes, and gets the food they like. We probably made enough food to feed a whole football team, but I know the girls will live off this for the next week while I'm in Palm Springs. I stand at the other side of the island, waiting for everyone to get their food first.

"Save some for the rest of us," Evan mutters to Scarlett, who's taken one of the last pieces of bacon in the foil tray. She looks over at him, her face plastered into a fake smile.

"You're right, sorry," she says sarcastically before picking up her bacon and shoving it into his mouth. He doesn't fight back. He lets her shove more into his mouth until he can't take it anymore. "Do you want some syrup with that?" He shakes his head vigorously, but he smiles behind his full mouth. He *smiles*? Weird. "Yeah, I thought so."

I tear my eyes away from them because I've never seen two people that crazy before. I'm waiting patiently for the day that whatever is going on between them will eventually bubble over and they'll become... friends? Or something.

We eat mostly in silence until we're all so stuffed we spread out in the living room. Everything feels so natural here, like we were all made to be friends in some weird way. Evan and Xavier lie out on opposite ends of the couch while Kennedy sits in her beanbag with Scarlett's head in her lap. Miles and I sit on the smaller couch, my head resting on his shoulder as his fingers draw lines up and down my arm.

I knew that moving into this apartment with my girls would make this place feel like a home, but now, it feels even better. As if the word "home" is screaming off the walls at full volume. I look around at everyone, and it just feels perfect.

Home.

"So, what did you guys get for Christmas?" Xavier asks. Evan sits up with a smug grin on his face. "Not you, Branson. Nobody wants to hear about what car Daddy bought you."

Evan slouches back down, and I giggle, feeling the champagne running through my body.

"You guys did Secret Santa, right?" Miles asks, and we all hum in agreement.

"I got these books from Scarlett," Kennedy beams, holding up her new prized possessions. I know she's not going to shut up about this until Jasmine's new book comes out.

"I got an all-inclusive access to my favorite hotel from Wren and Daddy Hacks," Scarlett says proudly, flashing a toothy smile at me. "If you're lucky, Miles, maybe she'll sugar momma you too."

Everyone bursts out laughing at her remark, and I stick my tongue out at her. I keep quiet. Saying what I got in front of these boys might be the stupidest thing I could do, so I keep my mouth shut.

"What about you, Wren?" Xavier asks when the laughter has died down.

"What about me?"

Evan's eyebrows raise. "What did you get?"

"Uh, nothing," I reply, cheerfully.

Xavier and Evan look at me confused, and I swallow, looking around the room as I try to find something that I can say to change the subject. It's too late to rush off and pretend the food's burning. Miles rubs my shoulder, turning to look at me.

"I know my gift is pretty killer, but I don't believe that none of your friends got you something," Miles says, his eyes narrowing at me. I shake my head, bite my lip, and look away.

"I got her a vibrator. The best one in town," Kennedy says,

and I shoot her an evil look along with Scarlett. "What? She was too scared to say it. A woman's pleasure should not be an embarrassing topic."

"You two having trouble in the bedroom, Davis?" Evan asks, laughing.

Miles ignores him, and the conversation around us moves on, but Miles's grip on my arm tightens. It's better that he didn't say anything. It's better that *I* didn't say anything.

What would he say?

No, she fucks like a god, or *Yeah, finger fucked her once and we've not spoken about it because she's too scared for this to get real.*

I feel him bring his mouth closer to my ear, his breath tickling my neck.

"Are you trying to make me jealous, or are you just trying to turn me on even more? Either way, it's working," he whispers, and my breath gets caught in my throat, and I end up coughing like a maniac.

Luckily, I'm saved by Evan of all people.

"Let's play truth or dare," he suggests.

Scarlett scoffs and rolls her eyes. "Are we in middle school?"

"I never said it was going to be PG," Evan argues. She raises her eyebrows at him, sitting up out of Kennedy's lap. "Truth or dare?"

"Truth," Scarlett responds, holding his stare. The energy between them is lethal, and I'd do just about anything to put out this fire.

"Where is the weirdest place you've had sex?"

Kennedy and I exchange knowing glances. Kennedy clears her throat, attempting to smother her laugh while Scarlett gives her a wicked grin before turning back to Evan.

"In public or in general? Or both?" Scarlett asks innocently.

"Let's go with both."

"Our business class. A few weeks ago."

Evan practically chokes on air while Kennedy and I finally burst out laughing. Miles lets out a "Jesus Christ" under his breath while Xavier's mouth hangs open. Scarlett's sexual pursuits have always been a topic of conversation between us, and as long as she's safe, I love this for her.

"I'm afraid to ask, but were there people in there?" Xavier asks, grimacing.

"No. Well, I don't think so anyway. It was pretty dark," Scarlett answers with a shrug.

"With who?" Evan asks when he gets his voice back.

His face is unreadable. It's hard to tell whether he's angry, dissatisfied, turned on, or all three. You could cut the tension between them with a knife, and I'm this close to whipping one out to see if I could. They're way more alike than either one of them wants to admit.

"That's for me to know and you to never find out," Scarlett says, tapping her nose.

"Okay, moving on," Evan drags out, turning toward me and Miles. "Wren, truth or dare?"

"Dare."

"I dare you to kiss the hottest guy in the room," Evan says with an evil smile. I'm beginning to think he just enjoys stirring shit up. Before I can retort, Kennedy butts in again.

"God, if you want someone to kiss you so badly, just say it. You're starting to sound desperate," she says with a groan.

"I'm not. I just want her to do what you've all been dying to since *I* got in here," Evan drawls. I feel Miles shift beneath me, his grip on my shoulder tightening again. "You could at least make it interesting."

Evan's a good-looking guy, but there is no way I'm going to kiss him.

"Well, obviously, it's not you, Evan. And sorry, Xavier, it's not you either. I love Michelle too much to do that," I say, and he shrugs happily. I move out of Miles's grip as I scramble on top of him, straddling him in my new favorite shirt and Christmas shorts.

"Uh, hi?"

"Hi," I whisper back, smiling at him before my fingers snake into the back of his head, pushing it gently onto the headrest and my mouth covers his.

It's the kind of release I've needed since he last had his hands on me. It's slow at first and patient, our mouths getting used to the sensation again. His hands instinctively grip my hips, pushing me further into him until my front is flush against his hard chest.

I let myself drown in him, letting his lips fight over mine. Everything around us blurs when his tongue slips into my mouth, and I whimper.

I'm surprised I don't explode into oblivion when his hands slip under my shirt, wrapping around my back. His warmth seems to seep into my bones, and I want to feel like this forever. I bite on his lip as I pull away from him, leaving the both of us panting.

I stay straddled on him, his hands still under my shirt when I turn back to the rest of them.

"God, he said kiss, not whatever that was," Xavier says, retching. This is why we work well together. Xavier is the voice of rationality.

"You get what you wanted, Evan?" Miles asks, his voice breathy from behind me. He bites my collarbone gently; his eyes connect with Evan across the room.

"You guys are so boring. You didn't have to choose him just because he's your boyfriend," Evan whines. I climb off Miles and try to ignore the throbbing I feel between my legs as I sit beside him, nuzzling my face into his shoulder.

"Even if he wasn't, I still would have," I whisper, only loud enough for Miles to hear.

THEY CONTINUE to play truth or dare while I slip away into the kitchen, cleaning up some of the plates and dishes that we ended up using.

Today has been another perfect day. Our friendship groups are so different that they make so much sense, and I couldn't think of anything more special. I might not get to spend the holidays with my family, but having my friends to celebrate it with feels even better.

I'm putting dirty dishes into the sink when Miles comes through from the living room. He doesn't say anything. He just stands beside me, waiting for me to wash the plates, then he dries them.

"Did you mean what you said earlier?" he asks in the midst of the comfortable silence.

"What?"

"Earlier. About you wanting to kiss me even if we weren't together."

I shrug. "You're not a horrible kisser." That doesn't get the reaction I wanted. I thought he'd laugh and say something flirty, but he just groans. "What? Are you annoyed?"

"No," he says with a slight edge to his voice. "I don't know. Maybe. I guess I'm a little frustrated because you know how badly I want you. How badly I've wanted you since the beginning. But whenever I try to make a move, you run away. Like you did the morning after the game."

"I didn't run away. I stayed with you."

"If I wasn't in pain, would you have stayed?"

I blink at him because the truth is, I don't know if I would have. If I didn't know how badly he needed someone to be there for him after we fooled around, I probably would have thought of some excuse to get out of there.

"That's different," is what I end up whispering.

"Is it?" I open my mouth to speak, but I'm interrupted by Xavier, Evan, and Scarlett walking into the kitchen. The boys look absolutely fucked. I don't know when everybody got so drunk, but I was focusing on pacing myself.

"If you're staying, Miles, I'm going to drive these two home," Scarlett groans, patting Xavier on the chest. He makes a strange noise from the back of his throat. "You guys gonna be okay?"

"Yeah," I reply. I look up to Miles, but he's not looking at me. Panic settles in me like a stomachache festering in my abdomen.

"Actually, I'm going to go too," Miles says, walking away to get his jacket. Scarlett nods as she opens the door. I walk toward him, trying to reach for his hand, but he pulls it away.

"Miles," I say. He turns around to me, his expression unreadable. "You're still picking me up tomorrow, right?"

"Yeah. I'll be here." He shuffles closer toward me and kisses me on my forehead. "Merry Christmas, baby."

I sigh, the nickname running through me like water. "Merry Christmas, Miles."

32

MILES

I'm so fucked

WE ONLY HAVE SIX DAYS.

Sunday until Saturday.

That's all we get. That's all the time I get with her until the new year and things start to get more serious for the both of us. That's why when we're on the plane and Wren falls asleep, I make a plan of what to do to make this a good vacation. A much-deserved break for her. I book us in for massages, hikes, and saunas, and I look around for a nice restaurant. I'm really cutting deep into my savings for this, but I need to do something nice. She's been on edge since her showcase, and if I can erase that worry for a few days, then I'll do anything I can.

On the drive to the airport, on the plane, and even when we drive from the airport to the hotel, we both ignore what happened last night. I shouldn't have gotten annoyed with her, but I'm getting tired of pretending I don't want her. I'm tired of her ignoring the obvious fact that I want her for real.

I don't want to ruin these next few days because after this, we could be done. If my first few games go well and she qualifies, we'll have no reason to be doing this anymore. She'll go back to skating regularly and I'll go back to playing.

It'll be over.

By the time we check into the five-star hotel, we're both exhausted. We throw our bags down and settle in. She's the kind of person to unpack all of her stuff immediately while I usually live out of my suitcase for the first two days.

This room is a lot bigger than the one that we stayed in at the gala. Instead of a massive bedroom, the room is smaller sized, but it has two huge bathrooms on each side of it. The kitchen and living room are connected in another room, with the refrigerator filled with drinks and snacks.

We spend the first two days in a haze, going through all the things that I booked for us to do. We go for massages, mostly for Wren. We spend our days out in Palm Springs, visiting the most touristy places we can, and we spend our nights binging bad movies and eating room service, talking about everything and nothing.

I could get used to this—the two of us sitting in robes, eating ice cream, slouching on the couch, and watching movies. Sometimes, she talks about whatever book she's reading, and I'm only half listening. I just like watching the way her mouth moves. I'd let her talk about a ten-book fantasy series if it meant I could watch her talk.

This morning, we decided to go down to the beach to read. I'm *still* making my way through the book Wren got me, but I brought my trusty hockey book as backup. I'm doing a lot more staring than I am reading. I'm lying on my back, slightly angled toward Wren, who's lying on her stomach, her head propped up on her bag while she reads. The sun has blessed her with faint freckles along her back and arms, and I'm fucking obsessed with every single one of them.

She's wearing a lilac bikini with a white knitted cover-up. She looks ethereal. I don't think I could tear my eyes away even if I wanted to. Being with her is like watching the ocean crash against the shore. It's like looking straight into the fucking sun.

"Can you stop ogling?" she asks without looking up from her book.

I pick up mine and pretend to read it. "I'm not ogling, I'm reading."

"Really?" She turns to me, squinting her eyes, her head resting on her hands. "What are you reading?"

"The McDavid Effect." She snorts, smothering her laugh in her arms. "What's so funny?"

"It's not funny. It's… typical, that's all."

"What's typical about a hockey player reading about hockey?"

"Everything." I roll my eyes and grab the book out of her hands, and she tries to reach for it.

"And what are you reading? *Romance*? Isn't this the book that Kennedy got for Christmas?"

"Yeah, she's letting me borrow it since she has a million copies. Give it back." She tries to reach for it again and looks adorable while trying to. I push my hand up higher so she can't see it. I skim the page she was reading and gasp loudly.

"Amelia Wren Hackerly, this is straight-up porn." Her face turns even redder than it was earlier from the sun.

"It's *not*. Jasmine is a great author. She writes about her own real experiences with love. It's entertaining. You could learn a thing or two," she retorts as she snatches the book out of my hand, putting it into her bag.

"It's filthy is what is," I say, and she shakes her head with a soft laugh.

"It's *inspiring*," she murmurs before turning her sun-kissed face away from me and resting back on her arms. I can't even argue with her anymore because the sight in front of me is so fucking worth it.

"WHY DON'T we go out tonight?" I suggest later that night after we're both tired from hiking on the Araby trail. I stand over her from the back of the couch while she lies down, her gorgeous eyelashes resting against her cheeks.

"I'm exhausted, Miles. We've done, like, everything on everyone's bucket list *ever* in the last few days," she says, sighing deeply. She opens her eyes and pushes herself up on her elbows.

"Don't you want to go out for some real food? We've been living off room service for four days," I say as I walk over to her side of the couch, and her eyes follow me.

"Aren't we going out on New Year's Eve? We can wait until then."

"Yeah, but it's going to be packed with people," I say as I crouch down next to her, batting my eyelashes at her. "Don't you want to go out somewhere nice? Somewhere where we can eat *good* food. Just us. Just one night, Wren."

"Jesus, you're so fucking dramatic." She groans before standing up.

I go into one of the large bathrooms to get ready. I'm lucky I packed a nice outfit in case something like this were to happen. Okay, nice might be stretching it, but it's decent.

I try to brush out my hair, but it looks wild. I've never known how to deal with my curly hair, so it just does its own thing. I put on a white button-down and black pants, rolling my sleeves up my forearms.

I wait in the kitchen area for her to finish getting ready because, as always, she takes hours. I stick my head into the fridge to find something, but there are only tiny bottles of tequila, so I close it.

"Ready to go?"

I turn, and the wind is knocked out of me. Literally. I think I've died and come back to life.

Wren is dressed in a silky black evening gown with tiny

straps. She holds a silver purse in her right hand, which matches her stilettos and earrings. Her hair is slicked behind her ear as it falls onto her back.

She walks toward me, and I can't take my eyes off her.

"You look beautiful," I whisper. She blinks up at me, and I wrap my arms around her waist, pulling her into me as if it's the most natural thing in the world. My hands feel so at home on her body. As if they just belong.

"You look really good," she murmurs, trailing her palms up my chest before wrapping them around my neck.

"You're not lying to me, are you?"

"Unfortunately not."

Watching her try to fight herself just makes me want her even more. She takes in my outfit, her eyes roaming all over me. God, I could sit down and let her look at me all day. I'd let her use me for whatever she wants if I could have her eyes on me.

I got us a table at the hotel we're staying at, so we only have to walk down past the lobby. I hold her hand even though we don't have to pretend out here.

"What are you doing?" she asks, looking at our linked hands and then at me.

"I just want to hold your hand," I admit, squeezing hers in mine. "That a problem?"

"No," she says quietly and doesn't bring it up again.

The restaurant is built to hover just over the LED pool with a cozy cabin vibe. Our seats are on the patio outside, giving us a perfect view of the live band that plays smooth blues music. People gather around them, glasses in their hands as they sway to the music under the sunset.

When we sit down, we both order steak with fries and a cherry blossom lemonade. I'm starting to think that my bad eating habits have rubbed off on her. We go through the never-ending list of questions to ask each other as we eat. It's been a while since we've done them, and they're my favorite part about our relationship.

"Okay," she says, popping a fry into her mouth before scrolling through my phone. "These are pretty personal. Is that okay?"

"Sure." I grin at her, but she frowns a little as she locks my phone and slides it over to me.

"What's one thing you would change about your family if you could?" She bites her bottom lip as if she's regretting asking the question.

"I wish my family were more upfront with each other. Instead of being too scared to say things, you know? It'd be a lot easier than whatever it is we're pretending to do now."

"What do you mean?"

"I've always been a pretty dramatic kid. I would get really attached to things and people, and I wasn't afraid to express that, but my family has always been weird about it. My dad ignores things that he can move on from, my mom pretends like they don't exist, and Clara is good at mediating the tension and making everything seem okay when it's not. I don't know, I think they just feel better hiding things," I admit.

As I say it out loud, my stomach twists as if I've just finished binging shitty food. I hate how uncomfortable it makes me. I hate that whenever I talk about them, I can feel my chest tightening. That's why at the Christmas dinner, I kept quiet.

Even when my dad and I were alone, we stuck to talking about sports and boring things instead of what we were really thinking. I knew that if I tried to say anything, I'd ruin the night. Or they'd back me up into a corner and tell me to calm down. That I was overreacting.

"I think they just find it easier to ignore problems. They've been treading on eggshells around me since I found out about Mom and since Carter died," I admit, and she keeps listening to me. "You know how much I talk. I can't move on easily, and I can't just ignore things that are clearly there. I know my parents love each other, but sometimes, that doesn't feel like enough. They're not *happy*. It's worse to be unhappy with somebody and still stay with them."

"I'm sorry," Wren says quietly. I shrug, smiling. "But you know you can always talk to me, right? Even if it's utter nonsense. I like hearing you talk."

"You do know I'm going to use this against you in the future. You can't ever tell me to shut up again," I joke. She smiles wide. "What about you?"

"I wish there was less pressure to be perfect all the fucking time," she says immediately. She tries to laugh, but the noise doesn't come out properly as she fiddles with her fork. "Austin's pregnant, and she told me to tell my mom for her."

I almost choke on my food. "What?"

"Yeah, she told me a few weeks ago. It was just after we went to the game, and I was planning on telling her after my show. Then my mom missed half of my performance, pissed me off, and I didn't tell her, so now we're here." She gestures to our surroundings. "Pity trip."

I'm quiet for a minute, and I have no idea what to say. I can't imagine having that weight on your shoulders. She looks out at the crowds of people, smiling softly at the music playing.

"Do you want to know what the worst part is? She didn't even think about my side of it. Austin wanted me to tell her after the showcase because she thought that if I told her, she'd have all of her focus on me and forget it. It's like me skating trumps her getting pregnant. Like she knows that Mom would fixate on me instead of her."

"That really sucks. I'm sorry. Do you know when you're going to tell her?" I ask after a while.

"I don't know," she says, sighing and falling back deeper into her chair. "I'm hoping that Austin will suck it up and tell her herself. I can't deal with that kind of drama. Not so close to comp season."

"Yeah, that's fair."

We both dig back into our food before it gets cold, neither of us asking any questions before she sits up on her chair, her arms resting on the table, her head in her hands. "Next question."

"They just get worse," I say, picking up my phone to scroll through it.

"I'm a big girl, Milesy. I can handle it."

"Okay." I close my phone, mirroring her position. "Do you believe in love?"

"That's easy." She laughs, pushing her hair over her shoulder before giving me a dead look. "No."

"What do you mean no? You *only* read romance books."

"Don't get me wrong, I *love* love. Does it exist? Sure. But do I want it? Definitely not."

Her candor shocks me. This whole time, I thought she was a romantic underneath all the stubbornness. A hopeless one at that. I thought that after reading all those romance books, she'd aspire to that. That she would crave it. *Hope* for it at least. She looks out to the band again as they play *At Last* by Etta James.

"I love the idea of love. The way it's written about in books and movies. But actually, being in love—it's scary. It's all-consuming. Falling in love is so easy, but it's just as easy to fall out of it or for it not to work out. My parents did. They acted like everything was fine. They went on pretending. And then one day, it was just gone. All the sparks, all the reasons they had to stay together just ceased to exist. I don't want that. I don't want to be constantly waiting for the day my partner doesn't want me anymore. The torture. The anticipation. I just couldn't live like that."

"I don't think you should be scared. It's a powerful thing, being in love. We're young, and we're going to feel things that are more than lust, and sometimes, the only word to describe that is love."

"Have you ever been in love, Miles?"

I swallow. "No," I say.

What I really want to say is: *I've never been in love, but the more time I spend with you, the more time I spend getting to know you, the more I feel like you're going to be my first and only love.*

"Neither have I," she admits. She turns to me now, tears lining her eyes. "We use the word love for everything. I *love* my friends. I *love* my shoes. I *love* this food. It doesn't *mean* anything anymore. Can't there be something that has the same meaning, carries the same weight but doesn't feel indefinite? Binding. Something that doesn't have to tie you down to that person and suddenly change everything. When you're in love with a person romantically, you can't go back. But when you change your mind, it becomes a big thing. But I guess that's what people want though. Something tangible to change in their relationship. To make it more serious or some shit."

We both look at each other for an extended moment. The way her brain works blows my mind, and I'm obsessed with it. I want her brain. Her mind. Her everything. Anything that she's willing to give me.

She doesn't look away from me as she says, "If I ever feel anything remotely close to being in love, I just want to *exist* with that person. I don't want to ruin it by binding us together by a word. An emotion."

I'm shell-shocked for a minute, not sure what to say. This girl has flipped around nearly every single thought that I had about her. I finally muster up the courage to ask, "Does that mean you were never in love with Augustus?"

She shakes her head. "I knew he loved me, and I appreciated it. I knew I had some strong feelings for him, but I definitely didn't love him."

I nod. "Do you think you feel this way about love because you feel like you don't trust it or because you don't deserve it?"

"Both?"

"Well, that's bullshit, Wren. You're worthy of everything good in this world."

Her eyes shine. "Even love? Even if it breaks my heart?"

"*Especially* love," I say, "even if it breaks your heart."

We're quiet for the rest of the day. Neither one of us wanted to say more than a few words after we just bled out our emotions onto the table. Something shifted. I don't know when or how, but something else had changed between us. Like the string that was holding us together has pulled us even closer without us realizing it.

The only thing that's running through my mind is the fact that I'm falling head-over-heels, no sign of turning back kind of in love with this girl, and I'm not sure if I'm enough to make her stay.

I am so fucked.

33
WREN

It must be something in the air

"SURFING?"

I have the urge to say yes just to see his reaction, but I don't have the energy. I came here in the hope of a relaxing vacation, not to go on an adventure every day.

Miles and I are on opposite ends of the huge couch in the hotel room. He's flicking through a list on his phone while I try to finish reading my book. Which I've been trying to do for the last two hours, but he won't stop bothering me.

"No," I say again.

"Yes."

"No."

"Maybe?" he says, leaning over and pulling my book from my hands, grinning at me. "Come on, Wrenny. You're only in Palm Springs once."

"I could be here next week if I wanted to."

"Right, I forgot. Scarlett said that you'll sugar momma me if I'm good," he says. "I'll be a good boy, Wren."

"Shut up." I laugh, pushing him away from me, but he's a lot stronger than me, and he clasps my wrists together, kissing them like he loves to do.

"I'll be so good for you, baby. So good."

His voice is so fucking tempting and inviting that I know I won't be able to fight him off for much longer. I sigh and soften my tone as I say, "Do you *really* want to go surfing?"

He nods, suddenly excited like a puppy. "More than anything."

"Fine, but I want to be back here before lunchtime."

WE DON'T MAKE it back before lunchtime.

In fact, we don't make it back until the surf instructor has had enough of us and the sun starts to set. We were both terrible at it, and it only got worse when the instructor suggested we tried tandem surfing. I can't tell if I'm disgusted or impressed with Miles's determination to actually catch a wave. We were out there for what felt like hours, sweaty, sticky, hot, and every other disgusting feeling you get after being out in the sun all day.

Instead of going back to our room like I suggested so we could order room service, I'm being dragged down a street to a dive bar, still in my skirt cover-up and bikini top while Miles is shirtless in his swim shorts.

"I need to shower properly. Please don't tell me we're about to eat here," I say, letting Miles pull my exhausted body into the near-empty bar. I take a look around and it's a nearly deserted space with a few people scattered around and a karaoke machine in the corner. "No."

"Oh yes, Wrenny," Miles says, pulling me onto the dance floor.

"Is it Opposite Day or something because it feels like you've been ignoring everything I've said no to all day?" I say, and he pulls me into him. He doesn't say anything as he winks over to someone at the bar. "Miles Middle Name Davis, what are you doing?"

"Harlan," he says, wrapping one arm around my waist and clasping his other hand in mine.

"What?"

"My middle name is Harlan," he explains, and I snort. "Don't ask. I have no idea where my mom got that name from. I think she was expecting me to turn out to be some big CEO or something."

I laugh, throwing my head back. "It's cute. It's giving hard-core grandpa vibes."

"Glad to know it's grandpa names that get you going," he starts, spinning me out and then pulling me back into him. We're not even dancing properly to the fast-paced music that is playing but I'm having too much fun to care. "And not my amazing looks."

"You're so full of yourself. You know that?" I say, laughing as he makes me spin again.

"You could be full of me too if you're nicer to me," he retorts, and I gag. "I'm kidding. The rules and all that."

"Glad to know that it's you putting your dick inside me that will breach rule number three and not this very romantic, very up-close dance we're doing," I say when the song changes to slow, smooth jazz. He pulls me into him, and I rest my head on his chest as he holds my hand and I wrap my other hand around his back.

"This," he says, gesturing between us, "is only whatever you want to call it, Wren." He continues to sway us, out of beat to the music.

"That's not confusing at all," I murmur, wrapping my arms loosely around his neck. I almost forget that we're both practi-cally naked, our sweaty skin clinging to each other until my front is flush against his. God, has he always felt and smelt this good? He's almost too perfect that it hurts. "Can I ask you something?"

"Anything."

"And you've got to be honest with me," I warn, listening to the rhythm of his heartbeat.

"Always."

I take in a deep breath. "Would I sound stupid if I said that I want to stay here, in this little bubble, forever?"

"I think that's the best thing you've said to me all day, Wren," he whispers. "You don't have to follow it up by explaining to me how you mean it in a platonic way or because we're pretending to date because I get what you mean. In whatever way you meant that, I'm right there with you."

"Okay, good."

"Great."

"Perfect."

"Do you have any hobbies other than skating?" he asks, and I look up at him, resting my chin on his chest. "I know that was a real one-eighty, but I've been thinking about it, and I want to know."

I nod, resting my head back down on his chest. "I like to read, obviously. A lot. And I write sometimes."

"And you find that fun?"

"It's the best. Getting lost between pages, finding myself within characters, and getting so caught up that I forget to look outside for a second. It's the best type of consuming feeling. Don't you ever feel like that about something that isn't hockey?" I ask

"I feel like that about music. I think," he says. "Maybe not as intensely as you do, but I do enjoy listening to music. Sometimes, it's the way certain songs sound and how they make me feel, and other times, it's the words that are so well written. But most of the time, it's both."

It feels like my heart is expanding. Is that possible? Or is that even a real thing? Because when Miles speaks to me, it feels like my heart is about to burst out of my chest, not only because it is beating so fast, but because it's being talked to, cared for, and understood so deeply that it just wants to jolt right out.

"That's why you made that playlist for me that you didn't really make for me," I tease.

"Exactly," he says through a laugh. "What's your favorite song?"

I think about it for a second. I change my favorite song the same way I change my outfits. It depends on what mood I'm in or where I am. "Right now, it's *Carry On* by Norah Jones."

He laughs a little, pulling away from me to hold me at arm's length. "You're going to have to sing it for me because I don't know it."

"I already told you, Davis, I can't sing," I say, shaking my head.

"If you do one, I'll do one," he says, walking over to the karaoke machine. He holds out the microphone to me. "Deal?"

I grab the mic off him. "Fine."

I stand next to the machine, looking at the tiny screen for the lyrics, mentally preparing myself for embarrassment. It's only Miles and a few other strangers in here, but it feels like everyone's eyes are on me. In some weird way, the strangers don't matter because I can only see him.

He stands across from me, his ankles crossed and his arms folded across his tanned chest, grinning. I start to sing. It's not my best, but it's something. It's a pretty slow song, but it's one of my favorites. I even do a little dance between the small interludes of piano, and Miles dances along with me, clearly enjoying himself.

It's so easy to just be with him like this. At the end of the day, it's his bed that I'm going to be crawling into and his arms that are going to wrap around me throughout the night. Because, here, we're untouchable. And whatever we do or say is going to be contained into this tiny bubble we've built, and that makes this less terrifying.

When my song's over, Miles takes the floor, psyching himself for the song he's chosen. He does a mini warm-up, jumping up and down and pretending to crack his neck before the song starts. When the song starts, I immediately burst out laughing. Obviously, because Miles is Miles, he chose *My Shot,* from *Hamilton* the musical.

He can't fucking sing to save his life; I've known that. But he can sort of rap.

I watch as he has the whole place captivated while rapping every single line of the song. There aren't many people, but it makes this whole thing feel like a real performance. I've never seen him so at home. I never would have pegged him as a theater kid, but from the way he's clearly memorized these lines, I might have been wrong about him. He keeps his eyes on me the entire time, giving an Oscar-worthy performance, pointing at me at any chance he can get until I'm crying-laughing so hard that I need to sit down.

I don't know how I didn't realize it earlier. Maybe weeks ago, when he picked me up from that bar and looked after me, or maybe it was way before that, but I might have real feelings for this guy. Like, feelings I definitely shouldn't have. The kind of feelings that I have not only between my legs but also in my chest.

When his five-minute rap is done, he stumbles toward me, out of breath and chest heaving. "That was the most tiring workout I've ever done in my life," he says, falling into me.

"Okay. Come on, big boy," I say, pushing his weight off me and onto the bar stool beside me. "I'm hoping that five minutes isn't how long you always last."

He gasps, holding a dramatic hand to his chest. "Are you making a sex joke?"

"No," I say, fiddling with my straw in my lemonade.

He tuts at me, shaking his head. "Didn't want to get me a drink?"

"And miss another second of that toe-curling performance? No way," I say, pushing my drink toward him. "You can have mine."

"Wow, Wren. Making sex jokes and letting me drink some of your drink? If I didn't know any better, I'd think you're finally warming up to me."

"You *don't* know any better," I murmur. "Plus, I warmed up to you a long time ago. It just took a vacation and a day full of surfing for me to show it."

"Nah, I think I figured you liked me when you let me finger fuck you until you came on my hand," Miles murmurs, sipping on my drink innocently.

"Are we talking about things because I remember you were the one who begged for it," I say, my cheeks flashing at the memory. We *both* asked for more, but I'm not going to admit that right now.

"Okay, fine. I'm admitting it because I'm not going to deny the fact that I wanted you badly that night, and you let me have you," he whispers so low that I can feel it in my stomach.

All I can focus on is *that night* because that is all it was. It was a moment of weakness. We were both turned on and reckless. That's it. It might have driven me insane for weeks, but I'm over it now.

I think.

WHEN WE GET BACK into the hotel, Miles immediately goes into the bathroom, desperate to get the smell of the ocean and the bar off him. I've become comfortable in my sticky bikini top over the past few hours, and I don't want the smell of the beach —or the smell of him—to come off me just yet. Instead, I sit outside on the balcony, letting the last of the summer breeze flow through my hair.

I pull up my phone and call Kennedy, knowing that she should be with Scarlett right now. They pick up on the second ring, their bright faces filling up the screen.

"Hiiii," Kennedy coos. "We miss you!"

"I miss you guys too," I say, smiling at them. "What are you doing?"

"We just came back from Miles's house. Apparently, hockey players want to party every night. You should know the kind of lifestyle you're getting yourself into," Kennedy warns.

"Well, it depends on how long you're planning on keeping this up for," Scarlett adds, trying to keep her whole face in the tiny screen.

"Yeah. I'm not exactly sure where we're going with this," I say, glancing back into the bedroom to make sure he's still in the shower. When I turn back to the screen, both of the girls are looking at me confused.

"What does that mean?" Scarlett asks.

"You guys have to promise not to kill me," I say. They both cross their hearts, holding up their Girl Scout promise.

Before I can speak, Kennedy pipes up. "You're falling in love with him, aren't you?"

My eyes widen, and I turn down the volume on my phone. "No! God. What? Don't be ridiculous."

"You totally are," Scarlett adds in.

"I'm not," I say as confidently as I can. "I just like him a lot more than I thought I would, okay? He actually listens to me and makes me feel valued and seen. He forced me to go surfing with him, and then we went to a bar to do karaoke, and I think I've had one of the best days of my life."

"And your tan is looking gorgeous," Scarlett says, pulling the phone closer to her face. "I bet those freckles are driving him insane."

"I don't know. I haven't—"

"You're getting off-topic," Kennedy chimes in. "Are you going to tell him?"

"Are you stupid? I'm not going to tell him anything. I don't even know what I would say. It's not like they are even real feelings anyway," I say.

"Who said they're not real? Because if you're telling yourself that then you *are* fucking stupid," Scarlett says, and I hate how right she is. "Don't tell him if you don't want to, but don't invalidate your own feelings. If you don't know what those are yet, that's cool. But that doesn't mean you have to pretend you're not feeling them."

I nod, taking in her advice. "When did you get so wise?"

"I always have been, you're just too stupid to realize it," she says with a shrug. We really are throwing around the S word today. "Anyway. We've got to go and binge-watch Love Island. We'll see you in a few days."

I say my goodbyes and end the call, trying my best to listen to what Scarlett says. I hate how she's able to see right through me and understand exactly what it is that I need. I don't need to tell him right now, but I do need to figure out my feelings before they start to turn into something bigger. The glass door to the balcony opens, and I flinch, turning around to a freshly showered, topless Miles, who is leaning against the door frame.

"Hey. You okay?" he asks, crossing his arms against his chest. "You seem a bit jumpy, so I'm guessing there's going to be no scary movie tonight."

I laugh. "No, because then I'd have to put up with your screeching."

"That was one time," he says. It happened more than once, but I don't say that. He scratches his stomach, and my eyes are desperate to memorize every inch of his chest. My mouth practically salivates at the sound. "Are you hungry?"

Yes.

"What?" I say, snapping out of my trance.

"I asked if you were hungry," he says, coming closer to me. He places his hand on my forehead. "You sure you're okay? Are you sick?"

I shake my head, letting his hand fall. "I'm perfect, Doc. Just tired. All that singing and surfing has really got to me."

My face splits into a huge yawn and so does his. "Me too. I'll set up the TV in the room and we can have an early night."

He walks back into the room, and I'm left with no idea what to do.

34
WREN

Happy fucking new year

I DON'T KNOW how we got here. I don't know how I went from wanting to rip his head off at that party a few months ago to being in a bar in Palm Springs on New Year's Eve with Miles Davis.

The strangest part isn't that I don't know, it's that I don't care.

For some reason, being here, in a crowded bar with Miles's hand on my back doesn't make me scream. It makes me want to melt into him. We don't have to pretend here, but being close to him is comforting and calming enough that I don't question it.

The last week has been heaven. I know I should be training and preparing myself for competition season, but I'm sure I can spare a week. I *deserve* a week, and Miles has spent the last few days proving that to me. We've been eating, talking, traveling, and doing more talking. I've learnt a lot more about him and myself being here than I have in the last four months of knowing him.

We've still tried to keep up with working out and using the gym in the hotel, but we stay for an hour at most before running back to the room or the beach. It feels like nothing can touch us here. All the pressure, the stress, the grief. It feels like the world is at our fingertips. Or maybe I'm just starting to feel the shots we took earlier.

It's half an hour until midnight, and we're desperately trying to speak over the loud music that's reverberating off the walls.

"What was that?" Miles basically shouts in my ear, his hand on my waist, leaning his face to mine.

"I said that I'm going to stop being strict on drinking," I shout back to him. A crooked grin splits across his face.

"Really? *That's* your New Year's resolution?"

"Yeah. I kind of like how it feels now. I feel like I'm floating," I say.

"You've had, like, two shots, Wren. I hate to be the one to break it to you, but you're a lightweight."

"I'm not!" I shout, pushing him in the chest.

"I put some water in your bag. Drink some, please. I can't have my girl passing out on me," Miles says, moving me with him as we walk around the room. If I could form real thoughts, I would thank him for being so responsible. For taking care of me. But all my thoughts latch on to those two words. *My girl.* "Do you want to go somewhere quieter?"

"Does such a place even exist?" I ask.

"There's a small room over there." Miles points down a corridor with brighter lights than the dark ones in the main bar. I stand still, not willing to go down the sketchy hallway.

"I think that's where all the orgies and murders happen," I say, shuddering.

"There's only one way to find out, Wrenny." He smiles. "I got you."

But as we start walking, someone shouts his name. He looks back at me, thinking it was me who called him. I shake my head and shrug.

"Miles!?" the shrill voice from behind us shouts again. We

both turn this time. A dark-haired woman walks toward us in a bejeweled silver dress, and I instantly recognize her.

My stomach tightens.

Miles has never been closed off about his ex-girlfriend, Emily Fraser. Mostly because she comes up a lot when he talks about Carter. She's a shortish woman with dark-brown hair that cuts off at her shoulders. She studies marine biology at Drayton Hills, so she's smart *and* gorgeous. She's the opposite of me, and I can't figure out if that's a good thing or not. I take a little step back, and Miles's hand wraps around my waist, pulling me into his side.

"Oh my god, it *is* you!" she shrieks, and before either of us can register, she pulls Miles into a hug, his hand slipping off me.

"It's good to see you, Emily," Miles says when she pulls away from him. His hand returns to me again. "This is Wren. My girlfriend."

"So I heard," Emily says as she gives me a once-over. Her fake smile doesn't even reach her eyes. She turns back to Miles, ignoring my presence. "Are you staying in town for a bit?"

"Yeah, only until Monday. Our flight's in the evening," Miles explains.

"Aw, that's tomorrow. If I had known, we could have hung out," she says.

She comes closer to him, her hand resting on his chest. *Okay.* So we're doing this. Miles doesn't look at her. In fact, he looks straight over her head. It doesn't take a genius to know that she's drunk, and he's too nice to tell her to fuck off.

"I miss you. I miss your body," she murmurs, and that's where I draw the line. I grab her hand and push it off him, pushing her back gently.

"Hi, I'm sorry, but I'm right fucking here. If you wanted to flirt with my boyfriend, you could have *at least* waited until I slipped away," I say, coming in her face.

The darkness of the bar and the LED lights have given me a

lot more confidence than I should have. I'm lucky I just tower over her in my stilettos or else I'd look ridiculous.

He might not be my real boyfriend, but he's still mine in every way that counts. Anyone else looking at him like they want him is driving me crazy, and I hate myself for it.

"Miles, can you tell your girlfriend to chill?" Emily scoffs. She blinks up at Miles, but he steps back away from her, pulling me into him again.

"No, she's right," Miles says, looking at me and then back to her. "You don't have the right to say shit like that anymore."

"I can say what I want," she retorts, spluttering.

Miles groans, lowering his voice so only we can hear. "And Emily, you're lucky I'm talking to you nicely because the last thing you deserve is nice. I don't want to shout at you and cause a scene because I'm a decent human. So please, step back so me and my girlfriend can leave."

She blinks at us, and I want to laugh so badly.

"Happy fucking New Year," I say to Emily before grabbing the cuffs of Miles's shirt and getting us the hell out of there. I know it was a petty thing to say, but it made my blood boil. Exes like that are not good for anybody. The kind of ones who want you back when you've moved on. That shit sucks.

We wait outside of the bar for a cab, not saying anything as we sit down on the sidewalk. There is something comforting about being around Miles in this setting, watching cars drive past and drunken strangers howl behind us. He's sitting next to me, sighing loudly as he throws his head back, probably as frustrated as I am.

"Thank you for doing that," I say quietly. I don't know how it came out, but it's New Year's Eve, and I'm feeling emotional.

"Doing what?" he asks, turning his head to me.

"For not pretending I wasn't there."

"Why would I do that?" he asks, sounding genuinely confused. I shrug. "Have people done that to you before?"

"Not on purpose," I admit. "I've always felt like I take up too much space because I'm so busy, and people poke fun at how I never have time for them. But when I was with Augustus, it was like he was trying to compete with me. Like he wanted to make me feel small and insignificant to make it easier. Sometimes, he'd just pretend I wasn't there."

The words fall out of my mouth at a stupid pace, spilling all my secrets like it's nothing. It's definitely the darkness. I don't like oversharing this much, but with Miles, it seems too easy.

What shocks me is that he pulls me into a tight side hug, his strong arm tightening around me, and I fall into him for a second. "I would never do that to you, princess. Ever. You're way too important to me."

My heart does a weird flip at his words. "*I'm* important to you?" He nods. "As in, *me?* The girl who almost bitch-slapped your ex-girlfriend two seconds ago?"

"Yes, Wren," he whispers, laughing quietly as he presses a kiss to my forehead, "You're important to me."

WE GO BACK to the hotel in silence, walking past people as they go down to get ready for the countdown in the lounge. We go back to our room, standing outside on the balcony, watching the early fireworks in the sky.

"That was hot," Miles says, nudging me with his shoulder as we lean against the rail, looking out into the darkness. I turn to him and laugh.

"You're like a horny teenager. You think everything is hot."

He smirks. "Only when you do it."

"Someone needed to get her in line," I murmur. He turns to me, his left arm resting on the railing. I mirror his position and shudder as I say, "I *hate* that it made me so mad."

"Can't you just admit that you wanted to defend me? That

you, not my fake girlfriend, but *you* wanted to defend me," Miles says. His serious expression catches me off guard as he closes the space between us.

"What are you talking about?"

"Why can't you just admit that you want me— like you said at Christmas? That you want me for real. Just as badly as I want you."

"Miles," I whisper, a half plea.

He steps closer toward me, our noses grazing as his breath hitches. "Tell me, Wren. Does this feel fake to you?"

I don't say anything because it's getting harder to deny the heavy want building inside me. That the past few days have been the most fun I've had in my life. That being with him makes me better. Happy. Whole. And I've never felt more alive in my life, and I never want that feeling to stop.

The countdown to New Year's begins outside.

Ten.

"Miles, I *can't* want you. You know that."

Seven.

"That's not what I asked. I'm asking you what you feel. What do *you* want, Wren?"

Two.

"I want you," I whisper.

One.

Fireworks explode beside us as he grabs my face and pulls me into him, catching my lips with his.

Something magical and indescribable happens when our lips meet. I gasp at the suddenness of the kiss, and he uses the opportunity to slide his tongue into my mouth. I can feel myself floating. As if we're existing outside of this moment. Maybe it's the alcohol I had earlier or the heat between my legs, but I feel myself slipping away.

He pushes my head back, deepening the kiss as I moan into his mouth at the force of him. He's not rough, but it's hard enough that it shocks me a little and makes the intensity in my lower stomach build.

When I realize my hands have fallen limp at my sides, I reach up for the nape of his neck, curling my fingers into his hair. The hair that I have not been able to stop thinking about since I ran my fingers through it a few weeks ago. He guides us to the railing and pushes my back against it.

I come up for air, the wind blowing into my face as I tilt my head back. This time, I go back in gently, my teeth skimming his bottom lip. He smiles into the next kiss; even when his warm mouth touches mine, I can still feel him smiling.

God, we're barely even kissing anymore as we just smile at each other like goofy high school kids, and I love it. One of his hands snakes around my waist, pulling me into him, my dress getting caught in the wind.

"You're too good," he murmurs, kissing along my jaw.

"Hm?"

"This— You— You're too good, Wren. I think you might ruin me," he replies, his voice shaky. The heat of his mouth and his words send another rush of pleasure through me.

"Let's go inside," I pant, locking my eyes with his. He responds by picking me up and wrapping my thighs around his middle, the fireworks still exploding behind us while more burst behind my eyelids.

35
WREN

Falling

AS HE CARRIES me into the bedroom, I kiss at his neck, inhaling his cologne, and I've never felt more obsessive. That's the only way I can describe it. Being with him just makes me want more and more until it's all I become.

I'm completely and utterly *obsessed* with Miles Davis.

He drops me down onto the edge of the bed, my dress pooling beside me. I reach down and slip off my sandals as he unbuckles his belt before I lay back down, staring at the ceiling, waiting for whatever is going to happen.

This is a good idea, right? We could do this, get it out of our systems, and if this plan works, I'll never have to see him again. No matter how badly I want to.

"Are we doing this?" Miles asks, kneeling in front of me. I push up on my elbows and nod frantically, panting. "Wren. It's fucking great that you're enthusiastic, but I need you to tell me with your words."

"Yes. *Yes*. We're doing this, Miles," I say. He pulls the material of my dress upward, exposing me to him, but he hesitates at the foot of the bed. "You sure you don't need step-by-step instructions to find my clit because you seem to be struggling there, pretty boy."

He laughs, the sound deep and throaty as he presses a kiss to my thighs. "I'm sure I found it easily last time with how you came all over my fingers."

One of his hands wraps behind the back of my thigh, tugging it around his chest while the other splays across my breast. He kisses up my thigh until he gets to where I want him the most, but he doesn't go all the way. Instead, he makes his journey back down.

"Miles. If you're not going to put your mouth where I want it, I'm going to deal with it myself," I say after he brings his mouth to the edge of my panties for the third time without doing anything. I look down at him, but I can only see his hair, his face buried deep into my thighs.

"You're very impatient, baby," he mumbles against my skin. "I've been waiting for this since I met you, so I'm going to savor it."

He still doesn't move anywhere near my panties. I groan, standing up, and he falls back onto his heels, looking up at me. "You're taking too long."

I reach behind me, struggling slightly as I reach for my zip and drop my dress down to my ankles. His mouth falls open when he notices I'm not wearing a bra as I stand there in nothing but my pink panties. The cool chill of the wind hits me, and my nipples go hard. I roll my eyes, bend down, and start to unbutton his shirt.

"I can do it myself," he mumbles when he gets his voice back, blinking up at me.

"Can you?"

He shrugs off his shirt and takes off his jeans. I take my time to memorize the curves of his tanned chest with my fingers, feeling him tense beneath me. I'm about to make a snarky comment, but he brings his hands around my waist. The skin-to-skin contact makes all my nerves and senses sing, and I step backward slightly until the back of my knees hit the bed.

"You're so beautiful, Wren," he whispers, and he presses an open-mouthed kiss to my chest, just above my breast. "So, fucking, beautiful. I want to worship you."

"Then do it if you're not all mouth."

My voice turns into a yelp when he pushes me onto the bed. He climbs over me, looking at me with a sexy, evil smile. He kisses me once before slowly making his way down my body. His lips catch onto my nipple, eliciting a moan from my throat. He laughs against my stomach, and I dig my heel into his back as payback. His glorious journey down my body stops at the waistline of my panties.

He looks up at me as he hooks his fingers into the sides and pulls them down. I wiggle slightly as he pulls them over my ankles. I close my eyes, but he doesn't move. For a second, I think he's moved off the bed, but I open my eyes, and he's just staring at my bare body in front of him.

"That's it," he whispers. "When I touch you, Wren, you keep your eyes open. I don't want you thinking about anything else other than us right here. I need all your attention when I take care of you in the way that you need. Got it?"

I'm not going to get used to the fact that everything Miles does is just so he can take care of me. It isn't to ruin me or break me even more. It's like he wants stitch me back together with his bare hands and then look at his handiwork afterward. He just wants to look after me and I'm still trying to get used to the fact that there's a person in this world that actually wants to do that. For *me*.

"Do you understand what I'm saying, baby?" he asks, and I realize I've just been staring at him with his face between my legs.

"Yes," I whisper. He brushes his thumb against my clit, and I cry out. "Please."

He strokes me again, murmuring, "So polite, aren't you?"

Before I can reply, two fingers slip inside of me in one quick motion. I clench around him, the size of his fingers filling me up. I roll my hips as he pumps in and out of me faster. It's not the fireworks that make me see sparks fly, it's him. It's all *him.*

"Miles," I cry when his tongue covers my clit. His mouth and his fingers move inside me in a practiced motion as I squirm beneath him. The sounds that I can hear myself making mixed in with the slick sound of his fingers inside of me are obscene. His free hand braces on my thigh, keeping my legs clamped around his face as he devours me.

"Wait," I say, panting, and his fingers immediately pause as I pulse around him. "Go slower, please. I'm going to come if you keep doing that. I want this to last longer."

He listens to me, and he's a quick learner. Before I know it, my whole body is shaking with need as his mouth and fingers taunt me in the way I like. "Like this?" he asks, laying his tongue flat against my swollen clit slowly, and I moan. "That's it, baby."

I grip onto the sheets, turning my head to muffle my cries into the pillow. I can't remember the last time I had a real orgasm before Miles gave me one. He's so fucking good at this that it pisses me off.

"Such a good girl," Miles murmurs into my skin, "So wet for me. You're making it so easy to fill you with my fingers."

My heartrate skyrockets. "Miles, I—"

"Come on my tongue, baby," he murmurs, and I explode. My entire body trembles, and he continues licking me, tasting me as my eyes roll back in my head. I'm still trying to catch my breath as he kneels over me. "You're a sight, Wren. Just fucking perfect."

"You're not too bad yourself," I say, looking down at his length straining against his boxers. "Do you want to do something about that or just keep looking at me?"

"Such a smart mouth." He runs his thumb across my bottom

lip, shaking his head. "If I didn't know any better, I'd be starting to think that you just want me to shut you up with my cock down your throat."

I swallow at the image he's just painted because, *god,* he has a mouth on him. He might give off this golden retriever energy to everybody else, but I know that this is how he speaks to me in private, and I fucking love it.

"Is that what you want, baby?" he murmurs, still running his thumb against my lips.

I shake my head. "No, Miles, I want you inside me."

"You want— You—"

"Yes." I groan. "Stop pretending to be shy and fuck me. Fuck me however you want. I don't care. I need—"

"Someone to make you feel good and fuck that bratty little attitude right out of you?"

"*Yes.*"

He smiles to himself at the way he's managed to turn me inside out. He takes off his boxers, rolls on a condom, and teases his cock at my entrance. He's big and hard and so fucking ready for me, but he keeps teasing me like he wants to draw this out.

"Do you need me to guide you, pretty boy? Or do you know what you're doing?" I bite out, shaking my head as he continues to torture me.

He stares at the place our body is connected, slipping himself in and out of me so fucking slowly, filling me up just to pull back out. "So fucking needy," he mutters. I'm all for foreplay and edging, but this is where I draw the line. I feel like I've been waiting for years for this moment, but he's right in front of me and he's not giving me *everything.*

I shift up the bed and grab his shoulders so he's beneath me. "What are you doing?" he asks when I rub myself over his length, and he hisses. I coat his dick with my wetness as he shifts beneath me, his hips bucking upward.

I roll my hips again, and he hisses. "I'm doing what you're clearly incapable of."

"I was trying to savor it."

"Savor it, my ass. When I tell you to fuck me, I'm expecting you to do just that," I say, kissing him. I use one hand to guide him into me, sinking onto him, taking every inch slowly until my ass drops onto his thighs. "If not, I'll have to take matters into my own hands."

His hands circle my waist, and I lean forward, grinding on him. "I think I like it when you take matters into your own hands," he whispers, looking down to where we're connected. His fingers dig into my skin, moving me up and down as his hips buck and I meet his every thrust. "I want you to use me. Fuck me until you get what you need, baby."

If I knew he would be so generous in the bedroom, I would have taken the initiative a long time ago. I do exactly as he says, riding him hard as his hands and mouth brand me everywhere. I want nothing more than to be in this moment with him, tethered to him, close to him, and I could even excuse the hickeys if he gives me more.

We move in sync as he guides my hips around him, moving in circles and forward and backward. I don't think I could think of coherent words if I tried, so I let myself get lost in him, the sound of our moans filling the room.

He thrusts into me deeper, his pace quickening as he leans forward to fit my breast into his mouth. I moan his name louder than I expected and press my clit to his skin, chasing the release. I greedily grab onto his hair, shoving his face deeper in between my tits as his hips thrust forward into me while he whispers into my skin.

"You feel so good."

"Shut up," I whisper back, breathless and exhausted. "If you keep talking, I'm going to come again."

He chuckles, sucking my nipple into his mouth. "It's almost like that's the whole point."

He keeps talking to me even when I tell him to stop, and I've never been with someone who is so vocal during sex. He's not just quiet and makes me do what he wants. He tells me what makes him feel good, he compliments me, and his moans are the hottest sounds I've ever heard.

The high ripples through us at the same time as I clench around him, his name slipping out of my mouth. His thrusts become sloppier as his orgasm soars through him, and he groans. Sparks burst behind my eyes as I collapse on his chest.

"I don't think I'm going to be able to skate anymore if my legs don't work," I pant, propping myself up on my forearms on his chest. He laughs and kisses me on the forehead, our breathing still heavy as he wipes my hair out of my face.

After we settle down, I slip out of the bed to pee. To think. When I look in the mirror, I see a puffy-faced Wren blinking back at me. I almost want to laugh at how insane this feels. I should be more concerned. After resisting him for so long, I finally succumbed.

This could be the start of something dangerous. Something all-consuming. Something that we'll both get attached to. A habit I won't be able to kick. The distraction that I can't afford.

I COLLAPSE beside him again onto my back for what feels like the hundredth time. Only this time, I can actually feel myself falling asleep. It's well into the morning now, and small slithers of sunlight are starting to peek through the windows.

I look over at Miles for a second, watching his heavy breathing subside.

The weight of the day comes crashing down onto me. I knew

that if we did it once, we wouldn't want to stop. And we've done it plenty of times in several different places tonight alone.

I roll over onto my side, my back facing him.

"Miles?" I ask. He responds by wrapping his hand around my stomach, pulling me into him, his head nestled in my shoulder. "I'm scared."

"Of what?"

I swallow. "I think I'm falling for you."

"I know," he whispers, pressing a kiss to my shoulder. "I've been falling for you for a long time, princess."

"So, now what?"

"If you fall, I'll catch you. That's the way this works."

Tears sting my eyes, and I try my hardest to hold it together. "You promise?"

He hums against my skin. "I promise."

I know his words should help. That they should erase all the fear I have about trusting someone again, but they don't. I'm hopeless when it comes to Miles, and falling for him might be the stupidest thing I can do right now. Well, it would feel stupid if it didn't feel so damn good.

36
MILES + WREN

"I'm your idiot."

MILES

> Where are you?

WRENNY

Went for an early swim. I'm going to read at the beach before our flight.

> Am I invited to come read with you?

WRENNY

If you mean to stare at me while I read, then no. I just want to be alone for a bit.

Is that okay?

> Of course, it is.

> Is everything okay with us?

WRENNY

Of course it is.

I don't know what I was expecting to happen this morning, but it wasn't to wake up in bed alone.

There is no doubt that we both had a good night last night, so Wren running off from me was not expected. I know she's probably got all in her head and let the last week's worries crash down on her when they don't need to. I don't know how many more times I have to tell her and prove to her that I'm right there with her in whatever she's feeling because I am.

Maybe sleeping together was a dumb idea. As good as it was at the moment, we both have a lot to deal with right now. With the pressure on Wren from her sister and my own struggles with trying to get back my captaincy on the team, complicating our relationship is the last thing either of us needs.

Our flight isn't until tonight, and I have no idea what to do with myself until she comes back. I tried calling her, but she clearly doesn't want to be disturbed. Usually, I'd push her on this, but I have a strong feeling that she doesn't want to be pushed right now.

I catch a cab into town to a good bar-restaurant so I can let myself think. I know she's at the beach closest to the hotel, and the best thing I can do is to give her space to figure out what she wants. Whatever the fuck that is.

I'm not surprised when I walk into the bar and it's completely deserted. It would be crazy for anyone to be up this early on New Year's Day anyway. The air inside is thick with the energy of last night, and the bartender is nursing a hangover as he wipes down the counter. I knew my fake ID would be accepted in a place like this, so he doesn't look twice when I take a seat and ask for a soda.

I stare at the soda, my fingers tracing patterns in the condensation on the glass. My mind won't stop spinning. The drinks are right there, and it would be so easy. Just one shot to take the edge off.

I've worked too hard to fuck it up now.

I look around, the shadows of the bar feeling like they're closing in on me. The polished wood of the bar, the clinking of bottles as the bartender restocks, the faint hum of a distant television. It's all too familiar and too tempting. I can almost taste the burn of whiskey on my tongue and feel the warm numbness spreading through me.

I grip the edge of the bar, my knuckles whitening. The urge to order a drink claws at my insides, a restless itch that won't go away. I know it would only take a moment, a simple word to the bartender. Just one drink to make everything fade, to silence the chaos in my head.

I pull out my phone and flick through my photos as a distraction. My entire camera roll has been consumed by Wren the same way my brain has.

I've always been a picture-taking person. I love having these kinds of memories on my phone to look through over the years. Whenever I post any pictures of Wren and me, my followers go insane as if we're the new celebrity couple. It's got to the point where I'm basically a Wren Hackerly fan page, and I love it.

One of my first pictures of her is when we went to meet up at the gym one cold morning. I forgot to give her my keys before I told her to go to the car so I could pee quickly. When I walked back out, she was standing at the side of my truck with the most ridiculous look on her face. Her hair was braided into two pigtails, and she was wrapped in a huge puffer jacket, a beanie, and a scarf while she sulked at the camera as I snapped pictures of her. "It's for the memories," I said, and she pushed me, almost making me topple over in the snow.

I catch myself smiling and don't bother to hide it.

I have tons of candid pictures of her in the library, at the rink, in my room, and in her car. And my favorite picture of us: a candid taken by Kennedy on Christmas Day. In the photo, I'm leaning on the sink, drying the dishes while Wren washes them, but the picture is a small moment caught where we both look at each other, smiling as she passes a dish to me. Kennedy sent it to me on Instagram, and I didn't get it until I was in bed that night. *To add to the photo album for your kid*s, the message read.

Another of my favorite photos is the one we took when it was snowing. She's straddling me, wisps of her blonde hair falling out of her beanie as she smiles at me. It isn't one of those fake smiles she gives to the camera when we're in public, but it's one that she reserves just for me. In contrast to the white snow covering the background, Wren looks like she's in screaming color, and I didn't want anyone else to see it, so I've kept it to myself. My girl is so gorgeous it almost hurts.

In all the ways that count, she's still my girl, and her running away from me isn't going to change that. Being with her this week has stopped this constant orbit that I have been in, trying to get her to pull me into her. To get her to notice. But when that happens, she pushes me back out again and I'm stuck circling around her.

I sit there, scrolling aimlessly through my camera roll, smiling to myself like a loon. I'm so caught up in listening to her laugh that I don't notice the tall, dark-haired guy who sits next to me. He looks around my age, maybe a little younger, but definitely not allowed to be drinking.

"Is that your girlfriend?" he asks, nodding toward my phone. Instinctively, I lock my phone and turn it face down on the table.

"Yep. I think," I reply, but my voice sounds distant. The drinks must be getting to me, and I'm too far in to stop.

"What do you mean, 'you think'? Is she or not?" He looks at me with kind eyes. His features seem boyish and friendly, a lot like Carter's. A huge part of me is telling me not to talk to strangers, but there's something about him that's so familiar. I gesture to the bartender for a drink

"Do you want to hear a story?"

WREN

As soon as I opened my eyes this morning, I knew I had to get out of that room. I have to stop pretending like this is my life. That living off room service and good sex was my lifestyle. I thrive off routines, not whatever this is.

I need to be in the rink, in the gym, training and eating well. I need to get my head on right so I can tell Austin to suck it up and tell Mom about her pregnancy. My mind hasn't been the same since last night, and I hate how out of control I feel. How helpless. So I got my ass up, showered, and got myself down to the beach to try to help settle my brain.

I know leaving without saying a proper goodbye probably pissed him off, but I didn't expect him to be gone too. I came back to the room, started packing up our things, and an hour went by with no text. Maybe he's taking some time for himself, too, which is understandable. I wouldn't blame him, but I at least thought he'd tell me if he was leaving.

The rapid knock on the suite door drags me away from my thoughts.

The door swings open as I cross the living room to answer it. My heart drops through my ribs as I take in the sight in front of me. An elderly black lady in a flower sundress stands in the doorway with a very sad and very drunk Miles on her shoulder.

My stomach turns.

This is the first time I've seen him drunk in months. The lady looks around the room before her eyes settle on mine and they soften. I rush over to them, pulling Miles's weight off her. He's sweaty and a lot heavier than I remember. He sinks into me, and I can smell the alcohol on him. It's so strong I'm sure he could start a fire.

"I'm so sorry to bother you. He was wandering around, and

he said that he was staying here. You're Wren, right?" the lady asks in a thick Southern accent. I nod, swallowing the lump in my throat. "Okay, good. He might not look like it right now, but he said some really nice things about you. Take care of him."

"I'm sure he did," I say as I look down at him, his face buried into my chest. "Thank you so much."

I try to keep calm as I walk with Miles's arm over my shoulder, but my mind and my heart are racing. He's avoided my eyes since he got in here, and I don't know how to make this better for him. What to say. I know he wouldn't drink unless he had a reason to, which is probably my fault for leaving this morning.

He stands, leaning against the sink even though I've told him to sit down, when I return to the bathroom with some water and painkillers. He takes a few pills and chugs half the bottle of water.

His movements are so slow and jerky, but I rub his back as he bends down to the floor, leaning over the toilet and throwing up. My stomach flips as I kneel next to him, rubbing his back in smooth circles while he leans his head on his arm on the toilet seat.

"It's okay. Everything is okay. Just let it out," I murmur. He doesn't say anything, just mumbles indistinctly as he sits back up. "You're okay, Miles."

He groans as he sits up. I pull his arm around my shoulder and wrap my hand around his middle to help him stand up. "C'mon, let's get you in the shower."

Like I expected, he doesn't reply; he just mumbles something in agreement. When he's able to stand, I stand across from him, and part of me wishes I couldn't see his face right now. Tears that are starting to dry stain his pale cheeks.

I inch closer, reaching my hand out to pull off his shirt. He helps me take off his shirt and his trousers, still staying quiet. I lean over to turn on the shower as he takes off his boxers and steps into it. He sits down, pulls his knees in, and hugs them close to his chest.

"I'm sorry. I'm so sorry, Wren," he mumbles as I run the shower over his hair and back. I place my hand on his cheek, rubbing my thumb under his eye, and he melts into my touch. "I'm trying to be good for you, I swear."

"I believe you. You don't need to be sorry. I shouldn't have run away," I whisper.

"I thought… I thought you hated me. That you regretted last night and that you didn't want me anymore. And I saw— I thought I saw Carter."

It feels like someone has taken a pin to my heart and deflated it. "We'll talk about this later, okay? We need to get you feeling better right now." He nods, some of the color coming back into his face as I run my hand through his hair. "I'm here, Miles. I've got you."

'You've got me?" he mumbles, and my heart tears.

"Yeah, I've got you, Miles. Always."

We don't talk as I help him to feel better. We don't talk about what happened. Why he went somewhere to drink or why he thought he saw Carter. I don't push him to tell me, so he doesn't bring it up. I ran away from the problem and so did he. We're clearly both to blame and have more important things at hand to deal with.

When we get back to Salt Lake, the winter air hits us as we run to find a taxi to take us back to our houses. The second my body warms up to the temperature in the taxi, we're already outside Miles's house, and I'm struck by another brush of cold air.

I almost forgot it was New Year's Day until I took in all the decorations in the house. Gold and silver banners hang from the ceilings. Beer cans and SOLO cups litter the floor. There's even a makeshift photo wall that I saw in Kennedy and Scarlett's pictures from last night.

They were not happy with me missing New Year's with them, but I convinced them to go to Xavier's party, and from the way Kennedy was cuddling up to one of Miles's teammates, Harry, I can tell they had a good night.

"Finally," Xavier exclaims when he sees me and Miles. "Dude, it's been hell without you."

"Can't talk. Head hurts," Miles mumbles, acting worse than he is. He sulks and brings his drama queen ass up the stairs. I laugh, and Xavier pulls me into a side hug.

"What's wrong with him?" he asks, turning to me with a funny look.

"He's hungover. Kind of," I reply with a shrug. He laughs and walks in the other direction. I run up the stairs after Miles as he hides away in the bathroom.

"You're such a drama queen. You know that, right?" I shout to him as I fall onto my back on his bed. The tap stops running, and I make myself comfortable.

"I'm not. My head *does* hurt," he whines, walking back out of his room in nothing other than gray joggers. He sits beside me, brushing my hair out of my face. "Are you going to stay here tonight?"

"I think we both know that's not a smart idea," I say. "I haven't seen Scar and Kennedy in a week. I miss my girls."

He moves from over me and rests his back against the windowsill next to his bed. I push myself up next to him. "I'm sorry, Wren. About earlier. I was freaking out, and the last place I should have gone to was a bar. Especially after we've spent so much time trying to avoid me getting to that place again. I was feeling sorry for myself, and I let myself slip."

"It's okay," I whisper. "You're allowed to have bad moments, Miles. You're allowed to freak out and lose your head a little. It's my fault too. I know I shouldn't have just left. That was a shitty move on my part." I turn my head to him, but his eyes are already on me. "I meant what I said last night. I am scared. I know you said you're going to be there, but what if one day you're not? Trusting people is terrifying. I can't depend on someone for them to let me down. I really don't think I've got it in me to get heartbroken again."

He pulls my hand into his lap and encloses his hands around mine.

"That isn't going to happen. I'm all in. For real," Miles says, turning over my hand in his. He traces the lines in my palm with his finger.

"I've got qualifiers coming up. Then the competition season begins, and you've got the hockey team counting on you. If we do this and something happens, we're *both* going to go down-hill," I ramble, my voice wavering. "Aren't you worried about that?"

"I know that this is what I want. I want *you,* Wren. You're worth it."

"What if you change your mind?"

"I'm not going to."

"But what if you do?"

"I'm. Not. Going. To," he snaps.

He brushes a strand of hair out of my face, the small gesture making my stomach do that annoying flip thing it's done nearly every day since I met him. I nod, but it's still a hard pill to swallow. It can be easy to say you're not going to stop feeling this way, but it happens. I've seen it happen right in front of me.

"Why don't we take it light and breezy and see what happens? If this gets too much, we'll tell each other, okay?"

"Light and breezy," I echo. He nods. "That sounds stupid."

"You're stupid," he mutters. I narrow my eyes at him, and he sighs. "You're not stupid. I'm drunk. You're gorgeous."

I grip both sides of his face, shaking him slightly. "You're an idiot, you know that?"

He grins, and it's enough to make my heart stop. "Yeah, but I'm your idiot."

I can't help it.

I press my lips to his, and he practically steals the air from my lungs.

"Yeah, you are," I mutter into his mouth.

He holds out his pinkie to me. "Promise?"

"You want me to promise that you're my idiot?" He nods, and I roll my eyes, linking my pinkie with his. "Promise."

37
WREN

He fucking winks at me

IF SOMEBODY HAD TOLD me a year ago that I'd be watching my sort-of-boyfriend play ice hockey, for *fun* and not be complaining, I would've laughed in their face. But that's exactly what I'm doing, and I have the stupidest smile on my face.

I've always thought hockey was a cool sport. I even tried it out a few times in middle school, but it was the boys and the typical culture that threw me off sticking with it. There were too many rules that I didn't understand, and I was too focused on skating to get into it.

After I finished practice, Miles insisted that I come to watch him practice. He's been having FaceTime calls with my dad, helping him get back into the swing of things, which they're both loving. It turns out my dad has a lot more knowledge and experience than he's let on. I think he was nervous that Miles wouldn't want to take any of his advice, but he's been more than willing.

The girls and I are sitting behind the bench; Scarlett is on one side of me, her feet up against the board, Kennedy on the other, her legs crossed, drawing on her iPad, and I'm in the middle, strangely very invested in the game. I put my feet up to the board, leaning back as they huddle together while Coach Tucker explains some very confusing tactics to them.

Maybe it's just because I've never seen Miles play in person. Or maybe I'm just finding an excuse rather than admitting that I could watch him here all day as he shouts at people on the team.

He hasn't regained his captain status yet, but he's acting like it. He's barking out orders, getting himself riled up as he takes off his helmet to run his hands through his hair. I never thought this could turn me on, but the more time I spend around him, the more he continues to prove me wrong. It's getting harder to pretend that everything he does isn't attractive.

He looks so at home on the ice. It's like he just belongs there, and I couldn't be happier for him.

"Are you *actually* enjoying this?" Scarlett asks, completely horrified.

"I think I am," I admit, unable to hide the smile on my face.

"Dick-whipped," Kennedy murmurs, not looking up from the sketchbook she has on her iPad.

"I'm not," I say back to her, but she shrugs. I turn to Scarlett. "I know Jake is an asshole, but didn't you ever feel that way about watching him play? I mean, all hockey players are hot without even trying."

She laughs. "God, no. I didn't feel anything for him other than the way he did when he was inside me. I never went to see him practice. Those weren't a part of the terms and conditions of our arrangement."

"And what exactly was your arrangement?" Kennedy asks.

"The same as it always is," Scarlett says. "We were just sleeping together, but when he started to parade me around because of my family, I called it quits. That doesn't mean it didn't hurt when he cheated on me. That fucking sucks no matter who the person is."

"I'm still really sorry about that. He's just an awful person," I say, remembering the way he acted at Sophia's house for the interview. The way his slimy gaze has landed on us too many times today. "You don't have to be here if you don't want to, you know? If seeing him is hard."

"It happened a long time ago, Wren. I'm over it but thank you." She sighs, leaning back in the seat and crossing her arms against her chest. "Besides, I like watching your boyfriend shout at him."

We all look back to the ice, and Jake pushes Miles in the chest, but he doesn't fall back. Instead, he pushes back, causing Jake to fall into a few other people on the team like dominoes.

"You better watch your mouth, Callahan," Miles warns. His loud, deep voice echoes off the walls of the arena, and it runs right through my body.

"What are you gonna do?" Jake retorts. I inch closer toward the boards, trying to see them better. "Your girlfriend's watching. You wouldn't want her to see you get your ass handed to you, would you?"

Miles steps closer to him; my heart is racing, but Coach Tucker holds his stick between them, pushing them apart. "You guys better keep it friendly or else you'll *both* be on the bench or the second line."

I can hardly see their faces, but I'm assuming they're glaring at each other as they skate away, getting ready to do the drills Coach Tucker has asked them to do.

"Also," I say, turning to the girls, trying to keep my voice low as I resume our conversation. "He's not my boyfriend. I don't know what he is, but we've never actually talked about real labels."

"Maybe you should before your manic brain starts to think of every possible thing that could go wrong," Scarlett says, digging into a packet of M&M's.

"Believe me, I've already started doing that," I mutter.

"Do you *want* him to be your real boyfriend?" Kennedy asks.

"I want everything that comes with having a boyfriend. But

we're both so busy." I explain. "I just don't think I'm emotionally and physically available for a relationship right now."

"But are you physically and emotionally available for a fake one?" Scar asks.

I sigh. "It's different when it's fake. There are no real feelings at stake, and we know we have to make it work if we want to get what we want. When that becomes real, there'll be more dependency and commitment."

"Wren. I'm sick of you saying that your feelings aren't real because they are," Scar says. "You've slept with him. Correct?" I nod. "And you somehow find his personality charming?" She grimaces, and I nod again. "And he looks after you, you look after him, and he's not the worst company to be around?" I nod. Again. "So what are you so afraid of?"

"Of it not working out," I blurt out. "Of him realizing that I'm not what he wants."

"I hate to sound like a cliché," Ken starts, "but isn't it better to have tried than not to have tried at all?"

"In movies, TV shows, and books, yes. But these are my *real* feelings, and there's a very *real* possibility that if this becomes more serious, he'll realize that this isn't going to work out," I say, feeling the weight drop off me the second the words pass through my lips. "We're just taking it light and breezy."

"Ah, yes," Kennedy says in her posh British accent. "The classic *light and breezy*. What are you? Advertising a summer drink at Florentino's? As a romance writer, you couldn't think of anything better to determine your relationship status?"

We all laugh at that, and I force myself to bury those feelings down for a time when I can actually process them. Competition season qualifiers are coming up soon, and I need to work on perfecting my routine with Darcy.

We watch the team go through their drills, Miles taking the lead once again. I can't tell if he just enjoys telling people what to do or if it's actually part of his role.

They start to play a quick game, zipping up and down the ice. It's hard to keep track of who is who with the amount of gear they have on, so I'm only guessing. Kennedy has finally put down her iPad, and Scar is doing the thing where she's pretending that she doesn't care, but I can hear her muttering under her breath every time Miles's team misses the shot.

When Miles gains control of the puck at one end of the ice, he hardly looks up as he dodges the opposite team, moving quickly and efficiently. He looks so fucking hot as he does it. The other team has basically given up at this point, not even trying to defend his shot. But right before he has the perfect opportunity to get the puck into the goal, he maneuvers closer to where we are sitting and picks up his stick, pointing it right at me, and he winks.

He fucking winks at me.

Dimples popping out and all.

I almost die.

"This one's for you, baby," he says before regaining control of the puck again and hitting it straight into the net, right past Harry.

Half of me wants to scream in embarrassment as the rest of the team laughs, and the other half of me wants to get down onto the ice and kiss that stupid grin off his face. Instead, I sit there and smile at him, feeling on top of the world.

When they go back to playing, Scarlett leans into me, whispering, "Whether he did that for show or not, that boy is head over heels for you, babe."

In some weird way, I think she might be right, and I'm right there with him.

38
MILES

Whatever it takes

SLEEPING the night before a game is the same as trying to go to sleep the night before Christmas. I haven't had this feeling in such a long time. Last season, it was exhilarating, but nowhere near as much as this.

Since we came back from Palm Springs, I've been training like crazy to get back into shape for this season, and the games we've played so far have been going well. I know we've got to keep working hard to make our way through the tournaments to the regional championships, but I'm more than happy to put in the work. Our game tonight is the first of the critical February matchups, and I'm committed to putting in my all like I have been these past few weeks.

There's a certain type of rush in the crowd, and having the first years' experience for the first time makes this more thrilling.

Weirdly, my mom's message has been comforting. Her birthday is coming up in a couple of weeks, so I know I'll have to speak to her again at some point. Knowing that she's keeping track of my games and has been looking out for me has been nice since I saw her over Christmas. It's good to have her back in my corner even if talking to her is still hard.

We all huddle in the tunnel, psyching ourselves up to play. Most of the team rough each other up a little, bumping their chests together and howling. Others take a moment to pray to their god to guide them through the game. Gray, Harry, Xavier, and I stand in a huddle, working out the logistics of the game. We had a team meeting earlier in the sports classroom to work on tactics, in which we looked at game tapes to plan how to improve.

I'd be lying if I said I wasn't nervous. I know how important my position is on the team, and I can't afford to mess it up. The last few games have been perfect, and we're getting closer to the regional semi-finals. If I mess this up, they're going to blame me because they know how in my head I've been. I'm the weakest link right now according to them. I have to lead us to victory. For myself. For Wren. And for Carter. He's the only reason I'm back out here doing what I love.

"Don't fuck this up, Davis," Jake mumbles as he walks past our huddle, jabbing his stick into my side. Since the fight at the playoff game, he's gone back to his usual self, annoying me at any chance he can get. I ignore his stupidity and turn back to the guys.

"As long as we play our best, that's all that matters, right?" Harry asks, looking between us. He's got the most worried look on his face like he does before every game. I don't know why he gets so nervous. He's the best goalie our team has ever had. Xavier bumps him in the shoulder playfully.

"Drayton is an easy beat," Xavier says. "Out hustle, out work, out think, out play, and out last."

We all nod, chanting along with him. We've been doing these rituals for as long as I can remember. Just saying encouraging words and affirmations helps us get our heads in the game. It works like magic. That, and my pre-game playlist that helps me when I sit in the locker room with my head down and try to focus on something else.

"Whatever it takes," Grayson shouts at the top of his lungs; this time, all the guys join in with the chant.

"Whatever it takes!"

I recite lyrics in my head to keep me relaxed as we stand in the tunnel. Everybody cheers and chants over the commentator as they introduce the line-up for the visitors' team. We start to make our way out of the tunnel as they call out our names, and we take our positions on the ice.

I stand in the right wing, trying to focus on my breathing as they play the national anthem. I attempt to ignore the tightness in my chest and close my eyes. Flashes of our last game with Carter cross my mind. I can see him skating around the ice in celebration after everyone left. "We fucking did it, Davis!" he shouted, patting me on the back.

My helmet suffocates me, but I keep on breathing. I can do this. I *have* to do this. For Carter.

When the national anthem is finished, I look up into the stands and see her. Wren's sitting down, wearing my jersey, which she stole the other night. She sees me and smiles wide. I swear my heart almost falls right out of my chest. Kennedy sits beside her, smiling too, but Scarlett frowns. I tear my focus from them when the whistle blows.

Whatever it takes.

"I JUST CAN'T GET over that shot. It was, like, completely legendary," Kennedy exclaims for the hundredth time.

Wren, Scarlett, and Kennedy invited themselves over to my place after the game, and I couldn't say no. I'd have rather gone out for food with my girl and explained to her how hockey works a million times, but I don't mind hanging out with our friends. Gray, Harry, and Xavier tagged along too, and I'd get better luck trying to take a kid from a theme park than get them out of my house.

While we were in Palm Springs, both of our friend groups got a lot closer without us, which is good. I kind of like the way our friends merge together with how different everyone is, but I love it. Despite how much they've hung out, Kennedy is still not over the way hockey works and how my shot wasn't at all "legendary."

I was able to get in two goals while Xavier and Gray got one in each. Gray needs to learn how to chill more on the ice because he was in the penalty box for half of the game. We all helped each other assist along with Tyler and Bryan. Overall, it was a really good game. I thought we were guaranteed a shutout in the first period, but Drayton were a lot better than they were last season.

Today's game seemed to ease some of the pain in my chest. My first game back was hard, and I struggled to flow with the team like I did last season, but something shifted today. I didn't feel that suffocating pressure or get distracted by thoughts of Carter. If anything, thinking about him only pushed me to play better, and that's the feeling I've been searching for for months.

"Calm down, Ken. You're going to boost his ego even more," Wren says, giving me a small smile. She leans her head on my shoulder as I wrap my arms around her waist while she sits in my lap, now wearing the shirt I got her for Christmas. Across from us, Kennedy and Scarlett give each other knowing glances.

"I don't mind it one bit," I say proudly. I turn to Wren. "It's not like you've even *told* me congrats since the game was over."

Wren's face turns red at my teasing. She *has* said well done. Once with a huge hug and a kiss when she ran up to me when the game ended and then again when we got home, on her knees in my bedroom with my hand in her ponytail.

"It was a good game, though. It helped that they couldn't play for shit." Gray laughs. "They looked like they only just learned how to skate."

Wren snorts. "You spent more time in the sin bin than you did on the ice, so can you even say that?" she retorts, seeming genuinely disappointed with his performance, and everyone laughs as she shakes her head.

I look at her, unable to hide my grin and the raging hard-on I'm sporting. "What did you just say?"

She tilts her head. "What? About the penalties?"

"Nah," I say, shaking my head. "I want to hear you say it again."

"You want me to say sin bin again? Is this a new kink of yours, Davis?" she asks, innocently batting her eyelashes at me.

"It might be," I admit, having to readjust my jeans just at the thought. I lower my voice and groan. "Fuck me."

"I can make that happen." She bites softly on my ear. I press my fist to my mouth and groan again. I'm convinced she is determined to torture me for as long as we both live. Everything about us now feels so natural. She fits in so well with my friends, and the way she hasn't been able to stop touching me since we left campus makes me think that maybe I'm not the needy one in the relationship anymore.

"Please don't," Kennedy cuts in, grimacing.

"Yeah, please don't," Harry agrees, dismissing us with a wave of his hand. "Can we move on past the game? As much as I love hockey, I don't want to talk about it all the time." He takes a swig of his beer. "How about truth or dare?"

All the girls look at each other and smile.

Scarlett groans. "Been there and done that. Not the smartest idea with this bunch."

"Why not?" Harry asks, clearly oblivious to the 2021 Christmas Incident.

"Because it brings out a lot of shit that no one needs to know about. Like how Scarlett had sex in the business classroom and how these two can't keep their hands off each other," Kennedy explains with a waft of her hand in our direction.

"That is not true," Wren retorts, sliding off my lap and trying to sit beside me, but there isn't much space, so half her leg is still on my thigh anyway. She pulls her hands in between her thighs and squeezes them together. "See?"

"See, what? That you can last two seconds without making out?" Kennedy says, raising her eyebrows. "It's gotten a *lot* worse since you came back."

"I second that," Scarlett announces, but she's grinning.

"Me too," Xavier and Gray say in unison.

Gray stands up and walks toward the kitchen, no doubt to raid my fridge. He's going to be disappointed when he notices that Wren threw out all of our junk food. He fiddles with the speaker and changes the song to *Save Your Tears* by the Weeknd.

"Whatever. At Christmas, it was a dare. It's not like we were doing it for no reason," I say, looking over to Wren, who has the biggest smile on her face.

"Exactly. At least someone agrees with me." She points at me, wiggling her finger in my face. Instinctively, I bite at the end of her finger before gripping her wrists and kissing them. She laughs, her pretty cheeks glowing as she slides back into my lap. God, I can't remember the last time I was this happy.

"You two are impossible," Scarlett grumbles, slouching back in her seat and throwing her hands up in defeat.

"Okay," Harry draws out, looking at me and Wren before turning to Kennedy. "Ken, truth or dare?"

"Didn't we just say we're not playing that?" Wren asks, bending over me to look over at Harry.

"Yeah, *we* are, but not with you two," Harry replies, returning his attention to Kennedy. Wren nods and snuggles herself deeper into me. "Truth or dare?"

"Truth."

"If you could have three wishes, what would they be?" We all start laughing at how different this question is compared to Evan's ones at Christmas. Kennedy rolls her eyes, pushing her long, curly hair over her shoulder.

"I'd wish for endless film in my camera, an endless supply of ice cream, and... a person, like an assistant, who can tell me endless conspiracy theories so I'd never run out." Kennedy lifts her chin up and grins.

"That was a boring answer," Harry says.

"It was a boring question," Kennedy argues, raising her eyebrow. Harry shakes his head with a laugh.

"Why are they all endless?" he asks.

"What would be the point of having wishes for them to run out?" Kennedy responds but Harry shrugs. She leans up in her seat, trying to peer over into the kitchen. "Grayson! Truth or dare?"

Gray leans in the doorway of the kitchen, giving Kennedy *that* look that he does when he's trying to flirt without really flirting. It would be sleazy and gross, but he's got the face of a baby, so he just looks stupid. "Truth."

Kennedy pulls her bottom lip between her teeth, thinking for a moment before saying, "What is one thing I don't know about you?"

"How much time I spend thinking about you," Gray drawls. All the girls gag. Harry coughs, punching his chest a few times like his comment sent dust straight into his throat. "I'm kidding, Ken, jeez. Anyway, it turns out Evan is not the only child prodigy. I play piano too."

Scarlett's eyes widen. "Evan plays piano?"

Gray nods. "Yeah, I caught him once in the music rooms on campus. Apparently, he was born into it like me. But he takes it a lot more seriously. I do it to impress the ladies." Gray winks at Wren, and she snorts.

"Thank you, Gray, for that pocket of information about Evan that I can now use against him," Scarlett replies, beaming.

"How are you going to use the fact that he's a pianist against him?" I ask.

She shrugs. "I dunno. I just will."

I swear those two will kill each other one day.

Gray turns to me and says, "Davis. Truth or dare?"

Wren looks up at me, her blue eyes dancing with mischief. "Dare," I say, turning back to Gray. He quickly chugs the bottle of water that has materialized in his hands.

"Pick a vegetable," he demands.

"What?"

"Just pick one, you dimwit," he retorts.

"Fine. Celery."

"Ooh, bad choice, Davis," Gray tuts. He goes into the fridge, rifling around for said vegetable before holding up a stick of celery. He throws it to me, and I catch it with one hand. "Since your beautiful girlfriend, here, threw out all your good food, you can brush your teeth with that and see if she'll kiss you."

I think about it for a minute, but with the way my girl's eyes light up at the suggestion, I can't say no. I do as he says, feeling disgusting as the green stick rubs against my teeth. I don't know why I chose it. It's the worst vegetable. The girls look at me in horror, and Wren laughs, finding joy in my pain.

"You are *not* kissing me with that mouth, Davis," Wren demands, holding her finger in my face at a distance. I make a pouty face at her, and she grimaces.

"Baby, you're forgetting that there's a million different ways I can get you off without my mouth. But trust me, you'll be begging to kiss me by the time I'm done with you," I whisper for only her to hear. She rolls her eyes at me, pushing me away again.

The game continues around us as Kennedy asks Harry, "Truth or dare?"

"Dare," Harry replies, leaning forward to look at her better.

"I was kinda hoping you'd say truth," Kennedy says, a smirk playing on her lips.

"Why?"

"So then I could ask if you were single or not." Everyone, except those two, exchange glances, smiles creeping up our faces. I knew there was something going on with them, but they're clearly both too chicken-shit to do anything about it. Besides, they seem like good friends.

"Smooth, Ken," Wren mutters under her breath when Scarlett looks at her with wide eyes. Harry still hasn't recovered from the question, and his mouth is open wide, blinking at Kennedy.

"He's single," I say. He's usually fine with girls, but for some reason, I think Kennedy scares him a little. "*Very*," I add, watching the confusion on his face.

"This feels like a perfect opportunity to play seven minutes in heaven," Xavier suggests, trying to stifle his laugh. "Should we spin a bottle? I'm not playing, obviously."

"We don't need a bottle," Kennedy says happily as she stands up. She waltzes over to Harry and grabs his hand as he blinks up at her, pulling him away from the living room.

"Do you think that's a good idea?" Scarlett asks quietly. "I'm in real protective older sister mode."

"He's a good guy," I say, reassuring her.

"You better be right," Scarlett says, pinning me with a Kubrick stare. "Or I'll kill you."

I raise my hands in surrender as Wren smiles and stands up in front of me. "Leave him alone. Kennedy can handle herself. She completely flamed a guy at Coachella last year without our help," she says.

"I forgot about that," Scarlett laughs.

"What's this Coachella story?" Gray shouts from the kitchen.

"That's a story for another time," she shouts back before she pulls me up from my seat. "I want to see if what you said is really true."

Everyone groans as she drags me up the stairs to my bedroom. There are very few things I can say no to when it comes to Wren, so I follow her like the dumb puppy I am.

39
MILES

Boyfriend of the year

I CAN'T REMEMBER the last time I celebrated Valentine's Day.

It always felt like such a stupid holiday to me. Especially when you're single. No one wants to walk into Target to see Valentine's Day-themed banners everywhere when you've just been broken up with. No one wants their timeline to be flooded with pictures of people in love when their idea of being in a relationship is physically repulsive.

Well, I *used* to think it was a stupid holiday. Now, I think the gods have blessed me with the best girlfriend in the world, who is currently sprawled out on my bed like she owns it. I'd have her in my bed every night if I could, but she only stayed over last night because I picked her up from her semi-final competition yesterday. I spent the entire time during the competition on the literal edge of my seat, watching her glide and turn on the ice. I truly don't think I've seen anything more beautiful. She's worked her ass off for these competitions, and she competes in them like it's no big deal, coming out on top with flying colors because she's just that fucking good.

Wren's lying like a starfish on her stomach in her underwear and a tank top. She passed out the second we got in last night, and I'm almost too afraid to wake her. I bet she's exhausted from the competition, but it's almost eleven and I'm afraid she might not function if she doesn't wake up before twelve.

I set the breakfast tray down on my bedside table, smiling at the concoction I made. I did have to take some pointers from Evan, who scolded me in the kitchen as I prepared some pancakes, sausages, and eggs for Wren's breakfast-in-bed surprise. The pancakes don't look as heart-shaped as I had hoped, but they're something. I'm new to the whole boyfriend thing, but I think breakfast in bed and some hand-picked flowers are a good start.

Did my neighbor turn on their sprinklers when I picked daisies from his garden? Yes. Yes, he did.

Did I regret it? Not one bit.

Leaning forward, I poke Wren in the cheek. "Wren, baby," I say softly, stroking my thumb against her cheek to wake her. I don't know what it is, but watching her sleep makes me feel weird. Overwhelmed, almost. I just keep staring at her, and it's hard to believe that she's real.

"What?" she grumbles, shoving her pretty face into my bed sheets.

"Are you awake?"

"What do you think?"

I laugh, pushing on her shoulder until she turns around, lying flat on her back. She opens one eye, peeking at me, and I smile at her. She closes her eyes again, but she twists her mouth to the side like she's trying not to smile back.

She drops her arm over her face, clearly trying to hide herself from me. "Hi?"

I grin. "Hi."

She peeks at me through her fingers. "Stop watching me sleep, you weirdo."

"Then stop sleeping," I say, dragging her arm from her face, and she frowns at me. I glance at my bedside table and then back at her. Her eyes widen in shock, and I press a kiss to her cheek. "Happy Valentine's, sweet girl."

"Oh my god," she whispers, looking at the breakfast, then at the flowers, and then back at me. Her expression is priceless. "Miles, this is— I didn't— It's the fourteenth. Oh my god, it's the fourteenth."

I laugh, throwing my head back. "I'm glad you know what day it is."

She frowns. "I didn't know we were doing Valentines. I didn't get you anything."

I shrug. "You've been busy. It's okay."

She shakes her head violently. "No. It's not okay. You're my fa— real sort-of boyfriend and I—"

I wink at her. "Nice save."

"I didn't get you anything," she whispers, her shoulders dropping. I press a kiss to the corner of her mouth because I know she hates kissing me before she's brushed her teeth.

"Just consider it a congratulations for winning yesterday and a pre-celebration for when you win the whole damn thing," I say, shrugging.

"These are heart-shaped pancakes," she argues, pointing to her breakfast.

"You really think they're heart-shaped?"

"No, but I don't want you to feel bad."

"Look, I don't want to make you feel like you have to be all lovey-dovey and coupley because it's the fourteenth," I say, even though I know that's not what I want. I want to do all the embarrassing and cringey couple things with her just because we can.

"No, this is great. We can celebrate it as long as you let me get you a gift too," she says.

"Deal."

I SHOULD HAVE KNOWN that when Wren meant she was getting a gift for me, she was talking more about getting a gift for herself. I knew taking her to an actual bookstore would be a good idea since I never got to actually buy her books on our first date, but I didn't expect to be roped into buying every new rom-com that's on sale and letting Wren pick one out specifically for me.

"Oooh, this one's about a professional hockey player and his kid's nanny," she says, picking up a book and showing it to me. She flashes me the title for a second before turning it around to read the blurb and then just shoves it into the basket.

"What makes you think I'd enjoy that?" I ask as we continue walking through the shelves.

She just points at my outfit. "You. Hockey. The two things kind of go together," she says before turning back around. "Besides, it would be good to see where your future might take you in the fictional world of the NHL."

I grin. "Do you think I'm going to make it to the pros?"

"Miles, have you *seen* your stats? I only had a glimpse when I was stalking you, and I don't know how you don't make a bigger deal out of it. You definitely have bragging rights. You're a really fucking good player, and I have no idea how you haven't got signed on to anyone yet," Wren says, shaking her head.

Honestly, I have no clue either.

The reality is my odds aren't great.

I've got the stats to back it up, sure. So far, this season, I'm averaging 1.5 points per game, leading the team in assists, and my faceoff percentage is sitting at a solid 57 percent. But college hockey isn't the NHL. There are over 4,000 NCAA hockey players, and only about 300 of us get drafted each year. Of those, an even smaller percentage make it to actually play in the NHL. Most of us end up in the minors, grinding it out in the AHL or overseas.

Even if you're good, it's not just about stats. It's about

timing, luck, and being in the right place at the right time. And then there's the draft. The NHL draft is a beast of its own. You've got scouts watching your every move, analyzing your every shift. They're looking for the total package—skill, work ethic, potential, and a bit of that X-factor.

Recently, I haven't been giving anyone a reason to prove that I'm anything special, but I have enough confidence in myself and my skill that I'll be able to pull something off. I've worked way too fucking hard to give up now.

"Yeah, maybe," I say to Wren, slinging my arm over her shoulder and trying to seem more confident than I feel. "Even if I don't, I'll still have hockey in one way or another. And I'll have you. I think I'll live."

I know saying that is suggesting that we'll be together for years from now, but I mean it. In some way, I can see us going to hockey games together and going book shopping just for Wren to force-feed me a romance novel I don't want to read.

I sway us to the side. "What about you?"

"What about me? I'll be an Olympian before I'm twenty-five," she says easily.

"Someone's cocky."

She pins me with a look. "Confident."

"You could be competing for Team USA right now if you wanted," I say. She shrugs, and I narrow my eyes at her.

She sighs, her green eyes sparkling. "I think I've just stopped waiting for something magical to happen for some random day when a scout is going to find me and suddenly see the potential in me. Because, like you, the chances are slim, and I'm not delusional enough to think that just because I'm close to winning this year's championship that guarantees me entrance to the next Olympics." She takes in a deep breath, shaking her head as if to reorganize her thoughts. "I just... I just work so hard, you know? And I just think that the more I keep working, the more it'll pay off. And the more times that I get looked over for opportunities, it's just a better story to tell. And then people will realize I was right under their nose the entire time, and then I'll have this great success story. Tell you the best part?"

"What?"

"Even if I *don't* make it to the Olympics, every single moment I've had throughout my skating career will be worth it because I love what I do. If I get to skate for fun or compete and still write my silly books on the side, I'll be happy."

The smile she gives me now is pure bliss. She seems so sure of herself. So confident in every single thing that she does. What she's saying is realistic, and I don't think I've ever met someone who is so aware of both their potential and the realities of how it could play out.

"Do you think you'll publish your books?" I ask.

She shrugs, running her finger against the spine of the book in her hands. "Trust me, I'd love to see my name on the spine of one of these books in the store, but sometimes, I just want to keep all my work to myself. Like, hoard it and just keep it hidden from the world so no one can ruin it for me. When I have a story I *really* want to tell, like Gigi did, then maybe I'll consider it."

"Has anyone ever told you how brilliant you are?" I say in complete and utter disbelief of the woman in front of me. Her cheeks flush, and she brushes her hair out of her face.

She gives me a coy smile. "Once or twice."

I shake my head. "I'm being serious, Wren. I want to live inside your brain."

She scoffs. "Oh, no, you don't."

"I do."

"No, seriously," she says, lowering her voice as if she doesn't want anyone to hear. "There's very terrible thoughts up in here. It's just straight-up doom and gloom and self-deprecation with a sprinkle of delusion."

"I'm sure there's other things going on in there," I say, laughing. She blinks at me. "There must be something else that you think about."

She steps closer, looking up at me with a smile. "Hm. There's one other thing."

I swallow when that fucking dimple pops out. "What is it?"

"You."

If it's possible for a person's heart to fall right out of their chest, that's exactly what just happened to me. The thing about Wren is that she doesn't notice how important she is to everyone else in her life. She doesn't know that just being around her makes me feel better. She makes me feel like I can breathe again after years of holding my breath. If I could erase every person from her life that has made her feel unimportant, I'd do it in an instant. I think I'd do anything for this girl.

Of course, I don't know how to say that to her while she looks up at me, so I just lean down and kiss her and pray she lets me continue to prove to her that I'm the kind of person that deserves her.

40
WREN

Mommy issues? Me? Never

MOM

I need to see you.

THE SECOND I get a text from my mom, I know something is wrong. I don't know how, but I do. Maybe it's the fact that I felt a weird chill down my spine when I finished first in the regional finals for soloists at the end of last month. I've been working my ass off like a maniac, and I've hardly had a second to breathe over the last month and a half, and I'm a step closer to winning the national collegiate championships if all goes well.

I was expecting to come out on top, so I wasn't surprised when I did. Darcy greeted me by the boards with a bouquet of flowers, Miles came up to me and kissed me senseless in front of all the cameras, and my mom just sat in the stands. She didn't say a single word to me. She didn't even smile or whisper "congratulations" when I slipped past her. All she's thinking about is how well I'm going to be able to compete in regionals and the championships in the next coming weeks. It's all that's been on my mind, too, but with Miles taking over nearly every thought in my brain, I haven't been stressing out about it as much as I usually would.

Maybe I should.

Maybe that's what she wants to talk about. She's probably going to talk me into breaking it off with him to focus on my performance, and I can't blame her. I might think I'm doing good, and my scores reflect that, but that means nothing in my mom's eyes. I'm pretty sure she'll have the same bored expression on her face when I win Olympic gold.

I make my way to her house, and I can still feel that weird sensation running down my spine, but I can't figure out what's wrong. It's probably just nerves. Yeah, that sounds about right. I've hardly spoken to my mom since I've been so busy with homework and skating. I also haven't spoken to my sister in hopes that she'll realize that Mom doesn't know and she'll have to tell her about the baby herself. It's not like she'd be able to hide for much longer since the baby will be due in less than two months.

Mom's house is quiet when I get there, but that's nothing unusual. Two ex-divorcees living together constitutes a quiet home. The only time it's ever full of life is when my mom and I would have lunch by the pool, and she'd give me unsolicited advice until it made me so sick I'd have to go home and cry.

I've always felt off being here since the divorce. I know it's never been my home, but something else hangs in the air. It's like walking into a house that hasn't been used, loved, or had any visitors in years.

"Mom?" I call out. Nobody responds. I walk through the kitchen, and it's deserted. I wander through the bright living room and the den, and still, nobody is there.

When I get to the dining room, which leads to the backyard and pool, I spot the back of my mom's blonde head first. She's standing next to one of the lounge chairs, staring out to the pool.

When I get closer, I hear another voice. A female voice. I slide open the door, walking carefully out onto the patio.

"Austin?"

I don't know why I ask because I know it's her. My sister has always had the most striking features, and now, standing next to my mom I'm almost too shell-shocked to say anything. She's wearing leggings and a white top, her small baby bump showing. She's got my dad's brown hair and his brown eyes to match. I always wished I looked like her instead of taking after my mom so much. I used to think she was the most stunning person I had ever seen, and she still is.

"What are you doing here?" I ask, stepping closer to them.

"You didn't tell her," Austin says, and her voice cracks. *God.* I can't even remember the last time I heard her voice in person. It's been *years* since I've seen her, and the least I want is a hug hello. My mouth opens and closes, and my mom scoffs. "I asked you to do one thing for me, Wren, and you didn't do it."

My hands shake, and I bring them to my lips. "I-I'm sorry. I had a lot going on. I've been busy."

Mom turns around, her cobalt-blue eyes narrowing at me. "Too busy to tell me that your sister is carrying a baby? Too busy to call and check in once in a while? Too busy to take a free vacation with your boyfriend?"

I blink at her and press my nails into the palms of my hands, willing myself not to cry. "What are you talking about? I don't see how this is my fault."

"You think just because you're skating at college now, you can shirk your family responsibilities? Your sister trusted you with this, and you let her down," Mom explains.

"How are you mad at *me* about something that should never have been my responsibility?" I ask, but I don't know why I do. I shouldn't have run away. I shouldn't have pretended that it didn't exist and put my big girl boots on and told my mom the truth. Maybe the fallout wouldn't have been this bad if I did.

Austin looks down, her eyes filling with tears. "I thought you would help me, Wren. I can't believe you didn't tell her."

The guilt crashes over me like a wave. "I'm sorry, Austin. I really am. I just... I thought you would tell her yourself eventually, and I got caught up in other things."

I have the urge to tell them that I have a life too, but I know that won't get me anywhere. I'm starting to realize that maybe they've never cared about me and my life outside of skating. Maybe I've just been a pawn in some stupid game for years and it's taken me this long to notice it.

"You always think someone else will clean up your messes," Mom interjects. "Just like in skating, you rely on everyone else's hard work to make you look good."

"That's not true," I say, my voice barely a whisper. "I work hard. I've *always* worked hard. It's all I fucking do."

"Not hard enough," Mom says coldly. "Your sister is standing here, pregnant, and you didn't even have the decency to be honest with me."

"Why would I be honest with you, Mom? All you do is pretend. You pretend to care. Pretend to be there for me. Pretend that what you're doing is making me a better skater, but you don't even *care* about me," I shout. My voice shakes, and it's taking everything not to break down right now. "You've never once asked how I was doing or checked in with me *just because.* You just expect me to perform. Perform for you and be this perfect little skater that you think I am. I'm *not* perfect, Mom."

She holds her chin higher like my words have had no effect on her at all. "It takes skill, dedication, and time to be perfect, Wren. If you wanted to be, you would."

I let out an incredulous laugh. "What else do you want from me? What else do you want me to do? Please tell me, Mom, because it's killing me trying to figure it out. I always play by your rules. I always do what you say when you say it. I've always performed at my best to make *you* proud, and I don't know how long I can keep doing this until you realize that I'm never going to be perfect." Austin sits down like my words have knocked the wind out of her, and if I wasn't so full of energy right now, I would sit down too. "I convinced a hockey player to date me so we could get some more recognition for the team. I put myself out, did everything I could because you asked me to, and I don't do this *one thing* and the entire world is on my case. It makes no fucking sense."

My mom blinks at me, and her eyes narrow even more, a dangerous glint forming. "What did you say? About that boy?"

"I thought it would help. He's popular, and I thought if people saw us together, it would get more attention for the team," I say, and I sound stupid as fuck trying to explain it to her. "I thought that's what you wanted."

A cold, bitter laugh escapes her lips. "You really are desperate, aren't you? You really thought pretending to date some boy is going to make you a better skater?"

"I didn't do it to be better. I'm more than capable of becoming a better skater on my own. I did it for the *team*"—my voice wobbles—"I did it for *you.*"

She scoffs. "What makes you think that he'd even be interested in you for real?"

I feel the sting of her words deep in my chest.

"It wasn't like that," I mutter, "What we have is real now."

"*Real,*" she says, sneering. "Don't fool yourself. A boy like him would get bored of you in days. He's using you, Amelia, just like you're using him."

I can't hold back the tears anymore. They spill over, hot and uncontrollable. "That's not true," I say, but my voice is weak, and I can't believe my own words.

"One of the things I admire most about you, Wren, is how selfish you are," my mom says, her voice low and thick with condescension. "You always put yourself first. You do whatever it takes to push yourself to the top regardless of who you hurt in the process. You think this fake relationship is about helping the team? It's about making you look good, about getting the attention you crave. You got too caught up, and you've forgotten about the people who actually care about you."

Admire.

Admire, not love.

The words hit me harder than any blow. For so long, I thought my mom's harshness was her way of pushing me to be better. But now, I see it clearly—she's been using me to relive her own failed dreams, to recapture the glory she lost. Every critique, every manipulation, it was all for her. She doesn't think of me as her daughter. Wren her daughter and Wren the figure skater are clearly two different people to her, and I honestly don't know if I truly exist as my own person without skating sometimes.

I don't want that. I don't want to do this for her. I've always told myself I skate for myself because *I* want to do better. Because *I* want to be the greatest in the fucking world. Not for her.

I look at Austin, hoping for some support, but she's still looking down, silent and complicit. She looks pathetic. How can she just sit there and let my mom speak to me like that? Let her rip me apart like I'm not her daughter. The weight of it all crushes me, and I feel like I'm drowning.

"You're wrong," I whisper, my voice trembling. "I'm not selfish. I've been doing everything to make you proud and to live up to your expectations. But I see now that it's never been about me, has it? It's always been about you and your dreams."

Mom's eyes flash with anger. "How dare you? Everything I've done has been to make you the best. To give you the life I never had."

"No," I say, finding strength in my realization. "You've been using me to chase your own glory. I'm done living for your approval. I'm done being manipulated."

For a moment, there's silence. Then, with a final, cold look, Mom turns away. "You'll regret this, Wren. When you fail, and you *will* fail, don't come crying to me."

Austin's eyes are filled with tears, but she remains silent, caught in the middle of our storm. I turn to her, my heart aching. "I'm sorry, Austin. I truly am. I should have been there for you, but you staying here, taking her side, is pathetic. I know you won't realize it now, but I need you too."

She nods slightly, her tears mirroring mine. "I know. I'm sorry too."

THE DRIVE HOME feels longer than ever, each step a heavy burden as I replay the confrontation with my mom in my mind. Her words, like daggers, pierced through the armor I had built around myself, exposing the raw vulnerability I'd kept hidden for so long. And Austin's silence, her compliance with my mom's accusations, cuts me even deeper than her words.

As I step into the dimly lit apartment, Kennedy and Scarlett's concerned faces greet me, and just seeing them here eases the pain a little. I called them on the way back saying that something had happened, but I could hardly get the words out. The facade I had desperately tried to maintain crumbles at their concern, and I can't hold back the flood of emotions threatening to drown me.

Kennedy's arms envelop me as I collapse into her embrace, the weight of everything crashing down on me at once. The tears flow freely now, unstoppable, as I bury my face in her shoulder, the sobs wracking my body with each breath.

Scarlett rushes to my side, her touch gentle as she tries to offer words of comfort, but they fall on deaf ears. All I can hear are my mom's accusations echoing in my mind, each word a painful reminder of the love I had craved but never received.

"I thought... I thought I was doing everything right," I

manage to choke out between sobs, the words barely audible through the pain gripping my chest. "But it was never enough. It was never about me."

Kennedy's arms tighten around me, a silent gesture of support as I finally let go of the facade I had clung to for so long. It's only because I'm surrounded by my friends that I feel a glimmer of hope flicker to life within me.

But as the tears continue to fall, I can't shake the overwhelming feeling of being unlovable, unworthy of the love I so desperately crave. I feel utterly broken, the weight of my insecurities crushing me under its grip, like there's forever going to be a gaping hole in my chest. And in that darkness, I can't help but wonder if I'll ever be able to find my way back to the light.

41

MILES

Spinnin' out waiting for ya

"YOU'RE lucky that I haven't cracked your head open yet, Davis." Jake shouts another threat to me from the showers while I finish getting ready in the locker room.

Some of the team shout a "Yeah" in agreement, and the howling begins. *Again*. We've just finished another qualifying game, which we *almost* lost. It was a close tie until the last few minutes of the third period, and we managed to pull through. We're one step closer to the semi-finals next month.

On top of all this unnecessary shit from the team, I've got to go to my mom's fiftieth birthday party later, which I've been dreading all week. Clara has been verbally bullying me for the last week, making sure that I attend. She told me to bring Wren, too, but she's been busy with nationals, and I know that it would just stress her out rather than help her. We've hardly spoken over the last few weeks with us both being so busy with sports and college, and I don't blame her. I know what she needs to do to get in the zone, and I don't get in the way of that, so I've kept my distance. I didn't realize how difficult it would be to be dating another athlete with a season as competitive as mine and it's been a hard adjustment not seeing her every day like before. We still text, but it feels like there's still this disconnection between us like I'm not fully pulled in again.

"God, can everyone chill out? We didn't lose. In fact, we did the opposite," Tyler says with a sigh. They nod at me before dapping me up and walking past me.

"We *almost* lost because you acted like you were out of your fucking mind," Jake spits out, walking around from the showers.

"But we *didn't,* that's the whole point. Give him a break," Xavier retorts, drying himself off. Jake inches toward me, a nasty look on his face.

"I'm sick of giving poor Miles Davis a break. He needs to man up and get his head in the game," Jake shouts, squaring up to me. I'm sick of his shit. I tower over him and glare. "What are you gonna do, Davis?"

"You know exactly what happened last time we did this, Callahan," I say calmly. "Step the fuck back."

He stares at me for a minute, resisting to back down. Most of the team are gathered around us, ready for a fight to break out. Luckily for him, he steps out of my face and turns back. We both know it would be a stupid idea to fight and get suspended.

"Listen, we've got one more game closer to the semis," Coach begins, standing at the door of the locker room. "There's no point trying to blame each other. All you need to do is work together on doing better. Understood?"

"Yes, Coach," we all say in unison.

"Out what?"

"Out hustle, out work, out think, out play, out last," we all chant back.

I survive the rest of the time in the changing room, and a few more sly comments are thrown my way on the bus back to campus. Each game day with the team has become another opportunity for them to berate me, and I've gotten used to it. It's stupid when they complain because it doesn't affect my performance. The only thing I can think about is Wren and if something has happened to upset her.

I've become an easy target after losing Carter. After he died, the whole team was disappointed in me, but with Wren's help, I was able to turn that around. I can't shake the feeling that we've stopped talking as much because we're busy or if there's something else I'm missing out on. I know she'd tell me if something was wrong.

She has to.

I pull out my phone and shoot her a text.

> Hey, Wrenny. I miss you.

WRENNY

Hi. Sorry. I've been super busy.

> Do you want to grab lunch next week when you're free?

WRENNY

Sure.

I KNOW that her agreeing to take some time off and have lunch with me is a good thing, but the only thing I can focus on is that she didn't say that she misses me too.

I TRY to be on my best behavior with my mom. It's her birthday, so it would be shitty of me to cause a scene. I know that she's been trying to foster a better relationship with me, but part of me thinks that it's too late. I've spent so much time not trusting her. So much time keeping all my feelings and my grief bottled up within myself, that opening myself up feels like opening up a fresh wound.

My parents' main priority my whole life was making sure that I was happy. No matter how many arguments we had or times me and Clara fell out, they were always there for us, which is why it makes what my mom did even worse.

They busted their asses for me and Clara to pursue what we wanted to do. Whatever I was doing, they just wanted to make sure that *I* wanted to do it and not for any other reason. Part of the reason I started to play hockey was because I enjoyed it, but I also wanted to do it because it's what made Carter and I grow closer.

Our families supported us from junior league right until college. Carter's brother Ethan was a dick to the two of us growing up, and I think he was just jealous of the attention Carter was getting. He was a smart kid, and not only was he smart, but he was talented and good at everything he did. Their parents always brushed it off as sibling rivalry, but I know Carter always wished he had a better relationship with Ethan deep down.

As much as I'm grateful for my parents, I can't stand birthdays in the Davis family. Every year, no matter whose birthday it is, we have to have some sort of celebration. For as long as I can remember, birthdays have always been a sacred tradition within our family.

There's something about bad music and shitty birthday cake that turns my family upside down. We have stupid rituals like the cake flip, where the birthday person has to flip their cake and catch it the right way around. When the party has died down and it goes from neighbors to close family, we each have to say one thing that we love about the birthday person.

As a kid, *that* was always my favorite part. Maybe it was an ego thing, but it was the part I remembered the most when I went to sleep that night. Every year before I moved out, my mom would tuck me in and ask what the best part of the day was. It was those little things that made me appreciate my family even more.

When I get to my parents' house, as expected, the lawn is littered with neighbors, distant families, half-naked kids running up and down, and babies passed out in strollers. One of my older cousins is working the barbecue, powering through even though it's not quite spring yet.

Kids run and scream on the front lawn, chasing each other with sticks. Old R&B songs blast from speakers through the windows as I walk through the lawn, stupidly carrying a bouquet of flowers and a card.

The first person to spot me is my mom's sister Whitney. She's a few years younger than my mom, but she has almost a hundred kids and hasn't aged a day since I was born. She's a short, tanned woman with a sleeve of tattoos on her right arm, making her by far my coolest relative.

"Ay, Miles, you're almost as tall as the doorframe," she exclaims, squeezing me into a suffocating hug around my middle.

"It's good to see you too, Auntie," I say when I'm free. She squeezes my cheek with her thumb and forefinger, turning my face at ridiculous angles. "Do you know where my parents are?"

"Yes, they're through there," she sighs, pointing down toward the living room. "They're speaking to an older couple. It looks kind of private."

"An older couple?" I ask.

"Yes, I've seen them around here a few times. They are all speaking Spanish, if that rings a bell," she explains before rushing past me to save one of her boys from burning themselves on the barbecue.

I don't have to ask anything else because I know who they are.

Carter's parents are here.

Before I was born, my parents became close friends with

Elena and Mateo Reyes since they lived next door and Ethan is around the same age as Clara. Growing up around them, they taught me and my family how to speak Spanish, and it's become useful in so much of my everyday life. Even though they're both fluent in English, Carter's parents wouldn't let me into their house unless I greeted them in Spanish.

I've hardly seen them since Carter died. I saw them regularly the first couple of weeks, but it got harder for the both of us for me to always be in their house. I was best friends with their son; I can only imagine how hard it must have been to look at me and miss the child you had. I tried to keep in contact with them as much as I could, but we lost touch a few weeks after the funeral.

I walk into the kitchen to keep my distance while they talk. I know my parents have been checking up on them regularly, but I have no idea why they'd choose today to have a private conversation.

I scan the fridge to find something to eat, but it's filled with uncooked seasoned chicken and cold mac and cheese stocked in containers. I look through the cupboards and grab a packet of Cheetos to snack on while I wait. I could go out and greet my thousands of cousins, but they're too chaotic for me right now. I already checked that Bryan, my favorite cousin, who's my age, couldn't make it from LA today, so there's no point talking to all the little kids.

"Miles?" I turn around to see Mrs. Reyes, and my heart drops.

I try to swallow my chip as she looks at me, scanning my black jeans and hoodie. She inches closer toward me, her hands shaking a little as they come to rest on my arms.

Es bueno verte, Tía, I say, my Spanish sounding so strange on my tongue.

Tú también. "Ay, you've got so big." She tries to smile, but it doesn't quite reach her eyes. "How are you, *amor*?"

"I'm doing okay."

"Good. That's good," she replies, her eyes drifting away from me. "Are you still playing hockey?"

"*Sí.* We're hoping to win the championship," I say softly.

"That's good," she says again. "That's good." I wiggle out of her grip a little to place my hands on her arms, trying to steady her.

"*¿Estás bien, tía?*" I ask softly. She nods slowly and opens and closes her mouth. As she takes a sharp inhale, Mr. Reyes comes around the corner. He notices what's happening and shakes his head gently. "It's good to see you, *tío.*"

"You too, Miles," he says, walking toward us. He puts an arm around Elena and mumbles something in Spanish to her. Her eyes don't move as if she hasn't even registered whatever he just whispered. "We better get going. It's getting late."

Mr. Reyes nods at me, and they walk out of the kitchen, leaving me confused. The sun is still up, but I don't say anything to stop them. I haven't known how to act around them since Carter died, and I don't know when it's going to get better for them.

My parents walk around the corner into the kitchen, and when they see me, they act as if I've not seen them in years. I haven't been around here since Christmas Eve, but we've spoken on the phone. Although the conversations were short, the communication has been better than it was a few months ago. They both embrace me in a hug at the same time, my dad practically crushing me.

"Happy birthday, Mom," I say, reaching over to pick up the flowers I got her. She looks down at them and then at me with a grateful smile.

"Aw, thank you, Miles," she replies. My dad winks at me from behind her before sauntering off to contain the raging party behind us.

"It's no problem. Are you having a good day so far?" I ask, shifting from one foot to the other.

"Oh, it's been wonderful. I wasn't expecting this many people to show up," she says with a huff. "It's a lot better now that you're here. I'm really glad you came."

"I wouldn't miss it," I say. Clattering sounds behind us, and my mom's head shoots back on instinct. She rolls her eyes, knowing she's going to have to see what that was. "Do you want me to go take care of that?"

"No. No," she says, shaking her head and gesturing to the seat by the kitchen island, "Sit. I want to catch up. How are you? How have you been holding up?"

I don't know why her kindness shocks me. I guess a stupid part of me thought we'd skip over this part and pretend that we've been speaking regularly for months. I take a seat, dragging a paper plate toward me so I have something to do with my hands.

"I've been okay. Keeping busy with school and hockey," I say, and she smiles. "I'm sorry for not checking in as much."

"Don't be," she replies, pressing her hand over mine. "The phone works two ways. I should have checked in on you more, but I just..." She heaves out a heavy sigh, and I blink at her. "I didn't think you'd want to hear from me, and I didn't want to push you into speaking with me."

My heart stutters at her words. "I always want to hear from you, Mom. I've been really stuck in my head these last few months, but I don't want that to dictate our relationship anymore. I acted like an idiot, and I'm sorry."

"I'm sorry too, my love," she whispers, "for everything."

I swallow, and my eyes meet hers. "I know."

She wipes the corner of her eye and laughs quietly. "Come on. I don't want to cry on my birthday. Let's get you some food."

I know it's going to take a while for us to get back to how we were, but this feels like a step in the right direction.

IT'S NOT until after one in the morning when the party is finally over. The only people left to clean up are me, my parents, and Clara.

Even though I was dreading it, the party didn't turn out to be that bad. I got to see tons of my family that came from up and down the globe for my mom's birthday. She was constantly showered with compliments and given hundreds of presents, which were mostly wine and flowers. The cake flip went well after years of practice, and the speeches made my mom cry.

We all said something nice about her too—even me. I cheated a little and just said that I'm grateful to have her as a mom. Because I am. As much as what she did is still going to take time to heal, I'm ready to give myself that time and the space for healing.

Clara has taken the backyard to clean up, and dad's taken the front. I don't know what mom has done, but the living room is spotless again. She's a magician, I swear. I've been trying to clean up the hallways, picking up paper plates and SOLO cups until I walk down the left corridor where the bedrooms are.

The door to my parents' room is cracked open a few inches, and when I walk closer, I spot my mom in there. She's sitting on the bed, still wearing her birthday sash and crown as she looks through photos spread out on the bed. I try to look without being seen, ready to walk past this private moment.

"Can you believe you were this small?" she says quietly, not looking up from the photo in her hand. "I can tell you're there, Miles."

I walk into the bedroom cautiously. I sit down on the king-sized bed, and I'm instantly reminded of waking up here on Christmas morning.

The bedroom is filled with large boxes as if they've just moved in. It's really just a lot of childhood memories like our baby clothes, birthday cards, and some of our old toys. They're both too afraid to keep them in the basement, and they said it makes them feel closer to us when we're away from home. Some people would think it's cluttered, but I think the sentiment is sweet.

I take up one of the photos, and it's of me and my dad, riding my first bike down our neighborhood street. The memories look brighter and even better than I remembered them.

"I remember this day," I murmur, holding up a picture of the first hockey game I went to. I'm in a jersey five sizes too big for me, sitting on my mom's knee with a hockey cap on her head.

"I do too. You couldn't keep still, but *every time* I tried to pass you to your dad, you didn't want to go to him. You were such a momma's boy," she says ruefully.

"Yeah."

A wave of comfortable silence settles over us as we look through the pictures. The memories seem so close yet so far away from where I am now. I'm turning twenty in a few months, and a huge part of me still feels like a kid. A huge part of me still *acts* like a kid.

"I'm sorry, Miles," my mom murmurs, snapping me out of my trance. She's still looking down at the pictures, running her finger across one of them. "I ruined this bond between us last year. It would be unfair of me to keep ignoring what has happened between us."

"I didn't make it easy for you either. I just… I thought you guys loved each other," I whisper. She looks up at me, and I can see the tears lining her eyes. It's hard thinking you know someone your whole life, then realize some of it was a lie.

"I *do* love your dad, and I love you and Clara more than anything. I made a mistake, but your dad and I found each other again. The most important thing is that we're happy now."

"Are you though? Happy, I mean."

"More than anything. That's all that matters."

"Yeah, I guess you're right."

"I'm always right, my love," she says, squeezing my face

between her hands. "I thought Wren was coming with you. Could she not make it?"

I shrug, trying to play off the hurt that I feel because she isn't here. "She's deep in competitions. We've both been busy with school, and I didn't want to push her."

Mom hums, rubbing my knee. "You're a good boyfriend, Miles."

"Am I? I feel like I'm not doing enough. Every time I think we've reached a new point in our relationship, something else happens and I feel like she's pushing me away," I get out. I'm sure my mom doesn't want to hear about my internal drama right now, but I have no one else to talk to about it. "She's not used to people looking after her, Mom, and it breaks my heart. Every time I try to be there for her, she freaks out and runs away."

My mom's eyes soften. "And you're there for her when she needs you?"

"Always."

She hums. "I know that feeling—being too scared to let good things happen to you. I was the same with your dad, but I came around. As long as you're showing up for her, making sure she knows that you're in her corner, that's all that matters. Sometimes it's all you can do," Mom says, a smile tugging at her lips. "I've seen the way that girl looks at you. She looks at you like you hung the moon."

My heart swells at the idea. That's exactly how I look at her. Wren Hackerly is everything to me: the light in the darkness, the warmth in the cold. But lately, it feels like that light is dimming, like I'm losing her bit by bit, and I don't know how to stop it.

"Why were you talking to Carter's parents?" ask, changing the subject.

There's a softness in my mom's eyes, a hint of sorrow that cuts through the mask of composure she wears so often. "They wanted to ask for your approval on a memorial the college is considering for Carter," she explains, her voice laced with a quiet sadness that echoes the ache in my own heart.

The name alone is enough to send a pang of grief coursing through me, a sharp reminder of his absence has left in my life. But what stings even more is the realization that his parents sought solace elsewhere, turning to my mother instead of reaching out to me directly.

"Why didn't they mention it to me?" I ask.

My mom's gaze meets mine, her eyes brimming with unspoken emotions that threaten to spill over at any moment. "They see so much of Carter in you, Miles," she murmurs, her voice heavy with emotion. "It's hard for them to separate the two, especially after everything that happened."

Her words hang heavy in the air, a reminder of the loss we all still carry with us, a burden we can never truly set down. And as the pieces of the puzzle start to fall into place, a wave of guilt washes over me, the weight of missed opportunities and unspoken words holding me down.

"I'm sorry, Mom," I whisper for what feels like the hundredth time. "I didn't mean to shut you out."

Mom's hand finds mine, her touch gentle yet reassuring as she squeezes it gently. "You don't have to apologize, my love," she murmurs, her voice filled with unconditional love and understanding. "We all have our own ways of coping with grief. But remember, you're not alone. I'm always here for you, no matter what."

"I know," I say, swallowing before meeting her eyes again. "I think they should do it. The memorial. I know they're hurting, but it would be a good official reminder of him on campus."

My mom smiles. "That's exactly what I told them."

Having us both agree on something like this makes the future of our relationship seem way less daunting. It's like we've finally set down some stepping stones for our future and we're going in the right direction.

It's good to be home.

42
WREN

"You've got me?"

I DON'T MEET Miles for lunch like I said I would.

I don't see anyone I'm supposed to be friends with for two weeks unless I accidentally bump into them on my way to the rink, the gym, or on the bus to another comp. Competing in the championships is hard enough, and having my mom's words still ringing in my ears isn't helping. It only took one conversation with her to prove how completely and utterly unlovable I am. How easy it is for people to lose interest in me when I'm no longer performing for them and bending over backward to change into a person that is more digestible for them.

I never even wanted to experience romantic love until I met Miles. I was so content with it just being me and my girls, and I didn't need a man to fill that gaping hole inside of my chest that has never fully healed. But, deep down, I crave it now more than ever.

As much as I love my friends, as much as Kennedy and Scarlett have been my anchors in this storm, it's not the same. There's a part of me that still craves romantic love. The tender moments, the whispered words of affirmation, the feeling of being someone's priority. I want to know what it's like to be cherished in that way, to be the person someone chooses every single day, not out of obligation, but out of genuine love.

I thought Miles was that person for me, the one who could see past the walls I've built and love me for who I am, not who I pretend to be. But now, I can't shake the fear that maybe my mom was right. Maybe I'm too much work, too much trouble, and not worth the effort in the long run. Maybe Miles will get tired of me too, just like everyone else.

I try to focus on my routines, on the precise movements that have always given me a sense of control. But the ice feels colder beneath my skates, the applause emptier, and the victories hollow. Pushing Miles away might have been the stupidest thing I've ever done because every piece of happiness that I get falls short of what it would have been like if he was there. I don't get his stupid jokes, his smiles, his ridiculous singing, and his inability to keep his hands off me. I didn't think I'd miss him so much, but keeping him at arm's length has been good for my performance, although not so much for my personal health.

I can deal with that later.

Right now, all I want to do is continue watching *Modern Family* until my eyes close. I've spent the entire day at the gym, and I planned on ignoring Kennedy and Scarlett's nagging to leave the apartment. I'm giving myself tonight to wallow and feel sorry for myself because if I spend another second in my brain, stressing over things that are beyond my control and trying and failing to get my medication to actually *do* something, I might go legitimately insane.

I've managed to deal with my anxiety over the last few months, and just when I think everything is going great, something else happens and I find myself falling back into a dark place. I hate it when that happens because I can quite literally *feel* myself falling. I know when it's going to get bad again, but I can't do anything to stop it, and I just let it be until it crushes me. A stupid part of me thinks that the more I look at self-help websites telling me that this feeling will pass, the more I might start to believe it.

Of course, my wallowing doesn't last for long because I have two golden retrievers as best friends.

"Wrenny? Do you want something to eat?" Kennedy asks, knocking on my door.

I sigh, pausing the episode I've been smiling like a loon at. "No, I'm good."

"Are you sure? You haven't left your room all day," Scarlett insists. Her voice is an octave higher than usual, which only happens when she's extremely stressed. I know I've put them through hell for the past three weeks, and they've been checking up on me, trying to talk me off a cliff at any chance they can get, and I love them for it.

"That's kinda the plan," I shout, rolling my eyes as if they can see.

They both mutter to each other, sounding like evil geniuses as they do so. I don't have the energy to listen to what they're saying, and I press play on the episode and get lost in the fictional world I desperately want to be a part of.

I'm deep into another episode when they knock on my door again. I groan, shutting my laptop and burying my head under the covers. If I didn't have a highly competitive to finish, I would stay here forever. No drama. No friends. Just me and my comfort blanket forever.

As much as these girls have saved my life these last few weeks, sometimes, just having a conversation with them is exhausting. Pretending to be interested in things when I'm so caught up in my head is one of the hardest things I've ever had to do. I *want* to engage and be present, but just existing has felt like a chore, and whenever I get a second alone in my thoughts, I can't stop thinking about how incredibly unlovable I might be, just like my mom suggested. It feels like a spiral is coiling tighter and tighter until it suffocates me.

"Wren," Kennedy presses, her voice softer than before.

"What?"

"Can you come to the door?" she asks, sighing. I weigh the options. I'll either have to listen to them nagging me from behind the door for hours on end or actually answer it and see what they want from me. They know when I get like this, but they're persistent fuckers.

"Why?"

"We just want to make sure you're alive," Scarlett adds.

I groan, slipping out of the bed. "You know that me talking to you suggests that I'm alive, right?"

"I need to see it to believe it," Kennedy says, and I walk toward the door. They're both bickering about something, and I open the door to find the two of them with wide eyes. "You look like shit."

"Thanks, Ken. Truly," I say flatly. I know I look terrible. I've been burning the candle at both ends for weeks. I've only worn makeup for my competitions, and if I'm not studying or at the gym, I've been cooped up in here without a smidge of makeup and in sweats.

Scarlett beams. "Don't be mad at us, okay?"

I narrow my eyes at them. "Why would I be mad at you?"

Before I know it, Miles appears behind them, and they shove him into my room, closing the door behind us. He almost falls right into me as his tall frame makes my average-sized room look tiny. My cheeks instantly flame with heat. My room is a mess, *I'm* a mess, and he is the last person I want to see right now.

I cross my arms against my chest, looking up at him. "What are you doing here?"

"I came to hang out with my girlfriend." He's not got that flirty smile like he usually has, and his words have an odd punch to them as he asks, "We are still dating, right? I guess I'm just confused since you've been ignoring me."

I blink at him. "What are you talking about?"

"Don't play dumb with me, Wren," he spits out. "If you wanted to break it off, that's all you had to say."

"I-I don't. I just have a lot going on right now," I splutter out, trying to busy myself by picking up clothes off my floor and placing the books back on my shelf. His gaze is harsh, and he follows me around the room as I do so.

"What is going on? I told you that pushing me away isn't going to work on me, remember?" he says, his voice weighty with sincerity.

That catches my attention. I stop what I'm doing and sit at the edge of my bed, and he follows me, but he doesn't sit down. He just stands in front of me, looking down at me and waiting for an answer.

Then I remember what my mom said.

He'll get bored of you.

What makes you think that he wants this for real?

Admire, not love.

I shake my head, staring down at my thighs. "You can stop pretending you care about me, and you can go, Miles." A desperate scoff leaves his mouth, and I shut my eyes. "You don't have to feel obligated to check in on me."

"Obligated? What the fuck does that mean?" I shrug, playing with my hands. I feel him step closer to me and his fingers brush my chin. "Wren, baby, look at me."

I push his hand away. "No. Just go."

His grip tightens on me, and I can feel my throat burning. I *can't* cry. I look up at him and instantly wish I hadn't. He looks tired. No. *Exhausted.* He's got a slight stubble on his chin that wasn't there a few weeks ago. There's a hurt in his eyes that I've never seen before, and it breaks my heart.

"I'm not leaving when you're clearly upset," he says roughly, his thumb rubbing my chin.

"God, I'm not upset. I just don't want you here right now.

I'm not in a good place, Miles, and you're making it worse," I say, my temper rising.

He doesn't back down. "Why?"

"Because you're driving me crazy!"

"No, *why?*" he presses, his tone sharp. "Why do you shut people out when they want to help you, Wren? Can't you see that's all I'm trying to do? I know that you might be used to it, but you don't have to do things on your own."

My lip quivers, and I will myself not to cry. I need him to stop. To stop trying to peel back the layers of me I haven't had a chance to look at myself. I need him to stop trying to break down walls that I've put up for a reason. I know just how bad it hurts when someone leaves or lets me down and it's going to hurt a thousand times more when it's him.

"Stop," I whisper, my voice shaking.

"No, Wren, I won't stop until you believe what I'm telling you," he says. He drops to his knees in front of me, and it's even harder to look at him. He rubs my thighs reassuringly, running his hands up and down as he looks up at me. "How many times do I have to tell you how enthralled I am by your presence? How many times do I have to lay myself bare for you so you can realize that I'm in this for keeps? How many times do I have to embarrass myself to prove that all I want is to spend time with you, find out things about you that no one else does, and just *love* you?"

My voice cracks as I speak, tears spilling down my cheeks. "You don't mean that."

"Who?" His grip on my thighs tightens, and the anger in his voice is unmistakable. "Who is telling you that I don't mean that, baby?"

"Miles," I whimper.

"Who is hurting you, princess? Tell me, and I can make it better. Who is making you believe that bullshit?"

I gasp for air, needing it quicker than it can get to me. "No one is hurting me. It's just— It's my mom. Austin came back and told her about the pregnancy, and they turned it all on me. I told her about our plan, and she said that you don't want me, that you'll get bored of me, and maybe she's right."

His jaw ticks. "You believed her?" I nod, and another sob rips through me when he shakes his head, dropping it to my knees. "Jesus Christ, Wren."

Not looking at him makes it easier to talk, but it still hurts. It's like the words burn to get out of my mouth, but I know I need to say them. "I thought that shutting you out would help, that it would make what she said feel less real. I thought it would give me more time to focus on my performance, but it just made it worse, and I stopped taking care of myself and pushed you away, and I fucking missed you."

My voice cracks on the last two words, and his head shoots back up. "Then why didn't you talk to me?"

"I was scared. I was embarrassed that I let her get into my head, and I couldn't stomach the idea that she might be right," I say.

"If you had let me, I would have been there for you."

I sniffle. "I know."

"Do you?" His eyes soften as he drinks me in. "Because if you knew that, Wren, you wouldn't have iced me out. I told you *months* ago that you've got me. That you don't have to be alone when things get hard. If you had told me, I would have told you a thousand times over that I could watch you just being you and never get bored. I think you're single-handedly the most brilliant person I have ever met, and I feel lucky to even know you. I am constantly in awe of the person that you are, you know that?"

Trying to think about what he just said makes the weight on my chest finally give way, and it crushes me. I crumble, my entire body shaking with sobs until Miles's arm wraps around me and he pulls me to the ground with him. I curl myself up so small in his arms, and he holds me like he's afraid to let go, like he's anchoring me to reality in the midst of my storm. His warmth seeps into my bones, and for the first time in weeks, I feel a sliver of safety, a promise of solace.

Miles's hand strokes my hair, his touch gentle yet firm. "Wren, you don't have to be perfect. Not for me, not for anyone."

I cling to him, my sobs gradually subsiding into hiccups. "I thought... I thought if I showed you the messy parts of me, you'd leave. That you'd see I'm not worth it."

"Baby," he murmurs, the word so soft and smooth I start to hate the nickname less and less. He angles my head toward him, and I struggle to look at him, but I do it anyway. "You, just existing, is enough."

His words are almost enough to make me break all over again, but I don't let them. I bade that feeling of belonging welcome home.

"I'm sorry," I say, "I hate crying."

He smiles softly. "Why?"

"Because it makes me feel weak. I'm not weak." I bite the words out and wonder if I'll ever stop feeling this way. I prefer to keep these emotions inside. Everything has always worked better that way. But maybe they don't need to.

"You're the strongest person I know, but crying doesn't make you weak," he whispers, brushing my hair out of my face. He lets out a soft chuckle. "I cry all the time."

That jolts me right in the chest, and I hold him tighter. "I'm sorry for not being there for you. I should have had your back too. I've been so caught up in my own shit that I didn't check in on you, and that's a real dick move from me. I'm sorry."

He lets out a heavy sigh. "It's okay to take time to process your own thoughts." He taps the side of my head a few times. "Just let me in here sometimes, okay? I want to know what's going on in there too."

I scoff. "It's not all sunshine and rainbows, Miles."

"I know," he says, grinning. "You just tell me when you need a minute, for whatever reason, and take time for yourself. I won't judge you. I just want you to know that I've got you."

I swallow. "You've got me?"

"Yeah, I've got you, sweet girl. Always."

He holds me tighter, and in that embrace, I feel the weight of the past few weeks lifting, replaced by the steady, reassuring beat of his heart against mine. The world outside might still be chaotic, but in this moment, with Miles holding me, I know we'll be okay. We have to be.

For the first time in a long time, I feel seen. I feel valued. And most importantly, I feel loved.

43

MILES

Is bullying really a love language?

"DO you think you'll get an award?" Wren asks, coming up behind me in the mirror while I brush my teeth. She's wearing my shirt and nothing else as she bends over me to pick up her toothbrush. God, I don't think I'm ever going to get tired of this. I watch her in the mirror, holding tight onto my toothbrush.

"Considering how I was on the bench at the start of the season and I've only just got back on the team, I'm not expecting to," I say through a foamy smile before spitting in the sink and rinsing.

"Well, it's your help that pushed you guys to the finals, right?" she asks.

I shrug. In all honesty, I wasn't expecting the Bears to do so well this season, but we've somehow made it to the conference final next week. Despite Jake's unnecessary insults that he spits out on the ice, we've been stronger than ever, and I can't wait for us to bring this championship home. We've been through a lot as a team. We deserve it.

"I guess you could say that," I say, and she grins. I move behind her, and she nods, placing her toothbrush back in her mouth. I wrap my arms around her stomach, resting my chin on her shoulder like it belongs there. "Do you think you will win?"

She rinses, but I can see the smile creeping up on her face.

All the sports students look forward to NU's sports achievement evening every year. It usually happens every April, awarding medals and certificates to the students who have performed well that year. I almost forgot about it until Wren reminded me last weekend to find another decent outfit since we'll be going together.

I got to watch my girl last weekend completely smash the competition at her national championship final. She performed a complicated as fuck routine to Stephen Fry's *Flying,* and I was on the edge of my seat the entire time. She wasn't nervous or anxious about it, and she got up there and won the entire thing. It helped that all of her friends were in the crowd; even Sophia and a few of her friends were there too. Her dad came with a huge banner and almost threw up next to me as he went on about how excited and nervous he was. Miss Hackerly didn't show up, but after Wren explained to me what went down between them, I wasn't expecting her to. Regardless, she did her best, and she came off the ice with a smile.

"I mean, I was crowned the winner of the National Collegiate Championships, so maybe," she says, turning and leaning against the sink. "It's not like Darcy has many options."

"Cocky," I mutter.

"Confident," she corrects, and she flashes that cocky–confident grin at me, and it's the sexiest thing I've ever seen.

"You're going to win, for sure," I say, and she rolls her eyes.

"Of course you're going to say that. You're biased because we're sleeping together," she says.

"Sleeping together?" I echo, taken aback. She bites the inside of her cheek and nods, trying not to smile. I know she's saying that just to get under my skin. "You're my girlfriend, Wren; we're not just sleeping together."

She feigns innocence. "Am I? I thought I was your fake girlfriend."

I grip her chin, tilting her face up to mine. "Baby, this stopped being fake a long time ago."

Her mouth parts, but before she can leave me a snarky comment, I press my lips to hers, ready to prove to her over and over that I can be exactly the kind of man that deserves her. If I have to worship her on my knees every day, I'll gladly do it.

HOURS LATER, I step out of my truck with Kennedy, Scarlett, and Wren all unbuckling their seatbelts. We're only allowed to bring one plus one to these events, but Wren thought it would be better if we each took one of her girls as our "dates" since she wanted them both there. It's not a problem for me. The only thing I don't like is how much Scarlett and Kennedy bully me.

Wren says it's because they like me, but I don't see how that makes any sense. I thought after they helped me get to see Wren when she was going through a hard time that they'd warmed up to me, but they haven't.

I open the back door to let the girls out of the car, holding my hand out for Kennedy. "Wow, you're such a gentleman," she coos as she slips out of the car.

"I try to be," I say coyly.

Scarlett rolls her eyes, and when I hold out my hand to her, she grabs it with unnecessary force. "Only when he's not fucking Wren's brains out and ruining my meal."

"That was one time," I mutter, narrowing my eyes at her.

"One time too many," she bites back.

"Does Wren know you're such an asshole to me?"

"Yes," she says, stepping out of the car, "and she encourages it."

I roll my eyes and step away from her. I sometimes think that

Scarlett is insane enough to either cast a spell on me or get her family to ruin my life. I know she's just protective, and it's sweet that Wren has friends who have her back like this.

Wren rounds the car, meeting us on the other side, and she slips her arm around mine. "You look good," she murmurs as we make our way to the building that's holding the event.

"You've said that already," I reply, pressing a kiss to her hair.

"I know, and I actually mean it."

"Actually? What's that supposed to mean?"

Kennedy turns around, laughing at me. "It means that she was lying all the other times."

"Is that true?" I ask Wren, who's trying her absolute hardest not to laugh.

She shrugs. "This tux is hot. You should wear one more often."

I scoff. "I'm not Evan. I don't wear a tie unless I actually have to."

That catches Scarlett's attention as we push open the thick wooden doors to one of the oldest buildings on campus. "What's up with that? Does he think he's going to get photographed every time he leaves his house?"

"Probably," I say. I don't think I've seen my housemate wear anything but a suit. It's weird.

"What a loser," Scarlett mumbles, and we all follow her into the building.

Holy fuck.

I don't think I've ever walked into this building before. The foyer is made with rich, dark wood paneling and historical portraits of past university luminaries. Crystal chandeliers hang from the high ceilings, casting a warm, golden glow over everything. The air is filled with a mix of excitement and formality as students mill around wearing their Sunday best.

We walk down a wide corridor lined with crimson carpets, our footsteps muffled by the plush fabric. The walls are decorated with old photographs and trophies, showcasing the university's rich sporting history.

At the end of the corridor, we enter the main hall, which has been transformed into an Oscar-like setting. Rows of elegant, upholstered chairs are arranged before a grand stage, draped with deep-blue velvet curtains. Spotlights highlight a podium at the center, flanked by large screens that display the event's logo.

The tables are set with fine china and sparkling glassware, centerpieces of fresh flowers adding splashes of color. Waitstaff in crisp uniforms move efficiently, placing hors d'oeuvres and drinks before the guests. A live band plays softly in the background, adding to the sophisticated ambiance.

"Wow," Wren exclaims beside me. "They really went all out."

"Yeah," I agree. "This is impressive."

She nudges me. "Better not spill anything on that tux. It'd be a shame."

I roll my eyes. "Don't worry; I'll be on my best behavior."

We find our seats near the front, joining other athletes and their dates. The excitement in the room is palpable, everyone dressed to the nines and ready to celebrate the year's achievements.

As we settle in at our table with Xavier, Michelle, Tyler, and their partner Beau, I glance at Wren. Her eyes are wide with wonder, a small smile playing on her lips. I squeeze her hand, and she looks up at me, her smile widening.

"You're the most stunning person here, Wren," I whisper just for her to hear. She doesn't respond; I honestly don't think she needs to. The way her eyes shine and her smile widens, I know she knows it just as much as I do.

As I settle into my seat, the reality of the evening starts to hit me. It's not just any sports achievement evening. It's *the* sports achievement evening, and I'm about to meet Josh Raymond.

Josh Fucking Raymond. I can feel my heartbeat quicken just thinking about it.

I've idolized Josh since I was a kid. He was the standout player for the NU Bears, and now he's tearing it up in the pros for the Utah Grizzlies. I've watched all his games, memorized his stats, and even tried to mimic his moves on the ice. He's the reason I started playing hockey in the first place. The idea of meeting him in person is enough to make my palms sweat.

Wren notices my silence and gives my hand a squeeze. "You okay?"

I nod, forcing a smile. "Yeah, just... you know, big night."

She laughs softly. "You're going to be fine. Just be yourself."

Be myself. Easier said than done when you're about to meet your hero. What if I say something stupid? What if he thinks I'm just another fanboy? I take a deep breath, trying to calm my racing thoughts.

Across from me, Xavier laughs. "Dude, you look like you're going to have an aneurysm."

"You do know that Josh Raymond is coming tonight, right?" I ask, scanning the room again. As expected, he hasn't arrived in the last three seconds. Xavier shakes his head, letting out an incredulous laugh.

"Don't act like you weren't like that last year, Z," Michelle says, laughing before taking a sip of her punch. "You practically shit yourself when you met Dean Mayer, and you wouldn't stop talking about it for weeks."

"She's got you there," Wren mutters, and Xavier shrugs happily. We've all got our particular favorites for the NU Bear's team of '15. Mayer was the left defense, and Raymond was the center and the captain, and they both play for the same team now. "I'm obsessed with your dress, Michelle. Where did you get it?"

"I made it myself, actually," Michelle replies with a soft smile, pushing her braids over her shoulder. Michelle, Wren,

Scarlett, and Kennedy float into a conversation about fashion and a bunch of other girl shit that I don't have a clue about.

Wren keeps her hand on my leg the entire time as she talks to them, constantly reminding me she's still there while I listen to another one of Tyler's boring stories. Don't get me wrong, Tyler is one of the funniest people I know, but there is one thing they can't do: tell a good story.

"And that's how I almost got arrested." Tyler ends the rant, and Xavier, Beau, and I exchange knowing glances.

"So, you went through that entire story——plot twists and all——just to tell us how you didn't get arrested?" Xavier asks, running his hands down his face in exhaustion. Tyler nods with a cheesy grin pulling at their cheeks.

"Yeah. Well, you had to know the contexts, obviously," Tyler begins before diving into another deep conversation about how things didn't happen.

The doors swing open, and the entire gym erupts into a thunderous cheer, saving me from another one of Tyler's stories. Legends of NU's sports history—basketball, football, soccer, and ice hockey players—stride in, dressed to the nines as if attending the most prestigious event of their careers. They take their seats at designated tables under the watchful eyes of the current students and faculty.

The screech of microphone feedback grabs everyone's attention, redirecting it to the makeshift stage at the front of the room. There stands Billy Carhart, assistant head of the sports department, behind a podium. I thought Hacks would have presented the event, but she's in a corner with the other faculty and hasn't looked our way all night. What a coward.

"Good evening, everyone," he begins, prompting another round of enthusiastic applause. Wren glances at me, beaming, completely unaware that I heard her earlier conversation. I press a kiss to her forehead, and she turns back to face the stage, nestling into my chest.

"As you've noticed, tonight, we welcome back generations of North's sports stars. But tonight is not about them. It's about each one of you—our current students—whose dedication to your sport is unparalleled."

He continues, praising our commitment and expressing how fortunate he feels to have such talented individuals playing the sports he loves. My mind drifts, excitement building within me as I anticipate talking to Josh Raymond. Carhart passes the mic to the basketball and soccer coaches, who proceed to present awards to their top students.

I snap back to attention when they announce the skating team's awards. Wren's shyness from this morning is nowhere to be seen as she strides confidently toward the stage even before her name is called. Of course, she knew she'd win.

Our entire table rises, clapping for her. She throws us an embarrassed smile as she accepts her certificate, while a projector plays her best moments on the ice. My girl is incredibly talented.

Kennedy and Scarlett tear up like proud parents, and I put two fingers in my mouth and whistle. Wren's eyes widen as she descends the stage, clearly loving and hating the attention simultaneously.

"See? I told you you'd win," I whisper when she's back at the table, snuggled into my side. "You are brilliant, baby."

She looks up at me, tears lining her eyes, but she doesn't let them fall. She opens her mouth, but no words come out. Instead, she kisses my cheek. "Thank you," she whispers.

The host's voice pulls me back to the present as he announces the next award. The spotlight shifts, and there he is— Josh Raymond—walking up to the stage to present the award. He looks just as cool and composed as ever, a testament to his years of experience under the spotlight.

The award is for one of the star players this season, and even though we might not have won just yet, I'm not surprised that

Xavier wins. He works harder than most people on the team, and granting him captaincy instead of me was the best decision Coach Tucker ever made. He deserves this, and I'm so proud of him.

My mind starts to spin with a million thoughts when he steps down and Josh returns to the corner he was in.

What do I say to him? Should I mention that game-winning goal he scored against Denver? Or maybe talk about the time he single-handedly turned around a losing streak for the Grizzlies? I don't want to come off as too intense, but I also don't want to miss this chance to connect with him.

The ceremony continues, but my focus is split. Half of me is trying to pay attention to the awards being handed out, while the other half is rehearsing lines in my head. By the time the final award is announced, I'm a bundle of nerves.

Wren leans in, her breath warm against my ear. "Relax. You're going to do great."

I nod, taking another deep breath. The lights come back up, and people start milling around, chatting and congratulating each other. This is it. My chance.

"Do you want to come with me?" I ask Wren, itching to get out of my seat.

"Sure. But you've got to promise not to freak out," she says, grabbing both sides of my face and shaking me. "You've got this, Milesy."

The moment we approach Josh, my heart feels like it's about to burst out of my chest. He's engaged in conversation with a couple of other athletes, but when he sees us, he smiles and extends his hand. "Hey, I'm Josh Raymond. Nice to meet you."

I grasp his hand, hoping mine isn't too sweaty. "Miles Davis. It's an honor to meet you. I've been a fan of yours since your college days."

Josh's smile widens. "Thanks, man. That means a lot. You play hockey here, right?"

I nod, trying to keep my voice steady. "Yeah, I'm a forward for the Bears."

He nods appreciatively. "That's great. I've heard good things about the team this year. Keep working hard, and who knows where it'll take you."

I glance at Wren, feeling the need to introduce her. "This is my girlfriend, Wren. She's the captain of the figure skating team."

Wren smiles warmly and shakes his hand. "Nice to meet you, Josh. We're both big fans."

Josh nods at her. "Likewise. I've heard a lot about the figure skating team's achievements. You guys are killing it."

After a brief exchange of pleasantries, I take a deep breath and dive into the topic that's been on my mind. "Josh, I wanted to ask... how do you keep pushing forward after losing someone close to you? My best friend, Carter Reyes, passed away at the end of last season. He was a huge fan of yours too."

Josh's expression softens, and he nods slowly. "I'm really sorry to hear about Carter. Losing someone you care about is never easy. When I lost a teammate back in college, it hit me hard. What helped me was remembering why I started playing in the first place and honoring his memory by giving my best every time I hit the ice. It's about channeling that grief into something positive, something that keeps their memory alive."

I swallow hard, feeling a lump in my throat. "Carter was my rock. He believed in me more than I did myself sometimes. I just... I don't want to let him down."

Josh places a reassuring hand on my shoulder. "You won't. Just keep playing with your heart, and you'll make him proud. And don't be afraid to lean on the people around you. It's okay to let them help you through it."

We talk for a few more minutes, with Josh offering advice on improving my game and sharing some stories from his own career. By the end of the conversation, I feel a mix of exhilaration and relief. I did it. I met Josh Raymond, and I didn't make a complete fool of myself.

As Wren and I walk away, she grins up at me. "See? I told you you'd be fine."

I smile back. "Yeah. Thanks for believing in me."

She squeezes my hand. "Always. And Miles, Carter would be so proud of you."

Her words bring a tear to my eye, but I blink it away, nodding. "Yeah. I hope so."

The remainder of the night goes by perfectly, and I couldn't be happier to be spending time with my teammates, my girl, and her friends. Everything about just being here with them feels natural and like it's always supposed to be like this. I just wish there was one other person I could share it with.

44
WREN + MILES

Are you trying to kill me?

WREN

SETTLING BACK into a routine post-season is usually one of the hardest things for me to do. Since the season has ended, we're now working on performance reviews and preparing for the off-season. I always feel a little lost when I don't have something to be skating for or looking forward to, but I think I've finally realized that I need time for myself.

After the awards night ended, we all went to Nero's Pizzeria and stuffed ourselves with as much pizza as humanly possible. My cheeks have been hurting from smiling too hard and laughing with my friend, and they hurt even *more* when I try not to smile. Especially since Miles's eyes have been on me all night.

I've never felt more loved and appreciated than I do when I'm with him. I don't feel scared of it all crumbling down and ruining me; I feel like I'm being lifted up.

Like right now, as I unpack some more of my things into the drawer he cleared out for me in his room. *A drawer.* I didn't want to be one of those clingy girlfriends who demands a space for her shit when we first start dating, but Miles just told me to pack a bag a few weeks ago and leave some stuff at his place. It didn't feel like this huge, monumental thing. It just *was*. And I'm grateful for that.

"Hey, can I ask you something?" Miles asks. He's sitting on his bed while I walk from his room to his en suite to unpack more of my things.

"Sure."

"Are you annoyed that your mom didn't speak to you today? I saw the way your eyes dropped a little when Carhart took the stage instead of Hacks," he says. I take in a steadying breath.

Honestly, not having to watch my mom pretend to be the perfect Melanie Hackerly like she has been pretending to be for months was like a breath of fresh air. I haven't heard a single thing from her in weeks, and I don't plan on speaking to her anytime soon. I need time away from her. I need time to really think about what I'm doing this for without her unnecessary opinions and expectations. Austin has texted me a few times, apologizing profusely, but I can't even think about her without picturing the way she stood by and let my mom speak to me like that.

"Nope," I say to Miles as I pass him again.

"Are you sure?"

"Yeah, it's cool. She'll get over herself eventually, and I might finally be able to look at her without wanting to murder her," I say cheerfully. He groans, and I turn back around to him. "I promise you, it's fine. I think we both just need some time away from each other. We're not going to have a perfect relationship, and maybe there's no real solution to whatever is going on. Trying to patch things up might take a while."

He nods. "That's understandable. But if you do want to reach out to her, you should."

"I don't."

"Okay," he says, nodding at me. Confrontation clearly gets

nowhere with that woman, and I don't want to put myself in that position just to get manipulated again. I like to believe I'm smarter than that and that I can learn from my mistakes. Miles must know I'm still thinking about it after I've put away all my things because he's still watching me. "Come here."

The corner of my mouth tips up, and I step between his legs, resting my hands on his shoulders as he looks up at me. He runs his hands over the back of my thighs reassuringly. "I'm going to be fine, you know," I whisper, laughing quietly.

"I know," he murmurs, "I just don't want you to think that you're alone. I know what it's like to not talk to your mom, but over the past few weeks, things have gotten better, and I'm glad she's back in my life again. I just don't want you to make any mistakes that you'll regret."

His words pinch at my heart. "Thanks for the concern, Milesy, but I promise you I'll figure this out on my own. Time is the best thing for the both of us right now."

"Okay," he whispers, pressing a kiss to my stomach. Since we started staying at each other's houses, I usually go to sleep in one of his jerseys, and I bet there's some weird alpha-male thing that makes Miles go wild. His hand skims across my stomach before reaching up and cupping one of my tits, pinching my nipple. "Fuck. I'm never going to get used to this."

"Yeah?" I tilt my head to the side, and he grins, looking back up at me, still toying with me.

"You're fucking perfect, Wren," he whispers, looking at me with complete disbelief. I have the urge to tell him he's joking or that he's just saying it to make me feel good, but I don't. I push him back on the bed and grip both of his hands as I straddle him.

I lean down and kiss the corner of his mouth before retreating.

"The jersey stays on, and you can't touch me," I say. His eyes flash with desire, and I smirk. "You're going to be a good boy and watch me play with myself. Understood?"

He swallows. "Understood."

In all honesty, I have no clue what I'm doing, but I'm in the mood to have some fun, and from the way I can feel Miles's dick pressing into me, he clearly is too. He tilts his head to the side to catch my lips, but I avoid him, and he pants, his hands writhing against the grip I have on them between our bodies.

I slide off him, moving to look through one of my bags that I dropped off here. I search through my pile of clothes, and I hear Miles shuffle on the bed. "What are you doing?"

"You remember that present I got for Christmas?" I glance over my shoulder, and he's leaning back on his hands, studying me as I move to the other bag and find what I'm looking for. He swallows, nodding. "Well, I haven't had much time to use it since you've been doing all the heavy lifting. But I just don't think it's fair that my toys should miss out just because I've got you now."

I turn around with the pink vibrator in my hand, and Miles's eyes go comically wide as he glances down to it and then to me. "You brought that here with you?"

"Of course I did," I say, laughing as I kneel back down on the bed beside him. "Here's what's going to happen. You're going to sit here and watch me fuck myself with all seven inches of this toy, and you're not allowed to touch me."

He keeps his eyes on me as I make myself comfortable on his bed, sliding down my panties as he kneels over me, haphazardly throwing away his sweats. I press the button on the vibrator, and it whirrs to life.

He swallows and I try not to laugh at the pure shock on his face. This is going to be a fun night.

MILES

I must be a masochist, because there is no way I'm about to watch Wren masturbate knowing I can't touch her.

I stare at her pussy, and it's so fucking wet, so ready, and I can't even be the one to touch her.

I close my eyes and groan. "Are you trying to kill me?"

She tries and fails to hold in a laugh. "You said you have more self-control than me, right?" I nod. "Well, this is a test of that. Whoever asks to touch the other person first loses. And if you come before I say you can, you lose."

I close my eyes, taking a deep breath. "So there's really no way for me to win. Perfect."

"There is," she says, lifting the oversized jersey to her stomach so I get a much better view of her pussy. I suppress another groan when she brings to toy to her mouth, wrapping those perfect lips around it before pushing the head against her clit. *Fuck me.* "All you have to do is listen, Miles. Do you think you can do that?"

I nod, but my gaze is still fixed on her pussy. I'm fucking mesmerized. Entranced. She could tell me to jump off a fucking cliff right now and I'd do it.

"Take off your boxers and touch yourself," she whispers, her voice hoarse. I do as she says, shuffling closer to her with my cock in my hand. It's hard and so fucking ready for whatever it is we're about to do. "I knew you'd be a good boy if I told you what to do."

I don't know what it is about the way she's completely taken control of the situation that fucks me up inside, but it's enchanting. I'm almost spellbound as I watch her, listen to her, and do everything she tells me to.

She moves the vibrator through her pussy slowly, watching as I pump myself at the same speed. I watch as she slowly eases the toy into her tight pussy, keeping her eyes locked with mine. She slides it in inch by torturous inch, and I have to slow down the pumps of my shaft. Her chest starts heaving, her thighs shaking as the vibrator moves inside her. My gaze is fixed on her face, watching the way her expression transforms into pure bliss.

If I'm not careful, I'm going to blow before the show has even started.

"So perfect," I murmur, stroking myself slowly as she whimpers. "So fucking perfect for me."

She keeps one hand on the base of the toy and the other trails under the jersey, lifting it up enough until she covers one of her breasts, teasing her nipple. I want to touch her just as badly as I want to watch. It's maddening. Her back arches, and she starts moving the toy in and out of her, the slick sounds making my eyes roll back.

"Miles," she moans. My head spins and I can't help but think how good it would feel if I was inside her instead. How I would touch her, tease her, make her feel good. I pump myself faster, applying more pressure as she picks up the speed with the vibrator. "I need—"

"What do you need, princess?" I ask, my voice gruff. She only moans in response, her fingers still playing with her nipple. "Do you want me to touch you?"

Wren shakes her head violently. "No. No. Just keep doing that. Keep looking at me." She reaches down to play with her clit instead. Jesus. The way she knows exactly what she wants and how to get it is a whole other turn on. I let out a tortured groan, shutting my eyes and dropping my head back as my pace increases. "Eyes on me, Miles."

"So fucking hot," I murmur, my eyes raking over her entire body. "Look at you, wearing my jersey, fucking yourself and letting me watch."

"God, Miles," she cries out, her eyes fluttering shut.

"Are you pretending it's me fucking you instead of that toy, princess?"

"*Yes.*"

The sound of the vibrator kicks up like she turned up the speed by accident and it's clear she's losing control. I know her. I know how badly she hates losing even though she suggested this little game. I'm close, too, and I'll probably come before she says I can. I'm trying my hardest to keep it together, but she keeps letting out this little moans and gasps like her self-control might snap any minute.

"Oh, fuck," she mutters, her voice shaking. We've got closer now, my knees on both side of her legs. All I would have to do is kneel a little, move that vibrator slightly out of the way and fill her with my cock. But I don't. She surprises me by saying, "You can come now." She's panting, chest heaving as she plunges the toy in and out of her needy pussy. "Please."

I swallow. "You sure you don't want me to hold on a bit longer?"

She shakes her head. "No."

I smirk. "It seems like you're losing, Wren."

"I don't care."

I look at our position again, and my eyes soften as I meet her desperate gaze. "You know that if I come right now it's going to go on you, right?"

She snorts. "It's almost like that's the whole point."

"But—"

"I have the implant, and I'm clean. If you'd rather not, we can just—"

"*No.* I'm clean, too, and I trust you, I just wanted to make sure... Fuck, I'm killing the mood, aren't I?" I roll my head back, but neither of us has stopped moving.

"Miles?"

"Yeah?"

"Can you just come on me, or I might legitimately die," she bites out. I don't know what it is about her words that spurs me on, but it only takes a few more pumps of my shaft before I spill over her stomach and onto the toy. She works my cum inside of her, moaning as her own orgasm slams through her.

Holy fuuuck.

I watch as she tries to breathe through it, deciding between looking at me or looking at the mess we've made. I can't remember the last time I jerked off and it felt that good. Having her here was like an out of body experience.

"What are you thinking about?" she asks, still trying to catch her breath.

"How I'm supposed to have a normal conversation with you after I just witnessed that," I whisper, shaking his head. Wren rolls her eyes and I pull her jersey over her head before pulling her up to stand. I turn us around toward my en suite, and when she looks in the mirror, taking in how utterly disheveled we look after such a long day, she smiles. I lean down to kiss her shoulder from behind, keeping my eyes locked with hers. "You've ruined me, Wren."

Her mouth twists to the side. "That was always the plan, pretty boy."

All she gets from that is a smack on the ass before I haul her into the shower and make sure she knows that I'm going to take care of her. She needs to realize that it's okay to have someone in your corner and to help you take on the load when things get hard. I knew from the moment I met her that I wanted to be that person for her, and I'm going to continue to prove that to her forever.

45

WREN

Pregnancy brain

AUSTIN

Are we still on for tonight?

Yes.

AUSTIN

Do you want me and Z to pick you up?

I can drive there.

AUSTIN

Okay. See you tonight, Emmy.

See you.

ALTHOUGH MY SKATING season is over, Miles has his final game against Carlton University in a few days, and his schedule is packed. I know what he's like before a game, so I do my best to support him the best I can while also giving him enough time to be on his own. It works out perfectly with both of our schedules and the end-of-year exams that are coming up. It also means I get to spend more time with my girls.

Without skating every day, I've had more time to work on my novel, Stolen Kingdom. I've had hundreds of late-night FaceTime calls with Gigi, and we've been working together so I can get through the first draft of the book. I know how busy she is with her own stories, so I'm so grateful that she's taken the time to help me out with mine.

I've managed to write another thirty thousand words of Stolen Kingdom over the last month, which is a hell of a lot more than I was doing monthly before. Now, I spend lunches in between classes with Kennedy and Scarlett at Florentino's, reading over the latest chapter. I don't know how Kennedy is not sick of being here all the time when she still works here most days. We use half an hour of our one-hour window talking over major plot lines and the other half trying to study. Emphasis on the word trying. We have exams coming up, but our priorities are very clear.

"You can't end it like that!" Kennedy shouts, almost knocking over her coffee. A few people turn their heads and flash us a dirty look. We should probably be banned from eating here.

"I'm not ending it like that. It's just a draft of the ending. It could change," I say, taking a bite of my scone. "I am open to suggestions."

"The only logical ending is that Carmen runs away and starts a new empire," Scarlett suggests with a shrug.

"Yes, that sounds better than her dying," Kennedy says dramatically. "Wait, you're making a sequel, right? Please tell me you're making a sequel."

"I'm thinking about it. I need to focus on real work for class instead of this. It's not like I'm going to get it published," I admit.

"You could. I'll design a cover, and you can self-publish like

Gigi," Kennedy replies, almost falling out of her chair as her eyes widen. "Thirteen-year-olds would eat that shit up."

"It's a possibility, but it's also a lot of work."

"Since when are you afraid of hard work?" Scarlett asks, wiggling her eyebrows. "Maybe not now, but I really think you should in the future. With a bit of editing, it would be perfect. I'm sure G would help you."

"Maybe," I say, trying to mentally add that onto my thousand-word long to-do list. "Anyway, I'm thinking of making Carmen fake her death and then run away to start a new empire."

"I hate that idea a little less," Kennedy says thoughtfully before her face lights up again. "Will she have a sidekick?"

"I'm thinking that Vita will go with her," I reply.

"Isn't she, like, a million years old?" Kennedy asks, flicking through the printed sheets of my book in front of her.

"Yeah, but she's in a middle-aged woman's body. She's basically a Cullen," I say with a waft on my hand.

"Oh, that's cool," Kennedy agrees, nodding her head. "I give you permission to end it that way."

"Why, thank you," I reply, nodding my head toward her. Scarlett pulls the paper out of Kennedy's hand and looks over it with a serious expression. They are both my harshest writing critics, but Scarlett looks more at the intricate details than anything. Kennedy just worried about how hot the protagonist is going to be.

"So, talking about boys..." Kennedy drags out with a whistle.

"We weren't," I say with a bored tone. She ignores it anyway.

"How are you and Milesy?"

I raise my chin. "How are you and Harry?"

She's been spending a lot of time with Miles's teammate, and anytime I bring it up, she denies that anything is going on. Apparently, they're just really good friends, but I'm finding that hard to believe. He looks at her like she hung the fucking moon, and she looks at him the same way.

"Fine," she says, sighing, "Let's not talk about boys."

So we don't. We spend the rest of Kennedy's lunch break talking about books and the fictional boyfriends we wish we had. I can't complain much though. I think Miles Davis is even better than all of them.

AFTER MY CLASSES ARE DONE, instead of going back to the library with them to study, I have to put on my best face and meet up with my sister.

I've been putting it off for weeks, but it's about time. I can only imagine how isolating this experience is for her being pregnant and not really having anyone to talk to. I don't know what the situation is with her and my mom at the minute, but I know my dad said he's excited for her. He passed on the news to me that she's having a boy, and I've been secretly buying clothes whenever I see them. She's due within the next few weeks and I don't want the first time I see her after what happened to be when she's had the baby.

We've never had any babies in our family, and we're so disconnected that I might just have not realized. I think kids are adorable and probably the funniest part of our world, and I've always wanted a younger sibling. The thought of having a nephew to spoil makes my heart swell. As uptight as Austin can be, I know she and Zion will make great parents. Zion has always been kind to me, and even though we don't have much of a relationship like we did when he still lived here, I know he's doing everything he can to make sure she's comfortable and happy.

I nervously adjust the silverware for the third time, my fingers tracing the patterns on the napkin. The cozy, softly lit bistro feels strangely foreign despite its familiar surroundings. I check my phone again, hoping for a distraction, when I hear the soft chime of the doorbell and see Austin step inside.

She spots me almost immediately and offers a tentative smile as she approaches the table. My heart races, a mix of anticipation and apprehension churning within me. This pregnancy has really done wonders for her. She's practically glowing as she walks with one hand on her bump, which has gotten impossibly larger since the last time I saw her.

As she takes a seat across from me, I can't help but notice the exhaustion etched into her features, the way her eyes seem heavier, and I already start to feel bad.

"Hey," she says softly, her voice tinged with nervousness.

"Hey," I reply, trying to muster a smile.

For a moment, we sit in an awkward silence, both unsure of how to breach the gap that has grown between us. A server comes to take our orders, and we're left in another round of silence. It shouldn't be so hard to talk to her. She's my sister for God's sake.

Finally, Austin takes a deep breath, her hands fidgeting with the edge of the tablecloth.

"I'm sorry, Wren," she begins, her voice trembling. Okay. I guess we're jumping right into this. "I should have stood up for you that day. I was just... so scared. Mom, she has this way of getting into your head, making you doubt everything. But that's not an excuse. I let you down when you needed me the most."

I feel a lump form in my throat, but I swallow it down, nodding slowly. "I get it. She's done the same thing to me for years. But it hurts, you know? It hurt feeling like I was alone when you were right there."

"I know," Austin says, her eyes glistening with unshed tears. I really hope she doesn't cry because then there'll be no stopping my own tears. "And I hate that I made you feel that way. I want to make it right." She takes in another deep breath, her eyes meeting mine. "I'm staying in town for a while. For the baby. Zion's parents are here, and it makes more sense than going back to Russia. I've had some good days with the company, and maybe in a few years I'll get back into ballet, but for now, I just want to settle down. I want to be here for you, for us, and for the baby. I want to have a better relationship with you, if you'll let me."

My heart skips a beat at the revelation. I didn't know that Austin was planning to stay. I hadn't even considered that we might have a chance to rebuild our relationship. It's been years since we've both been in the same country, and now, she's just going to be *here*. "You're staying?" I echo, the words feeling strange on my tongue.

Austin nods. "Yeah. I realized I can't keep running from everything. I need to face it, to be there for my child when he comes, and for you. I want us to be a family, Wren. A real one, not the broken mess we grew up with."

My eyes well up with tears, a mix of relief and hope flooding my system. "I want that too, Austin. I've missed you."

"I've missed you too."

We share a tentative smile, the first genuine one in what feels like forever. The server comes with our orders, and we eat mostly in silence. I talk a little about Miles since he's been the only thing on my mind lately and how excited I am for his game. She tells me about the baby name options she and Zion have been trying out, but they're not sure yet.

It's only after we've eaten that Austin broaches the subject that has been looming over us.

"So, what are you going to do about Mom?" she asks, her voice gentle but probing.

I sigh, picking at my nearly empty plate. "I don't know. Part of me wants to cut her off completely, to protect myself from her toxicity. But another part of me can't shake the hope that maybe, just maybe, she could change."

Austin reaches across the table, taking my hand in hers. "She might never change, Wren, and you need to know that. She's been this way for so long. But you don't have to make a decision right now. Take your time. Do what feels right for you."

I nod, appreciating the support. "I've been thinking about talking to her, setting some boundaries. I need to make it clear that I won't tolerate her manipulations anymore. If she can't respect that, then... I'll have to figure out what to do from there."

Austin smiles. "I think that's a good idea. I've got your back, okay, Wrenny?"

"Okay."

Things definitely won't be perfect for a while, but slowly mending this relationship with my sister is finally a step in the right direction. I want this with her. I want my big sister back, who I used to look up to, the one who would always protect me. And maybe we can find our way back to each other. For now, that hope is enough.

After dinner, everything feels weirdly normal. Like hanging out with Austin is just a casual thing that we do. As kids, I'd kill to have one-and-one time with her. We'd always be at our respective dance classes, or she'd be away for recitals. Now, it feels like that separation between us never existed.

The apartment that she and Zion are renting is a thirty-minute walk from here, but Austin insisted on walking. She's got her arm slung in mine, the other holding onto her bump as we take slow steps on the sidewalk.

"I think this baby is trying to kill me," she mumbles.

I laugh. "I'm pretty sure all kids are like that."

She flashes me a glance. "No, Wren, at my last scan the doctor told me that he's *huge*."

That makes me laugh again. It's so weird seeing her pregnant. She's always been thin and a little frail because of how seriously she takes ballet and seeing her with this massive bump is a weird adjustment. I spot a bench a few steps ahead of us and ask, "Do you want to sit down for a minute?"

She shakes her head. "I've put my body through hell since I was five. I'm sure I can manage a few more minutes of walking. We're close by, right?"

"I can still see the restaurant sign, so no," I say, grimacing.

"Seriously?" she groans, turning back and we're not even a block away from where we just ate. "Pregnancy brain is the worst."

We continue walking for another five minutes before she needs to stop again. Honestly, I don't mind all the stopping and starting. I'm just glad we're in the same place at the same time. When we get going again, she grips my arm a little tighter than before and stands still.

Her eyes widen, and she looks at me with panic. "I think my water just broke."

"Your what?" I blurt out, glancing down at her leg.

"My water! You know, the thing keeping this baby inside me. Either that or I just peed myself really bad," she says, glancing down to the wet stain on her dungarees. "Nope. Definitely baby goo water."

My heart starts racing and I have no fucking idea what to do. She must register the confusion on my face because she hands me her phone, leaning against the wall. "Call an ambulance and then call Zion. This baby is not waiting for anyone."

I HAVE no clue how long this process is supposed to last, but I've been pacing the hallway of the hospital for the last two hours. We managed to get here in one piece and Austin got hooked up to all these machines just as Zion walked in. She screamed at me the entire time we were in the ambulance, but just as they wheeled her through the doors she shouted, "I didn't mean any of that. I love you, sis." And I think it might have been the sweetest thing she's ever said to me. The doctors taken her in for an emergency C-section because of the way the baby is positioned, and my mind won't stop telling me the hundreds of things that could go wrong.

I called my mom to let her know, and she said she was too busy to come down now and will come to visit when the baby is here. I don't know what I was expecting from her, but I'm pissed on Austin's behalf. My dad was able to make it so he's sitting in the waiting room chatting with Miles and the girls.

"Wrenny, baby, can you sit down? You're making me dizzy," Miles says, rubbing his eyes dramatically. I stop in front of him and heave out a sigh. He was in the middle of an evening practice when I called him, and he got here just before Zion did. I didn't exactly want my boyfriend to meet my sister whilst she was in labor, but I guess the world doesn't always work out in my favor.

"What if something goes wrong?" I ask for the thousandth time.

"She's in a room full of trained professionals. She'll be okay," my dad says, laughing quietly. "They do this every day."

"Do you think she's scared? What if she's scared?" I whisper, finally taking a seat between Kennedy and Miles. Miles rubs my knee reassuringly, the pressure of his hand soothing me for a second. "I just want everything to go okay."

"And it will," Miles says, dropping his head to my shoulder. "We just have to be patient."

Of course he's right. It's not long before Zion walks through the doors to tell us that the baby is here, and that Austin is doing well. I swear my heart triples in size when we all walk into the room and she's sitting with the gorgeous baby boy in her arms.

We let my dad walk in first and he immediately starts crying. I can't imagine what it must feel like to see your little girl have a kid of her own. I watch them have their moment and it suddenly makes me excited to be in her position one day. To be able to hold a child that I created in my arms and instantly fall in love. My dad steps out the room to compose himself and Miles and I shuffle closer to get a better look.

He's got golden brown skin, lots of curly hair and the cutest little face. "He's perfect," I whisper, smiling at my sister and then to Zion. "The perfect mix of both of you."

"I'm hoping he gets your sister's talent. I've not got much to offer," Zion says, laughing quietly.

Austin frowns at him. "You're spectacular, babe. He'll probably have your brains. He'll be able to read before he can even walk."

"We can only hope," he replies, kissing my sister on the forehead. "Wren, do you want to hold him?"

"Seriously? Already? Isn't there like rules about when you can hold babies? He's quite literally fresh out of the womb. I don't want to break him," I ramble, my hands shaking. I don't know why I'm nervous. I don't get to be around kids much, but this one is already extra special. I can feel it. And I don't want to give him my bad luck.

"Just sit and hold your nephew, Amelia," Austin snaps and I listen. Zion walks around the bed, picking up the baby and placing him in my arms as I sit in the chair next to the bed. An overwhelming feeling washes over me when I look down at him as he sleeps. I didn't think my heart could get any fuller, but it can, and it is. It's like my heart is being bumped with helium and at any moment I could float away.

I don't know when I started crying, but my tears fall onto his baby blanket, and I tilt my head back. "He's so cute and perfect and sweet, and I just want to love and protect him forever," I sob.

"Jesus. Are you crying?" Austin asks, her eyes widened with panic.

I just sniffle and Miles comes beside me. "You and your cute baby made my girlfriend cry. Awesome," he deadpans, and everyone laughs.

Miles looks down at me and I try to stop myself from crying again, but there's no use. I have the strongest urge to let him put a baby inside me. I want it to be all him. All his good parts, all his bad parts. Because I'm convinced this man is the most perfect person on the planet. "I really want a baby," I wail, sounding and feeling ridiculous. "Can we have one?"

"In a couple years, sure. We can have as many kids as you want," he says. I watch the look my sister gives him, and he clears his throat. He kneels to my height and whispers, "But right now, I kinda want you all to myself."

I sniffle again. "Yeah?"

He grins. "Yeah. Just me and you, sweet girl."

I like the sound of that.

I like the idea that my sister gets a fresh start with her new family even more. And the fact that *my* family are all in this hospital right now makes me feel a thousand times better. These people are all I'm going to need forever.

46
MILES + WREN

The alchemy

MILES

THERE'S nothing like the atmosphere in the locker room before a big game.

The anticipation of the upcoming game mingles with the nerves churning in my stomach. Lacing up my skates, I run through the mental checklist of everything that needs to fall into place for tonight's match against Carlton. It's not just about winning the championship; it's about proving myself on the ice, especially with my parents in the stands for the first time in what feels like ages.

Coach paces back and forth, delivering a fiery pep talk to the team. I listen intently, my focus sharpening with each word.

But there's a knot of nerves coiled tightly in my stomach. This is the first time my parents will see me play in a while, and the pressure to perform weighs heavily on me. I check my phone, making sure everyone has a ride to the game. Away games always come with their own set of logistical challenges. I want to make sure everyone is coming tonight, and the thought of looking into the crowd and not recognizing anyone hurts. I excuse myself from the locker room, walking down the hallway before Coach tells me not to.

I call Wren, and she picks up immediately. "Hey, Miles." Wren's voice comes through, warm and comforting. "Shouldn't you be ripping each other's shirts off or doing whatever pre-game ritual you guys do?"

"We don't do anything like that," I reply, "but if you want me to take my shirt off, that's all you have to say."

"Pass." Just hearing her voice is enough comfort for now, and it slowly helps settle the nerves that are running through me. As if she can read my thoughts, she says, "You've got nothing to worry about, baby. You're going to do great."

"I know," I sigh. "Are you and the girls on your way yet?"

"Yeah, we just got here. We're grabbing some food and then going to our seats. We'll be right by the boards, don't worry."

"And my parents?"

"Clara said they're already here. I think they came before the arena even opened because they didn't want to miss the game," Wren says, laughing softly. That helps me let out a genuine breath of relief. "Hey, stop worrying. Your parents are excited, and surprisingly, so am I. You guys are going to kill it."

Her unwavering faith in me fills me with determination. I need to get my head in the game within these last few minutes before we make our way to the ice. Tonight, I'm not just playing for the championship; I'm playing for my team, for my family, for Wren, and for Carter.

WREN

The game is about to start, and I can feel the anticipation thrumming through my veins. I glance around at the faces of Miles's parents and his sister Clara, all here to support him. My friends are here too, their excitement contagious as we wait for the puck to drop.

The first period begins, and I watch as Miles takes to the ice with his team. The game is intense right from the start, both teams moving with speed and precision. Carlton is known for their aggressive play, but our team matches them stride for stride. The puck moves back and forth, a blur of motion as players weave through defenders and make sharp passes.

Miles's mom leans over, her face tight with nerves. "He's doing well, isn't he?" she asks, her voice tinged with worry.

"He's doing great," I reassure her, squeezing her hand. "Miles is one of the best players out there. He's got this."

Clara nods enthusiastically. "Yeah, Mom, he's fine. He's been training for this his whole life."

Miles's dad, on the other side of Clara, smiles confidently. "They'll be fine. Our boy knows how to handle the pressure."

The first period ends with no goals, but our team has held their ground. The defense is solid, and Miles is skating like he's got wings, blocking shots and making crucial passes. The tension in the arena is palpable as the second period begins.

The puck drops, and the game resumes with even more intensity. Carlton's offense is relentless, but Miles and his teammates are a well-oiled machine. They anticipate each move, countering attacks with swift, precise plays. I watch as Miles executes a perfect breakaway, skating past two defenders before taking a shot on goal. The puck flies past the goalie and into the net, and the crowd erupts in cheers.

Kennedy and Scarlett are in the row behind me, and they've been quiet the entire time. Kennedy has had her eyes on Harry in the goal the whole time, and though Scarlett acts like she hates it, I know she's just as entranced as I am as we watch them zip up and down the ice.

"You're really enjoying this, huh?" Scarlett asks, leaning forward to tug on my ponytail.

I turn back around to her for a second, not wanting to miss

anything even though Miles isn't on the ice right now. "Dude, this is intense. I'm genuinely having a good time."

They both laugh behind me, but I don't have the time to even speak with them. The minutes go by quickly in every period, and I can't take my eyes off the ice for longer than a few seconds.

As the second period continues, our team maintains its momentum. Miles is everywhere, intercepting passes, setting up plays, and maintaining a strong defensive presence. Carlton scores once, but our team quickly answers with another goal, keeping the lead.

During a brief pause, Clara leans over to me. "He's really in the zone tonight. I've never seen him play like this."

"He's definitely on fire," I reply, watching Miles skate to the bench for a quick breather. "I think knowing you all are here is giving him an extra boost."

Miles's dad chuckles. "He's always been a clutch player. When the pressure's on, that's when he shines the brightest."

The second period ends with our team up by one goal. I decide to stretch my legs and head to the concession stand for a drink. The girls have been making small talk with Miles's family, and I feel like I need a breather. The atmosphere is intense, and I want them to win so fucking badly.

As I make my way through the crowded concourse, I catch sight of two familiar faces: Darcy, and my mom. I thought my mom would be here, being head of the sports department, but Darcy being here is a shock. I always thought they were friends of sorts, but where my coach is sweet and supportive, my mom is the opposite.

It's the first time I've seen her since the blowup at her house, and part of me wants to walk straight past her. She's not even visited her daughter who just gave birth. Austin and Zion finally landed on a name for their baby boy, and Marley fits him so well. I've cried nearly every time I've held him and I think I'm just going to have to get used to the fact that I might be one of those people that cry a lot now.

My mom catches me walking by and calls out to me. I almost ignored her, but the Band-Aid needs to be ripped off immediately.

"Amelia, wait," she says, her voice carrying over the noise of the crowd.

I stop, my heart pounding in my chest. Darcy looks between us, sensing the tension. "I'll give you two some space," she says, squeezing my shoulder before walking away.

I turn to face my mom, the weight of everything unsaid pressing down on me. Her eyes are softer than I've seen in a long time, but I don't let myself be fooled. "What do you want, Mom?" I ask, my voice steady despite the turmoil inside. All the messages exchanged between us over the last few weeks have just been pleas to talk—like everything can be solved through a simple conversation. One where she'd try to make me feel small.

"I wanted to see how you were doing," she begins, her tone cautious. "It's been weeks, Amelia. You've been avoiding me when you know we need to talk."

"I'm fine," I say, crossing my arms. "I'm here to watch Miles play. That's all."

"Is it really?" she asks, stepping closer. "Because I know you're still holding a grudge against me for what happened. I know I hurt you, but we need to move past this. You're my daughter, and I love you."

I take a deep breath, trying to keep my emotions in check.

Love, not admire.

I can't remember the last time she said those words to me. We were never the emotional, tell-each-other-I-love-you-everyday type of family, and that was fine. I learned to deal with it, but it wouldn't have hurt to hear those words every once in a while.

"Do you? Because it hasn't felt like love, Mom. It feels like control. Like manipulation. I can't keep living like that." She opens her mouth to speak, but I cut her off. "No, listen to me. I'm not here to rehash old arguments. I want to make something clear. I love skating, but I need to do it for myself. Not for you, not for anyone else. Just for *me*."

"Wren, I was only trying to help you be the best—" she starts, but I shake my head.

"Being the best at skating doesn't mean anything if I'm miserable," I say, my voice gaining strength. "I want to enjoy my life. I want to be with Miles without you telling me he doesn't care about me or that I'm not good enough to make him stay. I need boundaries, Mom. If you can't respect that, then I don't know how we can have a relationship."

Her face crumples slightly, and for a moment, I see a flicker of vulnerability. I just want what's best for you," she whispers.

"Then trust me to know what's best for myself," I reply. "I have to go. The game's about to start again."

Without waiting for her response, I turn and walk back to my seat, feeling a mix of relief and sadness. It's not easy standing up to her, but it's necessary. I can't keep doing everything on her terms. Not when this is *my* life.

The third period begins, and the intensity on the ice ramps up. The players are moving faster, hitting harder. Carlton's team seems desperate to even the score, and they're not above playing dirty. I watch as one of their players trips Grayson, our defense-man, sending him sprawling to the ice. The referee's whistle blows, and the crowd boos as a penalty is called.

Miles is right in the thick of it, his focus unbreakable. He takes control of the puck, weaving through Carlton's players with a skill that takes my breath away. The crowd is on its feet, the tension almost unbearable. I can see the determination in his every move, the fire in his eyes as he skates down the rink.

Another penalty is called, this time on Carlton for slashing. It's a power play for our team, and the energy in the arena is electric. Miles's dad leans over to me, grinning. "This is it. They've got the advantage now."

I nod, unable to take my eyes off the ice. Miles is coordinating the play, passing the puck with precision, setting up the perfect shot. And then it happens—a beautiful slap shot that sends the puck sailing into the net. The crowd erupts, and I find myself jumping up, screaming in excitement.

The final minutes of the game are a blur of motion and noise. Carlton tries to rally, but our defense holds strong. Miles is everywhere, blocking shots, making passes, and leading his team with a fierce determination. When the final buzzer sounds, signaling our victory, the arena explodes in celebration.

Miles's family and I hug, caught up in the joy of the moment. As I look down at the ice, I see Miles looking up at us, a triumphant smile on his face. Our eyes meet, and I can see everything we've been through reflected in his gaze.

The announcer's voice booms over the PA system, calling everyone's attention to the center of the ice for the awards ceremony. The players form a circle, and a small stage is set up. Conference officials and sponsors make their way onto the ice, holding the gleaming championship trophy.

Seeing the trophy, I feel an overwhelming urge to be closer to Miles, to share this moment with him. I start making my way down from the stands, his family and Scarlett and Kennedy behind me as my heart pounds with excitement. We maneuver through the crowd, pushing past people who are just as eager to celebrate.

As we reach the edge of the rink, I see Miles standing proudly at the front as the team captain, his eyes shining with pride. God, he's never looked more attractive. The official steps forward, ready to hand him the trophy, but Miles's gaze locks onto mine. He doesn't hesitate. Instead of reaching for the trophy, he breaks away from the team and skates directly toward me.

My heart races as he gets closer. The next thing I know, he's lifting me off my feet and spinning me around, his arms wrapped around me tight. I'm wearing his jersey, and I've never felt prouder to sport the school's colors.

"You did it!" I exclaim, wrapping my arms around his neck.

"*We* did it," he says, his voice filled with joy and emotion. "I couldn't have done it without you, princess, seriously."

Our eyes meet, and everything else fades away. The noise, the crowd, the flashing cameras—none of it matters. It's just us.

"I'm so fucking proud of you," I whisper, my voice choked with emotion.

Miles's eyes glisten as he pulls me even closer. "Thank you for being here," he says, his voice trembling slightly. "Thank you for everything."

"I'll always be here," I reply, my heart swelling with love and pride. "Always."

We pull apart just enough to look into each other's eyes, but neither of us lets go. The moment is perfect, and I can feel the depth of his love and gratitude in his embrace.

"Go get your trophy, hotshot," I say with a smile.

He grins and gives me one last kiss before skating back to his team. The official hands him the trophy, and the team erupts in cheers once again. Miles lifts it high above his head, his face beaming with pride. The team gathers for the official photos, posing with the trophy, their smiles wide and genuine.

The team takes a victory lap around the rink, holding the trophy high for the fans to see. The arena is a sea of cheers and applause, and I can't help but feel overwhelmed with pride and love for Miles and everything he's accomplished. He deserves this and so much more. I can't wait to see what the future has in store for him because I have a strong feeling it won't be long before he'll be playing in the pros.

47
MILES + WREN

**"You're being nice to me.
Are you sick?"**

MILES

BEING CRAMMED into a back booth of a restaurant with my best friends, my sister, and my parents is exactly how I saw tonight going after the championship. The room is buzzing with excitement, laughter, and the faint sound of clinking glasses from the other patrons celebrating their own victories and milestones.

My arm is draped around Wren's shoulders, her warmth grounding me as I soak in the scene around me. Kennedy and Scarlett are sitting across from us, animatedly recounting their favorite moments from the game despite neither of them being huge hockey fans. Their excitement is contagious, and it's clear they had a good time.

"To be honest," Scarlett says, leaning in with a conspiratorial grin, "I didn't understand half of what was happening, but seeing Miles score that goal was pretty impressive."

Kennedy nods vigorously. "Yeah, and that hit you took in the second period? I thought you were done for, but you bounced right back. Like, how do you even *do* that?"

I chuckle, feeling a swell of pride. "Thanks, guys. It means a lot that you were there. Even if hockey isn't your thing."

My parents are beaming with pride when I look over at them. Being with them both today has felt like a dream. It felt like old times when they'd go to mine and Carter's games and take us out for food afterward.

My dad lifts his glass. "To the North Bears, and especially to you, Miles. You played one hell of a game."

"To the Bears!" Everyone echoes, raising their glasses.

My sister, sitting next to our dad, smirks at me over the rim of her drink. "So, MVP, how does it feel to be the hero of the hour?"

I roll my eyes playfully. "It was a team effort. Everyone played their hearts out."

"Don't be so modest," Wren chimes in. "You were incredible out there, Miles. I was literally on the edge of my seat the entire time. I couldn't be prouder."

I squeeze her shoulder, my heart swelling with gratitude. She put up a hell of a fight to wear my jersey a few months ago, and now she's wearing it with pride. I can't wait to rip it off her tonight.

"I couldn't have done it without you cheering me on," I say.

As we continue to talk, my mom's eyes glisten with emotion, and part of me is too afraid to know what she's thinking. Our relationship has strengthened since her birthday, and I couldn't be happier. I forgot how good it feels to have my mom in my corner, and I don't want her to leave there again. "I have to say, Miles, seeing you play tonight, after everything we've been through... It's just... We're so proud of you."

My dad nods, his voice thick with emotion. "We really are, son. And Carter would have been too. You did him proud tonight."

Mentioning Carter brings a lump to my throat, but I manage a nod. "I hope so. This win is as much for him as it is for us."

The table falls silent for a moment, each of us lost in our thoughts about Carter. His loss has been a heavy burden, but tonight, I feel a sense of peace, knowing that we honored his memory with our victory.

It's not long before the night starts to wear on, and the more alcohol Clara has, the more embarrassing childhood stories she wants to share. If it was any other night, I would have told her to stop by now, but I don't. We're all so happy and tired, and it feels too good to ruin some good fun.

Clara teases, "Remember that time you tried to build a hockey rink in the backyard and ended up flooding the lawn?"

I groan, shaking my head. "I was ten, Clara."

She laughs, her eyes twinkling with mischief. "Oh, come on, it's a classic Miles moment. Mom and Dad were so mad, but you were so determined to make it work. You even tried to freeze the water with a fan!"

The table erupts in laughter, and my mom shakes her head. "I remember that. You were convinced that if you just got it cold enough, it would turn into ice. We had to explain the concept of freezing temperatures to you."

My dad chimes in, grinning. "And don't forget the part where you tried to recruit Clara to help you carry buckets of water from the kitchen sink. She was just as determined as you were."

Clara rolls her eyes. "Yeah, because I thought it was a brilliant plan. We were going to have the best backyard rink in the neighborhood."

Kennedy and Scarlett are laughing so hard they're nearly in tears. Kennedy wipes her eyes and says, "I wish I could've seen that. It sounds like something out of a movie."

Wren nods. "Definitely. Little Miles, future hockey star, flooding the backyard."

I shake my head, chuckling. "Alright, enough about my childhood disasters. How about we talk about something else?"

Wren squeezes my hand, a warm smile on her lips. "I think

it's adorable. It shows how passionate you've always been about hockey."

Clara isn't done yet though. "Oh, and what about the time you tried to make your own goalie pads out of couch cushions and duct tape? You looked like a marshmallow man."

Everyone bursts into laughter again, and I can't help but join in. "Those were innovative. I was ahead of my time."

My dad chuckles. "You were always resourceful, I'll give you that. And look where it got you. Conference champion."

The mention of the championship brings a proud silence to the table, everyone reflecting on the journey we've been on. I look around at my family and friends, feeling an overwhelming sense of gratitude.

There's no place I'd rather be right now.

WREN

Seeing Miles this happy almost makes me want to cry.

From the annoying hockey hotshot who I met at the party, he's grown on me. He's still annoying, but my heart yearns for him sometimes. It feels pathetic when I think about it. Even when I'm with him, like right now, basically sitting in his lap, I still want to be closer to him. If it was possible, I'd sew myself to him so we wouldn't have to be apart.

Which is probably why I insist on driving back with him, holding his hand the entire time while Kennedy and Scarlett pretend to gag in the backseat. They've told me multiple times they feel "violent" when they look at us, and if it wasn't me in the situation, I'd be grossed out too. I don't *love* PDA, but I love being close to Miles. I love it when he brushes his thumb against my hand when he's driving before he lets go to hold the wheel. Or when he always guides me when we walk with his hand on my back. Or when he grabs my wrists and kisses them like it's some sort of weird game we have.

I think— no, I *know* I love him.

It's a love that scares me, but not because I'm scared it will disappear. It scares me because of how much I want it to last, how much I've come to rely on it, how much it means to me. It's the kind of love that changes everything, but not in the way I feared. It doesn't tie me down or trap me; it lifts me up and makes me want to be better.

I used to think that love should have another word—something that carries the same weight but doesn't feel binding. But now I realize that love is supposed to be binding, in the best way possible. It's a commitment, a promise to be there for each other, to grow together, to face the future as a team.

Miles has shown me a side of love I didn't believe in before —a love that is steady, supportive, and unwavering. It's not just about the grand gestures or the fleeting moments of passion; it's about the everyday acts of kindness, the constant presence, the feeling of being truly seen and understood.

I think about all the times he's been there for me, always ready with a reassuring word or a comforting embrace. I think about the way he looks at me with a mixture of admiration and tenderness that makes my heart swell. It's not just that he loves me; he respects me, cherishes me, and wants the best for me.

When we pull up outside my apartment, the girls go in first, and as Miles goes to open the door, I reach for him. He turns back to me, and I grip both of his cheeks, his eyes widening with surprise.

"You're incredible. You know that, right?" I say, and I hate the way my voice shakes.

He grins. "I know."

"I'm being serious. You're genuinely the best person I've ever met."

"You're being nice to me. Are you sick?" he mumbles.

I roll my eyes, dropping my hands from his face. "No, you idiot, I just mean it."

"Are you sure you're okay?" He narrows his eyes at me.

"Does something have to be wrong for me to be nice to you?"

He shrugs. "No, but it's scary. It's our whole thing. You pretend to hate me; I pretend like I don't care. You bully me; I let you. It's our dynamic. When you're nice to me, I get worried."

"That's stupid," I mutter, and he just grins. I take in a deep breath. "Well, I'm going to say something *really really* nice, so here's a warning, okay?"

He swallows. "Okay."

"I love you, Miles." The words leave my mouth with a whoosh, and Miles's eyes soften as he looks at me intensely. "I should have said it weeks ago, but I didn't know how to say it, so I've just come out with it." He blinks at me, and more words keep spilling out of my mouth. "You're my favorite person in this universe, Miles, and if there are any more universes out there, you'd be my favorite in each of those too. You're my best friend. You make me feel like I'm the smartest person in the room even when I'm not. You made me realize that I don't want to do things on my own anymore. I want to do things with *you*."

My voice cracks on the last word, and I tell myself to hold it together. Miles stares back at me like what I just said was the wrong thing. He takes a deep breath, and instead of responding, he wraps his arm around my neck and kisses me. He kisses me like it's the first time, and I could drown in him. His mouth moves against mine softly at first, then with growing intensity. It's like every emotion we've both been holding back is pouring out all at once, and I can feel my heart pounding in my chest. His hands move to cup my face, his touch gentle and reassuring, grounding me in this moment.

When we finally pull apart, we're both breathless. Miles rests his forehead against mine, his eyes closed, and I can see the faintest trace of a smile on his lips. He opens his eyes and looks at me with a mixture of tenderness and wonder.

"I love you, Amelia Wren Hackerly," he says quietly, his voice steady and full of conviction. "You're my best friend, and I love being around you. I love being there for you and protecting you even when you don't want me to. I don't just love you, I'm *in* love with you. So desperately. I don't think I would ever be able to stop loving you. If you try to push me away again, I won't let you. Because I'm in this, okay? Me and you."

I try to breathe, but it's hard. His words are like a balm to my soul, soothing all the fears and insecurities I've been carrying for so long. I feel my eyes well up with tears again, but this time, they're tears of relief and overwhelming happiness.

"I don't want to push you away," I whisper, my voice trembling. "I was so scared, but now... now I know. I know that I want you in my life, forever, if you'll have me."

He pulls me into a tight embrace, his warmth seeping into my bones, grounding me in the reality of this moment. "Forever sounds perfect to me, princess," he murmurs against my hair.

There's something about the severity of his voice that makes me realize that I won't have to spend another day guessing my worth. That every day can be a great one if I let it. And I want to spend all of those days with him.

EPILOGUE - AUGUST
MILES

"ARE YOU NERVOUS?"

I run my hands from her shoulders down to her waist as I stand behind her in the mirror, losing my mind over how good she looks in her dress. I'm sure we're breaking every wedding ritual right now, but I can't bring myself to care. I know Kennedy would have my head if she saw that I was with Wren in her dress already.

I rest my chin on her shoulder, and she beams in the mirror. "No, I'm excited. One, I've never been here before, and two, I've never been a maid of honor before," Wren says.

We've been in Jamaica for the last few days, trying to catch up on sleep as well as helping Wren do her bridal duties to her sister. Zion proposed to Austin earlier this summer and Wren cried literal tears when she told me. I know things have been hard between them, but they've been making it work.

As soon as we came off the plane, the humidity hit us worse than it was in Palm Springs. We were greeted by Zion's large family and Austin and baby Marley, who flew out a week before. I don't think I've seen a cuter baby than him, and he's only a couple months old. He's got the chubbiest little cheeks and the cutest dimples.

Ms. Hacks is still not open to the idea of Austin's new life, but their dad has shown up like has been doing for the past few months. Talking to Wren's dad is always the highlight of my day. He always has some story to tell about how crazy Wren was as a kid and I love it.

"I'm mostly excited for the food," I say with a sigh. Wren turns around, her bright-green eyes staring into mine. "Do you know how long the service is going to take?"

"I hope you're joking. This is a very special and romantic day," she protests.

"I know, but can't it be special and romantic *and* short?"

THE CEREMONY IS special and it's overly romantic, but it is *not* short.

Wren had to stand in her light-blue maid-of-honor dress at the front of the wedding aisle. I had to sit in the line of chairs in the blistering sunlight as we waited for more guests to arrive. We exchanged private moments since we couldn't speak while Wren and the other bridesmaids waited for the ceremony to begin. Even when Austin came down the aisle in a white wedding dress, all I could focus on was Wren, beaming, with fresh happy tears welling up in her eyes.

Even when Marley started crying on Zion's mom's knee, I still couldn't tear my eyes away from her. Being here in the sun, her freckles have appeared on her face and down her arms, and it's the most beautiful thing I've ever seen.

When we finally get out of the heat, we're moved into a large room with the AC on—*thank God*—where all the food and drinks are served. Jamaican food is incredible. I've always been a big eater, and I would sit by the food table all day if it were socially acceptable.

I follow Wren around like a lost puppy, holding her bag as she greets all of Zion's family and some of her family too. She gives an emotional and funny maid of honor speech, which has almost the entire room in tears.

When Zion and Austin have their first dance to *Is This Love* by Bob Marley, we dance from a distance, her head resting on my shoulder as I rest my hand on her hip, swaying us to the music.

"They look so happy," Wren whispers to me. I brush her shoulder with my hand reassuringly before she starts to cry for the hundredth time today.

"They do. But for the love of God, stop crying."

"I can't help it," she says, sobbing into me. For someone who hated crying when we first met, she's cried a fuckton in the last few months. I rub circles on her back and change the subject.

"I like that they have a song just for them. Do we have one?"

She looks up at me as if I offended her. I can't help but laugh at her sudden change of expression as she continues sniffling.

"Of course, we have a song, Miles, and you know which one it is," she demands. "Do you really think I'd be still dating you if we didn't have a song?"

"I'll try not to take that personally," I murmur.

She rolls her eyes. "Come on."

She pulls at my arm as she starts to walk through the crowds of people in the room and leads us through the door. She drags us down the corridor of this fancy hotel until we get to a dark corridor. She looks into some of the rooms as if she knows her way around, and the thought crosses my mind that she's secretly a spy.

When we get to the end of the corridor, she jingles the door handle to the right and opens the door, which leads to a flight of stairs.

"Where are we going?" I ask as she starts to sprint up the stairs.

"I know a shortcut," she pants.

"How? We've literally been here a week."

She ignores me with a laugh until we reach the top of the first flight of stairs to another door, which she opens with ease. We're in darkness for a few beats before a light turns on and we're somehow back in our suite.

"How?" I ask breathlessly as I cross the bedroom into the open living room and kitchen area, looking back to the door that we came out of.

"I have my ways," she says with a shrug, looking through her bag from under the couch. She pulls out her speaker and holds down the button to connect it to her phone.

"You're insane," I say, walking over to her. Her blonde hair that she curled especially for today falls down across her face, and I brush out a strand from her eyes before pulling her further into me.

"I know," she says cheerfully as she sets the speaker on the kitchen island. "Come and help me move this out of the way."

We take a while to move the couch and the coffee table out of the way until there's a large space in the middle only holding the carpet. Now we're both sweatier than before as I huff and stare at her. She has a daring look in her eyes as she grabs her phone from the kitchen before returning to stand in front of me.

"You can have one guess as to what our song is," she demands as she tugs on my tie and pulls me into her.

"I'm guessing it's a Taylor Swift song based on your excitement." She nods, waving her phone between us suggestively. "I don't know, baby. I'm sorry."

"Don't be sorry. Just be grateful you have a super cool girlfriend with impeccable music taste," she says with a flourish as she hits play to the song she's chosen. My heart expands as soon as the instrumental begins, and the moment that she played this to me for the first time hits me. "See."

She throws her phone on the couch and snakes her hands around my neck as the first verse to *You Are in Love* plays over the speakers. I wrap my arms around her waist as she brings her body closer to mine, our bodies fitting together perfectly.

"Do you remember what happened when I played this for you?" she asks as she sinks into my chest, her arms falling loose around my neck.

"I was driving us back from the gym, and you insisted on putting a song on because, apparently, my music taste is shit. You put this on, and I said it was good, but it felt like you were trying to subconsciously convince me to fall in love with you. Like you were trying to manifest it or something. You then told me that that's never going to happen, but you thought it was one of the best love songs," I explain as we sway back and forth to the music.

"And then what happened?" She starts to laugh into me, knowing what I'm going to say. I press a kiss to her head and chuckle into her.

"Then *you* fell in love with me."

"I did." She laughs softly before breaking away to look up at me. "I really did and hard too."

We stay close to each other as the song plays on a loop, letting the words settle around us.

You can hear it in the silence.
You can feel it on the way home.
You can see it with the lights out.
You are in love.
True love.

That's exactly what it feels like being so desperately in love with Wren. I can feel her everywhere. It feels like no matter where I go, where we are, there's always something tying us together.

There's always that true, consuming kind of love that lingers between us whenever we're around each other. If a pink heart was a person, it would be Wren. She makes me so happy that it almost makes me queasy when I think about it too much.

I don't get time to think right now because her phone starts to ring through the speakers. She groans into my chest as we waddle toward the phone, her arms tightly around my waist, not daring to look at it.

"It's Scarlett," I say when I catch a glimpse of her phone. She groans even louder. "Maybe something's wrong. You should answer it."

"Fine," she replies, pulling out of my grasp to answer the incoming FaceTime.

She falls onto the couch, which is now at the far end of our suite, and I sit next to her, sweeping her into my lap. The phone lights up with a puffy-faced Scarlett as it balances on the kitchen island of their apartment while she stands across from it, leaning against the sink with her arms crossed.

"Hi, Scar. What's up?" Wren asks, smiling into the camera.

I lean my face into the frame and wave. Scarlett rolls her eyes at me.

"Hi," she says sharply. "I have a question to ask."

"Shoot," Wren replies, pushing her hair out of her face.

I notice her necklace in the camera screen, and the clasp has fallen to the front. I move my hands over it and pull it around the right way. She presses a kiss to my cheek as a thank you before turning her attention to Scarlett.

"You guys are disgusting," Scarlett huffs. "Anyway, have you seen The Whiteboard anywhere? I don't know how I can't find it. I only have the one that I use for school, not *our* one."

"How could you lose The Whiteboard? It's huge," Wren replies, and Scarlett shakes her head with a short laugh. "I haven't seen it in a while. Our lives have been pretty put together recently so we haven't needed it."

She's right. Since we finished our exams, we settled into a comfortable rhythm with our friends where we can actually get work done as well as hanging out.

Kennedy is always working on a new project for class and giving us free drinks from Florentino's. Xavier and I have still been training like crazy and going on double dates with Michelle and Wren. Evan and Scarlett are still constantly arguing about whatever assignments they need to do for business class, finding new ways to insult each other.

Wren is working the hardest out of all of us as she works on her writing and skating while trying to juggle the relationship with her mom. She has laid off Wren recently, but it's still tense between them, but that's just the reality of their relationship. It's never going to be perfect and that's okay.

"Huh," Scarlett says disbelievingly. "What about you, Miles? Have you seen it? At your house, perhaps."

"Uh, no... Why would it be at my house?" I ask with a skeptical look. Wren looks up at me and widens her eyes, and I realize what she meant. She probably thinks Evan has taken it. Typical. "Have you asked Ken?"

"No, Miles, I haven't asked the one person currently living with me right now," she retorts sarcastically. "I have a feeling someone has taken it, but they won't own up to it."

Something catches her eye above the screen, and she glares as if she's talking to someone indirectly.

Wren and I give each other a suspicious look before we turn back to Scarlett, whose face has suddenly turned a deep-red color. I can't tell if she's blushing or if she's pissed.

"What? Do you think Evan took it?" Wren asks. Scarlett waits a beat before turning her attention back to the screen.

"I *know* he took it," she bites out.

"Scar," Wren says slowly. "Please don't tell me you're holding him hostage right now."

"I'm not holding him hostage," Scarlett says, rolling her

eyes. "I asked him to come over, and he was stupid enough to agree."

She slowly pans the camera around to face the other way, and that's when we both see him. Evan is sitting in a dark blue suit in their apartment with his arms crossed against his chest. He doesn't look like he's being held hostage. He looks too comfortable. Like he's enjoying it. He smiles at the camera before blowing air up to push his blond hair out of his face.

"Hey, guys. I hope you're having a good time," Evan begins with a smile. "Jamaica is beautiful. I've been a few times and—"

"Shut up," Scarlett demands, turning the phone around, but she holds it closer to her face.

"Scarlett, you're insane," Wren says, laughing. I can't help but laugh too at the fact that she seems so used to this. As if this is a completely normal Scarlett thing to do.

"Whatever. I need to get it back, like, now." She pulls the phone closer to her face so we can see straight into her green eyes as she lowers her voice. "I'm having a crisis, Wren."

"I'm sorry, Scar. I'm sure Kennedy can help you out. I'm coming home in a few days. Can you hang on until then?" Wren asks, scrunching her nose up. Scarlett opens her mouth to speak, but Evan butts in.

"What's the crisis?" Evan asks loudly. "I'll help."

"I would rather gouge my eyes out than ask you for help," Scarlett replies with a disgusted glare, shuddering before ending the call.

THE END.

ACKNOWLEDGMENTS

Writing my acknowledgements are always the most terrifying part for me. You'd think stringing together a 137,000 word novel would be the hard part, but you're wrong. This, what you're reading right now, is by far the scariest part about writing, drafting, editing and completing a novel.

I always feel a strange wave of emotions when I get to this part of the writing process. For this book especially. I'm sure most of you know the lore behind the creation of this book, and how I've taken the time to rewrite my debut novel for it to become what you've just read. I'm not going to bore you with the details, but after writing the Drayton Hills series, I knew I had it in me to do better. So that's what a did. It was a long few months of pulling apart Fake Dates & Ice Skates while also pretending it didn't exist so I could give it a shot with a completely new lens. All that's to say, the book that it turned out to be in the end has been everything I wished it could be, and I'm so grateful that you all let me take you on this journey and allowed me the time and space to make this huge change.

I want to thank Emma, Ella, and Maine for being three of the first people who truly connected with Fake Dates & Ice Skates an entire year ago, and you weren't shy about reaching out. You are some of my closest friends to this day, and I'm so grateful for you sliding into my DM's. Thank you Emily for listening to me cry about quitting every week and always having faith in me when I struggle to have some in myself. I love you all more than life itself.

Thank you to Sophia for always being there to hype up my stories and to cry over my characters with me. You are a genuine light in this world, and I would not have been able to get through this without you.

Thank you to my wonderful and amazing PA, Morgan. I would be falling apart right now if it wasn't for you. You do all the things that I dread doing, and I'm so happy that you chose to be apart of my team. I'll forever be grateful for our friendship and your support.

Thank you to all my Bookstagram girlies: Zarin, Ellen, Ami, Mylla, Haya, Megs, Grace, and everyone I forgot to mention. The fact that you allow me to act the way I act on my close friends is insane. You're always there for me with outstanding advice and general good vibes. I love you!

A huge thank you to every single person on Instagram, TikTok, or anywhere else that you're able to see my books or my content. Interacting with readers is always my favourite part about this whole thing, and getting to see reactions updates means the world.

Thank you to my incredible cover artists Emily, Marta, and Layla. Your talent is out of this world. Thank you for brining my visions to life in such an incredible way. Thank you to the amazing Louise at KLS for proofreading this book— you and your team are amazing.

Thank you, reader. This book is nothing without you.

Printed in Great Britain
by Amazon

47406034R00310